John Connolly

A Game of Ghosts

HODDER &
STOUGHTON

First published in Great Britain in 2017 by Hodder & Stoughton
An Hachette UK company

3

Copyright © Bad Dog Books Limited 2017

A CIP catalogue record for this title is
available from the British Library

Hardback ISBN 978 1 473 64186 0
Trade Paperback ISBN 978 1 473 64187 7
EBook ISBN 978 1 473 64188 4

Typeset in Sabon LT Std by Palimpsest Book Production Ltd,
Falkirk, Stirlingshire
Printed and bound by Clays Ltd, St Ives plc

Hodder & Stoughton policy is to use papers that are natural, renewable
and recyclable products and made from wood grown in sustainable
forests. The logging and manufacturing processes are expected to
conform to the environmental regulations of the country of origin.

Hodder & Stoughton Ltd
Carmelite House
50 Victoria Embankment
London EC4Y 0DZ

www.hodder.co.uk

For Lucy Hale

I

Indeed, as things stand for the present, the Land of Spirits is a kind of America . . . filled up with Mountains, Seas, and Monsters.

Joseph Glanvill, *A Blow at Modern Sadducism* (1668)

1

A new fall of snow had settled upon the old, like memories, like the years.

It would freeze too, according to the weathermen, adding another layer to the ice that blanketed the city, and another day or two to the slow thaw that must inevitably come, although any release from the cold seemed distant on this February evening. Still, at least the latest snowfall, the first in more than a week, hid beneath it the filth of earlier accumulations, and the streets of Portland would look fresh and unsullied again, for a time.

Although the air was chill, it held no clarity. A faint mist hung over the streets, creating penumbrae around the streetlights like the halos of saints, and making a dreamscape of the skyline. It lent the city a sense of duplication, as though its ways and buildings had been overlaid imperfectly upon some earlier version of itself, and now that shadow variant was peering through, the people of the present within touching distance of those of the past.

Charlie Parker walked up Exchange Street, his head lowered against the rawness of the dark so that he progressed like a ram between sidewalk drifts. He didn't need NBC to tell him that winter was tightening its grip. Some ancient personification of the season seemed to sense the approach of spring, even if no one else could, and was determined to cling to its white kingdom for as long as it was able. Parker could feel it in his bones, and in his wounds. His left hand was curled into a ball of hurt in his pocket, and the scars on his back felt tight and uncomfortable. His head ached, and had anyone asked, he could have pointed to the scattering of odd markings in his hair, silver-gray along the lines cut through his scalp by the shotgun pellets, and ascribed a locus of agony to each.

Older injuries troubled him too. Many years before, he had thrown himself into a frigid lake in the far north of the state rather than face the guns that would otherwise surely have ended his life. He had still taken a bullet for his troubles, although the pain of the strike was dulled by the greater shock of immersion in freezing water. He should have died, but he did not. Later, the doctors would throw an array of medical terms in his direction – hypothermia, hypotension, hypovolemia, high blood viscosity – none of which was of any great benefit to the human body, or its prospects of immortality, but all of which applied, at some point, to him.

On top of being shot, he had then violated just about every piece of post-immersion medical management by continuing to fight his tormentors, and that was before someone tried to kick his teeth in. One of the attending physicians, a specialist in maritime medicine, wanted to write a paper on him, but Parker had politely declined the offer of free ongoing treatment and therapy in exchange for his cooperation. It was a decision he sometimes regretted. He often thought that his body had never quite recovered from the trauma it had endured, because he had since felt the cold in winter with an intensity he could not recall from youth or young manhood. Sometimes, even in a warm room, he would be struck by a fit of shivering so violent that it would leave him weak for hours after. Even his teeth would hurt. Once, they chattered so hard that he lost a crown.

But hey, he was still alive, and that was good, right? He thought of the old commonplace about how giving up vices didn't make you live longer, but just made it *feel* as though you were living longer. Nights like these made him feel as though he had been in pain all his life.

It was the first day of February. Parker could recall arguing with his grandfather about the months of winter, shortly after the old man had taken in the boy and his mother, permitting them to escape New York and the ripples from his father's death. For Parker, those winter months were December, January, and February, but his grandfather, who had roots in another continent, always thought in terms of the old Gaelic calendar in which November was the first month of winter, and so for him February meant the start of spring. Even decades spent enduring the grimness of Maine winters, and the icy darkness of February in particular, had not shaken him in his conviction. As time went on, Parker came to suspect that the old man might have been wiser than his grandson realized. By embracing February as the birth of a new season, instead of the slow death of the old, his grandfather was demonstrating a degree of psychological acuity that enabled him to tolerate one of the worst months of the year by regarding it as the harbinger of better times to come.

Parker stopped outside Crooners & Cocktails. The bar was Ross's choice. Parker wasn't sure why. It wasn't as though the FBI man was intimate with Portland's restaurant scene. Then again, Parker had come to accept that Edgar Ross was more attuned to unfamiliar rhythms than might be considered advisable, even for someone directly involved in matters of national security.

Actually, Parker kind of liked Crooners & Cocktails. The name might have been a bit hokey, but the interior was a throwback to another era, and the food and drinks were good. He stared through the glass, fogged by the heat inside, and thought he could make out Ross's figure at the back of the room. The agent had a half-filled glass in front of him, and what looked like a tray of oysters. Parker hated oysters. As for his feelings about Ross, the jury was still out.

Parker turned away from the window. He could hear music drifting up the street from Sonny's, and across from him figures moved in the bar of the Press Hotel, a building that had housed the *Portland Press Herald* until the newspaper relocated to One City Center back in 2010. He'd only been in the hotel once to take a look around and meet Angel and Louis for a drink. He thought it might be an okay place to stay, even if, like Crooners & Cocktails, it was a carefully cultivated exercise in nostalgia. Then again, maybe nostalgia was an understandable response to a world that appeared to be going all to hell, as long as everyone remembered that the past was a nice place to visit but nobody should want to settle in it.

One of the cars parked opposite was a black Lexus. Two men sat in the front. To avoid conflict, they would be listening to something neutral, Parker guessed: Classic Vinyl or Deep Tracks on Sirius. Both would be armed. He had informed them that Ross was coming. They were curious, just as Parker was. Ross rarely ventured so far north.

Parker's cell phone rang. He answered, and Angel spoke.

'He arrived in a limousine,' said Angel, 'but not one with government plates. The car dropped him off at this place, then left. I stayed with Ross, and Louis followed the car. It's parked down on Middle Street. Private hire, but nothing flashy. The driver's in Starbucks, playing games on his cell phone.'

Parker hung up and adjusted the pin on his tie. He hated wearing ties.

'You still hearing me?' he asked.

From the passenger seat of the car, Angel showed him an upraised thumb. At least, Parker hoped it was a thumb. With Angel, one could never be sure.

With that, Parker entered the bar.

It struck him, as he was escorted to the table, that he knew almost nothing about Ross. Was he married? He didn't wear a ring, but Parker was aware of men and women in risky professions who chose not to advertise their marital ties. He could be separated, or divorced. Given his work, that would make sense. Did he have children? Parker thought not, but he'd been wrong about such matters before. Children mellowed some men, but made no difference at all to others beyond adding to their burdens. He'd read an interview with a novelist whose estranged daughter traveled thousands of miles to somewhere in Africa in order to mend their broken relationship, only to have the door slammed in her face. The novelist justified his actions on the grounds that he was not trained to deal with 'problem children', but Parker didn't know of any parent who was trained to deal with children, problematic or not. Actually, that wasn't entirely true: he knew a couple of child psychologists – one in particular – and they were terrible parents.

Ross stood to shake Parker's hand. He had spilled Tabasco sauce on his shirt; just a speck, like a pinprick of blood. Parker didn't comment on it, but he would find his eye drifting repeatedly toward it over the course of the evening, as though it represented an aspect profound that otherwise refused to reveal itself.

Parker handed his coat to the hostess but kept his jacket on.

'I figured you wouldn't mind if I ordered some oysters before you arrived,' said Ross, once they were both seated. 'I know how you feel about seafood.'

'That's gracious of you,' said Parker. His general distaste for shellfish and seafood had, he realized, hardened into a phobia. He might have been tempted to see a therapist about it, were he not afraid of what a distrust of bivalves could suggest about his personality.

'What are you drinking?' he asked Ross.

'A Dewar's and Disaronno. It's called a Godfather.'

'I hope you're being ironic.'

Parker glanced at the cocktail menu, found a drink he wasn't too embarrassed to order – a Journalist, mainly Bombay

Original and vermouth – and set the list aside. He barely sipped the cocktail once it was in front of him. He still had an aversion to hard liquor, but he'd learned long ago that when in the company of just one other person who was drinking, it paid to have something similar in turn, even if not a drop of it passed one's lips. Coffee, beer, wine, Scotch, it didn't matter: the act of ordering relaxed the other party, and that relaxation was important for the eliciting of information. Then again, Ross probably knew this already. If he didn't, he shouldn't have been working for the FBI.

He and Ross made small talk for a time – politics, the weather, Parker's health – before ordering entrees: monkfish for Ross, steak for Parker, with glasses of Riesling and Malbec, respectively, to go with them. The waitress left them. Music played low, a counterpoint to the hum of conversation.

'So,' said Parker, 'why are you here?'

2

They were surrounded by people having a good time, cocooned against the cold beyond the glass. Portland eateries were adept at making customers feel cozy in winter. After all, they had a lot of practice.

Ross sipped his drink.

'Have you ever crossed paths with a private investigator named Jaycob Eklund?' he asked. 'That's Jaycob with a "y".'

'Out of where?'

'Providence.'

'I don't believe so. Does he have a specialization?'

'Not officially. He does whatever it takes to make ends meet: errant husbands and wives, bail skips, process serving – a little like you did, before the federal government began contributing to your finances.'

Only a few months had passed since the retainer had started to appear in Parker's account, but it was already making a difference to his standard of living and the kind of cases he accepted. The paperwork, though, had taken a while to complete. Parker's lawyer, Aimee Price, refused to have anything to do with the arrangement, regarding it as an error in judgment on his part, and quite possibly on the part of the FBI as well. Also, Price had finally tied the knot during the summer, after an engagement that had gone on for so long that the ring, although bought new, now practically counted as an antique. She was pregnant with twins, and intended to cut back on her workload, or so she said, but Parker knew that she was more concerned with putting some distance between herself and her most notorious client. As a mother-to-be, she wanted to take no risks with her safety or that of her nascent family. Parker couldn't blame her, and had transferred his business to Moxie Castin, who had no such qualms.

Moxie gave the consultancy agreement with the FBI such a reworking that it now bore more resemblance to a monthly charitable donation from the government than any payment for services, current or future. But the words on the page weren't the issue, and their true meaning lay hidden behind the legalese. Parker understood that he was tied to Ross, and Ross to him. Any favors asked or granted would always come with a price. Now, Parker sensed, he was about to begin earning some of that money.

'And unofficially?'

'Eklund was an occasional recipient of our – of *my* – largesse,' said Ross.

'In return for what?'

'Watching. Listening.' Ross finished his cocktail, washed his mouth out with water, and moved on to wine. 'Did you think you were the only one?'

'You're making me feel less special,' said Parker.

'I suspect that may be beyond my skill range.'

Parker managed a smile.

'Eklund has gone missing,' Ross continued. 'I want him found.'

'You're the FBI. That's a little like a miner asking me to help him find coal.'

Ross didn't answer. He just sipped his wine and waited. Their food came. It looked good, but neither man touched it, not yet.

'Unless you can't get the feds to do it,' said Parker at last, once it became clear that they wouldn't be able to eat, or move the conversation along, until he demonstrated to Ross his understanding of the situation. 'You don't know for certain what Eklund was looking into when he disappeared. If you put him into the system, and he was on your dime, you risk drawing attention both to him and to whatever it is you might currently be cooking up in that cauldron brain of yours.'

'Very good.'

'It's sad that you don't have faith in your fellow agents. I mean, if we can't trust those who spy on their own citizens for a living, who can we trust?'

'You,' said Ross. He carved a slice of fish, carefully added some lobster and spinach risotto, and forked the combination into his mouth. He nodded his approval. 'That's a very fine piece of fish. You really don't know what you're missing.'

Parker ate some steak. It was perfect, but Ross's presence at the table – in fact, in the state of Maine – was inhibiting his enjoyment of the dish.

'You could just have called and asked me to look into this,' said Parker. 'You didn't have to come all the way up here to do it.'

'I look upon you as an investment. I wanted to see how it was maturing.'

'And Eklund is just some small-time investigator who's dropped off the radar, leaving you mildly concerned.'

'You have it.'

Lies, all lies. Eklund was important. Ross wouldn't have been here in person if he were not.

But then, this was all a game. Parker had in his possession a list of names retrieved from a plane in the Great North Woods. The list contained details of men and women who had been compromised in ways large and small, individuals who had made a pact, either knowingly or not, with the servants of an old evil. Parker was drip-feeding some of those names to Ross, and Ross would occasionally complain about the pace at which this information was being shared, but Parker felt certain that Ross was doing little more with it than memorizing those identified, and perhaps moving discreetly against them when the opportunity presented itself.

Mostly, Ross was waiting.

In theory, Parker could have handed over the list in its entirety, enabling Ross to run it through some massive computer in the FBI's basement, at the end of which process a name would be spat out, for they were both convinced that hidden in this directory of human failings were clues to the identity of a single individual. That person, male or female, was leading a search for the Buried God, the God of Wasps, the One Who Waits Behind the Glass. If God existed, then this was the Not-God, but the names ascribed to it were irrelevant. Even whether or not such an entity might actually exist was relatively unimportant. What mattered was that those who believed in it, or simply professed to do so, used it to justify acts of immense depravity. Yet if the one who manipulated them all could be neutralized, that search would be set back for generations, perhaps forever.

But Ross was unable to carry out such an operation alone, no matter how quietly, because he couldn't be sure that his search would remain a secret. Some of those being hunted occupied positions of power and authority. They were wary, and vigilant. They listened. For now, these people believed the list remained lost. If they knew it had been retrieved, they would act to secure it.

So for all Ross's concerns about Parker, he acknowledged that Parker's continued possession of the list, and his investigation of those on it, might be their best chance for success. That was why Parker's retainer was so generous. Through it, Ross was funding a search in which his own agency could not be trusted to engage.

And now here he was, spearing fish with his fork and speaking of a missing investigator while Tony Bennett played in the background.

'How long has Eklund been missing?' Parker asked.

12

'He was scheduled to get in touch four days ago. I let it go to five before I contacted you.'

'Don't you know about the importance of the first forty-eight hours in any investigation?'

'I tend to eschew alarmism.' He gestured at Parker's plate. 'You've barely touched your steak.'

'I think I'll ask them to bag it for me. I may have it with eggs in the morning.'

Ross's own plate was already just a scattering of greens interspersed with fragments of white flesh. He dabbed his mouth with a napkin, finished off his wine, and called for the check. There was no suggestion of dessert or coffee. His business in Portland was almost done.

'What makes you think Eklund isn't just taking some time to himself?' Parker asked.

'Because that's not the arrangement I have with him. The conditions of our agreement are very clear.'

'I wish I could say the same.'

'I don't think you'd care much for the kind of errands Eklund runs.'

Another lie. Ross had put just a little too much effort into being dismissive.

'I've placed the relevant information on Eklund in a drop box,' he told Parker. 'You'll find a series of e-mail links to it when you check your in-box.'

The check came. Ross paid it in cash. When he had finished counting out the bills, he wrote down a cell phone number on a piece of blank paper that he took from his wallet.

'If you need to contact me, use this number,' he said. 'You'll be reimbursed for any expenses. I don't need receipts, just an estimate. I'll also make an ex gratia payment to your account to cover any incidentals. If you could avoid drawing too much attention to yourself, I'd be most grateful.'

He stood, but told Parker not to get up.

'Stay. Finish your wine.' His hand rested uncomfortably

heavily on Parker's left shoulder as he leaned down and spoke his next words very softly.

'And if you ever try to record one of our conversations again, I'll set the dogs on you and your psychotic friends, and let them tear you all apart.'

He patted Parker on the shoulder, then left.

A few minutes went by before Angel and Louis joined Parker.

'Where did he go?' asked Parker.

'The car was waiting for him,' said Louis. 'He obviously had the pleasure of your company timed to the minute. We didn't figure he was worth following. You want to talk to him, you can always knock on the door of Federal Plaza and ask if he can come out and play.'

'And we didn't hear a word either of you said after something about oysters,' Angel added. 'All we got was dead air.'

Parker reached for his tie and detached the pinhead microphone before removing the tie as well. Recording Parker's interactions with Ross had been Moxie Castin's idea. Even in its amended form, Moxie regarded Parker's contractor's agreement with Ross as being as close to toxic as it was possible for a document to come without requiring the addition of a biohazard symbol. Federal law permitted the recording of telephone or in-person conversations as long as one of the parties consented, which in this case Parker, as one of the parties, did, although Ross clearly held dissenting views.

'He knew, or suspected,' said Parker. 'He jammed me shortly after I arrived.'

'I think he has issues with trust,' said Angel. 'And charm, although we always figured about the charm part.'

'He called you and Louis psychotic, by the way.'

Louis scowled, or at least his permanent scowl deepened slightly.

'I'm hurt,' he said. 'I'm not psychotic. I'm sociopathic.'

Angel, who didn't seem bothered either way, pointed at Parker's steak.

'You eating that?'

'I—'

Before Parker could reply, Angel took Ross's seat, drew the plate toward him, and commenced feeding. Louis borrowed a chair from the nearest table and began scanning the wine list, 'since we're here.' A couple of the other diners glanced at them in mild alarm. Angel in particular looked like he might have been called to fix the boiler and become distracted by patrons' unfinished meals. One woman nearby was now huddled protectively over her lobster thermidor.

Louis ordered a glass of the Malbec and some bar snacks: bruschetta, meatballs.

'So,' he said, once he was done, 'what did Ross want from you?'

'To find a private investigator named Eklund who's gone off the reservation.'

'You going to do it?' asked Angel through a mouthful of steak.

'You know,' said Parker, 'I don't think I've been given a choice.'

3

As Ross had promised, the links to the Eklund file were waiting in Parker's in-box when he returned home that night. They required him to jump through some hoops to download the material, but eventually he retrieved everything. It didn't amount to much. Eklund was fifty-two, divorced for five years, with no children. He had been a licensed private investigator for nearly a decade, having first served time with law enforcement in New Hampshire and Rhode Island without ever rising very high in the ranks or, it seemed, serving with any particular distinction. Parker could find no tales of bank robberies foiled, no shoot-outs with hardened gunmen, no murderers apprehended in the course of routine traffic checks. It was a standard law enforcement career. Eklund had simply served his twenty, retired, and gone into business for himself. What might have drawn him into Ross's orbit, Parker did not know. Eklund appeared to be remarkably nondescript, but maybe that was the point. He wouldn't attract attention, and Parker only had to glance in a mirror to figure out why that quality might have appealed to Ross.

Nevertheless, he wondered if Eklund had ever come to regret striking his deal with the FBI man. At least Parker knew what he was getting himself into, or hoped that he did. He was playing Ross, but he was also being played. Parker was the bait on a hook, the tethered goat in the forest, while Ross waited to see what might come to take a bite. But what was Eklund's role? He watched, he listened, or so Ross had claimed. But whom was he watching, and to whom was he listening?

If Ross knew – and Ross must have known – then he wasn't telling Parker, and the bare details of Eklund's life contained in the drop box file offered no clues. Ross had supplied little more than business and home addresses, license plate number, the name and address of Milena Budny, Eklund's ex-wife, professional affiliations, bank account details – that much was useful, in any case – along with the access code to Eklund's cell phone. Parker wasn't about to ask how Ross had secured the latter information. The bank accounts he could understand, especially if Ross was paying Eklund for his services, but the code was another matter. Either Ross did not entirely trust Eklund, or this was simply the preferred operating procedure in all of Ross's dealings with those outside, and possibly even inside, the bureau. Whatever the reason, it made Parker glad he had gone to some lengths to secure his own computer, and was careful in the use of his landline and cell phone. In addition, he had his laptop and desktop computer regularly swept for viruses or Trojan horses; changed his passwords on a weekly basis; and, most adroitly of all, recorded little that was important or essential on-screen, preferring instead to rely on notebooks, his own system of shorthand, and a memory that was, as yet, showing no signs of decay beyond an occasional inability to recall the names of actresses in old movies.

With nothing else to do, Parker called Eklund's cell phone. It went straight to voice mail, but he used the code provided to access the messages. He listened to eighteen, including one from Eklund's ex-wife expressing concern at not hearing from him in a while, two from old cop buddies looking to meet up for a drink, and the rest from clients, either actual or prospective. Most left numbers, which Parker noted down, but none of the messages stood out as significant. He was also under no illusion that Ross was not already familiar with their contents, probably having accessed them without causing their deletion, and had come to the same conclusion as Parker had: if there was anything of use, it was well hidden.

Parker returned to the phone messages. They might have appeared mundane, but that didn't mean they contained no interesting information, merely that Ross – or someone acting on his behalf – hadn't been able to spot it. The same might well be true of Eklund's computer, once it was found. Ross's notes indicated that both the laptop and the phone were missing, and it didn't take a trained investigator to assume both were wherever Eklund currently happened to be. Parker knew he'd have to go to Eklund's office and home and perform a thorough search of all material he found in those locations, as well as track down each of the callers who had left messages in order to ascertain if Eklund had been in touch since they'd tried to make contact with him. The messages covered a period of five days, just as Ross had indicated. Eighteen messages over five days, almost a quarter of them personal. It wasn't much for a working private investigator.

Parker set what little he had learned aside, turned off his office light, and went to bed. It was late, and he couldn't do much for Eklund at this hour. He wasn't even sure he would be able to get started in earnest for a day or two, at least. He had promised Rachel, his former partner and the mother of his daughter Sam, that he would travel to Burlington for a meeting with Emily Ferguson, the child psychologist who had been dealing with Sam in the aftermath of her recent abduction.

Parker had met Ferguson twice before: once at the start of Sam's sessions, and the second time a week or so later, when he'd come across Ferguson and her children at the Maine Mall. Apparently her mother lived in Falmouth, and Ferguson had taken the opportunity to combine a visit with some shopping. As far as Parker could tell, Emily Ferguson had given birth to three monsters; that, or she had taken three kids and turned them into monsters. Either way, they were monsters.

Given the time and opportunity, they could probably have reduced the Maine Mall to a pile of rubble and twisted metal. Rachel thought highly of Ferguson, and Parker bowed to Rachel's professional knowledge, but he doubted that she had ever met the Ferguson tribe at its marauding best. If she had, it might have caused her to reconsider.

Sam: his daughter's problem, at least as far as her mother and Ferguson were concerned, was not that she was traumatized by her abduction, but that she appeared almost entirely untroubled by it. A man had taken her from her home, locked her in the trunk of his car, and brought her to a remote motel, but he had suffered some form of hemorrhage before he could visit any harm on his captive. Sam had been very lucky, but an element of post-traumatic stress might have been expected. Instead, it was as though nothing had ever happened. Both Rachel and the psychologist were convinced Sam was burying her true feelings. Parker wasn't so sure, but he kept his own counsel. He knew only that his daughter was stronger, and far stranger, than even her own mother could have suspected.

He lay in the dark. He hadn't bothered to draw the drapes, and through the window the snow-clad Scarborough marshes shone in the moonlight, white on black, like a landscape image in negative. He opened and closed his left hand, stretching the fingers, just as he had been doing all evening. The action hurt, but it would mean less pain for him in the morning, or so he hoped. Sometimes his entire life felt like a series of such trade-offs, a little suffering now for the possibility of a reduction in suffering down the line. Perhaps it was a vestige of his Catholicism. In a past life, he might have been an ascetic, or a mortifier of his own flesh.

He fell asleep to the sound of waves lapping at the shore, in this world and another.

4

In a house far to the west, a conversation ensued as blood was washed from skin to sink, and swirled away in a rush of pink.

'Others may come.' It was a man who spoke.

'Let them' was the reply. A female voice, but colder. 'They'll get the same.'

The woman stared out the window. Snow swirled as the storm moved east. She was glad that her brother could not see her face. She did not want to add to his concern. He did not like this part of their lives. Neither did she, but unlike her brother, she was capable of doing what was necessary, however unpleasant it might be.

'Whose work do we do?' she asked, dredging up the question from their shared childhood.

The response came automatically, even though he had not used it in years.

'Our father's work.'

His sister came to him, and kissed him softly on the lips. His mouth opened, and her tongue found his.

From the shadows the Brethren watched, and smiled their approval.

5

Parker rose early for the drive to Burlington. Knowing that he would soon be in a car for hours, he poured coffee into a Thermos mug and walked the margin of the marshes, through pitch pine and red maple, through foxglove and winterberry holly, alone with his thoughts.

He was stricken by a fleeting sense of melancholy. He did not want to make the trip west, but could not have said why. He walked back to his house and reflected on how he missed having a dog. Dogs were generally incompatible with melancholy.

Before he left, he made a series of calls to those who had left messages for Eklund, confirming that they had not been returned. Finally, he called Milena Budny, who now lived in Florida with her second husband. He identified himself, and informed her that he was acting on behalf of a client who was concerned about her ex-husband after he failed to make contact at an agreed time and date.

'Has something happened to Jaycob?'

The worry in her voice sounded genuine. Parker didn't mention that he'd already listened to the voice message left by her on Eklund's phone.

'I really don't know,' said Parker. 'I've only recently been engaged to look for him.'

'I haven't spoken to him in more than a month.'

'Is that unusual?'

'Yes and no. We try to speak every couple of weeks, but a month without contact wouldn't be untypical.'

Not too many divorced couples stayed in touch in this way, or not in Parker's experience, an opinion he now shared with Budny.

'Our divorce was pretty amicable,' she said.

Parker picked up on something in her tone. 'Pretty' amicable wasn't the same as 'amicable', not by some distance.

'May I ask why you separated?'

'We'd been drifting apart for a long time.'

'Okay.'

'And I met someone else, someone with whom I wanted to be more than I wanted to be with Jaycob.'

'So you instigated the divorce proceedings?'

'Yes.'

'I'm reluctant to pry, Mrs. Budny, and anything you tell me will be held in confidence, but—'

'You can ask what you want. If I feel something is too private, I'll let you know.'

'Well, there are degrees of amicability. I'm wondering, I guess, if your husband was angry, or upset, when you informed him that you wanted to end your marriage.'

'It was all a long time ago.'

'Five years. Not so long.'

'You seem to know a lot about us.'

'I've been tasked with looking for your husband. It's kind of my business to find out as much as I can.'

'Sure, I understand. Jaycob was sad about the end of our marriage. Not angry, just sad.'

'Did he try to change your mind?'

A pause.

'Yes.'

'But your mind wasn't for changing.'

He could almost see her smiling.

'No.'

'Is Jaycob still sad?'

'Yes, I believe he is. I wish he'd find someone else, but he hasn't.'

'Some women would simply have cut off communication under those circumstances.'

'I fell out of love with Jaycob, but I never stopped liking him. Talking with him occasionally, checking that he's okay, makes me feel better.'

'Less guilty.'

'Yes.'

Parker didn't suggest that this situation might be contributing to Eklund's inability to move on after the divorce. He didn't want to alienate Budny.

'Does Jaycob ever talk about his work during your conversations?'

'No. But then, he never did. Perhaps that was one of our problems.'

'Any friends with whom he was close?'

'No. Jaycob was always pretty solitary. He stayed in touch with some of his old police buddies, but only in the sense of joining them for drinks once or twice a year. Jaycob doesn't have any real friends.'

'What about hobbies, or pastimes?'

'Ghosts.'

'Excuse me?'

'Jaycob has a fascination with the paranormal. He reads books on it, goes to conferences.'

'Is this a long-standing interest?'

'I think it's grown stronger since the divorce, but it was always present.'

'General, or something specific?'

'I can't really say. I just know he spends a lot of time and money going places, talking to people. He doesn't share the details with me. Not that I ask anymore.'

'Why not?'

'It gives me the creeps, and he didn't seem to welcome my interest.'

'And did Jaycob say why he preferred not to tell you more about what he was doing?'

This time, it took her a while to answer.

'Only in the last couple of months.'

'And what was his reason?'

'He said it would be safer for me if I didn't know.'

'Those were his exact words?'

'Yes.'

Parker thought that might have explained the anxiety in her voice on the message she left, but he had to be sure.

'Mrs. Budny, are you worried about your ex-husband?'

'Mr. Parker, I've always been worried about him.'

Before ending the call, he gave Budny assurances that he would call her if he discovered anything helpful, and she similarly agreed to get in touch with him if Eklund made contact.

He next called the number Ross had given him, and clarified one or two details from the Eklund file with the agent. That call lasted less than a minute.

His final call should, he thought, really have been made before he spoke with Milena Budny, but he didn't think the recipient would have appreciated an early wake-up. His name was Art Currier, and he lived up by Seboomook Lake, on the doorstep of the state's Great North Woods. Currier was retired, liked a drink, and enjoyed sleeping late. He was also a useful source of information on the area for men like Parker, and was willing to do legwork for twenty bucks an hour, as long as it didn't get in the way of his sleep.

Currier answered on the fifth ring, if a yawn could be considered an answer.

'It's Charlie Parker.'

'Uh-huh.'

'You could sound more pleased.'

'This *is* me sounding pleased.'

'No wonder you live alone. I have some work for you.'

'Then talk.'

According to Ross's file, Eklund owned a cabin near Baker Lake, ten miles or so from Seboomook. Ross hadn't checked it because the place was remote and didn't have a phone line, but he obviously assumed that Parker would. It was a hell of a drive to take in winter on the off chance that Eklund might be there, which seemed unlikely given the current weather, but Art Currier owned a snowmobile and knew the whole area better than Parker. Currier agreed to check on Eklund's 'camp', as he termed it in true Maine fashion, and get back to Parker later that day.

With his calls made, Parker headed for Vermont. The weather was bad, although the storm was easing as it neared the coast. He listened to music on the drive, letting each album play in full, resisting the lure of the shuffle on his iPod. He thought this might be part of the reason for the resurgence in vinyl: at just twenty minutes each side, it wasn't worth leaving the room to go and do something else. You might as well just sit and listen and, hey, since you'd sat through the first side, what was the point in neglecting the second?

He let the music wash over him, and thought of Sam. He had not seen his daughter in two weeks, although he had spoken with her over the phone and via Skype, which was increasingly how they communicated. When Rachel first moved out, taking Sam with her, she and Parker had come to an informal agreement about access and visits, and the arrangement had mostly worked. But Sam had been put in jeopardy by her father's actions on two separate occasions over the past year. It had not been Parker's intention to place her in harm's way, and in neither case could he have antici- pated or prevented what transpired, but the blame was his to bear. Those two events had altered the balance of his relationship with Rachel. He knew she still cared about him,

25

and understood the depth of his feelings for Sam, but she was no longer as willing as before to entrust their daughter to his care. The negotiations were ongoing, and he was doing his utmost to ensure that they did not become fractious, an approach that seemed to surprise Rachel, as though she had somehow expected him to put up more of a fight.

But it wasn't about fighting. Sam was special. She had to be protected.

And she was, although the precise nature of that protection remained to be understood.

It was close to three thirty p.m. when Parker finally arrived at Emily Ferguson's practice on Spear Street, which was based in a house equidistant from the University of Vermont and the adjacent Burlington Country Club. Sam had already gone into Ferguson's room for her session. Rachel was sitting outside in the waiting room, flicking through the latest edition of *Vanity Fair*. She greeted him with a perfunctory kiss on the cheek, and they sat opposite each other with the table between, just in case either one of them needed to pick it up to use as a shield.

'I'm sorry I'm late,' he said.

'Don't worry about it. The weather's terrible, and Emily said she'd prefer to speak with us after Sam's session anyway.'

'How is she?'

'Still fine.'

'You sound almost disappointed.'

'Don't start.'

'Sorry.' And he was.

She fiddled with the drawstring on her hooded UV sweatshirt.

'It's not normal,' she said, not for the first time.

'I guess not.'

She dropped the drawstring.

'I've been offered a contract with the university,' she said.

'That's great.'

'Three years, with the likelihood of an extension if all goes well. I'll be attached to the Falls Laboratory as part of the biobehavioral subprogram.'

'Will I sound stupid if I confess I don't know what *biobehavioral* means?'

'It's the study of the interaction of behavior and biological processes. That's the simple answer.'

'Thanks for not overcomplicating it.'

'I'll be specializing in the neural systems underlying fear.' She looked at him now. 'I figure I've been dealing with so much of it that I should try to understand it better.'

'And get paid for it.'

She allowed him a smile.

'You're such an asshole.'

'I know.'

The smile faded.

'My father thinks I should go to court,' she said. 'He believes we need to formalize our arrangements for Sam.'

'Your father wants me to fall off the edge of the world and disappear.'

Rachel didn't try to deny it. Parker's relationship with her father was too far gone for that.

'He cares a lot about Sam. What happened with the abduction – well, it nearly broke him. It nearly broke us all.'

'You don't have to go to court.'

'Don't I?'

'You tell me what works best for you and Sam, and I'll agree. If Sam is concerned, I'll talk her round. She'll understand.'

'Why are you doing this?'

'Doing what?'

'Being reasonable. No, being – God, I don't know – so *neutral* about it all.'

There it was again. Sometimes he thought she might have

preferred it if he raged and shouted, or tried to stand up for his rights. If he did, it would probably have made it easier for her. It would have proved that her father was correct, and next thing anyone knew they'd all be knee-deep in lawyers.

'Because I want her to be safe as much as you do. Because I love her.'

There was no time for further discussion. The door to Parker's right opened, and Sam emerged. Ferguson stood behind her. She was a round, curvy woman who, for Parker, brought to mind a figure assembled from a selection of soft fruits. Aside from her apparent inability to raise children who were not a threat to the stability of nations, he found her patronizing, and strangely unyielding despite her fleshiness. *Smug* was the word that sprang most frequently to mind when he thought of her, although he tried to think of her as little as possible. All this he did his best to hide from Sam, as he didn't want to prejudice his daughter against a woman who, whatever her flaws, was trying to help.

Sam gave him a hug as he rose, and he ruffled her hair as he hugged her back.

'How you doing, Bear?' he asked.

'Good, Bear,' she replied.

'Bear' had become an occasional thing with her lately. He wasn't sure why.

'If you'll just grab a seat, Sam, we won't be too long,' said Ferguson.

Sam took the chair her father had just vacated and removed a book from her bag. She was working her way through the Encyclopedia Brown stories, and only had two or three left to go. Whenever they were in the car together, and someone cut them off or drove like an idiot, she would now order her father to 'tootle him with vigor.' It didn't matter if the driver was male or female: 'tootle him with vigor' was the standard response.

Ferguson greeted Parker, and invited him and Rachel to

join her in the consulting room. The space was bright and cheerful, with painted shelves that mixed clinical volumes and children's books. The pictures on the wall were mostly landscapes, along with some original illustrations from modern YA fiction, although nothing threatening or potentially disturbing.

The initial discussion with Ferguson went much as Parker had anticipated. Sam, much to the frustration of two-thirds of the people in the room, continued to show no signs of trauma from the events surrounding her abduction. She claimed to have little clear memory of what had occurred beyond being snatched and taken to a motel room. Before she could come to any harm, her captor had started bleeding from multiple sites, and Sam used this opportunity to run away and seek help. This was much the same as what she had told the police, and later Parker himself. When he tried to press her further, both over Skype and in person – although only in Rachel's absence – Sam responded to his questions with a single gesture: she placed a finger over her lips as an injunction to silence. Parker knew what that meant. He could recall the words she had whispered to him when he first became aware that his daughter was different.

'They're always listening. We have to be careful, Daddy, because they'll hear. They'll hear, and they'll come . . .'

Ferguson was speaking to him, but he'd missed it, so lost was he in his own thoughts.

'I'm sorry,' he said. 'What was that?'

Rachel glanced at him with barely concealed annoyance. Ferguson, meanwhile, was being even more patronizing than usual, as though Parker were a slow learner who had to be coaxed along the road to greater understanding.

'I was just remarking that I strongly suspect Sam worries about you.'

'Really? I try not to discuss my work with her.'

'Perhaps she's more aware of it than you believe.'

If only you knew, he thought.

Something of this must have revealed itself in his face, because Ferguson's placid expression faltered for the first time since the conversation had begun, briefly revealing a potentially more interesting side to her character; that, or she was simply wondering how anyone could be so dumb and still walk in a straight line without help.

'She watched a man die in your presence,' Ferguson continued. 'A man who was about to kill you.'

'I understand that.' He decided to give her a brief flash of teeth. 'It wasn't intentional on my part.'

'Jesus . . .' said Rachel.

'I'm not sure you understand the gravity of the situation in relation to your child,' said Ferguson.

'What do you want me to do?' asked Parker. 'Stop seeing her? I hardly see enough of her as it is.'

'I—' Ferguson began, but Parker interrupted her.

'I could find another profession, I suppose. Child psychology might be an option, except my tendency is to try to solve problems, not create them where they don't exist.'

Now Ferguson bared her teeth back at him. Good, thought Parker. For the first time he was being willfully difficult in his responses, even obstructive, but he was sick of this. He had enough guilt already without Ferguson trying to add to it. He knew his daughter better than any of them, and even he didn't really know her at all.

'I'm not sure that attitude is helpful,' said Ferguson.

Parker forced himself to relax. Through the window behind Ferguson, he watched a breeze carry flurries of snow from the bare branch of a tree. A robin alighted amid the flakes, its feathers ruffling. Most headed south for winter, but a few always stayed. This one was a mature adult. It was either lucky or tough, because robins were prey for squirrels, snakes, cats, ravens, crows and just about every kind of raptor. Few lived longer than a couple of years.

'Again, what do you want me to do?' Parker asked, and saw Ferguson exchange a look with Rachel. *Go away*, that was one answer, but Ferguson and Rachel were both smart enough to recognize it wouldn't make Sam happy. It wouldn't even make her safer. He was there to protect her until the time came when she could protect herself, even if she wasn't as vulnerable as she led others to believe. Nevertheless, it wasn't a responsibility that he planned to abdicate anytime soon – or ever.

'I think that's a discussion for you and Rachel to have,' said Ferguson. She and Rachel exchanged another look, and he knew that whatever Rachel might have to say had been the subject of a prior conversation between them.

'We will,' said Parker. 'And thank you for what you've tried to do for Sam.'

He meant it, too. He might not have cared much for Ferguson, but she believed what she was doing was right. Who knew, it might even have helped Sam to have an adult other than her parents or grandparents taking an interest in her.

But his sincerity was lost on Emily Ferguson. She had relegated him to the position of 'bad parent', maybe even 'dangerous parent'. It made Parker more determined than ever to avoid having anything to do with lawyers and courts when it came to Sam. If Ferguson were required to give expert testimony, it would not be in his favor.

'I think I should continue my sessions with Sam for the time being,' she said.

'I'm sure that will be fine,' said Rachel.

Parker didn't object. He saw no reason to, for now.

They both stood. Ferguson shook hands with Rachel, and clutched her arm in a gesture of intimacy. Parker got a dead fish in his hand. He was no expert, but he thought that constituted some form of bias. There must have been something in Ferguson's training advising against it, but she might have been sick on the day they covered it.

In the waiting room, Sam was immersed in Encyclopedia Brown, who was keeping Idaville safe from criminals.

'Can we go to Al's?' she asked.

Al's French Frys was nearby, on Williston Road. It had been producing damn fine fries since the 1940s, and a visit to it was part of Sam's post-session routine.

Parker looked at Rachel, but she was determined that any anger she might have felt toward him should not be obvious to Sam.

'Sure,' she said. 'Let's do that.'

Sam turned her gaze to Parker, then back to Rachel. She scrunched up her nose.

'Did you guys just have a fight?'

II

Yesterday, upon the stair,
I met a man who wasn't there.
He wasn't there again today,
I wish, I wish he'd go away . . .

William Hughes Mearns, 'Antigonish'

6

The boy's name was Alex MacKinnon. His family was of Scottish ancestry on one side, and proclaimed it at every opportunity, although no immediate member had set foot in the old country since the beginning of the previous century.

Alex was twelve, and had only recently begun cycling to and from school, with his mother's reluctant permission, although it was a freedom he had been given ample cause to regret over the course of winter. Yet only the worst of the weather forced him to abandon his bicycle. He was not about to let the elements undo, even temporarily, such a hard-won concession.

His bike had lights on both the front and back. He wore a reflective vest with a blinking red LED on the left sleeve, and another LED on the back of his helmet. He considered himself to be so well lit that a motorist would be more likely to collide with a fully decorated Christmas tree than hit him. On the other hand, the daylight was already fading as he left school, and although it was less than a mile from the school gates to his door, there were dark patches along the road, mostly where the woods lay.

That was where Alex saw the man, or what might once have been a man. He was dressed in black, but his head was bare despite the cold, revealing a bald pate fringed in red, the color of his hair matching that of his beard, which ran like the strap of a helmet from ear to ear.

He was walking parallel to the road on a bank of thick snow. The sight of someone marching bareheaded through

35

the trees would have been unusual enough at this time of year, because a cold wind was blowing, and the drifts hid hollows and tree roots, so it was easy to misstep and take a fall. But what made this particular individual even more distinctive, and caused Alex to veer into a ditch, spilling him from his saddle, was that he was not walking through the snow but over it: his shoes were clearly visible when he should have been buried in white almost to his knees. It was also clear to Alex, even in this poor light, that the man was leaving no footprints, not a one.

Alex lay on his back, the front wheel of his bicycle still spinning beside him. He hadn't hurt himself in the fall, but the air had been knocked out of him. More to the point, he was scared shitless.

The man stopped walking, frozen in midstep, like a hunter alerted to the presence of a deer. For a moment he remained entirely still, until his attention slowly began to shift in Alex's direction. His features were smudged and indistinct, as though a thumb had smeared itself across an ink drawing of a face. His head tilted slightly to one side, taking in the boy and his bicycle, then—

Well, Alex could only describe him as turning in upon himself. The man pivoted on his right foot so that his right side was now toward Alex, then took a step forward and was gone, leaving no sign that he had ever been there to begin with.

Alex scrambled to his feet, grabbed his bicycle, and made a running start along the road. He didn't look back. He didn't dare. And although he had never seen this apparition before, still he knew it for what it was, because he'd heard his father whisper to his mother of just such a figure, when his father thought he was going mad.

The Brethren shadowed Alex through the forest, watching him from the trees. Another haunting had begun.

7

The meal at Al's wasn't the most convivial that Parker could recall, although Sam didn't let the chill between her parents prevent her from enjoying her cheeseburger and cup of fries, as well as a strawberry milk shake. She declined to accompany Rachel when she went to the bathroom, and stayed with her father at the table, sipping the last of her shake and watching a small snowplow at work in the parking lot.

'Do I have to go visit with Emily again?' she asked.

'I think it might help,' Parker replied.

'I don't need help.'

'Are you sure?'

'Yes.'

She spoke in a tone that brooked no argument. It was a simple statement of fact.

'It might make your mom feel better about things.'

Sam considered this.

'Okay.' She sucked noisily through the straw. 'Did Mom tell you about the picture?'

'What picture?'

'Emily asked me to draw a picture of my house and my family. I did like she asked, and she just looked at me funny.'

'Why?'

'Well, I drew Grandpa and Grandma, and Mom, and you – and Walter, although dogs are hard. And I drew the house. I thought it was pretty good.'

'And Emily didn't?'

'She showed it to Mom after, when I was waiting outside.

She told Mom that she thought I felt like I wasn't part of my own family because I didn't put myself in the picture.'

'Why didn't you draw yourself?'

'I was the artist. How could I draw myself if I was the one drawing everyone else?'

Parker sipped his coffee. It made sense to him, but then he never claimed to be a psychologist.

'So,' Sam continued, 'I drew another picture and brought it to Emily today, and I put a girl in it. She asked if it was me.'

'And what did you tell her?'

'I just smiled. She figured it for a yes.'

Parker found that he was holding on too hard to his coffee cup. The sounds of the other people in the restaurant faded away, and there was only Sam, him, and the whiteness beyond.

'But it wasn't you, was it?' he said.

'No.'

Jennifer, he thought: she put her dead half sister into her drawing.

'Do you still see Jennifer?'

'You know I do.'

His throat hurt, and his eyes were warm. He blinked to try to keep the tears away. He couldn't help it. This was wrong. And yet:

'How often does she come to you?'

'A lot.'

'Is she . . . ?'

His voice trailed off. He didn't know what he wanted to ask, or nothing that could be captured in a single word. Happy, sad, angry, frightened – did these concepts even have any meaning for what Jennifer now was?

And Sam replied, 'She is.'

Yes, he thought: if there was only one truth, then that was it. She is. She exists. Anything else was purely incidental.

Sam was draining the last of her milk shake, assessing him

over the glass. He stepped carefully. He found that he did so more and more often around her. He looked to his left. Rachel had stopped to speak with someone over by the restroom. He couldn't see who it was from where he sat. Her body was turned slightly away from the other speaker, as though she was not inclined to linger. Whatever the nature of the conversation, she would be back at the table very soon.

'Sometime you're going to have to talk to me about what really happened at the motel,' he said.

Sam detached herself from the straw and opened her mouth to object, but he held up his hand to stop her.

'I know what you're going to say. You'll tell me about being careful, and people listening, and I understand all that. But I'm still your father, and I can't protect you if I can't talk with you about stuff.'

Rachel extricated herself, and began moving toward them. Only when she was almost – but not quite – within earshot did Sam speak again.

'But you're not protecting me, Daddy. I'm protecting you.

'And,' she added softly, 'the ones who are listening aren't people . . .'

8

The sky was gray as they emerged from Al's. Parker checked the forecast on his phone. More snow was due, and the meteorologists were advising people against unnecessary travel. He could leave Burlington and start driving, but the likelihood was that he'd be caught in the worst of the storm before he even got halfway back to the coast. It would be a slow, tedious, stressful trip. He was better off staying where he was for the night, and starting out early in the morning when the roads were clear.

He looked at Rachel. They'd made love when last he stayed in Vermont. He was injured at the time, and she was hurting from a breakup, and they cared about each other and loved each other enough to be able to draw comfort from a night together. That wouldn't be happening tonight, or perhaps ever again. Sam's abduction had altered the delicate balance between them, possibly irrevocably.

'I'm going to find somewhere in town for the night,' he told her.

Rachel didn't bother asking him where he was going to stay. She probably guessed: there was a little inn near the university that he had grown to like. He'd slept in enough motel beds to want to avoid them whenever possible.

'I'll be in touch,' she said.

'Sure.'

He hugged Sam. A little fragment of his heart came loose and was lost to him each time he had to say goodbye to her. He'd never believed it would come to this. He'd never wanted to be one of those fathers.

'Take care of your mom,' he told her.

'I will. Love you, Bear.'

'Love you too, Bear.'

He watched them drive away. He felt trapped in a strange dream from which he could not awaken; each time he opened his eyes, he found himself mired deeper in unreality.

And he was frightened of his daughter.

He got in his car and started the engine, then sat for a time to let the windows clear. The door to Al's opened, and a man emerged. He had neatly coiffed white hair, and the tanned skin of someone who could afford to escape much of the winter for sunnier climes. It was Jeff, Rachel's former boyfriend – asshole boyfriend, Parker corrected himself, although the asshole part was a given. Burlington was a small city; too small, sometimes. If it was with Jeff that Rachel had been talking in the restaurant, then why hadn't she mentioned it to him when she returned to the table? Actually, he knew the answer: any discussion of Jeff would only have darkened an already somber mood.

Parker's Mustang was distinctive enough to draw a second glance even in passing, but Jeff must have been looking for it. Parker saw him pause at the door and scan the lot before locking onto the car. His expression was one of restrained distaste, but he gave no other acknowledgment of Parker's presence. There was just the pause, and the look, before he walked off to the left and disappeared around the corner.

Al's wasn't Jeff's kind of place. He didn't much care for eating with his fingers, or being surrounded by folks who did. So what, Parker wondered, was he doing there? It didn't take a PI's license to figure out the answer to that one.

If Jeff starts dating Rachel again, Parker thought, *I'll have him killed.*

Slowly.

The inn was otherwise unoccupied by guests that evening. He was given a large room with a bay window overlooking the garden, and beyond it a view of Lake Champlain and the Adirondacks. He put his overnight bag in a corner. He always kept a canvas carrier in the trunk of his car, filled with a couple of changes of clothing, some toiletries, and a little medical kit. He took the room's wingback chair and checked his phone. He saw that he'd missed a call from Art Currier, which he now returned.

'Art?'

'That camp is way out in the willy-wags. Even in summer it'd be hard to get to.'

'Meaning?'

'It's empty, and I don't think anyone's been down that trail since before the first snowfall.'

'Did you ask around?'

'Didn't need to, but figured you might want confirmation. This Eklund doesn't have many neighbors, and up there most people incline toward minding their own business, but I rousted an old coot who thought the owner might have cleared out some stuff last year: furniture, bedding, and the like. He hasn't seen him since.'

Parker thanked Currier, and told him he'd send a check.

'Send cash. It was me who hauled his ass out there, not the IRS.'

Currier hung up, and Parker opened his laptop to go through e-mail. There was nothing from Ross to indicate that the missing Eklund had reappeared, so he pulled up a map of Providence, Rhode Island, saved a couple of screenshots, and booked a hotel room equidistant between the home and office addresses of the missing PI. Then, because it was on Ross's dime, he booked a second room. One night alone was enough, and he decided he might want some company in Providence.

9

Alex MacKinnon didn't eat all of his supper that night. He told his mom he wasn't feeling so good. May MacKinnon put her hand to her son's forehead and found it cool to the touch, but he was definitely shivering, and she was worried that he might have caught a chill. That bicycle: while part of her was pleased to see her son growing more independent, she hated the thought of him cycling to and from school. Some people just drove like jerks, and cell phones had made their kind into jerks squared. Every time she saw a dumb bitch or bastard texting or talking while trying to drive with one hand, she wanted to put a gun to someone's head and pull the trigger. She didn't want her son to end up dead in the gutter just because a seventeen-year-old was too busy with a phone to keep her eyes on the road.

She checked on Alex shortly after eight. He was lying under the covers of his bed, watching YouTube videos on his iPad. He was wearing earphones, so he didn't notice her at the door, and she decided not to disturb him. She considered keeping him home from school the next day. Alex wasn't one of those kids who complained of being ill when they weren't. She'd see how he was feeling in the morning and make a final decision then.

She went to the storage closet beside the first-floor bathroom, which was where they kept the laundry hamper. She'd noticed earlier that it was pretty full, and it wouldn't hurt to put up a load while she had time. It would mean she could transfer it to the dryer before she went to bed, and it would be ready to go in the morning.

Of course, there was less washing now than there used to be.

Mike, Alex's father, would be missing for a year come April. He'd been suffering from depression, and privately most people believed that he'd taken his own life. May didn't hold with that, though, not one little bit. Her husband might sometimes have been sad, but not only wasn't Mike the kind to do away with himself (although was there really such a thing as 'the kind', May often wondered, when she lay alone in their bed and wept for the absence at her left side), but he wasn't a man who would abandon his wife and son to pain and uncertainty in the aftermath. He had always been a gentle, courteous individual. He couldn't even accept a complimentary dessert at the Sovereign Grille without sending a thank-you card a day or two later. He wouldn't have killed himself without leaving a note for his wife and child, but she struggled even to envisage him writing such a missive. Mike was a quiet man, but he never kept his pain bottled up. They'd always been able to talk to each other, right from the start. He'd been open with her about every aspect of his life.

Even his family.

God, getting in touch with Mike's brother after Mike went missing was just about the hardest thing she'd ever done. Mike would have hit the ceiling, but then Mike wasn't around, which was the whole point, and May's fear was that his disappearance might be linked to his brother's activities. If that were the case, then his brother would know whom to approach, and where to look. But this, too, was a dead end. Mike's brother helped, or appeared to, but she couldn't really know for sure.

And as for that woman with him – Jesus, she gave May the creeps.

She'd held on to hope. Mike could have been involved in an accident, or suffered some type of stroke. For all anyone knew, he might have been stuck in Boise, Idaho, with no recollection of his previous life, living with the homeless, just another man who'd fallen through the cracks. Lately, though, she'd come to feel that he was dead. She sensed it as a severing of the bond between them, perhaps because they'd always been so close. Maybe her desire to have him returned to her alive had caused her to remain willfully blind to reality. It was as though she had been shot, or stabbed, during some incident of panic and flight, and the recognition of her injury was only emerging as the adrenaline subsided.

But Mike had been unhappy, even troubled, in those last weeks before he disappeared. He'd been scared, too. He thought he might have a tumor, or bleeding on the brain. He started getting bad headaches. He admitted to experiencing what he thought were hallucinations, both visual and auditory. He was seeing people who weren't there, hearing voices in empty rooms. His physician referred him for tests, but before he could be checked out, Mike was gone.

May opened the laundry hamper. Alex's clothes were in a wet ball on top, discarded from earlier in the day. *Funny*, she thought, *it hadn't started snowing again until he got home.* She picked up his trousers and saw that they were still damp, and marked with dirt along the left leg. There was also a hole in one knee. She knew then that he had fallen off his bike and hadn't told her. That child: it wasn't a chill he was fighting off – well, it might be a little, given how wet his clothes were – but shock. Good grief, he might even have hurt himself and been afraid to tell her. It would be just like him to keep it secret in case she forbade him to ride a bike ever again, not even when he left home and got married, because she'd say something about it at the wedding reception just to be sure that his new wife knew what a doofus he was when it came to two wheels and a chain.

She tossed the clothes on the floor and stomped back upstairs. She wasn't angry with him, or not very, but she was concerned. She'd have to insist on his letting her see that left leg. She had visions of it swollen and bruised under the comforter, maybe with a bend in it where no bend should be . . .

She opened the door to Alex's room, but he was no longer in bed. She could see that both of his legs were fine, too, because he was standing in his boxers and T-shirt with his back to her, facing the window. The drapes were open, and a pale version of her son hung in the darkness while snow fell around him. She felt a terrible sense of foreboding, as though she were experiencing a visitation by the ghost he must someday become.

'Honey,' she said, 'did you have an accident on your bike today?'

He didn't turn around, didn't even acknowledge her presence. That was his father in him. For all his openness, Mike would very occasionally pretend that he couldn't hear her when she got into one of her rages, especially if it was over something he had done, hoping it would all just blow over and obviate the need to deal with it. Actually, she believed that it might be hardwired into the whole male gender, because her own father had been like that as well. He'd even been known to sneak out the back door and head for the safety of town when his wife armed herself and went on the warpath.

'Alex,' she said, 'I'm talking to you.'

Only then did he turn. His face was milky white, his mouth like a red wound in his flesh.

'Mom,' he said. 'Mom.'

She went to him, her arms open to enfold him.

'What is it, Alex? What is it, baby?'

And she saw them even as he spoke.

'Mom, there are people in the woods.'

10

Parker ate dinner alone at the Farmhouse Tap & Grill on Bank Street. He was reading a biography of the writer John le Carré, and thought that le Carré would have made a very good undercover cop if he could just have learned to better accommodate himself to his secret sense of shame.

Parker limited himself to one glass of wine. He was feeling maudlin, and he didn't want to exacerbate it. He was worried about Sam, and Rachel. He was also worried about himself. He was glad for the distraction offered by Jaycob Eklund's possible disappearance. While he had a couple of cases open in Portland, they were routine bits of business for Moxie Castin and a couple of other lawyers, mostly involving the transfer of papers from his hand to another. It was dull, safe work. If he were smart, he'd have limited himself to juggling envelopes for lawyers, and then wouldn't have found himself eating alone in a bar in Burlington, Vermont, trying to figure out how to keep his former girlfriend from getting in touch with the Family Division of the Vermont court system.

Then again, if he were that smart, and that careful, he'd have been someone else.

The easiest money he'd earned all year had come from a woman named Thea Bentling, who was convinced that her husband, Steve, was cheating on her. As it turned out, Thea was right: Steve was seeing another woman called Sherri Sweetman, a name that would have suited a grade school teacher, which, conveniently, was precisely what Sherri was. She was also, as it happened, married to Dave

47

Ohlson, who was a client of Moxie's. Ohlson had recently approached Moxie because he believed that his wife – who had kept her maiden name, possibly because it was just so damn cute – was less faithful to him than he might ideally have wished. Moxie had put Ohlson in touch with Parker, who had already been engaged by Thea Bentling to follow her errant husband.

Parker followed Steve Bentling to a new boho coffee shop in South Portland, where Bentling met Sherri Sweetman, whose details Parker had been handed not an hour earlier by Moxie himself. Bentling and Sweetman took themselves to an inexpensive motel in which to spend some quality time together, while Parker snapped pictures of them with his phone and wondered how anyone could believe they might be able to keep an affair secret in a town so small. The cheating couple's idea of being discreet was to take the Casco Bay Bridge from Portland into South Portland, maybe because there were folks in Portland who seemed to regard South Portland as not just another city – which it was – but possibly another existential realm entirely, compounded by the fact that they had to cross water to get to it. When Parker met Moxie to tell him, the lawyer almost choked laughing, and Parker collected two fees for what was essentially the same job.

He finished a chapter of the biography and called for the check. He'd walked to the bar, and now he headed back toward his lodgings as the last of the falling snow thinned before ceasing. He felt the crunch of it beneath his feet. He wished Sam were with him. He kept one hand in his pocket and the other by his side, as though by doing so he might conjure up the sensation of her walking with him, her gloved hand in his, her small footsteps trailing beside his own.

His thoughts of Sam inevitably brought to mind his lost daughter, and he peered into the trees at either side of the street, and into the shadows between the houses, both hoping and fearing to see a flicker in the darkness as of a child shadowing him while leaving no mark upon the newly fallen snow. So lost in thought did he become that he failed to notice the car parked outside the inn, or the individual who emerged from it as he drew near the gate. Only when the man stepped forward did Parker stop and look into his face.

Rachel's father was standing before him. Frank Wolfe was wearing a long gray coat, and a trilby with a feather in the band. He looked like a dad from an old movie, right down to his gray mustache.

Parker and Frank had never gotten along, and recent events had done nothing to bring them closer together. When the identity of Sam's abductor was revealed, along with his connection to her father, it was all that Frank's wife and daughter had been able to do to keep him from outright physical assault on Parker. Since then, they had neither seen each other nor even exchanged a word over the phone, and yet Parker was not particularly surprised to see him. It was that kind of day.

'Frank,' he said. 'How long have you been waiting out here?'

'Couple of hours. I told them I was going to catch a movie.'

'What did you go see?'

'What?' He looked confused.

'When you get home, Rachel and your wife will ask what movie you went to see. You should have an answer. Unless you're going to tell them the truth.'

Frank Wolfe wasn't used to lying. While it would have been an understatement to say he and Parker did not see eye to eye, the detective did not doubt that Frank loved both his daughter and his grandchild deeply. Rachel's old man was a straight arrow, and it was not in his nature to be dishonest. He lived a comfortable, privileged life, which might have been part of the problem, but he would have been wealthier and more privileged still if he had been prepared to compromise his own moral code. He thought of himself as a good man, but truly good men never think of themselves in that way at all.

Frank looked at the trees, and the street, and his car as though he had suddenly found himself in an unfamiliar environment with no recollection of how he might have arrived there. He breathed out deeply, his breath pluming, and Parker caught the distinct smell of alcohol. Frank wasn't drunk, not yet, but he'd been drinking enough to earn himself a DUI if he were pulled over. If the cops didn't get him, then a combination of the weather and his own dulled reactions might ensure that a collision would.

'Why are you here?' Parker asked.

'I came to talk to you.'

Parker could think of few people with whom he wanted to talk less, but a conversation offered the possibility of clearing the air. Relations would simply continue to deteriorate if he sent Frank on his way, assuming he made it home alive, or without an involuntary detour to the nearest police station.

'It's cold. Why don't we go inside and sit down?'

Parker gestured to the inn. It had a couple of common areas where guests could work or read if they chose. The room at the front, to the left of the door, was empty. He could see it through the open drapes.

Frank nodded, and Parker led the way along the snow-covered path to the warmth of his lodgings.

11

May MacKinnon stood at her kitchen window and stared out at the woods that marked the boundary of her backyard. She thought about calling the police, but she wasn't ready to do that, not yet. Despite her husband's disappearance, and all the possible fates she had imagined for him, she remained inclined to think the best of people, and to trust in an ordered universe, because only in a universe in which people were good, and order was the natural state, might her husband not have suffered too much before he died.

She was also experiencing a readjustment of the senses, a selective distortion of her own memory and perceptions. She believed that she had seen figures in the woods, but had found herself struggling to keep them in focus. They resembled those tricks involving symbols on cards, in which the symbol momentarily disappeared from view when the card was placed in the blind spot of one's eye. When she tried to look directly at any individual form moving between the trees, that figure would seem to be swallowed by the shadows while the rest remained visible. If her gaze shifted, then the previously unseen man or woman would flicker back into sight at the periphery of her vision.

Now, downstairs in her kitchen with the lights deliberately left off, the better for her to hide herself as she monitored her property, May could no longer detect signs of movement. An atavistic part of her mind – seldom used, a relic of an older humanity – was sending conflicting messages: it was warning her not to go outside while simultaneously trying to suggest to her that she had been mistaken in what she supposed herself to have seen.

But Alex had been with her. He had seen them too, right? And the voice in her head, the one that spoke like a version of her absent husband, answered:

But you were worried about him. You were concerned that he might have injured himself, and he in turn was frightened because he had concealed his accident from you. Each of you communicated fear to the other, and each of you fed upon it in turn.

'And from that we both conjured up people in the woods?'

She said the words aloud, whispering them to an entity in her head, one that was doing a damn fine job of imitating Mike, right down to the foreign cadences of his speech, the way he always paused between sentences, no matter how angry, happy, or sad he was. He was a deliberate man, a mindful one. But the voice that was causing her to doubt herself was not quite right, for one simple reason.

Mike would never have tried to make her doubt herself.

Her skepticism drove it away. She was glad. She would entertain no phantasms of her lost spouse.

Then it came to her: gypsies. A group of them had passed through town earlier in the year – three interrelated families, according to the police, who monitored their presence from the moment they'd parked their motorhomes in the lot of the Walmart out by Airway Drive. They'd been a mix of ages, just like the folk she'd glimpsed in the woods. They hadn't caused any trouble – hadn't been given the opportunity to, according to certain people in town, since the cops and the mall guards sent them on their way after the second night, waking them in the darkness so they left with crying children and confused, barking dogs. May didn't care for this, since they didn't seem to her to be doing any harm. Then again, May was the only person in her family who thought that

Bernie Sanders would have made a good president, so what did she know?

Could this be part of the same group, or some other come to set up camp in the woods now that the mall had been ruled out as a possible halting site? May felt her liberal credentials being sorely tested. It was one thing having gypsies camped out at the mall, but another entirely having them lighting fires within sight of her own backyard.

Don't go out there.

It wasn't Mike's voice any longer. It wasn't any voice she had ever heard before. It spoke to her as a patient parent might speak to a child on the verge of doing something unwise, but May was already pulling on the gardening boots that always stood ready by the back door, and putting on Mike's old coat, the one he kept hanging in the closet by the laundry room, and which she refused to put away. Sometimes, when it was cold, she would wrap herself in it, sit on the kitchen floor, and close her eyes, imagining that it was Mike who was with her, Mike who was holding her.

Mike, Mike: why did you have to leave?

She heard a noise behind her. Alex was standing at the foot of the stairs, wrapped in a robe to keep out the cold.

'Mom? Did you call the police?'

'Not yet. We don't know who they are.'

Or even *if* they are, she wanted to add, but did not. *Christ, where did that come from?*

'Mom, I saw a man in the woods today.'

'A man? What man?'

'I don't know. He was dressed weird. One second he was there, the next he was gone. I think he was floating on the snow. He made me fall off my bike.'

He started to cry.

'I should have told you, but I was scared.'

Her saliva crackled in her ears, like the sound of bacon sizzling in a skillet.

I won't go far, she thought. *I'll step to the edge of the ring cast by the security light, and if I see anything, anything at all, I'll be back inside before you can say cock robin.*

'You lock the door behind me, you hear?'

'Mom—'

'It's okay. I just want to look.'

She opened the back door and stepped into the yard.

12

A Nespresso machine sat in a corner of the inn's library, beside a bookcase filled with the kind of works designed to be looked at, or flicked through, but never actually read. A couple of airport novels were interspersed, like yokels who'd stumbled in on intellectuals' night at the local meeting hall.

Parker had no idea what the colors of the Nespresso capsules signified, so he just found two that matched and made Frank Wolfe a double, then followed it with a single cup for himself. Frank unbuttoned his coat, but didn't seem willing to remove it until Parker took off his own jacket and tossed it on a couch. He asked Frank if he wanted cream in his coffee.

'Just black,' said Frank, then added, 'thank you.'

Which was something.

Parker brought the coffee and took a seat in an upright chair opposite Rachel's father. Frank didn't look well. The cold should have added some red to his nose and cheeks, but they retained only a kind of yellowish pallor. Parker had a vague recollection of yellow skin being a sign of liver problems. He wondered if Frank was seeing a doctor about it, then remembered with whom he was living: at the first sign of illness, Rachel and her mother would have taken him to a physician, at gunpoint if necessary.

Parker sipped his coffee. He could have tried to engage in small talk, but both men were long past that. It hadn't worked in the past, and nothing had changed between them to make it likely to work now. Eventually, Frank broke the silence.

'I hear it didn't go so good today, with Sam's psychologist.'

'The psychologist is doing fine. She couldn't be better. Sam seemed happy too. Your daughter and I were the problem.'

'Rachel might say you were the problem.'

Parker took a deep breath, and wondered if the world was determined to test his ability to control his temper right to the last. He was glad he hadn't ordered a second glass of wine. It wouldn't have mellowed him at all. Even now, completely sober after his walk back to the inn, he felt the urge to let rip at Frank Wolfe, but it would not have served any purpose.

'I think I did okay, but I admit I might not be the best judge,' said Parker. 'And I've had better days.'

'Yeah, well . . .'

Frank tried his coffee. He looked confused.

'It tastes like mulled wine,' he said.

'I don't know what the colors mean,' said Parker. 'I just grabbed the first two that came to hand. You want something different?'

'No, it'll do. It's just strange.'

'It's sophisticated, apparently.'

'Must be why I didn't recognize it. I drink instant at home.'

He sipped some more, and didn't frown quite so much the second time.

'What happened to Sam, the abduction . . .'

Parker waited. Frank used a thumb to wipe coffee drips from the rim of his cup, but didn't look up.

'I wanted to blame you for it,' he said. 'Still do.'

Now he lifted his gaze. Parker thought that he didn't look angry, or bitter, just bewildered.

'Do you blame yourself?' Frank asked.

'Sometimes,' said Parker. 'I couldn't control events once they unraveled, and couldn't have known what that man would try to do in the aftermath, but I helped to set them in motion, and they concluded with him taking Sam.'

'It might have ended badly. The way it did end was bad enough.'

'I know that.'

Frank nodded.

'I used to think we had nothing in common, you and I,' he said. 'It was what I wanted to believe, but all the time I saw something in you that I saw in myself when I looked in the mirror. I saw a man who'd buried one of his children.'

Rachel's older brother had been a state policeman, shot and killed in the course of a bank raid long before Parker and Rachel met. Parker knew that part of what had attracted Rachel to him was an echo of loss, but also of rage. Her response to her brother's death had been to try to understand, as though an exploration of the psychology of criminals might enable her to comprehend why her brother had been taken from her. But another part of her, one that it troubled her even to acknowledge, wanted to lash out, to inflict pain in return for pain. It was an aspect of herself that she had refused to indulge, but then Parker entered her life, and as he unleashed himself on those responsible for his own pain and loss, she allowed a little of her own anger to feed his. She didn't like the results, or told herself that she didn't, even as her secret self exulted.

'You'd think I'd remember it all,' he continued, 'but I don't. I have fragments, but I'm missing pieces of my memories. I remember being at the hospital, but I don't recall how I got there. I remember the graveside, but not the church. And when I try to picture my boy, I see him only as still images. He doesn't move.

'And I can't hear his voice,' he concluded. 'I can't bring it to mind. It's like death wiped the tapes.'

They had never spoken of this before. Parker wasn't sure that Frank had talked like this with Rachel, or even with his wife. Rachel always described her father's grief as silent and intensely personal. His inability to share or discuss it had blighted her mother's life, she said, because it forced her mother to grieve for her son alone.

'I thought about killing myself,' he said. 'That only came later, when the pain was no longer so bad, when it had dulled. But the problem was that everything had dulled, not just the pain. It all went gray.'

'And why didn't you take your own life?' asked Parker.

'Rachel,' came the answer. 'My daughter kept me alive. Not even my wife could do that.'

He put his cup down.

'But you didn't have another child, not then, and your wife died with your daughter. So how did you stay alive?'

'By hunting the man who had done that to me,' said Parker. 'By finding him and killing him.'

'And you did.'

'Yes.'

'Did it help?'

'That question doesn't have a simple answer. Less than I'd hoped, but more than was good for me.'

'But the loss stays, doesn't it?'

'Yes.'

'I don't ever want Rachel to experience that agony.'

'Neither do I.'

'But you continue to do what you do, and it almost cost us Sam.'

Parker remained silent.

'So why keep doing it?'

'That question doesn't have a simple answer either.'

'Try me.'

'I do it because I'm afraid that if I don't, nobody else will. I do it because if I turn away, someone else might suffer the way I have. I do it because it's an outlet for my anger. I do it for reasons that even I don't understand.

'But mostly,' said Parker, 'I do it because I like it.'

'You're not going to stop, are you?'

'No. I've tried. It never took.'

Frank wiped his mouth. It wasn't very warm in the room, but he was perspiring. He watched cars passing slowly on the street, the glow of their headlights catching one side of his face, freezing him half in shadow, half in light.

'But when that man abducted Sam, he planned to kill her.'

'Sam didn't die.'

'She could have!'

'She didn't. She won't. No harm will come to her.'

'You can't know that.'

'Frank, look at me.'

Frank turned away from the window.

'Rachel once told me that after your son died, you insisted on collecting her every day from school until she was sixteen. When you weren't in town, your wife had to do it instead, and you called her to make sure. You only stopped when Rachel handcuffed herself to a railing in protest.'

This was true. It was one of the things Parker loved about Rachel.

'They were plastic cuffs,' said Frank huffily, clutching at the nearest straw.

'That's not the point. There were countries under military rule with looser curfews than your home.'

'It's not the same thing. Rachel has been put at risk by your work. Now Sam has, too. Christ, she saw a man die because of it!'

'Frank—'

'No, I—'

'Frank!'

Frank Wolfe stopped talking.

'We can't leave these people to wander the world unchallenged. They're predators. If they can't feed in one place, they move on and find easier prey, and they continue inflicting pain until they're stopped. We can hide our children away, and lock our doors, and close our ears, but they'll just go after others instead.'

'But she's your child,' said Frank.

'They're *all* someone's children.'

A light went on in the hall. The innkeeper appeared in the doorway. His office was at the back of the house, where a trellised walkway curved to the property in which he and his wife lived. He must have heard them arguing and come to find out the cause.

'Is everything okay, gentlemen?' he asked.

'Sorry,' said Parker. 'Strong opinions.'

The innkeeper gave them both the hard eye before deciding that violence wasn't imminent.

'Well, at least you're the only guest,' he said. 'I guess you can be as strong as you want with them. Goodnight.'

He left them alone again. Frank stood.

'I should get home,' he said.

'I'm parked in back. I'll drop you.'

'I can drive.'

'I wouldn't,' said Parker. 'Just come by and pick up your car in the morning.'

He spoke gently. The coffee had helped Frank some, but Parker wasn't sure that it was enough. He was prepared for another argument, but didn't get it.

'Maybe you're right,' said Frank. 'But I can call a cab.'

Parker told him it was no trouble. He had his car keys in his pocket, and the Wolfe property was only a ten-minute ride away – twenty in this weather.

The innkeeper's intervention appeared to have put an end to any further discussion of Parker's vocation, but he wasn't so deluded as to believe he could change Frank Wolfe's mind about anything. Nevertheless, he felt that progress of some kind had been made. They had talked, and been reasonably civil with each other. And Frank was right: they were both fathers who had lost children, and somehow they had come through that loss – not without ongoing pain, and not without fractures, but they had endured, and each had a daughter whom he loved, and memories, however fragmented and imperfect, of the dead, memories that he cherished. The difference between them was that his departed child did not visit Frank Wolfe in the night – or, if he did, it was only in dreams.

They drove in silence to the Wolfe house, mostly because Frank began snoozing five minutes into the ride. The ice had been cleared from the center of even the minor roads, but stretches of it still remained at the margins, and the new snow meant that the car headlights couldn't pick out the telltale glisten in the dark. Parker drove carefully, and in time they came to the Wolfe property. A light burned in the hallway, and another illuminated the front step and a patch of the yard beyond. The converted stables in which Rachel and Sam lived were quiet and dim. Had it been earlier, Parker would have asked to say a last goodbye to Sam. It pained him to be so close yet not be able to hold her or speak with her.

Parker stopped the car but remained staring at the building in which his daughter slept. Frank came awake beside him, and the two men sat together without speaking. Eventually, Frank said:

'Rachel worries that Sam is hiding some kind of trauma over what happened. But I worry that she isn't.'

Parker turned to him.

'Sometimes,' said Frank, 'I hear her talking to another person. Not when she's playing with her dolls, or when the dog is in the room with her, but when she's entirely alone. She speaks, and she listens, and she speaks again. I know kids are supposed to have imaginary friends, but this is different. I can't explain it. It frightens me, if that makes any sense. There's an intensity to these conversations. Even her voice changes. It's older, somehow. More serious. It's like an adult's voice. Who can she be talking to in that way?'

'I don't know,' Parker lied, but he thought that perhaps the other man saw the lie and simply chose not to call him on it.

Frank opened the car door and got out.

'Thanks for the ride,' he said.

'It was no trouble. And Frank?'

Frank Wolfe leaned on the car door, waiting.

'Thank you for looking out for both of them.'

Frank nodded. No more was said. They were done.

13

May MacKinnon advanced through the snow in her yard and paused at the edge of the woods, where the light from the bulb outside the back door began to fade. She looked back to see Alex at the kitchen window, watching her. She waved at him, and tentatively he waved back.

May scanned the trees with the flashlight, trying to use it to pierce the shadows instead of create more, but the night simply swallowed the beam, like a light stick thrust into a pool of pitch. She could see no signs of movement, no people. She moved closer, advancing marginally into the woods. She didn't want to go too far because the ground was uneven and her boots only came up to the lower part of her shin. She'd had enough of cold, wet feet.

But neither did she wish to leave the light.

The flashlight was bugging her. It wasn't long since the batteries had been replaced, and she hadn't used it very much since then. The beam should have been stronger than this. She used it to examine the snow between the trees. It was an evergreen wood, but the coverage offered by the foliage wasn't perfect, and so most of the terrain was white. None of it had been disturbed, and no footprints were visible, but that didn't seem possible. People had been walking through it not minutes before. She'd seen them, for crying out loud: men and women, but no children. They'd all been adults, and some had even looked old enough to be grandparents.

May didn't believe in ghosts. She might have enjoyed Scottish ancestry, but that didn't mean she was prey to fairy

63

tales and midnight shockers. She didn't even go to church, although she was not entirely an atheist. Her view was that if a greater power existed in the universe, it did not look like an old man with a beard, and did not work through saints and angels. It didn't care if hymns were sung to it, and it didn't listen to prayers. It was a presence without name or form, but it was in everything that surrounded her, and every facet of her own being. She was a pantheist of sorts, but that word was unfamiliar to her. Now she would never hear it, and never learn more of it, because she would soon be dead. She would join her husband, and the truth of the universe would at last be revealed to her.

But she did not feel the imminence of her own mortality as she stood among the trees, not unless the chill of it was concealed by the night air; and the pain to come was one with the biting at her fingertips, and at the end of her nose, and at the lobes of her ears; and the tears she would shed at the end were inseparable from the two that fell to her cheeks as the cold touched her eyes; and a sudden sharp wind cut the air like the breath of a presence unseen, an expired creature with no warmth to it that exhaled only as part of its imitation of life.

There is nothing here, she thought. *I was mistaken.*

The house called to her with its light and its warmth. She backed away from the woods and did not turn from them until she was almost within touching distance of the door. Only then did she take her eyes from the trees, returning to the safety of her home.

And death entered with her.

14

It was the law of such things: having spent so much time talking with Frank Wolfe, Parker found himself unable to sleep when he returned to the inn. Instead he sat at the desk by his window and worked more slowly than before through the details of Jaycob Eklund's life and career. He had no particular hope of a pattern emerging at this early stage, or of spotting a single crucial detail that might have explained Eklund's disappearance, but this background knowledge would be useful once he began searching Eklund's home and office. It was groundwork, and one ignored the mundane at one's peril.

After half an hour he was no wiser than when he started, but had built up a picture that corroborated Eklund's ex-wife's description of a solitary man. Ross had come through with business and personal credit card statements going back two years, but they gave no sign of any great vices on Eklund's part. Parker saw some motel costs, the kind that would have been replicated on his own expenses – business trips requiring overnight stays on behalf of clients who might have begrudged any accommodations more expensive than a Red Roof Inn, and any repast more lavish than mall dining – but nothing to suggest a man indulging himself, or anyone else; gas; stationery; clothing. And books. Eklund ordered a lot of books.

Apart from the occasional blowout at an Olive Garden or Outback Steakhouse, and the growing library, Parker might have been looking at a version of his own life, which depressed him slightly. He closed his laptop and undressed for bed. His room was one of the more masculine at the inn, but only by the standards of the rest, which tended toward the kind of rustic chic that Parker associated with wealthy spinsters. His pillows had lace edging. If he died here in his sleep, his friends would never stop laughing.

Before he slept, he prayed for Rachel and Sam. He prayed for Frank Wolfe and his wife, too. Whether his prayers were in vain or not, he didn't care. It was the effort that counted.

But he knew that, somewhere, those prayers were being heard.

15

'Mom.'

The voice was a whisper at May MacKinnon's ear. She woke in shock, and felt a small hand cover her mouth. Her son was standing by the bedside in his pajamas, his face lit by the glow of the digital clock on the nightstand. It was eleven-thirty. He should have been asleep.

'Mom,' he repeated. 'I think there's someone downstairs.'

He removed his hand from her mouth. She listened, but all was quiet.

'Are you sure?' she whispered.

'I heard a noise.'

She climbed from her bed. She was wearing an old sweatshirt and a pair of leggings that were torn at the knees. Her feet were bare. The house wasn't very old, and didn't have the nightingale floor of her childhood home, a medley of sounds that plagued her late teens and early twenties, making it impossible to sneak in or out without causing a racket that could have woken the dead.

Alex tried to take her hand, but she pushed it gently aside.

'You wait here,' she told him. 'If you hear anything that sounds like—'

Like what? Like I'm being raped? Murdered?

She settled for 'If you hear anything bad' – whatever that might mean – 'you call the police.'

There was a landline by her bedside which Alex could use. She picked up her cell phone from beside the clock and slipped it into the pocket of her leggings, then reached under the bed and pulled out a hammer. She didn't like guns, and certainly didn't hold with keeping them in a house where a boy's curiosity might lead to an accident. There was a limit to how much damage Alex could inflict on himself with a hammer.

'Mom!'

He tried to hold her back by yanking on her sleeve, but she tugged it away from him. She would go to the hallway and listen. If she detected any sound that suggested the presence of an intruder, anything at all, then she'd lock the bedroom door and call the cops herself. The Millwood PD had a pretty good reputation for responding quickly to emergencies, especially if they involved a woman and child under threat, but she wasn't about to cry wolf too soon. Alex had the jitters and, truth be told, she did too. She'd been dreaming when he woke her. In her dream, she and Alex had been at his bedroom window, watching figures move through the trees. She had gone outside with a flashlight – she'd been reading about the gypsies at the mall and thought some of them might have been in the woods – but found no signs of footprints in the snow. Then she had gone back inside and—

That was when Alex had spoken.

Wait, she thought. *What was the dream?*

She was still struggling to separate the real from the imagined, two realms bleeding into one, as she walked to the bedroom door. She couldn't remember what had happened between returning to the house and going to bed. She was confused, and her head was throbbing.

She stepped into the hallway. The little night-light in the outlet between her room and the bathroom was working, but the lamp at the bottom of the stairs was dark. She always kept it lit, using one of those eco bulbs that were supposed to last for years and might help to save the environment in the absence of anyone else giving a rat's ass. It shouldn't have gone out.

Alex stood in the doorway. He was crying. Why was he crying? She wanted to hug him, but there wasn't time, not now. She held on to the doorframe as she listened. It was cold and damp to the touch. She rubbed the condensation between her fingers. The whole house was freezing. She hadn't noticed it in her bedroom because that room was always cold. The radiator had been on the fritz for a week, so she'd been making do with a heavy blanket over her comforter and a hot water bottle to warm the bed before she got in. She'd meant to call someone to take a look at it, but she was afraid it might be a sign of a larger problem with the heating system, and money was tight this month. Now it seemed as though her suspicions had been confirmed, and the whole house was about to turn to ice. Damn: that wouldn't be cheap to fix.

'Mom,' said Alex for the last time, but she didn't pay any attention. She pulled the door closed behind her, turning the handle so that it would make no noise, and her son's face was lost to her. The heating had given her something practical on which to concentrate. No more dreams; no more shapes in the woods, half glimpsed. And as for burglars, they'd be better off leaving before they froze to death instead of wasting their time trying to find anything of value in this house, although they could take the TV before they left. That was acting up as well, and the insurance would probably cover one of those new HD models.

She moved slowly down the stairs, the hammer in her hand. She saw more condensation on the walls. It made no sense. The heating had been fine when she went to bed. Could the temperature really have plummeted so fast? And she wasn't cold. That was the other peculiar aspect. The house might have been challenging the Arctic in the chill stakes, but she remained warm. How could she not be cold?

The moonlight poured through the glass pane above the front door, liquid and heavy. Instinctively she raised her hand to it, as though she might grasp it in her palm, raise it to her lips, and taste it, the sweetness of it trickling like honey down her chin.

Her hand stopped. Her breath stilled.

She heard movement in the living room.

16

Tobey Thayer had a gift. It was not one of which he spoke very often, and was as much a curse as a blessing – more the former, in fact, because it brought him little joy and great unease – but it was his, and it made him special.

Thayer was resolutely average in all other respects: average build and height, averagely handsome with an averagely good-looking wife, averagely wealthy by the standards of the circles in which he moved. His two kids, thankfully, were doing better than average, and both were now at college, one at NYU and the other at Amherst. Their combined fees and living costs were two of the reasons he wasn't wealthier, but most of the time he didn't mind.

He owned Thayer's Discount Furniture Sales, which had outlets in Pennsylvania, New Hampshire, and Connecticut. The bulk of his income was derived from the warehouse area in back of the stores, which was where he displayed the mismatched, end-of-line, and slightly damaged goods that he sourced from suppliers for dimes on the dollar, and sold to his customers at just enough of a markup to satisfy both his own needs and theirs, which was the trick to being a good businessman. Oh, he did well enough on new suites and armchairs, but they involved deposits and ordering. A great deal of the warehouse business was cash on the nail, with no returns. Rain or shine, the warehouse was always full of stock, as well as the buyers for it. All of Thayer's staff started out in the warehouse. It was where they learned their trade, just as he had learned his from his father, Freddie, although Tobey differed from his father in that his own home was furnished entirely from the best of the new, whereas old Pop Thayer had filled his family home with the kind of warehouse junk at which even the most desperate of his customers would have balked. Thayer blamed his back problems of late middle age on the family living room suite, having realized too late in life that the floor would have offered a more ergonomically advisable option.

At the precise moment that his father died, plowing his car into a massive bridge support on a clear summer afternoon while driving along a perfectly safe stretch of road, instantly decapitating himself, Tobey, then only seventeen, was sitting at the desk in his room, completing his geography homework. He blanked out for what he thought was just a few seconds, the way someone who is driving while tired might nod off before snapping instantly awake again, preferably in time to avoid the removal of his head from his neck between the C1 and C2 vertebrae. When Tobey looked down at the page on his table he found that he had drawn a pretty good picture of a mangled car at the base of a bridge support. He'd even managed to add the license plate, which was the same as the one on his father's old Buick. This was surprising on any number of levels, not least because Tobey Thayer couldn't draw for shit.

The call came within the hour. Tobey was left to deal with most of the funeral arrangements since his mother, who had loved his father dearly, was deep in shock, and would never really emerge from it. The mortician, John Welsby, who was an artist of a kind, suggested it might be possible to have an open casket, if the family so wished, as Freddie Thayer's face and head were remarkably undamaged thanks to the angle at which the metal had entered his neck. Tobey declined. The circumstances of his father's death were widely known, since his head had ended up on the grass verge, in full sight of passing motorists. He didn't want folks speculating on what might lie beneath the buttoned-up collar of the corpse.

Tobey did not mention to anyone the drawing he had made. He felt a dreadful weight of guilt in the aftermath of the accident, and feared he might somehow have been responsible for his father's death. After all, he had dozed off at precisely the moment his father's car left the road. The autopsy showed no signs of the kind of catastrophic attack that might have caused his father to suddenly lose consciousness, and Freddie Thayer had no reason, as far as anyone knew, to take his own life. Even had he wanted to do so, his son knew, he would have found a more reliable way to end his days than gambling on the angle of a metal shaft jutting from a bridge support. He had also disliked any kind of fuss: as much in death as in life, he would have chosen to avoid a spectacle. The investigators speculated that his father might have fallen asleep at the wheel. But his son, being a teenager and therefore the center of the universe, was concerned that somehow a link had been created between his father and himself, and by falling asleep at his desk he had also caused his father to nod off, thereby precipitating the accident.

It was nonsense, of course, except for the fact of the drawing's existence. He did not get rid of it, but kept it in a drawer, hidden among old school papers. His mother would never look there, not that there was much likelihood of a search. She spent most of her days weeping, and continued to do so until she went to join her husband not two years later. By then Thayer – no longer 'Tobey', but the surviving heir, and future of the business – had gone to work full-time at Freddie & Ron's Discount Furniture Sales, under the careful guardianship of his father's younger brother Ron, a bachelor who liked to vacation in South Beach, Florida, and who was, as one of the company's salesmen put it, 'queer as a Jewish Christmas.' When Uncle Ron died, Thayer inherited the company in its entirety, and it became his alone in fact and name.

But in the years since his father's death, Thayer had

continued to experience what he thought of as 'moments': a glimpse of a woman walking between hayricks, her feet suspended a good six inches above the ground, the day before a picture of that selfsame woman appeared on news bulletins after her bruised and naked body was discovered in a drainage ditch; the bleeding of the walls in his local DMV while he was standing in line to have his lost license replaced, as though the building had developed stigmata, just hours before a man named Linus Crewell – Crewell by name, cruel by nature, Thayer later thought – walked in with a semiautomatic weapon and sprayed the room, killing five people and injuring seven, just because, he said, his fellow staff members had forgotten his birthday for the third year running; a painful blistering on his right hand as he passed the drive-thru window of a fast-food joint, only subsequently to learn that a fire in the kitchen an hour later had killed one person and left another blind.

And those were just the major occurrences: he'd lost count of the little ones, the incidents that might almost, under other circumstances, have been dismissed as coincidence or déjà vu. He supposed that he was psychic, although he tended to avoid using the word, even in his own mind, and he didn't appear to conform precisely to any definition of the term that he could find.

And even if he was psychic, or telepathic, or whatever you wanted to call it, then it wasn't anything like the way it was shown on TV or in the movies. He always felt a sense of dislocation when he had his moments, as though he might be experiencing a kind of waking dream, and with them came terrible headaches, and the urge – no, the need – to lie down and sleep until the pain passed. His visions and flashes were also unreliable: he'd experienced moments in grocery stores and movie theaters, and then nothing happened. Nobody got shot, nobody died, and life went on. Well, that wasn't quite true: sometimes he'd pick up a paper and find that, in a grocery store or a movie theater hundreds, or even thousands, of miles away, someone *had* been shot, and someone *had* died. On those occasions, Thayer would take a sleeping pill and go to bed, because the possibility that he might be some kind of radar for death and suffering made him want to retire from life.

Thayer had done his research, although he'd been careful about it. He'd read up on Swedenborg, who believed in a spirit world that sat alongside our own, but remained beyond our comprehension, and had consulted the writings of John Wesley, whose strong belief in ghosts influenced early evangelical Methodism, a faith to which Thayer still adhered, if only gently. But Thayer was also interested in the medical and psychological theories surrounding his affliction. He reckoned he was the only discount furniture salesman who could discourse knowledgeably on the theories of Friedrich Nicolai, who argued that the appearance of ghosts might be linked to an imbalance of bodily humors, and John Ferrier, who viewed them as manifestations of a disordered perception. He knew of the experiments with magnetism of Mesmer and Puységur, and the idea of ghosts as projections of memory, of blasts of brain electricity, as reactions to electromagnetic disturbances. But none of these theories could explain what Tobey Thayer had endured ever since the day his father died.

His wife knew of his scourge. He'd revealed the fact of it to her after the incident at the DMV, and shown her the picture he'd drawn of his father's accident. She'd learned to spot when he was having an episode, or when something might have happened that found an echo in one, but they were all so different from one another that even Thayer struggled to find any kind of pattern in them.

All except one. Ever since the gift had first manifested itself, he'd experienced a recurring dream of figures moving through fields, woods, houses. Among them were older and younger people, but no children. The styles of their clothing spanned centuries, but they were as much a part of the present as the past. He sensed a profound malevolence emanating from them, and from their leader in particular, a thin figure with red hair and a red beard, his profile peculiarly flattened, as though there were not quite enough of him to fully occupy three dimensions.

And he knew what they called themselves.

They were the Brethren.

Tobey Thayer woke in his bed in Greensburg, Pennsylvania, his wife snoring gently beside him. The clock read 11:37 p.m. His head was pounding.

'Stop,' he said to the darkness, and to the fading image of the woman walking through it. 'They're waiting for you.'

17

May MacKinnon did not turn back. She did not return to her bedroom, where her son waited, in order to call the police. The presence in the living room called to her, summoning her in a hundred voices and none, a great dissonant harmony alien yet familiar, like a song that, once heard, insinuates itself into one's history, finding echoes in old melodies; a configuration once hidden, now revealed.

Step, step: warm amid the cold, rivulets of moisture running down the wood, the walls.

A great weeping.

In the living room stood a man, his pate bald, a ring of red hair hanging below it like the fingers of frosted ferns against the collar of his shirt, his neck beard leaving his upper lip bare, his age indeterminable. He wore a dark vest, trousers, and jacket, but each was part of a different suit. Even in the dimness May could tell that they did not quite match. His cheeks were ruddy, his lips fat, but his profile was flattened so that a plumb line might have been dropped from forehead to chin, touching the tip of his nose, and still have hung true. He was examining the photograph of Mike, May, and Alex that stood in a silver frame on the center of the mantelpiece. His tongue made a rhythmic clicking noise against his teeth, like the dripping of a tap or the ticking of an old clock.

Tck-tck-tck.

May tried to speak, but no words would come.

Tck-tck-tck.

A weight brushed against her back. She turned to see a

young woman, her fingers deep in the bowl of potpourri that stood on a side table. The woman lifted her hand, and fragments of dried citrus and cinnamon ran through her fingers. She put her palm to her nose and sniffed. Her hair was red, and singly braided. The braid hung over her left shoulder, and her left hand toyed with it while the right plunged back into the bowl once more to crush the material inside. Like that of the older man by the fireplace, her profile was abraded, and she did not acknowledge May's presence.

More movement: figures in the kitchen, the dining room, male and female. Some she thought she recognized from the woods. They were touching her possessions: sniffing, tasting, stroking.

Breaking.

And May found her voice.

'Stop,' she said. 'They're not your things.'

Instantly, all motion stopped. The voices in her head went silent. The man at the fireplace, still inclined in the direction of the photograph, stopped his clicking. Even the very dust motes in the air ceased to billow in their barely felt gusts. The only movement came from a winter moth, its wings beating so slowly that she could follow the agitation of them with her eyes, drawing a breath with their upward drift, exhaling with the downward. The insect came toward her, beat by beat, until it hung suspended before her eyes. It was banded in brown, beige fading to red at the forewings, gray at the hind wings, tipped in yellow. A male: the females were flightless, with stubs instead of wings. She was aware of them as an invasive species, capable of annihilating fruit orchards, and had no compunction about killing them.

She stared into its compound eyes. Its short antennae quivered. The clamorous voices faded from her head. There was only the beating of the moth's wings. She could hear them now.

Ta-dump. Ta-dump.

'Who are you?' she asked. 'Why are you here?'

Ta-dump. Taaaa-dump. Taaaaa-dump.

The moth's wings slowed their movement. *Surely it must fall*, she thought. *It cannot hold its position. It must drop, and die.*

A man ascended the stairs while the same man descended the stairs, two moments in time coalescing. He was not like the others. He was a pale blur, the impression of a figure against the dark, a ghost in the house.

Taaaaaaa-

The ghost on the stairs had a blade in his hand. A dark, sticky thread dripped from the tip to stain the oatmeal carpet.

Why am I not cold?

The moth froze.

In her bedroom, on the bed that she had once shared with her husband, the blood had turned the pillow red. May's heart beat for the final time, and she exhaled as she was released. Her son tugged at the sleeve of her sweatshirt. He was weeping.

'Stay, Mom,' he said. 'Stay.'

'Go with her,' said the voice of the man behind him, and Alex felt an awful sharpness enter his back and pierce his heart.

18

Parker left early for Providence. He toyed with the idea of dropping by to see Sam before he went, as she wouldn't yet be on her way to school, then decided that, hard though it might be, it was better to leave things as they were. He and Frank had parted on reasonably good terms, at least by their standards, and the more time he gave Rachel to cool down, the better. But he felt a tug as he passed the nearest exit to the Wolfe property, so he distracted himself with *Morning Edition* on Vermont Public Radio.

The roads had been cleared overnight, but that familiar soft haze of cold hung in the morning air; not enough to restrict visibility, just sufficient to bring with it a sense of unreality. He felt as though the shadow realm that had manifested itself on the evening with Ross was slowly encroaching, contaminating everything it touched, blurring the edges of this world. He killed the radio and traveled on in silence, as though by doing so he might better attune himself to the cadences of the transformation.

When he was only an hour out of Burlington, he took a call from Ross on his cell phone. The FBI man was seeking a progress report. Parker told him he was on his way to Providence as they were speaking, which didn't appear to impress Ross very much, who would have preferred if Parker were already there, and had been for some time.

'What have you been doing?' Ross asked.

'With respect, that's none of your business.'

'"With respect",' said Ross, 'is one of those terms that generally mean their opposite.'

'Honestly, I did not know that.'

Ross didn't rise to the bait.

'I engaged you to perform a task.'

'Which I've been doing, along with living.'

'Then, with respect, your work-life balance may be out of sync.'

Parker was still trying to explain the difference between private individuals and bodies funded entirely from the public purse when Ross ended the call. He wondered if he should have told Ross that Angel and Louis would be joining him in Providence, and on Ross's tab. On balance, he decided it was better that he hadn't. It would only have made Ross worry, which would have been terrible. Anyway, Ross seemed to be worried enough as things stood. For a man whose life appeared not a little sad and dull, Jaycob Eklund was exercising SAC Ross considerably.

Parker started picking up signs for Providence. He didn't know it very well. He'd been down to visit a couple of times, one of them with Rachel shortly before Sam was born. His memory was of a city that contained within itself the echo of the prettier town it once was, a past that took the form of old churches and buildings now scattered like pieces of a puzzle among anonymous apartment buildings and the big Providence Place Mall, at least until one headed across the river and into the streets around Brown University. He also vaguely recollected that a man's hair could go gray and fall from his head before the crossing signal went green for pedestrians, so the citizens of Providence had jaywalking in their genes.

And as he drove, he continued to wonder just how much Ross was keeping from him about Eklund, and why.

19

'This,' said Angel to Louis, 'is the best fucking idea anyone ever had since, like, Columbus bought a boat.'

The two men, along with Parker, were sitting in New Harvest Coffee & Spirits on Weybosset Street, part of the revived Arcade Providence, the nation's oldest indoor shopping mall. On the one hand, Parker thought, Arcade Providence was therefore to blame for the deaths of cities, the decline of communities, and the Mall of America in Minnesota. On the other, anywhere that specialized in offering a man a good espresso along with single malt Scotch and a slice of pie could be forgiven a great deal, although possibly not the creation of the Mall of America. Someone had also clearly put some thought into the redevelopment of the Arcade, and it was now home to the kind of businesses destined to be described as 'eclectic'. Harvest stood across from a store named Lovecraft Arts & Sciences, which reminded Parker, in a good way, of Strange Maine back in Portland. The world, he decided, would be poorer without such places.

'It is pretty fine,' Louis agreed. The single cube of ice in his glass clicked in an appealing manner, although it caused Angel to wince. The two men differed on many matters, fashion and politics not least among them, but it was generally accepted by those who knew them that Louis led the way in taste and discernment. Yet Angel had developed a certain appreciation for Scotch, linked in no small part to the theft of various interesting bottles and cases earlier in his criminal career. He and Louis could now afford to buy whiskies of considerable price and vintage, although Angel maintained that none ever tasted as good as those he had once pilfered for himself. 'Stolen waters are sweet,' he would say, 'and bread eaten in secret is pleasant', thereby proving that the devil could indeed cite scripture for his purpose.

Thus it was that Angel possessed very set opinions on the consumption of whisky, maintaining that ice detracted from the subtlety of the flavors. He liked to add a little water to his Scotch to open them up, but that was all. He had managed to whittle Louis down from three cubes to one, but it still pained him to witness its introduction. As for those who chose to pour soda or, God forbid, Coke into their whisky, Angel took the view that only a severe beating could set them straight.

Parker stuck to coffee. The server gave him a smile as she brought his Americano. It was a nice smile. It wasn't promising anything, kindness apart, but it was the kind of smile that made a man feel good.

'I think she likes you,' said Angel.

'Given the other choices are you and the dark lord over here, that's not saying much.'

They were killing time before hitting Eklund's office, which was based in a serviced building housing a variety of businesses, all sharing a small pool of secretaries and receptionists. It stood off North Main, in a new development that also housed a cosmetic dentistry clinic and a pet supply company. Parker had taken a look at it on his way downtown, and saw that the front desk was being taken care of by a woman who couldn't have been more than twenty. The building used a card entry system to permit access to the offices, although the receptionist could buzz visitors through. It looked like the kind of place that went quiet after five, and would be dead after six. The nearer they left their visit to the close of business, the more time they would have in Eklund's office. After that, depending on what they found there, they'd start on his home.

'You think we look like tourists?' Angel asked Parker. Angel liked to think he could blend in with the vast mass of humanity, even as that same vast mass instinctively took a step back from him and his partner. His desire to belong was touching in its hopelessness.

'It's Providence in February,' he replied. 'If you looked like tourists, they'd assume you were crazy. Instead, you just look like two guys with guns under their coats.'

'Then we'll fit right in if we try to steal something,' said Angel. 'This is a bent state.'

He was right. Parker had once read that you could fit every human being on the planet into the physical area occupied by Rhode Island. If that were true, then they wouldn't leave without having their pockets picked by a politician. 'Buddy' Cianci, who was mayor of Providence for a total of twenty-one years, was twice forced to resign because of felony convictions, and spent four years in federal prison for running a criminal enterprise out of city hall, although the jury found him not guilty of extorting a membership to the University Club, which suggested he wasn't entirely beyond redemption. Cianci tried to run again in 2014, but by that stage he was too rich even for Providence's blood. Add the former governor Ed DiPrete, who spent a year in jail for taking bribes from contractors, and Joseph Bevilacqua, the chief justice of the state supreme court, who resigned over allegations that he had ties to the Mob – and those were only the big names – and you had an almost admirable level of institutionalized corruption.

'Makes you seem almost honest by comparison,' said Louis.

'I don't mind people stealing,' said Angel. 'I just don't like them lying about it after. Shows a lack of pride in their work.'

They asked Parker how the meeting with Sam and her psychologist had gone, and he, in turn, told them of his talk with Frank Wolfe.

'You think he dislikes you any less because of it?' asked Angel.

'A bit less.'

'That's progress. Pity your ex-girlfriend now dislikes you more. Kind of cancels out the good work done with Frank.'

'Hey, thanks for that.'

'Don't mention it.'

Parker checked his watch.

'Guess we should be going.'

Angel called for the check. The server returned and smiled again at Parker.

Damn, he thought.

The check remained on the table, where Angel and Louis effortlessly ignored it. Parker glanced at the total without touching the paper. They had expensive taste in liquor, he'd give them that.

'No chance,' said Parker. 'Not in a million years.'

'Shithead,' said Angel, and reached for his wallet.

They emerged from the Westminster Street end of the Arcade and stopped for a moment to watch a peregrine falcon circle high above the old Bank of America Building – the Superman Building, as it was better known.

'You know what that bird's name means?' asked Louis.

Parker and Angel admitted they did not.

'Wanderer,' said Louis. 'Wanderer falcon. I like that.'

Sometimes, Parker thought, Louis exhibited disturbing signs of humanity.

20

Parker had made the decision to search Eklund's office first. Targeting the office still involved breaking and entering, but would require less time than searching Eklund's home, and so it made sense to get it out of the way first. He left his car in a parking lot, and the driving to Louis.

Serviced offices mostly hired cheap, in Parker's experience. It wasn't as though they offered many opportunities for promotion, and the work was dull. The receptionists to watch out for were the older ones, who were the human equivalent of junkyard dogs. But the young woman was still behind the desk, and appeared capable of a degree of civility, from what Parker could see of her smile.

Angel made the call from across the street. They watched the receptionist answer as she buzzed in a visitor.

'This is Mr. Eklund in suite seventeen,' said Angel. 'I'm expecting two clients to arrive in the next five minutes. You can send them straight up once they've signed in.'

If the receptionist noticed that the call was coming from an outside line, she didn't mention it. Most people were so attached to their cell phones that to receive a call from one, even from someone who had a landline in the same building, was unremarkable.

'I'll do that, Mr. Eklund.'

Angel thanked her and hung up. The oldest tricks in the book endured for a reason. Her reaction also told Parker something else: either she was new, or Eklund's disappearance hadn't yet been noticed. He just hoped it didn't cross her mind to check if Eklund's entry card had been used that day, but he suspected she wouldn't bother to try. Why should she? She wasn't guarding Congress.

It was close to five p.m. as Angel and Parker entered the building, leaving Louis with the car. They introduced themselves at the desk, told the receptionist – Carly, according to her badge – that they were here to see Jaycob Eklund, and were supplied with temporary entry passes once they'd signed a register and one of them had shown some form of official ID. Angel let her see a driver's license, although the name on it bore no resemblance to his own, even if the photograph was a close enough match to fool anyone who wasn't intimately acquainted with him.

'How many of those do you have?' asked Parker, as they stepped from the lobby into a corridor with an elevator bank and a flight of stairs to the right.

'I've lost count,' said Angel. 'Sometimes even I forget who I am.'

They took the stairs to the third floor. Along the way, Angel removed his jacket to reveal a shirt with MATCHLESS LOCK SERVICES INC. embroidered on the back. As it turned out, that particular layer of deception wasn't necessary. Eklund's office was close to the end of the hall, and nobody appeared from any of the other suites as Angel worked on the lock. He had it open in less than a minute. It would have been sooner had he used a pick gun, but there was no point in attracting attention with the noise. They went inside, closing and securing the door behind them.

Eklund's office was little more than a glorified cubicle. A cheap desk occupied the width of the room in front of a window with vertical blinds, leaving just enough space for the occupant to squeeze by on either side. Two uncomfortable-looking padded chairs faced the desk. A generic landscape print hung beside a calendar on the left wall, while the right was dominated by a four-drawer filing cabinet. Parker tried it, found it locked, and set Angel to work on opening it while he searched Eklund's desk. There wasn't much to search. Eklund didn't use a desktop computer, at least not in his office, and if he had a journal, he'd taken it with him. The drawers were unlocked, but yielded only stationery, stamps, assorted business cards, a jar of instant coffee, packets of sweetener, and some containers of powdered creamer. He didn't even have a bottle of cheap hooch and a pair of shot glasses, like private detectives in movies.

Parker pressed the blinking message light on Eklund's office phone and put it on speaker. There was some overlap with the cell phone messages, but he took down all the names and numbers once again. The last message was from a woman who didn't get to say much more than 'Hello' before the machine cut her off. The internal system seemed to be set to about a dozen messages. It was what you got for renting cheap.

By then Angel had succeeded in unlocking the filing cabinet. Parker spent the next hour flipping through folders containing copies of reports for clients, invoices, bills, and the other assorted paperwork that accumulates in a one-man operation. The cases were all mundane: insurance work, process serving, debt recovery, due diligence, some minor instances of fraud, a little employee surveillance, and a couple of child custody cases, the sight of which gave Parker a dull ache. None of them was current, meaning that Eklund probably kept details of whatever he was working on elsewhere, and only filed material away when he was finished with it. The office was a place for meetings and storage, but little else. Parker did notice that Eklund's hourly and daily rates were higher than his own, although Eklund probably needed the extra cash to cover the cost of his lousy digs. The room smelled musty, and the carpet needed a good cleaning. It reminded Parker why he didn't have an office of his own: if working meant coming to a place like this, he'd have been happier living on welfare.

It was dark outside. Through the blinds, Parker could see Louis sitting in his car. The building's parking lot had emptied considerably in the time they'd been searching Eklund's office, and Louis's vehicle now occupied a section entirely to itself. It was time to go. Parker didn't want some rent-a-cop taking note of the plate.

He looked around Eklund's workspace one last time. He still had little real sense of the man. Maybe a search of his home would change that, but the office left Parker feeling as though he had wandered onto a stage set. Had the initial approach come from anyone other than Ross, he might have suspected he was being set up. As it was, he was simply puzzled. Eklund mattered to Ross, but right now, Parker was no closer to understanding why.

The only personal touch was a framed photograph on the desk. It showed Eklund – prematurely gray-haired, nudging six feet, a few pounds overweight – with an arm around the shoulder of a much smaller woman whose smile made up for the plainness of her features. Thanks to the material supplied by Ross, Parker identified her as Milena Budny, Eklund's ex-wife. The photograph evidently predated their divorce – their wedding rings were clearly visible – but not by too many years. Ross had provided a picture of Eklund from the renewal of his driver's license the previous year, and he didn't look a whole lot different from the man in the photograph.

Parker continued to stare at the picture for a while. He didn't know of many men who kept photos of ex-wives on their desk – or, at least, not their own ex-wives.

'You find something?' Angel asked.

'Just regrets,' said Parker. 'I think we're finished here.'

III

Perhaps other souls than human are sometimes born into the world, and clothed in human flesh.
Joseph Sheridan Le Fanu, *Uncle Silas* (1864)

21

D onn Routh, known to the Brethren as 'the Cousin', had been traveling for hours, pausing only to catch some sleep in the cheapest motel he could find. He always felt the need for oblivion after killing. He did not know why.

Were it summer, he might just have pulled into a parking lot and spent the night in his car, but in winter that would have meant freezing to death or running down his battery to keep the heater running. He disliked wasting money on motels, just as he rarely ate out, and then only in the kinds of places that offered a salad buffet, or unlimited soup. His lifestyle was frugal, even miserable.

Routh worked as a supervisor in one of Kentucky's largest industrial laundries, although his job also entailed visiting on-premises laundries in hospitals, prisons, and colleges to ensure their equipment was properly maintained, and advise on chemicals, water temperatures, and cycle duration. He had spent so long working with detergents that he could no longer smell much of anything else, and his clothing and person always bore a faint chemical tang.

He still lived in his childhood home, although his parents had been dead for some years. He had sold most of their possessions after his mother followed his father into the ground. He'd considered holding on to their bed because it was bigger and more comfortable than his own, but decided that he would have felt odd sleeping in the same bed in which he was conceived, even if he disposed of the mattress. The bed went the way of their clothing, and their jewelry, and the rest of their furniture, for he was not a sentimental man. A visitor entering the house would have found it largely empty, with the exception of the kitchen, the living room, and one small bedroom. Outside of those rooms, none of the light fixtures contained bulbs, not even in the hallways.

The house was untroubled by books or newspapers, or anything other than the most rudimentary trappings of modernity: a gas stove, a refrigerator, an ancient toaster oven. Routh's only concessions to luxury were a widescreen HDTV on which he watched Blu-rays, and a top of the line hi-fi component system: a Clearaudio Concept turntable hooked up to a Rega Elicit-R amplifier and a pair of Mythos STS SuperTower speakers. He also had a Cyrus CD player, but he was mostly a vinyl aficionado. His father had built up a considerable library of classical music on vinyl during his lifetime, and his son retained it intact while continuing to add his own selections. He had built the shelves to house the collection, and it was one of the few facets of life that gave him unadulterated pleasure.

He didn't own an electric kettle, and the bath and shower were so seldom used that they spat brown water on those rare occasions when they were put into action. Routh usually opted to bathe at work – it saved money – just as he had his clothing cleaned by one of the laborers the company employed in conditions that would not have been unfamiliar to similar workers a century earlier.

Technically, the Asians and Africans who loaded the carts, sorted the torn and stained materials from those that were still usable, and washed, dried, and ironed amid relentless heat, steam, and moisture, all for thirty-five cents above the minimum hourly wage, were known as 'laundry associates', which the Cousin found risible. They didn't need a title, not for the jobs they did. They were nothing, nobodies. He no longer even bothered to learn their names, and not just because the position offered two pairs of overalls with the wearer's identity embossed on the left breast. If those overalls became damaged, the employee was required to pay for a new pair out of his or her wages. Few ever did, preferring to conduct running repairs rather than sacrifice part of their checks. Those who left, or were fired, were supposed to return their overalls for recycling, but most passed them on to the ones who remained, and they didn't bother to remove the stitching in order to add their own names to the uniform, and so the whole issue of nomenclature became even more nebulous. Not that any of the supervisors cared: the immigrants' names appeared to give no indication of their gender anyway, so who could tell if Afua or Abioye or Ling or Kwong belonged on overalls with tits underneath? It only became an issue when they screwed up, or were late, or didn't appear at all.

To test his theory that none of these people really mattered, and no one cared about them – or no one of any consequence – Routh, some years previously, had abducted a twenty-one-year-old Chinese woman named, according to her overalls, Meixiu, as she ran to make the last bus at the end of her shift. Routh deliberately delayed her in order to separate her from her fellow workers. He'd given her the job of laundering his undershirts and underwear, and then complained that she'd used too much starch, and the whole load needed to be done again. Routh not only had the power of hiring and firing, but he could also cut an employee's hours, or assign the kind of shifts that made it impossible for those with children to work. It didn't pay to cross him, and so Meixiu did as she was told. Only when Routh pronounced himself satisfied with the work did she hightail it across the lot without even bothering to remove her overalls, or her blue protective booties. There was a shortcut through some wooded wasteland that took five minutes off the journey to the bus stop, and Routh knew she'd go that way. He pulled her into the bushes as she was almost in sight of the road, clamping a thick-gloved hand over her mouth so she couldn't scream. She didn't weigh hardly anything, and Routh was a big man. He got her into the trunk of his car without any trouble, and slapped her once to keep her from struggling while he bound her legs and hands with duct tape.

Later, when he killed her, it was like breaking the neck of a bird.

The next day, some of the Chinese women came yabbering to the office. Few of them could speak any English at all, and Jun, their spokesperson, was only marginally better equipped than the rest to explain their concerns about the missing Meixiu. But it soon emerged that Meixiu was in the United States illegally, and the papers she'd used to get the job belonged to someone else, and it was explained to the women that if they continued to kick up a fuss then maybe the company would have to look closely at all of their paperwork, and if the police became involved then the immigration people would probably follow, and—

Well, who knew where Meixiu had gone? These people lived by their own rules. Meixiu wasn't even her real name. One of the women claimed it was Yingtai. When Routh heard that, he thought it sounded familiar. He thought the girl might have spoken it near the end.

The police were never called, and thus Routh was never questioned, although he thought he caught some of the women looking at him with suspicion in the days and weeks that followed. It didn't matter to Routh. There was no trace left of Meixiu, or Yingtai, or whatever she was called. It was one of the benefits of understanding chemicals and their uses.

Routh never harmed another woman from the laundry. He hadn't even raped the Chinese girl. He'd just been interested in proving a point.

Routh did not take vacations. For the most part, he used his annual leave to stay at home, listen to music, and watch documentaries and old movies. He was never ill, and consequently was the only employee in the company never to have recorded a sick day. He was polite to his fellow senior staff, and – with the notable exception of the unfortunate girl who had ended up dying in his bathtub – generally behaved reasonably toward the firm's associates. If nobody particularly liked him, then few actively disliked him either. Those who had once whispered about him, and cast suspicious glances in his direction, were long since gone.

He was not lonely. Sometimes, the Brethren came to him. He would open his eyes as he lay on his couch, a pair of Beyerdynamic DT 880s clamped to his ears, and watch as one of them glided through the room, or stood in a corner swaying to music that might have been the same as that to which he was listening, or possibly a tune from another time and place. Such apparitions did not disturb him. They were all of the same blood. Eventually he would take his place with them, and it would be for him to move between worlds. It was unusual for the men in his family to have this gift of sight. It tended to be associated with the female side, but then Routh was distinctive in many ways, not least of them his willingness to commit homicide, and those of his blood who had gone before owed him a great debt for his efforts.

Routh did not like leaving his house, beyond the requirements of his job. He was a creature of routines. He broke them only for family. Routh appreciated the irony of a man who worked for a laundry company being responsible for cleaning up loose ends. It was a duty, but not a burden. He took no pleasure in killing – he was no sadist – but did not dislike it either. He was a practical man.

Routh kept his distance from the rest of his kin. It was the pact agreed among them all, just in case, through some misfortune, he was ever apprehended, but Routh did not believe this would ever happen. He was meticulous, and he had the Brethren to watch over him. They would not allow any harm to befall their enforcer.

The road unfurled before him, the snowflakes catching in

his headlights as though the very world were disintegrating, burning in a cold fire that turned all to white ash. At short notice, he had requested three days' leave from the laundry. He was required to deal with the problems raised by the private investigator, Eklund, which included May MacKinnon and, inevitably, her son. It annoyed him slightly that his boss had huffed and puffed when Routh notified her of his wish to use some of his vacation time. The woman – her name was Wendy Bray, and she wore too much makeup and spoke too loudly for his liking – was new, and unfamiliar with his ways. He detected a vague hostility toward him on her side, although he had given her no cause for it. He wondered if some men and women were more attuned than others to a potential wrongness in those whom they encountered, a rudimentary recognition of a possible threat. He was not concerned, just curious. The provocation of unease was not a firing offense, last time he checked.

Bray consented to his request with bad grace, even though he had lied and told her that he wanted to attend a funeral. He even found a suitable bereavement on the East Coast to claim if required, but Bray showed no particular inclination to delve deeper into the matter, and signed off on his time; with the weekend, it would give him almost five full days to do what was needed, although he expected to be home with a day to spare. He might have been able to return sooner had he flown, but he disliked airports and airplanes. He was not afraid of flying, but the proximity of so many strangers was distasteful to him, and so he had driven first to Millwood, and now on to Providence, with a box of CDs on the seat beside him from which to choose his listening. The pleasure of the trip was disturbed only by his lingering sense of annoyance at Bray's attitude.

Somewhere around the southern New Hampshire border, he decided that he would kill the Bray woman: not this year, nor even the next. In fact, he was prepared to let a decade go by, and wait for her to move on somewhere else, or quit to raise a family, before he went looking for her. He was very patient.

Having determined this eventual course of action, his mood improved. He put on a recording of Ravel's Piano Concerto made in 1957 by the reclusive Italian pianist Arturo Benedetti Michelangeli, who had always been notoriously reluctant to commit his performances to disc. The recording took place in Studio 1 at the EMI facilities on Abbey Road in London. Later, the Beatles would colonize Studio 2, which the Cousin regarded as a sign of plummeting standards. The disc also included Benedetti Michelangeli's recording of Rachmaninoff's Piano Concerto no.4, and it was to the strains of Rachmaninoff that he entered Providence, making his way to the home of Jaycob Eklund.

22

Tobey Thayer sat in his office between the warehouse area and the main Greensburg store floor, struggling to maintain his concentration on the paperwork before him. The warehouse had just taken delivery of a new consignment of substandard furniture and oddments, which was why he was still at his desk with the clock nearing seven p.m. He rarely stayed beyond five. After all, what was the point in being king if you had to work like a serf? His father had never learned that lesson, perhaps because he was never happier than when he was on the floor, selling beat-up three-piece suites to people whose trailers could barely accommodate them. Then again, Freddie Thayer would have sold one of his own arms – or better still, someone else's arm – if he thought he could make a profit on it.

Thayer picked up his cell phone and pressed redial. He had lost count of the number of times he'd tried to contact Jaycob Eklund since he woke with that sense of the Brethren. He got the same message, which was that Eklund's mailbox was full. He wasn't having any more luck with the office number, and Eklund's home number just continued ringing. In this day and age, it seemed impossible that someone could be simply beyond contact.

Thayer experienced a brief flashback to his twentieth year, when a misunderstanding between himself and a girl named Laurie Naylor caused a serious rift in their relationship, one that he became convinced Laurie would attempt to widen by seeking comfort in the arms of Bobby Welbeck, who was a jock and a prick but exerted a strange power over the opposite sex. It was widely believed that more women had gone down on Bobby Welbeck than on the *Titanic*, which would have put Welbeck's current total somewhere north of 110. That had seemed like a lot to the young Thayer, but what did he know? Frankly, three would have been a lot to him.

Thayer tried calling Laurie's home the next day, which was a Saturday, then the homes of her friends, and finally resorted to going door-to-door in an effort to find her before she did something she, or certainly Thayer, would be likely to regret. In the end, it turned out that Laurie had just gone to a movie with one of her cousins, and so had not added her name to the Welbeck Wall of Fame. Thayer, eager to avoid a repeat of that kind of stress, promptly asked Laurie to marry him, which was one of the better decisions he'd made in his life. Now, as he tried to contact Jaycob Eklund, he felt a moment of empathic contact with his younger self: unwelcome, and still strangely painful.

'Mr. Thayer?'

He looked up. Eric Louvish, one of his better salesmen, was standing at the office door.

'What is it?'

'That damaged Ashton love seat? I have a guy on the hook, but he won't go more than one fifty for it.'

Thayer knew the love seat. He knew all of his stock.

'Is he bleating about the stain?'

It was oil, and nasty.

'Yeah,' said Louvish. 'Maybe if you could—'

'Take the one fifty.'

Louvish staggered slightly where he stood. The Ashton retailed for $399 new, and the stain wouldn't be visible as long as you kept the love seat in a corner so the back and the right side were concealed. The guy had another fifty in him, if the boss would come out and work his magic. Five minutes for fifty bucks. It would also help Louvish's total, because he was running neck and neck with Alyce Voycich for the additional bonus Thayer threw in each month to the salesperson who shifted the most stock. Alyce Voycich was racked like a Barbie doll, which gave her an advantage right from the start, although she was smart enough to do up an extra button when negotiating with couples.

'You sure?'

'Yeah. I can't be dealing with that shit right now. Record it as two hundred on your sheet, with a note about the difference. I'll take it into account at the end of the month.'

Louvish shrugged. It wasn't like the boss to stay stuck to his chair like this. He might not have been his old man, but he still had Thayer blood running through his veins.

'And close the door behind you, would you?' Thayer added. 'I need some peace and quiet while I take care of this stuff.'

He gestured at the delivery invoices on his desk, even though he could have checked them in his sleep. Louvish nodded and pulled the door shut behind him. The boss's door was hardly ever closed, but when it was, his staff knew that he wasn't to be disturbed. Louvish then returned to the warehouse floor, got the guy up to $175 for the sake of pride, and completed the paperwork before suggesting to Alyce Voycich that Mr. Thayer might be coming down with something.

In his office, Thayer closed his eyes, just for a moment. His head ached, and he was experiencing that familiar unpleasant tingling in his extremities. It hadn't entirely gone away since he'd woken up during the night. His fingers and toes felt swollen, and his shoes were too tight on his feet.

When he opened his eyes again, twenty minutes had passed, and Alyce Voycich was staring at him through the glass of the door, her hand poised as though unsure whether to risk knocking. Perhaps she had already knocked, Thayer thought, and he just hadn't heard because he'd been sleeping.

But he hadn't been sleeping, not really. His eyes might have been closed, and his conscious mind turned off for a time, but he had still been busy. A pencil was in his right hand, and his left was holding the blank side of an invoice sheet flat on the desk. On it he had drawn studies of the same faces, each in profile and each with a flattened aspect to the nose and chin. The pencil portraits were as good as any he had ever done. There was something elegant and old-worldly about them, even allowing for the ugliness of their subject.

Because he was ugly: ugly beyond appearance, ugly beyond skin and bone.

Thayer put the pencil down. The tingling had gone. Even his headache was receding. It was as though by drawing he had lanced a boil, allowing the pus to drain and thus ease his discomfort.

For a while.

He tried calling Eklund again. Nothing.

Just nothing.

23

Jaycob Eklund's house was a small bungalow-style dwelling in Fox Point, on the east side of Providence.

'Man,' said Louis, 'this place makes Williamsburg look like Salt Lake City.'

He wasn't far off the mark. Fox Point was so hipster that Parker felt as though he stood out simply by not having a beard, while Louis was conspicuous solely by virtue of being black. The only one of them who might conceivably have blended in was Angel, if only because he had three days' worth of facial growth and was wearing a wool hat. They'd passed a whole bunch of coffee shops along Wickenden and its environs as they got their bearings, alongside stores selling antiques, used records, sex toys, rugs, and jewelry. It was hard to believe all this had been farmland until the construction of the city's first port at India Point, after which Providence did its best to hasten the world's ruination by exporting large quantities of rum. That maritime and industrial past was now visible only in some of the older buildings, while gentrification, aided by the students from nearby Brown, had seen off most of the older residents.

Parker had performed a realty search on Eklund's property. Eklund and his wife had bought at a good time, before Fox Point became a beacon for the young and wealthy, and the value of the house had increased sufficiently by the time of their divorce to enable Eklund to leverage the equity and buy out his wife's share. The house still looked too big for a single man's needs, but Parker realized he wasn't in a position to criticize Eklund for not selling up and buying somewhere smaller, not when he himself was rattling around in his Scarborough home. And why should Eklund have sold if he didn't want to? He lived in a buzzing, interesting area, and his property wasn't about to lose significant value anytime soon. As long as he could eat the taxes, he'd be fine.

His home was the smallest on Arnold Street, twin rows of mostly nineteenth-century dwellings of various styles not far from the intersection with Brook. The house had a small yard front and back. A black wrought-iron fence marked the boundary, a low hedge surrounding it behind. A children's playground took up one corner of the intersection, and it was there that Parker and Louis dropped Angel before making another circuit and picking him up at the next corner.

'The house is dark,' said Angel, 'but it seems to have a monitored alarm. The main thing is to get inside and kill the siren before any of the neighbors become concerned and call the cops.'

He rummaged in his kit bag and emerged holding a black box about the size of four cigarette packs in one hand, and a pair of wire cutters in the other. He waved the box at Parker.

'Cell phone jammer. Big boy.'

Parker knew what it was. He kept one in his own car kit, just in case, although his was a modest device with a short range. Angel's looked like it could knock out a city block, and render every male in the vicinity sterile in the process. The jammer would take care of the monitoring service. Angel's first task would be to cut the landline connection between the alarm system and the security firm's monitoring station. When that was done, the alarm would try to send out a signal from a transmitter using the cell phone network. The jammer would ensure that this signal would be blocked.

Angel left them, and disappeared into the shadows at the side of Eklund's house.

'You know,' said Louis, 'for three guys supposedly doing a favor for the FBI, we're breaking a whole lot of laws.'

Parker couldn't argue. They were indeed engaging in a great deal of illegal activity on behalf of an agency of the state – or one of its agents, which was not the same thing. He was pretty sure Ross would just leave the cops to feed on them if they were picked up for burglarizing the home of a retired police officer, or make them sweat for a while for being dumb enough to get caught. Parker had been in jail cells in more states than he cared to enumerate. He didn't particularly want to add Rhode Island to his collection.

The alarm in Eklund's house began to sound. Even though they were expecting it, the noise was still shockingly loud. Parker started counting the seconds. It was still ringing after five, then ten.

'Shit,' said Louis. 'Maybe he wants to get arrested.'

Parker was at fifteen when the alarm stopped. A light went on in a building across the street, and he saw movement at a window. They waited. Parker knew Angel would no longer be in the house and was instead waiting somewhere close by, in case someone called the police. They gave it twenty minutes, just to be safe, but no Providence PD patrol car or private security company vehicle came by.

A light flashed once from the bushes to the right of the house, where Angel had first vanished from sight.

'Guess that's me,' said Parker. 'But we're going to be out of contact with you once we're in there.'

Knocking out the connection to the cell phone network allowed them to enter the house, but it also guaranteed their own phones would be useless, which meant that Louis couldn't warn them if anyone approached. The best he could do would be to sound the horn, but in that case he might as well just have cuffed himself before lying facedown on the sidewalk to save the cops the trouble. The next worse option was to set off the car alarm, so that was what they agreed on. Louis was wearing a gray Chesterfield coat with a velvet collar over a black Italian silk jacket and a turtleneck shirt, so he looked respectable enough to avoid a DWB – driving while black – in the event of attracting any police attention, and was close enough to bars and restaurants for it to be plausible that he might have chosen to park on a residential street. If he had to move, he'd wait for them on South Main.

Parker stepped from Louis's Lexus and patted the roof in farewell.

'So I'll just stay here with the car, massa,' said Louis. 'You see Miss Daisy, you tell her old Louis said hello.'

'If we get arrested,' said Parker, 'try to convince them you're our lawyer.'

'If you get arrested, I'll be in Massachusetts before they give you change for your phone call.'

Parker crossed the yard of Eklund's home and made his way to the rear of the house, where Angel had opened the back door in order to gain entry through the kitchen. The alarm was still sounding faintly from the box by the front door, but otherwise the place was quiet.

'The house is clear,' said Angel. From bitter experience, he'd learned that just because a building was dark, the doors and windows were secured, and the alarm system was activated, didn't mean it was unoccupied. He'd taken the trouble to give the rooms a quick check. 'The basement door is locked, though.'

The door in question stood to the left of the kitchen. Parker told Angel to get it open while he checked the refrigerator. If Eklund had been planning to leave home for any length of time, even if he hadn't chosen to share the details of the trip with anyone, then he wouldn't have bothered stocking up on food. But Parker found cold cuts, milk, cream, and a couple of chicken breasts in a Thai marinade, all with expiration dates that were either imminent or had just passed. There was also fruit in a bowl by the sink, and a sourdough loaf, carefully sealed, in the breadbasket. The garbage can had not been emptied, and had started to stink. Wherever Eklund had gone, he hadn't intended staying away for long.

Parker took a flashlight from his pocket and locked the beam to its smallest setting, which was little more than a bull's-eye spot. He was still instinctively cautious, even though Angel had pulled down the blinds on the windows in each room. Flashlight beams in an otherwise dark house were a sure way of attracting attention.

The interior smelled stale. It was relatively clean, but had the air of benign neglect that Parker associated with a certain type of single man. The kitchen cabinets contained some interesting and exotic ingredients, which suggested that Eklund enjoyed cooking, but otherwise the rooms were much as Parker might have anticipated, given what he knew of the investigator. A glass case in the living room displayed various trophies and awards, some dating back as far as Eklund's high school days, and others from his time in the New Hampshire State Police and the Providence PD. The case also held a lot of photographs, although the subjects, apart from his ex-wife, were exclusively male: cops, sporting buddies, and a couple of Eklund with local ball players. A signed and framed Providence Bruins hockey shirt hung on the wall behind the well-used couch, while a flat-screen TV dominated the wall over the fireplace, which was piled high with fresh logs. More logs rested in a red bucket nearby. A long bookcase contained a mix of very male novels and even more male nonfiction, including a whole shelf of volumes on JFK. The Blu-rays lined up in a separate case by the TV consisted of action movies, HBO shows, and comedies, along with a few sports documentaries.

'You got that door open yet?' he called to Angel.

'Patience. The first lock was easy, but he's also got a pretty good double cylinder deadbolt on this, and it's a steel door. The deadbolt can take ten door strikes. Add in the steel door, and the noise I'd make trying to break it down would be heard in Florida.'

Parker continued his search. The house had three bedrooms, one of which contained a twin bed, and closets stacked with men's clothing wrapped in plastic to guard against moths. Parker patted the bedspread and raised dust. It hadn't been used in a while. A smaller, second bedroom – which gave Parker mild claustrophobia as soon as he stepped inside because of the slope of the ceiling, the tiny floor space, and a window that reminded him uncomfortably of an oven door – was given over to gym equipment, including an exercise bike and some light-to-medium free weights. It had its own small bathroom, with clothing dumped in a laundry bag secured on a wooden frame. Parker opened the medicine cabinet and saw assorted medications, including metformin to tackle type 2 diabetes, and a prescription nonsteroidal anti-inflammatory, probably to help with arthritis. An open box of twelve rubbers occupied the top shelf. Three had been used. Parker checked the date on the box and saw that they'd expired in 2013. Either Eklund had given up on safe sex, or he was going through a dry spell on the dating front.

Parker continued his search, but found little of interest, apart from a small gun safe in one of the closets. The safe was open and empty. Wherever Eklund was heading, he'd gone armed.

He heard a sound on the stairs, and then Angel's voice called to him.

'I got it open,' he said.

The basement door stood ajar. Parker's flashlight revealed a set of wooden stairs, and a light switch to his left. The basement was windowless, which meant that they were in no danger of alerting a neighbor if they turned on the light. Parker hit the switch, activating a series of fluorescent bulbs, and together he and Angel descended, Parker leading.

They paused at the base of the stairs, and stared at the walls around them.

'Congratulations,' said Angel. 'You've just found someone who's weirder than you are.'

109

24

Donn Routh arrived in Providence, but was delayed in his approach to the Fox Point neighborhood by a traffic accident, and later by his own lack of familiarity with the layout of the city. He did not own a GPS system, just as he did not own a smartphone. His cell phone was an ancient, battered clamshell Nokia, the object of so many repairs that he could be certain of the originality of only the case itself. He liked the Nokia because the battery could easily be removed, and a phone with a removable battery was virtually untraceable, as long as one was careful of where and how one used it. For Routh, it was little more than a mobile answering service on which messages from the Brethren could be left for him, and then always couched in the most neutral of terms. He made all follow-up calls using calling cards and public phones.

Even being in Fox Point made him ill at ease; these were not his people, and never would be. He felt estranged from them by virtue of his own alien nature, as though these privileged young folk could detect his otherness, so that if he were to glance in his rearview mirror he would see only faces staring back at him, following his progress to make sure he continued on his way and did not attempt to infiltrate their ranks.

He turned onto Arnold Street and squinted at the numbers on the houses to his right. He carried Eklund's keys in his pocket, and had memorized the alarm code, so he had no concerns about gaining access to the house. He knew the names of Eklund's neighbors, and the state of the investigator's relationships with them. He was aware that Eklund did not get along with the man who lived in the house to the right of his own; it was something to do with a tree, and the extent to which it overhung his neighbor's property. Because of this, the two men had not exchanged a civil word in seven years, not since shortly after the neighbor, a young restaurateur, purchased the property. Relations with the couple to the left were better, although both worked long hours outside the city, and were rarely home before seven or eight. As for the rest, Eklund was on nodding terms with most of them, but close to none. It seemed unlikely that anyone had noticed his absence, or if they had, that anyone was worrying too much about it.

Routh parked within sight of Eklund's house and turned off the engine. He was armed with a Heckler & Koch USP 9, and the long-bladed knife he had used on May and Alex MacKinnon – the same blade, curiously, that he had also used on Mike MacKinnon, a killing that had brought much of this trouble down on the Brethren to begin with. Routh legally owned a number of firearms, and had acquired a few more which he kept as throwaways, but he carried a weapon only when he was convinced he might have cause to use it. Otherwise, the attention it might draw meant that carrying even a legally owned weapon was just not worth the risk.

For the Eklund business, he had decided to bring a gun. If he were caught in the man's house, he would be in trouble with or without a weapon. Armed, he would give himself a way out. The big tool kit in the trunk of his car was filled with various parts and implements, including assorted pieces of piping. Concealed among them was an Osprey suppressor, which was illegal in the state of Rhode Island. Routh was aware of this, but remained unconcerned. To any but the most expert eye, the Osprey blended in perfectly with the pipes.

His job here was simple: to remove from Eklund's home

any and all traces of the investigations he had been conducting into the Brethern. Eklund's laptop was already in their possession, since the investigator had conveniently brought it with him. Eventually, Eklund's disappearance would in turn be investigated, and the absence of his laptop, along with the purging of his records, might well be noted. The house would become a possible crime scene. If nothing else, the Cousin's work left him under no illusion about the capacity of human beings to contaminate, deliberately or inadvertently, the spaces through which they moved. With this in mind, he had brought with him a pair of fresh disposable overalls from the laundry, the feet protectors oversized in the manner of a onesie so that he would not have to remove his shoes. He was also in possession of a pair of Hatch protective gloves and a plastic dust mask. All were contained in a black backpack lying in the trunk of his car. If, by some small chance, he were to be pulled over by police, his job gave him the perfect excuse for having such materials with him. A pair of larger expandable bags would be used to accommodate whatever material he decided to remove from the house.

He was about to open the car door when he saw the dead girl in the road.

25

Louis did not enjoy acting as a lookout. Watching for cops made him feel like the dumb guy in the gang, the one who generally ended up dead. He understood the need to occupy the role of picket on this particular occasion, but it did not make him feel any happier.

Neither did he trust Edgar Ross. Louis's past activities, in addition to a number of his current ones, gave him no cause to wish to associate with the FBI or any other branch of law enforcement, but his loyalty to Parker had pulled him into Ross's orbit. He tried to look on the silver lining of the deal, but he had to skirt a lot of cloud to find it. The FBI, whatever its suspicions, was not about to move against him in the near future – Ross had seen to that – but as a consequence Louis had confirmed for them something of his own skills and proclivities, and made himself and Angel into Ross's creatures, just as Parker was. Despite all Ross's protestations about keeping his distance from the search for Eklund, Louis could not shake a sense of being observed, but to what end he could not say. He remained certain only that somewhere in the mystery of Eklund's disappearance lay a potential trap.

He scratched an itch on his left cheek. He glanced over at Eklund's house, and glimpsed a veil of mist that hung in the night air beyond the window of the car. He exhaled a cumulus cloud in the cold of the vehicle. He did not like a warm car at the best of times, but heat, or the drowsiness it brought, was potentially lethal on a surveillance detail. The vapor inside dissipated, but the haze outside remained. Curiously, he could only really see it when he did not look directly at it.

And then he was otherwise distracted, because the police car appeared.

26

The girl was sixteen or seventeen, and wearing a short jacket of gray tweed over a black dress. Her hair was more dark yellow than red, and hung loosely over her shoulders. Her right foot tapped a slow rhythm on the street, as of one who was not yet impatient but was gradually becoming so. Routh did not recognize her, but he knew her for what she was even before he registered the milky cast to her eyes; they seemed almost to glow in the evening dark. She was standing beside a late model Lexus, staring intently at the driver through the glass.

Routh remained in his vehicle. He took another look at Eklund's house. The blinds were drawn on all the windows. He could not recall if Eklund had indicated whether this was how he had left them. Routh went over what he had been told, and what he had subsequently asked to be confirmed for him. He was good on details. It was why he had kept his job for so long, even when the company rationalized a few years earlier, shedding employees at all levels like flakes of old skin.

Now he saw the Providence PD patrol car. It was moving slowly, but without lights. As it passed the Lexus on the opposite side of the street, the officer at the wheel turned his head, and just for a moment, Routh wondered if the cop might somehow have seen the girl. No, he thought, it was more likely that he was taking in the man or woman at the wheel of the Lexus.

The patrol car did not stop, merely continued on its way, then turned right before it reached the block on which Routh was parked. He waited for a time, but the car did not reappear, so he returned his attention to the Lexus and the house. The girl remained standing where she was, but now she gave her attention to Routh, confirming that he had seen her and, more importantly, had registered the object of her attention. Even after all these years, finding himself looking directly into the eyes of one of the departed Brethren still gave him a chill.

Routh blinked, and the girl vanished.

Louis put down the phone he had been holding to his ear as the patrol car approached. The only thing worse than attracting the scrutiny of a cop while you were sitting in a parked car was attracting the scrutiny of a cop while you were sitting in a parked car doing nothing. Cops had a natural suspicion of people who appeared to be doing nothing, as it usually meant that they were in actuality doing something, and often something they shouldn't have been doing.

Louis knew the cop would be back. Ten minutes, maybe fifteen at most. If Louis were still there when he returned, he'd be asked to state his business. The car could remain where it was, but it would be better if it were unoccupied the next time the cop swung by.

Louis got out of the Lexus and sniffed the air. He smelled a faint trace of burning, like the acrid aftermath of an electrical fire. The prickling at his cheek had ceased, and the faint haze had departed.

Louis decided he did not like Providence.

Farther up the street, he took in the most recently parked car. A big man emerged from it and removed something from the trunk. Louis didn't like that much either until the man closed the trunk, turned his back, and disappeared from sight.

Routh had taken the suppressor from the tool kit, fitted it to the H&K, and was debating how best to approach and kill the driver of the Lexus. The pack containing the mask and overalls remained in the trunk, but he had put on the gloves before handling the gun.

He watched the tall black man step from his car and take in his surroundings. Routh shopped only at JC Penney and Marshalls. He owned one suit that stood duty for formal business events and funerals. He had never attended a wedding, but assumed that the same suit would have served perfectly well had such an occasion arisen. He had no knowledge of fashion worth speaking of, but he could tell at a glance that the clothing worn by the man he was watching probably cost more than his entire wardrobe, including all his shoes. Routh had never seen a black man who was so well dressed, except on TV.

A number of explanations existed for this individual's presence. One was that it was simply coincidental, and his purpose for being in the vicinity of Eklund's house was entirely legitimate, although the minimal lapse of time before the arrival of the police car and the man's exit from his own vehicle suggested otherwise, as did the presence of the dead girl. The second possibility was that he was watching Eklund's home, perhaps to see who might display an interest in it in turn. The third was that he was the sentinel, and others were already inside.

The object of Routh's attention crossed the street. Eklund's house was near the corner of the block, but the man did not enter. Instead he followed the sidewalk around, keeping the house to his right. He cast a glance at Routh, an appraisal that appeared casual but which Routh recognized as something more loaded. Routh removed his tool kit, closed the trunk, and walked away from the car, not looking back, giving no cause to suspect surveillance. Only when the black man was gone from sight did he return to his vehicle. He started the engine and moved the car so that instead of being parked on the same side as Eklund's home he was now looking straight at it, partly shielded by a Dumpster.

From this vantage point, he resumed his vigil.

27

Three entire walls of Eklund's basement were lined with shelves, some of which were sagging under the burden of the volumes they held: hardcovers, paperbacks, lever arch files, and bundles of typewritten and handwritten pages bound with ribbon, string, and rubber bands. The room was dry and well insulated, so that it held the dense yet brittle scent of an old library. A metal desk stood on a red tasseled rug in the center of the floor, along with a black office chair. The desk was covered in piles of papers and strewn with photographs. A banker's lamp was available to provide additional illumination. Attached to its frame was a magnifying glass that could be moved into position when required.

Eklund's shelves were devoted almost exclusively to the paranormal. They included works by the Austrian-born paranormal researcher Hans Holzer and his predecessor Charles Fort, the American researcher who gave the world the term 'Fortean' to characterize phenomena that fell outside the picture of reality provided by science or common sense. Eklund had also collected books by prominent skeptics, among them David Marks and Joe Nickell, but the main body of his library was clearly weighted in favor of believers.

The main wall facing the desk and the stairs was not shelved, and was dominated by a map of the continental United States dotted with an array of pins. From each pin extended a thread that led beyond the borders of the map to a collection of notes, press clippings, photographs, even hand-drawn illustrations, all set against the whiteness of the wall.

Every cluster contained details of murders and disappearances dating back from the present day to the nineteenth century: individual killings, mass slaughters, kidnappings, unexplained vanishings. The oldest dated back to the 1850s, while the most recent was about a year old, and involved the disappearance of a family man named Michael MacKinnon from Millwood, New Hampshire. Between those two incidents, like ugly baubles on a chain, were accumulations of information on at least fifty other incidents, a minority distinguished by the violence inflicted on the victims – burning, slow torture, skinning, mutilation, the breaking of bones – while others appeared to have been carried out with the brutal efficiency of someone putting an injured animal out of its misery. Most, though, concerned disappearances: individuals who had passed from sight, never to be found.

The photographs alongside these accounts were of old houses or flat fields, stretches of river or expanses of forest. Some of the landscapes were marked with red dots as though to say 'Here: this was the place,' while others had sepia-tinted reproductions of older photographs linked to them by more of the ubiquitous threads, each showing a town, a family, or sometimes just an individual. Parker's attention was drawn to a picture of a pretty young woman with dark hair standing next to a man in a sailor's uniform, a blue pin and matching thread anchoring them to a photograph of a pond surrounded by dead and broken trees, like the fallen crosses and fragmented monuments in some abandoned and neglected cemetery.

Two names were written in block capitals on a piece of card above their black-and-white heads: RICHARD FILLER & HEIDI WOLKE. They had died in December 1945, shortly after Filler was discharged from the US Navy. He was twenty-four and she was twenty-two. Their bodies were found tied to a pair of trees in woodland near Burdette in Mississippi County, Arkansas, by a group of students and scientists studying the

group of little blue herons and great egrets that had begun
to nest in the area. Both Filler and Wolke were naked, although
according to one of those who discovered the bodies, an
academic from the University of Arkansas, quoted in a report
from the *Blytheville Courier News* next to the picture of the
victims, 'there was so much black blood on them, it was hard
to tell.'

If anyone had been charged with the crime, Eklund had
not recorded it, but a quick glance at the shelves revealed a
thick file related to the case. It was the same with the rest:
the details on the wall, the pins on the map, appeared to
function as a kind of aide-mémoire for Eklund, with the
substance of each atrocity contained in the carefully assembled
files on his shelves.

*The Huygens Family: murdered April 1962 in Grinnell,
Iowa. Chained together and burned alive.* Eklund's file on
them was easily an inch thick.

*Alicia Muny: abducted from her home in Farmville, Virginia,
in June 1969. Remains found outside Emporia, Virginia, in
November 1969, with all bones, major and minor, broken in
her arms and legs.* A smaller file, but this one containing a
copy of a handwritten letter from her mother to a named
detective in the Prince Edward County Sheriff's Office denying
that her daughter was a prostitute.

*Robert Damiani: murdered February 1975 in Cross City,
Florida. Cause of death: strangulation.* Barely a handful of
pages here, among them a copy of an internal FBI report
speculating that Damiani may have been killed due to his
older brother Jeffrey's links to the Colombo crime family in
New York.

But the atrocities themselves were not the strangest aspect
of Eklund's work, for bundled with each assemblage of factual
documents – newspaper articles, coroners' reports, crime scene
records – was a separate file concerning descriptions of hauntings: testimonies from clairvoyants, telepaths, and psychics;

letters, both copies and originals, from ordinary individuals recounting experiences that were far from ordinary, and for which they could find no rational explanation; photocopied extracts from books and journals; even carefully preserved reports from the kind of publications that made the *National Enquirer* look like the *New York Times*. Parker flicked through three of the case files, but these cursory examinations alone revealed similarities among the accounts. Two contained illustrations depicting what was clearly the same old man drawn by two different hands: the clothing, the hair, the eyes, the slightly flattened profile – all matched.

'What is Eklund, some kind of amateur parapsychologist?' asked Angel.

'A serious one, from the look of things.'

'Jesus, the guy must live for Halloween.'

'He lived for this,' said Parker, indicating the walls around them. The basement contained many years of work. 'How much time have we got on that alarm?'

'I can find an outlet for the jammer. You have as long as you need.'

Parker had no desire to spend longer than was necessary in Eklund's house. While he didn't doubt Angel's word on the alarm, it made no sense to linger illegally on the property. He also wanted time and space to work his way through this material in an effort to figure out precisely what had attracted Eklund to these crimes, and what had caused him to bundle them with paranormal investigations. It was possible, of course, that Eklund's absence had no connection to the contents of his basement, but the man's obvious obsession seemed like the most promising starting point.

'I saw a couple of suitcases in the bedroom at the front of the house,' he told Angel. 'Bring them down, and we'll use them to remove these files.'

Angel left. What they were doing was highly illegal, whether Eklund was alive or not, but particularly so if something bad had befallen him. Parker had no sense of the house as a crime scene – there was none of the disturbance associated with an attack or abduction – but what they were about to take from it might well be germane to any investigation. Then again, Parker had no intention of allowing Ross to hang him or his colleagues out to dry. If it came down to it, he'd use Ross's name, and let the FBI agent sort out any mess Parker might have left behind.

He went to Eklund's desk. He hadn't seen a computer in the house, which suggested that Eklund was either a Luddite or, based on the similar absence of a computer from his office, only used a laptop. The desk had a couple of drawers, but they contained nothing more interesting than spare pens and paper clips. Parker flicked through the papers and photographs on the desktop, and saw that most of them related to the disappearance of Mike MacKinnon, the most recent of the mysteries catalogued by Eklund.

Beneath them was a blue folder, which immediately stood out because all the others in the room were either brown or green. Parker opened it and found a copy of a pro bono contract between Eklund and a client named Oscar Sansom from Natick, Massachusetts, signed about a year earlier. The name was familiar to Parker, but he couldn't quite place it until he saw the newspaper clipping and a woman's picture under the agreement.

Claudia Sansom had disappeared three years earlier, and suspicion had long lingered among law enforcement that Sansom had killed her and disposed of the body, although nobody could ever find proof, or even a possible motive. Claudia's family had initially sided with her husband, certain that he could not have been responsible for their daughter's death, but gradually fractures had appeared in their relationship, possibly not entirely unconnected to the seeds of doubt sown by the police. The taint of murder stuck to him, but Sansom never left the state, even when it might have been easier on him to do so, and he became active in a number of support groups for families of missing persons. He never sought to remarry, never – as far as anyone knew – even started another relationship. He just waited, and ignored the whispering.

In January, the remains of Oscar Sansom's wife, Claudia, had been found buried in a shallow grave not far from Lincoln, New Hampshire, in the western White Mountains. A hunter's dog sniffed out a skull protruding from the earth of a shallow grave, and DNA tests confirmed Claudia's identity. The mystery of Claudia Sansom's fate appeared to have been solved. All that remained was to confirm the manner of her death, and apprehend the individual or individuals responsible. Within hours of the results of the DNA test results being confirmed, Oscar Sansom was in a room being questioned by both the Natick PD and the New Hampshire State Police.

Which was when it all got weird. Claudia Sansom had disappeared at the age of 36, but the body recovered from the ground was that of a woman closer to 39, at the best estimate. It was definitely Claudia Sansom – that much was certain – but where had she been for the three years between her disappearance and her burial? The initial analysis of the skeletonized remains showed no evidence of significant trauma or fractures, so there was no obvious cause of death. Forensic anthropologists were still examining Claudia Sansom's body in an effort to establish how she had died.

A lot of theories emerged in the aftermath. Perhaps Claudia had simply abandoned her husband and started a new life before finally coming to a bad end, because nobody who met a good one ended up buried in an unmarked shallow grave in woodlands. She could also have been abducted, but who abducts someone and then keeps her alive for three years?

Oscar Sansom was permitted to view his wife's remains. Some police investigators persisted in viewing him as a suspect, but most of those with detailed knowledge of the case by now believed him to be innocent, although the contamination from years of rumors and suspicion had marked him irrevocably in the public eye. After looking at the bones in silence for a time, Sansom simply returned to his home, the same home in which he had lived with his wife in the years before her disappearance, and in which he had remained ever since. He gave no statement to the media. He went about his business. If he mourned, he mourned in silence, and in private. Now it seemed that Sansom had engaged the services of Jaycob Eklund about two years after Claudia vanished, but no payment was exchanged.

When Angel returned with the suitcases, Parker was sitting in Eklund's chair, leafing through the Sansom file. Eklund was one of three private investigators who had assisted Sansom over the years, but he hadn't enjoyed any more success than the others. Eklund had reinterviewed various people, consulted with the police, and followed a couple of lines of inquiry, all to dead ends.

So what was the Sansom file doing sitting on Eklund's desk? He might, of course, have retrieved it from his records after Claudia Sansom's remains were found, perhaps in the hope that something in it, something he had missed, could prove useful to the police, and then forgotten about it.

Nevertheless, it was interesting.

28

Donn Routh was not a blunt instrument to be wielded indiscriminately; that was not how the Brethren operated. Perhaps in more distant times, when they dealt in routine savagery, such methods might have been acceptable, but not now. It was important for them to pass unnoticed, to be free to drift without fear of connections being made. That was why the appearance of Eklund had been so troubling. How long had he been working, researching, picking up on those details about the Brethren that others had ignored, accepting as a possibility – a probability, even – what most would have dismissed as absurd? Years, certainly.

Routh felt a kind of admiration for the man's persistence. Eklund was paying for it now, of course. He had received a confirmation long sought, and consequently understood the truth of the matter at last, but Routh was certain that Eklund might, in retrospect, have wished it otherwise. As far as Routh was concerned, all important questions ended in one final, implacable answer: death. Eklund would have been better advised not to pursue it with such avidity; it would have found him in its own time. Better not to summon it, to bring it down on oneself. Some might have said that death always comes at its appointed hour, the moment of its appearance embedded deep in the matter of every man at the time of his birth, but Routh knew this not to be true because he himself was an instrument of that very death, and was fickle in his approaches.

He checked his watch. Fifteen minutes had gone by. The patrol car had just appeared for the second time, and then departed. Moments later, the black man returned to his Lexus, confirming Routh's concerns about him. The stranger had clearly found himself a patch of shadow from which to watch both the Lexus and the house, knowing that the cop would return and understanding that it would be better to be absent when he did.

It would undoubtedly be useful to Routh to take him alive and determine his connection to Eklund, but like any predator Routh was attuned in turn to other predators, if only on a competitive level. He couldn't tell for sure how old the black man was – he might have been forty or sixty, although Routh thought he could pick out a halo of gray around his mouth. He walked on the balls of his feet, and a litheness and grace to his movements suggested he would respond quickly to any potential threat. He was about as tall as Routh, but less stockily built. In an exchange of punches, brute force against brute force, Routh would prevail, but he doubted that he would be able to get close enough to land the first crucial blow before his opponent reacted. He didn't look as though he'd respond particularly well to threats, either. He struck Routh as a man who had probably looked at his share of guns from both sides, and was still standing.

But Routh did not know as yet if there was anyone else in the Eklund house. To find out, he would first have to confront the stranger. Once the threat represented by him was neutralized, Routh would deal with anyone inside the house before emptying it of all clues as to the nature of Eklund's investigations.

In an ideal world, Routh would have taken a turn around the block in his car before pulling up alongside the Lexus, driver's side to driver's side, hemming in the target while emptying a magazine through the window, but such an approach only suited a fast getaway, and Routh would be remaining in the area. He would have to approach on foot, but it would still be better if he could persuade the man to roll down his window before killing him. Broken glass would alert anyone passing by, and Routh wanted time to complete his tasks in Eklund's home.

Routh left his car, but didn't bother to lock it. Whatever happened in the coming minutes, he'd be moving fast on his return, and didn't want anything to delay him. Even with the suppressor attached, the H&K fit easily into the deep false pocket of his jacket.

Routh stepped onto the sidewalk and saw a figure coming toward him on the same side. It was a male smoking a cigarette. He appeared absorbed in his own thoughts. His head was down, and his shoes were clearly unsuited to the weather, because he walked like a man afraid of falling. Routh didn't panic. He needed the bystander to be out of sight before he could move on the Lexus. He turned back to his car and opened the passenger door, leaning in as though he had left something in the glove box. He heard footsteps drawing nearer, then the sound of someone slipping. A voice swore. Routh raised his head from the interior of his vehicle and a white object caught the moonlight, like the wings of a small bird cleaving the darkness. Routh felt pressure at his neck, followed by a line of pain that swept from left to right and became a wet burning against his skin. A great gush of red shot into the air as he slumped back, his hands gripping the body of the car. Blood filled his throat as he released his hold on the car, sliding awkwardly down so that he ended up sitting on the ground with his head leaning so far back that the crown almost touched the passenger seat. The interior light had come on, but a gloved hand reached in and switched it off.

A face stared down at his. It had the yellowed, prematurely aged skin of a lifelong smoker, under a greasy swathe of black hair that hung in untidy curls to the neck of a filthy shirt. The man held in one hand a curved blade, like a raptor's talon. He stank of nicotine. Even in the last seconds of his life, Routh, a fastidious person, was repelled by the stench.

'Yingtai,' said the man. 'Remember her?'

There were other figures behind him now, gray men and women, their eyes dark hollows against the pallor. Routh's vision dimmed. Hands reached for him. He tasted their fingers in his mouth.

And as he died, he finally understood why the Brethren were so afraid of the next world.

29

The couple, Kirk and Sally Buckner, arrived in Turning Leaf, West Virginia, in 2009, at a time when the Turning Leaf Primitive Baptist Church was in severe difficulties. As one senior member of the congregation commented at the time, with some bitter amusement, 'our hard shell has cracked.' Their deacon, Elder Danny, had briefly left his wife for the spouse of Thomas Hooven, the illicit entanglement only becoming common knowledge when, during the ritual foot washing, Thomas Hooven upended an entire basin of water over Elder Danny's head, and then proceeded to beat the shit out of him with the basin in full view of the rest of the congregation.

The Primitives were already suffering a drain of members to the Bright Paradise Missionary Baptists on the other side of town, in part due to Elder Danny's unpopularity with many of his flock, Elisabeth Hooven being the obvious exception, but the whole business of the affair, and the embarrassing basin assault, put the kibosh on his time in office. Elder Danny did make one last attempt to save himself in a rambling sermon that invoked the doctrine of limited atonement in what could best be described as an innovative way, and followed a particular logical path: Jesus died to save his elect, who can never be lost; Elder Danny was one of those elect, and could not be lost; hence his affair with another man's wife did not affect this status, or render him any less able to carry out his duties as deacon. Finally, Elder Danny pointed out that he hadn't enjoyed the sex anyway, so he had endured guilt without pleasure. Elisabeth Hooven wasn't present to witness this last act of betrayal, although certain male congregants later whispered of how she had always seemed like a cold woman to them, and therefore they weren't particularly surprised to hear that part.

None of this was enough to save Elder Danny, who went to live in Hoboken and was last known to be working in a liquor store. His removal from office resulted in a split in the congregation between those who believed that the cuckolded Thomas Hooven had, in his use of the basin as a weapon, displayed the same kind of fiery zeal that Christ himself had shown in chasing the moneylenders from the temple, and was therefore a suitable candidate for deacon, and those who believed that being cuckolded by Elder Danny meant that Hooven was little better than a fool, and they would be even greater fools to reward him for his inability to keep his own wife under control.

It was the newly arrived Kirk Buckner, calm and quiet, and with no loyalty or obligation to either side, who acted as mediator in the dispute, with his wife beside him to offer counsel and work behind the scenes with the female members of the faithful to force their spouses to see reason. While a groundswell of opinion held that Kirk would make an ideal deacon, he graciously declined the honor, and instead pointed the congregation in the direction of Perry Garris, a man so unassuming, so unostentatious in his godliness, that he had been overlooked in the search for a more imposing figure. Only behind closed doors, and in the comfort and security of certain homes, were whispers of discontent to be heard, as the more worldly of the Primitives noted that, in a very short space of time, the Buckners had accrued a great deal of influence unto themselves and, in the person of Perry Garris, had found an individual who might easily be manipulated by them, although to what end none could say.

But it also had to be admitted that, church commitments

excepted, the Buckners, while not exactly reclusive, kept to themselves and showed no signs of vanity or ambition. They behaved modestly and were generally liked, even admired. Sure, maybe they could have mixed a little more, but most of those in the community – both the Primitives and the larger township – were content to let folks be, as long as they didn't stir things up for others.

So the Buckners were now settled in Turning Leaf, and few even bothered to recall that no stones in the local cemetery bore their family name, or took it amiss that the Buckners continued to carefully guard their privacy, and permitted no one to trespass farther than their front porch. It was Thomas Hooven, of all people, who spoke loudest among the naysayers when it came to the Buckners. Hooven had since divorced his first wife and was now happily remarried, having been assured by greater theological minds than his own that he was on sound biblical ground in the reasons for the separation, and the remarriage of the innocent party was never depicted in Scripture as adultery, bigamy, or polygamy. He had also since abandoned the Primitives for the Missionary Baptists, and something of the resulting distance probably enabled him to look upon the Buckners with a cold eye.

'It's some trick,' he would observe to his new wife, each time they drove by the Buckner house, 'to make everyone like you when you show no signs of liking anyone else in return.'

And his wife would tell him to hush, and hush he would, even as he stared at the Buckner residence receding in his rearview mirror, and wondered why he felt a prickling on his neck at the very sight of it.

Kirk Buckner heard the smashing of glass from the kitchen as he was upstairs trying to rehang a closet door. He swore in a manner that would have shocked even the most lax of Primitives: he had one screw inserted in the top hinge, but he didn't think it would be enough to hold the weight of the oak. He carefully shifted a block of wood into place to support the door before he released his hold, then went to the top of the stairs and called down to Sally to ask if she was okay. He received no reply, which was when he started to worry. He took the stairs two at a time and entered the kitchen to find the floor covered in pieces of broken glass and an uncooked vegetarian lasagna. Sally was standing rigid before the mess, her arms by her sides, her hands clasped into fists. Her whole body was trembling.

Kirk couldn't see whatever she was looking at, but he could almost sense it, even smell it some. The kitchen was noticeably colder to his right than to his left, and he caught the faintest hints of vegetal dampness and burning, like a fire in a swamp. It was how he always knew that one of *them* was present. Unlike his wife, he did not have the gift of seeing the departed. It tended to pass from mother to daughter, but not to sons. The menfolk did occasionally glimpse them, but only in the most exceptional of circumstances, most frequently on the deathbed – with the notable exception of the Cousin, Donn Routh, but Kirk preferred not even to think of Routh.

'What is it?' he asked.

Sally began to cry. This in itself was shocking to him. She never cried.

'He's dead,' she said. 'The Cousin is dead.'

30

Parker and Angel filled three suitcases with Eklund's files, including the one relating to Oscar and Claudia Sansom. Parker then photographed the map on the wall, and the surrounding material. He didn't want to risk taking it down and disturbing it. He would do his best to re-create it from the images when he was back in Maine.

With that, he and Angel turned out the lights and left the basement, although they could only close the door behind them because Angel had been forced to fry the locks to gain entry. Angel unplugged the jammer – the device heated up like hell's own oven after extended use, and he didn't want to risk incinerating the house – but left it switched on and concealed behind a bookcase. It would run down in an hour or so, at which point the alarm would activate. By then they'd be long gone, with no outward evidence of intrusion. With luck, the alarm would be dismissed as a false activation. Louis started the car as soon as he saw them emerge into the snow that had just begun to fall, and within moments they were gone from Fox Point.

But their departure did not go unnoticed.

It is said that a falcon, trained to the lure, has no affection for the falconer. The relationship between them is based, in roughly equal parts, on trust and food. Birds of prey are essentially lazy: to hunt for prey requires the expenditure of huge amounts of energy, which is why the bird must be precise in its death strike. To be otherwise is to deplete valuable resources, weakening the hunter. Weakness begets mistakes, which leads in turn to greater frailty. The ultimate consequence for the predator is its own death.

The man responsible for killing Donn Routh was known as the Collector, and it was he who watched as Parker and the others left the home of Jaycob Eklund. The Collector had moved Routh's car to a nearby lot. Routh's body lay in the trunk, and there it would remain. In the present weather, it might be days before the vehicle was noticed. Eventually the Collector would go to Parker and tell him of what he had done.

Perhaps.

The Collector was a predator, but he too only had limited resources on which to draw. His once solitary missions to locate, isolate, and slay his targets were time-consuming, dangerous, and not always successful. And so, reluctantly at first, he had allowed himself to enter the orbit of the private investigator Charlie Parker. The truth of Parker's nature might have been hidden from the Collector – just as, in reality, the essence of the Collector's own being was partly concealed from himself in order to protect the entity that dwelt within him – but he understood that Parker was both hunter and lure, driven to pursue depraved men even as others like them were pulled inexorably toward him.

Yet the Collector had been mistaken about Parker. At first he simply assumed that Parker had his part to play in the great unfolding, and was acting as an unwitting agent of the Divine. (And, the Collector occasionally reflected, with something resembling amusement, he was long overdue a conversation with Parker about the reality of God. The investigator had no idea of the truth, none at all.) But slowly it became apparent to the Collector that Parker was much more than a pawn on the board, although his position in the hierarchy of pieces had yet to be determined. Parker had died not once but three times following the shooting at his home, and on each occasion was brought back by the physicians. It would have been noteworthy even for an average man, but given what Parker had already endured in life, his survival qualified as positively miraculous. The Collector had begun to believe that perhaps Parker had not been kept alive by doctors so much as returned to this world by another agency.

But the man who came back was not the same as the one who had fallen under a volley of shotgun blasts and pistol shots. He had seen what lay beyond, and he *remembered*. He spoke of old gods awakening, and the Collector knew it to be true. He had felt it, and the Hollow Men had felt it too. The Hollow Men, the soulless residue of the dead, followed the Collector just as a trained bird of prey follows the falconer. He fed them the discarded husks of the ones he excised from the fabric of this world, permitting the Hollow Men to absorb them into their number. Their dependency on him was almost equal to their hatred.

Finally, Parker had come to the Collector, tracking him down to his last place of refuge, and there he had confirmed what the Collector had already begun to fear: the Collector thought he could use Parker, but instead he had stepped into a snare, and now he was tethered to block and glove. Worse, the Collector found that he was almost content in his role – or, more accurately, resigned to it. He retained some freedom to roam, but he remained Parker's beast, and the beast instinctively shadows the master, and will always return to his side as long as it is being fed.

But Parker had not been feeding the Collector as much as he might have liked – had not been feeding him at all, in fact – and so he had returned to his solitary ways. This led him, eventually, to Donn Routh, a minor malefactor by the Collector's standards, but worthy of a little time nonetheless, especially because the Collector had encountered such difficulty in tracing and tracking him. It was as though Routh were hiding in fog, and only revealed himself in the spaces between, the clearings in the mist.

That was why the Collector had not taken Routh on the road. He was curious to see what could have drawn Routh from the safety of his Kentucky lair, and perhaps discover what it was that allowed him to conceal himself in this way. In the end, as if to confirm the presence of the tether, and the guidance of a hand unseen, the hunt had ended within screaming distance of Charlie Parker.

But once he got close to Routh, the Collector understood that this man was more dangerous, and more interesting, than he had imagined. His lethality was instantly apparent, but so too was his strangeness. The Collector might have thought himself simply to be hunting a degenerate believed to have abducted and killed a young Chinese girl – and he knew that to be true, had detected it in the reactions of the Hollow Men as they circled – but Routh turned out to be so much more than that. The air around Routh shimmered as though from an unseen source of heat, and the Hollow Men had kept their distance until the Collector's knife began its work.

And then—

Ah: that was the oddest part of it.

After his death, Routh was not added to the Hollow Men's number. They had retreated from the body, like carrion birds detecting poison in a carcass. The Collector sensed their bewilderment and rage, for just as he was tethered to Parker, so too were the Hollow Men tethered to him. They had no love for him, because he had caused them to become what they were, and no loyalty beyond his ability to assuage their misery by introducing others to it, but they were his creatures regardless.

So Routh had been watching Parker – or maybe, like the Collector, he had come to Providence anticipating one outcome and instead had been presented with another in which Parker was involved. Whatever the truth, Parker was connected to the mystery of Donn Routh, and the Collector wanted to be near when, or if, an explanation was offered.

The Collector felt no surprise that Routh should be linked to Parker. He was long past such feelings.

I should have known, the Collector thought. *No matter how far I fly, it seems I must always return to Parker's glove.*

31

Parker considered returning to Maine that night. It was a question of balancing the risk of staying near what he was trying not to think of as the scene of the crime against the tiredness that he and the others were already feeling. In the eyes of the law, they had just burglarized both an office and a house, and engaging in burglary – as Angel in particular knew, from long experience – was a stressful way to pass the time. In the end, they compromised on leaving the state of Rhode Island. They retrieved Parker's car and drove in convoy until they found a small motel just over the Massachusetts border with what looked like a pretty decent bar adjacent to it. They took a booth by a window, where they ate hamburgers and drank bottles of Sam Adams on special.

As a precaution, the material they had removed from Eklund's house was being stored in compartments concealed in the trunk of Louis's Lexus, although Angel thought it unlikely that Eklund's alarm would have gone off yet, and Parker didn't believe anyone had noticed them removing the paperwork from the house. Still, nobody ever went to jail for being too vigilant.

Angel finished his burger, then took three bottles of pills from the pockets of his jacket, shook two tablets from each, and knocked them back with a mouthful of water. Parker watched the process with one eyebrow cocked high.

'That's a lot of pills,' he said. 'Who are you – Bill Cosby?'

'I've been getting pains.'

'The size of those bottles you're carrying around, I'm not surprised. What kind of pains?'

'Man . . .'

'Come on, what kind?'

'Pains in my insides. They come and go. Headaches, too.'

'You see a doctor?'

'No,' said Angel. 'I just stole all these pills.'

There was a pause. It took Angel a moment to realize that sarcasm might not be effective in this case. He'd stolen a lot of things in his life.

'Yeah,' he said, 'I've seen a doctor.'

Parker glanced in Louis's direction, but could not catch his eye.

'Anything I should know about?' he asked.

An awkward silence descended. Louis was staring out the window. Angel was spinning a beer mat on the table. Eventually he conceded, with palpable reluctance, 'The doctor said I ought to have some tests.'

'And, of course, you made the appointment straight away.'

Louis released a sound like a poison dart being shot from a pipe, but still didn't speak.

'I'm working on it,' said Angel.

'Working on it how, exactly?'

'Jesus, when did we get married? I don't see no ring. Look, I don't like doctors, and I don't like hospitals.'

'You'll like dying a whole lot less,' said Louis, intervening at last.

'I'm not going to die.'

'Yeah, 'cause you're immortal. Says so on your résumé, right beside "honest" and "values neatness".'

'You're spoiling my evening,' said Angel.

'You know what would really spoil your evening?' said Louis. 'Fucking dying because you were too scared to go get some tests. You need to do like the doctor said.'

'Fine! Okay! It's only been a week. If I'm dying, you think a week is going to make any difference?'

'Oh, so you an internist now?'

'Hey, I know my body.'

'*I* know your body, and the only surprise is that it's still upright and in one piece.'

Their server drifted over, drawn by the sound of raised voices. She was in her fifties, and if she didn't look like she'd seen it all, then she'd seen as much of it as she cared to.

'Everything all right, boys?'

'Our friend here has pains,' said Parker, 'but he won't go get tests like the doctor told him.'

'Oh, for the love of God . . .'

Angel folded his arms and let his forehead sink down on them.

'My first husband was like that,' said the server. 'Didn't matter how sick he was, he wouldn't see anyone.'

'And what happened to him?' asked Angel from the tabletop.

'He died,' she said.

'No shit,' said Angel. 'What of?'

'Someone shot him.'

Once again, there was silence for a time.

'We'll just take the check,' said Parker.

'Sure thing.' She patted Angel on the back. 'Go see a doctor.'

'I did see a doctor. That's how all this started.'

'Well, go see another.'

She left them.

'I hate Massachusetts,' said Angel.

'Because they speak wisdom,' said Parker. 'Make the damn appointment.'

'Tomorrow. Anything for peace.'

'We're going to stand over you to ensure that you do.'

'I hate you all.'

The server returned with the check.

'Is he making the appointment?'

'Yeah,' said Angel. 'You talked me around with your story. I don't want to get shot.'

Parker paid the check. He saw Angel wince slightly as he

got up from the booth, and tried to recall if he'd noticed it before.

'Quit watching me,' said Angel.

'You want us to get you a wheelchair?'

'Fuck you.'

'We could hire a nurse.'

'I said I'd call. Leave me alone.'

They left the bar and headed across the parking lot to the motel. A passing car illuminated a man stepping from the driver's seat of an expensive gray BMW parked by Louis's Lexus. He approached them slowly, and Parker felt as much as saw Louis tense instinctively, but the man held his hands out from his sides to show that they were empty. Parker scanned the lot, but saw no one else nearby. Whatever this was, it wasn't an attack, and unless someone in Massachusetts law enforcement had recently won Powerball and thrown a contribution into the state hat for some German engineering, it didn't look like police business. Louis relaxed a little, but Parker could see that Angel had shifted position to shield his partner's right hand from view. Parker guessed there was already a gun in it.

The man before them was just a shade less than six feet tall and wore a dark wool car jacket over black trousers. His leather shoes, only barely spotted with mud and slush, had thick rubber soles for grip. His hands were gloveless, and Parker could see that the final two fingers on the left were contorted, either as a result of some ancient injury or a birth defect. The tips sat against the palm, giving the impression that he was making an awkward pistol with his digits. He wore a wool cap with the peak tilted back. The eyes beneath it were very blue and very cold. Any capacity for warmth they might once have been capable of exhibiting had long since been excised from them. It was like staring into a clear, dead sea.

'Help you?' asked Parker.

'I'd like you to come back to Providence.'

The voice was peculiarly flat and vaguely androgynous. It

held no depth or roughness, no traces of individuality. Parker tried to gauge the man's age: the smoothness of his features suggested mid twenties at most, but he carried himself with a certain confidence, even arrogance. Apparently alone and without a visible weapon, he felt no compunction about confronting three strangers in a darkened parking lot – three strangers, what was more, who almost certainly numbered guns among their possessions.

'And why would we want to do that?'

'Your interests may intersect with those of my employer.'

He didn't elaborate. Either he had a flair for the dramatic, which was entirely possible, or he didn't think and behave like a normal human being, which struck Parker as being increasingly probable.

'And who would that be?'

'I work for Mr. Caspar Webb.'

Louis spoke for the first time in the conversation.

'Caspar Webb is dead.'

Those arctic eyes flicked to him.

'Yes, I believe he is.'

32

Organized crime – or the Italian variety of it – had been in decline in New England ever since the death of Raymond Patriarca in 1984. Senior figures expired, went to prison, or turned informant, and internal family feuds further weakened those who remained. Providence, which had been the New England Mob's base of operations since the 1950s when Patriarca ran it from the National Cigarette Company and Coin-O-Matic Distributors on Atwells Avenue, was abandoned in favor of Boston. And all the time, the FBI continued to hammer away at the Office, as the Patriarcas' operation was termed, leaving others to thrive in the shadows.

Caspar Webb's real name was unknown, and even his nationality was a matter of dispute, although it was generally agreed that he had roots somewhere in Eastern Europe. How he had come by the money that enabled him to establish himself in Rhode Island was also a mystery. He began as a smuggler, thus positioning himself as part of a long and noble tradition in the region's black market. He brought in cigarettes, narcotics, and women for the sex trade. Through intermediaries, he cut mutually beneficial deals with the Patriarcas while never meeting with any of their hierarchy, or even acknowledging that his operations were the source of their contraband.

Webb owned a vast property on the outskirts of New Shoreham, the only municipality on tiny Block Island, officially the smallest town in the smallest state in the Union, where the median house price was roughly $1 million. If he ever came to the attention of law enforcement, then nothing resulted from it. Slowly, carefully, and always through others, Webb insinuated himself into the interconnected political and criminal spheres of life in Rhode Island, and from there into the rest of New England. He was a malign and largely undetected influence on the economies of six states for decades, and left no bodies in his wake, because those who crossed him simply disappeared. When he died, his passing went almost entirely unremarked, publicly at least. In private, by contrast, most of those who knew of him quietly offered up a prayer of gratitude for his demise.

Now, as Parker and the others stood watching the man who claimed to be Webb's emissary, another BMW pulled into the lot and parked alongside the first. Four men could be glimpsed inside. They didn't emerge, and the driver didn't cut the engine. They just waited.

Webb's representative clasped his hands before him.

'Mr. Webb would have appreciated being informed of your presence in his state,' he said.

'Well,' said Angel, 'we forgot to bring a medium. Maybe next time you could organize a séance.'

Parker gave Angel a look. They were now outnumbered, and this wasn't helping.

'Who are you?' asked Parker.

'My name is Philip.'

Parker gestured at the new arrivals.

'I take it these guys are with you.'

'We really would be grateful if you would accompany us back to Providence,' said Philip. 'You can bring your own vehicle, if you'll permit me to travel with you. My colleagues will follow.'

A large group of young men and women emerged from the bar and looked in their direction. They were beginning to attract attention. It wasn't anything they were doing, but people were more sensitive to potential violence than they were often given credit for, and Louis's left hand was only barely concealing the gun in his right.

'Just for argument's sake, what if we were to refuse?'

Philip smiled. No wrinkles showed, so it was like watching plastic reshape itself.

'You're not going to refuse,' he said, 'so why sow disquiet?'

'"Sowing disquiet",' said Louis. 'I never heard it called that before.'

Parker didn't see what choice they had. If they stayed in the parking lot any longer, there was a chance that someone might call the cops.

'Then I guess we're going back to Rhode Island.'

33

Sally was in the bathroom. She'd retreated there shortly after Kirk discovered her in the kitchen. She hadn't spoken a word to him since, even though he'd hammered on the door to ask if she was okay. In the end he simply sat against the wall outside, and wondered what they were going to do now. It all depended, he supposed, on how Routh had died. If he'd expired of natural causes, then they had little to worry about, and his death would be more of an inconvenience than anything else. But if his passing was connected to Eklund, they could have a problem.

He heard the water running in the tub, followed by the sound of a body climbing in and settling. For a time silence descended – no splashing, no small noises of pleasure or relaxation – and he had a vision of Sally with vertical slashes on her arms, lying in a bath of bloody water. It had happened to others of their number in the past, when their burden became too much to bear. Mostly, though, the women of their family endured. Oddly, more males than females had taken their own lives down the centuries. It was guilt, Kirk guessed, or a form of madness brought on by the nature of the pact into which they had been forced. Either way, he did not really understand why they chose death. After all, they knew what waited for them beyond it.

And then, of course, there were those who had been about to turn, the ones who decided it might be better for all if the pact were brought to an end, but they were always sniffed out in time. They would be spoken to, and reminded of their obligations to all. On occasion, a period of restraint and isolation was necessary. In the most extreme cases, they were removed and dealt with, but such actions had been carried out only a handful of times over the years. The last occurred when Kirk was a teenager and Aunt Hattie was diagnosed with cancer. She'd started wondering aloud about repentance, which was fine while she was in her own bed but could have presented difficulties when she was transferred to a care facility, as would ultimately have been required. When it became clear that she posed a potential threat, Routh was summoned. It was quick and painless. It might even have been considered a blessing in light of how Hattie would have suffered had the cancer been allowed to take its course.

Kirk had never killed anyone. He didn't know if he could. He liked to think he'd be able to do it if worse came to worst, but he was happy to leave murder to others. Then again, he was still relatively young, and the prospect of his own mortality was not yet real to him. He'd noticed the years passing faster, though. His day would come, and like all the others, he wanted to be sure he would be safe when it did.

Sally could kill someone, he thought. He'd seen what she'd done to the private investigator, and that was worse than murder. She hadn't taken any delight in it, or none that he could see. She'd just gone about it the way she would with any other unpleasant chore that needed her attention. Still, her capacities frightened him. They reminded him of the now departed Donn Routh.

A single lamp lighted this end of the hallway. The bulb was bright – brighter than was needed for the space – but Kirk liked it that way. The bulbs in the basement and the garage were also very bright, and he kept them on even when the light was good. He avoided darkness as much possible, because *they* liked the dark. Even if he couldn't see them, he could often smell them, and he didn't care to have them around him, especially when Sally was absent. The light kept them away, and that suited Kirk just fine. Sally understood what he was doing, but never commented on it. It was different for her. They knew better than to intrude upon her against her wishes. It meant that he and Sally could turn off the lights when they made love, and when they rested. Otherwise, Kirk wasn't sure he could have performed at all, or slept without nightmares. On those nights when Sally wasn't with him – and they had been few over the years – he kept the bedroom brightly lit, and used a pair of airline shades to cover his eyes.

Kirk could see the telltale flicker of candlelight through the crack under the bathroom door. Maybe one of them was in there with Sally right now, staring down at her nakedness. Man or woman, it wouldn't trouble Sally. She claimed they didn't have those desires anymore, but Kirk wasn't so sure. They felt rage and fear, so why not desire, or even envy? Kirk suspected that envy might be the emotion that drove them above all others, even more than fear. How could the dead fail to envy the living, and these dead more than most? They were trapped, and they had to remain that way, because the other option was—

Well, the other option didn't bear considering. It was as simple as that. The choice was no choice at all.

And eventually – sooner, but oh-so-preferably later – he and Sally would take their place among them, and the whole damn cycle would continue for another generation, the stain of the sin growing with the years, and with it the punishment that would befall them all if their line faltered.

He heard a noise from the bathroom. It sounded like Sally moving in the water, and he waited without speaking in the hope that she would get out, dry herself, and tell him just what was going on.

But she didn't. He called her name again, if only to remind her that he was there, and then, like generations of the Brethren's males before him, he waited for a woman to guide him.

*   *   *

Reclining in the tub, the water slowly growing colder around her, Sally watched as the dead girl paced the tiles of the bathroom floor, back and forth, back and forth, like an animal trapped in its own madness.

34

The man named Philip sat in the front passenger seat, Louis driving, Parker directly behind him, and Angel at Philip's back. Philip consented to being frisked before joining them, because Louis was very particular about not allowing strangers with weapons in his car, and Parker confirmed him to be unarmed. The same probably couldn't be said of the four men who were escorting them back to Providence – one BMW in front, the other shadowing – but since Parker hadn't suggested frisking them as well, the truth would have to remain unknown.

Philip sat with his back turned slightly to the door so that he could keep staring at Parker. Seen up close, his face had a slight sheen to it, like the faintest of glaze on an uncooked pastry. He also had a distinctive scent, which grew stronger as the interior of the car warmed up. He smelled like dying violets. Philip ignored any questions, and didn't give any directions, content that Louis would follow the car before them. If he was aware of the gun that was now in Angel's hand, he gave no sign of it. The little .22 was the perfect weapon for the situation, because its bullets would kill without exiting the body, thereby avoiding embarrassing damage to the windshield or interior of Louis's car. Parker wondered idly if Angel simply happened to have the gun on him, or if Louis had somehow contrived to pass it to him. It never ceased to amaze Parker just how many weapons Louis could lay hands on at short notice. Parker had no idea where he kept them all, and decided that, on reflection, he really didn't want to know.

'It's strange,' said Parker, 'but I once broke up with a girl because she kept staring at me the way you do.'

Philip maintained his gaze. As far as Parker could tell, he didn't seem to blink. It was like finding oneself under the scrutiny of a stuffed bird. His attention was not hostile, or even particularly designed to disconcert, but Parker detected perhaps a hint of curiosity, and a certain amount of disappointment, as though the object of his scrutiny had failed to live up to rumor and reputation.

Eventually they re-entered Providence, this time heading south of downtown, through the small financial district and into the grungier area beyond the fringes of what had been christened an arts quarter, a designation common when a city had blocks of old buildings and not enough tenants for them. That situation didn't seem likely to persist for much longer. Most of the vacant lots appeared to have been flattened in preparation for development, probably by Johnson & Wales University, which was in the process of expanding.

But islands of old brownstones still remained, particularly around the Jewelry District off Ship Street, and it was to one of these old relics that their little fleet was drawn. They stopped before a five-story detached building with a brass plaque beside its black door, and a single ornate stained-glass window that gave no indication of what business might be conducted within but served to hide from public view whatever it might be. Louis pulled up behind the first car, and the second immediately boxed them in.

'You can't bring any weapons inside,' said Philip. 'Leave them in the vehicle. They'll be perfectly safe.'

Louis turned to Philip for the first time since he'd invaded the space of his beloved Lexus.

'Hell of a thing, asking us to trust you by walking in there unarmed.'

Philip's features melted and re-formed to create his approximation of a smile.

'I wasn't asking.'

'You got a way with people,' said Louis.

'Is that sarcasm?' Philip sounded genuinely puzzled, as though sarcasm were something of which he had heard but of which he had no direct experience, like an exotic, untested food.

'I'd like to think so.'

'Trust runs both ways. I trusted you not to kill me in your car. You now have to trust me not to have you killed beyond that door.'

'Since you put it like that,' said Angel, 'fuck you.'

The four men who had escorted them to Providence were now ranged around the Lexus. One of them was giving his attention to the weapon in Angel's hand. The expression on his face suggested he didn't like what he was seeing. There were no other guns in sight as yet, but Parker had a feeling it wouldn't be long before that changed.

Philip put his hand on the door handle.

'We just have some questions for you,' he said.

'"We"?' said Parker.

'Mother and I,' said Philip. 'There will be tea.'

He got out of the car and waited. Parker turned to Angel and nodded. Angel let the gun dangle from his finger by the trigger guard, raised it so the men outside could see, then set it carefully on the floor. Parker was not armed. He held his jacket open, inviting a search, but none came.

Louis sighed, and relieved himself of the weight of a Glock.

'Well,' he said, 'if there's going to be *tea* . . .'

The front door clicked and unlocked as they approached it, although nobody had produced a fob. The brass plate on the wall read Agave Associates. The plate was shiny and without blemish, at least until Angel ran a finger across the surface and smudged it. Instantly, a handkerchief was produced from the pocket of one of the quartet of escorts, and the stain vanished. Philip paused in the doorway.

'Why did you do that?' he asked.

'It was too clean,' said Angel. 'I don't like things that are too clean. It always means there's dirt hidden somewhere else.'

Philip considered this for a moment before filing it away for further examination later. Beyond them lay a small foyer and a glass door. As with the window outside, the glass was stained, but it was clearly a layer that had been placed against a thicker pane. The door looked as though it could take a grenade blast and not yield. Again, it opened without contact, revealing a hall with walls covered by antique mahogany on the lower half and expensive red-and-gold wallpaper above, decorated with what appeared to be death masks, waxen faces with closed eyes. Gas lamps were inset at regular points, and flames flickered inside them. The floor bore a blood-red wool carpet so thick that a small child could have become lost in its weave. It led to a massive set of wooden stairs that wound up to the next floor. The prints on the walls depicted scenes of Providence from centuries gone by, all of which had the patina of age.

This time, Philip held the door open for them to enter, but no one else joined them, so Parker and the others were alone with Philip in the hall. It smelled, not unpleasantly, of dust and woodsmoke. Combined with Philip's distinctive scent, it was reminiscent of a fire in a florist shop. Added to the old lighting, the thick carpet, and the peculiar wallpaper, the odors lent a turbid atmosphere to the place, so that Parker felt as though his vision were blurring.

This, he thought, *is what it's like to step back in time.*

The door was closed behind them, and Philip walked toward the stairs, not bothering to check that they were following him. With few other options available, they did.

'You live here?' Angel asked Philip's back.

'Nobody lives here.'

'Probably for the best.'

They passed a darkened landing on the second floor. A

door stood ajar, and through it Parker glimpsed furniture draped with sheets, and what might have been medical equipment, all of it barely visible in the gloom, as the shutters on the windows were closed. He caught a faint antiseptic tang, and the stink that underpinned it. It reeked of a hospital ward, and the last days of the dying. He saw, from a brief wrinkling of his nose, that Louis had picked up on it too. Maybe this was where Caspar Webb had made his last stand against the encroaching darkness.

They reached the second landing. Philip knocked softly on the first door to his left, then waited for a moment before opening it and indicating they should enter. Parker and the others paused, and each was thinking the same thing: if this was a trap, they were dead men.

Parker moved first. After all, the Eklund investigation was his responsibility.

The space was vast, taking up what must have been almost the entirety of the floor. A second door, closed, stood immediately opposite the first, and Parker saw another to his right, at the far wall. The room was unoccupied: Parker was the only person in it, at least until Angel and Louis joined him. To his left was a carved oak desk the size of a king's sarcophagus, inlaid with green leather and lit by a pair of ornate lamps. It stood before the window, but the heavy red drapes were drawn. The room was warm, but not uncomfortably so. A fire burned in the grate on the opposite wall, with leather armchairs at either side of it. The walls at this end were shelved to the ceiling, where an unlit crystal chandelier hung, one of three along the length of the room. All the light came from floor and table lamps, and the flickering of flames. The floor, visible at the margins, was wood, and looked like the original boards, or a very good re-creation of them using salvaged materials. A series of heavy Persian rugs, the largest at least ten feet in length, and almost as wide, helped to dull any sound.

The other half of the room contained some freestanding bookshelves, but the walls were mainly covered with paintings. All were landscapes, except for above the second fireplace where a life-size portrait of a man looked down on those below – figuratively as well as literally, from what Parker could see of the expression on the subject's face.

Philip took one of the chairs by the fire, crossed his legs, and clasped his hands in his lap.

'Feel free to look around,' he said. 'Mother will be with us momentarily.'

'Maybe once they've finished embalming her,' said Angel softly.

His voice was barely audible to Louis and Parker, and should have gone unheard by Philip, yet Parker noticed that he reacted. It was there in the barest narrowing of the eyes, and a twist of the mouth, but it was enough. Parker had been in Philip's company for less than an hour, but he was already pretty certain that the man was insane. He stood before Angel so that Philip could not see his face, and mouthed the words *Watch him*. Angel didn't even bother nodding.

Parker strolled around the room, browsing the bookshelves. They contained bound volumes of the proceedings of various institutions of the state, both legal and governmental, dating back to the start of the nineteenth century, but he also found a section devoted to artists' monographs and catalogues raisonnés, divided equally between twentieth century modernists and a variety of American landscape painters, from Ralph Earle and John Trumbull among the earliest to more recent artists such as Andrew Wyeth and Georgia O'Keeffe. Parker had identified at least one Wyeth among the paintings as he moved through the room, but Alfred Stieglitz and John Singer Sargent apart, most of the names among the monographs meant nothing to him.

Before the second fireplace, also lit, were a pair of leather couches, some occasional chairs, and a coffee table holding a tray containing a china tea service and a plate of the kind of tiny cookies that disintegrated into a storm of crumbs as soon as anyone tried to eat them.

Louis joined Parker.

'At least he wasn't lying about the tea,' said Louis.

'What are you thinking?'

'That they're not going to try to kill us.'

'Why?'

'They wouldn't have put out cookies.'

'Good point.'

'And that Philip is crazy.'

'I'd kind of come to that conclusion myself. I'm interested to meet his mother.'

'Yeah, bet she's quite the pistol.' Louis took in the paintings on the walls. 'Lot of money in this room, and Caspar Webb is dead. Smelled like he died downstairs, and died bad.'

'Did he leave any family?'

'Not that I heard.'

They both looked at the painting on the wall.

'Is that him?' asked Parker. He knew of Webb only by reputation. If any photographs of the man existed, he had never come across them.

'I only saw him once, a long time ago. But, yeah, that's him.'

'Remind you of anyone?'

Philip was watching them from his seat at the other end of the room. Neither man even glanced in his direction to check the resemblance.

'Now I *really* want to meet Mother,' said Louis.

And as if in answer to his wish, Mother appeared.

IV

Quis est iste qui venit?
What is this who is coming?

> After M. R. James, 'Oh, Whistle,
> and I'll Come to You, My Lad'

35

Sally Buckner could clearly recall the first time she saw a ghost. It happened when she was five years old, and playing in the sandbox outside her family home. A fence enclosed the backyard, and a heavy locked gate at the side of the house led to the front garden. She was in no danger of wandering off, and her mother could watch her from the kitchen window. She was playing with some of her older brother's toys, because Kirk was at school and she wasn't. She couldn't remember why. Sometimes, she thought that her mother might have suspected what was going to occur that day. Sally was always her mother's favorite – her father's too, come to think of it. 'Sickly' was the word their father used about Kirk, because he was frequently laid up with his chest. Sally would listen to him wheezing through the night, sometimes struggling so hard for breath that she feared he might die. On those occasions she would climb into bed beside him, hushing and calming him, and they would fall asleep in each other's arms.

Years later, she would wonder if their relationship might not have started had he been a stronger, healthier boy. Not that she minded being with him: she loved him. The Brethren didn't care either. There were others who would continue the family line, and they had their own plans for Sally. The appearance of the ghost had confirmed as much. Perhaps the whole family had understood how events would transpire for Sally and Kirk, even then.

Sally always did value boys' toys more than girls'. She

never had much time for dolls or miniature plastic kitchens. She liked guns and trucks. She enjoyed building colorful houses and bizarre vehicles using plastic bricks. On this particular bright sunny day, she was working on a series of great walls along one edge of the sandbox. She would build one, add battlements and a couple of Kirk's model soldiers, then run a metal truck through the whole construct with all the force she could muster, sending bricks and soldiers flying into the early summer air. Some of them went into the nearby bushes, but she decided that she'd go looking for them later, if she could be bothered. Kirk had plenty of bricks and soldiers to spare.

She was engaged in the raising of the most intricate defenses yet when a piece of plastic struck her on the side of the head. She looked to see where it had come from, and saw a girl standing in a small flower bed between a pair of shrubs. She was about seventeen or eighteen, with short dark hair and freckled skin. She wore a patterned denim pinafore dress, and her feet were bare. Her toes worked at the damp soil – Sally's mother had watered the beds less than an hour earlier – but didn't disturb it. They couldn't quite seem to grip the earth, as though a thin pane of glass had been placed between her and the ground.

But it was her eyes that drew Sally's attention. They were clouded, so it was hard to tell what color they might once have been, and encrusted with mucus in the corners, like the eyes of someone who has been asleep for a long time and only just woken up. The edges of her mouth were crusted too: when she opened her mouth to lick at them – with a hint of pale tongue resembling the raw flesh of a fish – her lips cracked, but no blood bubbled from the cuts.

And she smelled. It wasn't a bad smell, just odd and vegetal, with a hint of burning. It reminded Sally of the water that accumulated in the bottom of her mother's orchid pots, a kind of slow, wet decay. It seemed to roll off the girl like mist from the sea, and it fell on Sally's skin as a chill, even though the sun still shone brightly on her.

Sally had never seen a dead person before. She had no conception of death as such, and so struggled to factor the girl into her limited experience of the world. She was afraid, but only a little. The girl didn't speak, but Sally sensed her feelings as colors that manifested themselves as a glow in the air around her. The girl was currently calming her with greens and golds, urging her not to be frightened, and Sally understood that she meant no harm.

'You threw a brick at me,' said Sally.

The girl smiled, cracking her lips still further. Sally didn't care to see that, but said nothing about it. She didn't want to be rude.

'But your feet can't touch the ground,' Sally went on. 'So how did you move the brick?'

Blue, then – an admiring glow. Sally was smart. Everyone said so.

The girl lifted her right hand, and another brick flew through the air and landed where Sally knelt, almost touching her leg.

'Wow,' said Sally. 'Could—?'

But she got no further in her question, because the girl glanced back over her shoulder, as though summoned by a voice or presence unseen. She raised her right hand again, this time in a gesture of farewell.

'Wait!' Sally called to her. 'I don't know your name.'

The girl moved her shoulders in a small shrug, pointed to her mouth, and shook her head.

'Can I tell my mom about you?'

A single nod, then the girl appeared to turn in upon herself and was gone.

Sally got to her feet, wiping sand from her knees. She walked to the flower bed and examined it, just to confirm that no footprints marked the ground. The vegetal smell was stronger here, but it was already fading, and within seconds

161

it was only a memory. The chill remained a little longer before it too dissipated and all was warm once more.

Sally ran to the kitchen to share the news of her sighting. Her mother was sitting at the kitchen table, shucking black-eyed peas to add to smoked ham for the evening meal. She looked up as her daughter entered.

'Mom! Mom!'

'What is it, honey?'

'I saw a ghost. It was a girl.'

Her mother smiled, and opened her arms to embrace her daughter.

'Oh honey, I'm so proud of you . . .'

It all seemed so long ago now. She had been chosen to protect the Brethren – the dead, the living, and those yet to be born – and unless some weakness of character were later to reveal itself and render her unsuited to the task, it was a duty she would carry with her to the grave.

In the thirty-five years since, the girl had been Sally's near-constant companion. Her name was Eleanor Craig. Sally had discovered this early on by using the native intelligence that had led her to be chosen in the first place. Eleanor could not speak, and Sally didn't really want to spend hours or days trying to guess her name, so she wrote out the alphabet on a piece of paper, pointed to letters in turn, and marked them off according to the colors that the girl's reactions took: blue for yes, red for no, like a child's game.

When she was older, Sally learned more about Eleanor from Internet searches, as well as the knowledge of the Brethren passed down through generations. Eleanor was part of the original bloodline, daughter to the Magus himself. She had burned alongside him and twenty others in the nineteenth-century siege at Capstead that put an end to the Brethren's earliest predations. She would be Sally's shadow, her link to the rest, until the time came for Sally to cross over and become like them. The prospect, in truth, gave Sally little pleasure, but the deal had been struck a long time ago and could not be undone.

The water in the tub was now little better than tepid. Sally could see the wrinkles forming on her fingers and toes, but she did not want to get out, not yet. Kirk would be looking for answers and reassurance, and she had none to give him. She reached forward and turned the faucet, releasing more hot water. Eleanor was radiating black for rage, and a kind of pale blue for grief, but rippling through both was a dark indigo that Sally had glimpsed only rarely in the past, most recently just before she summoned Routh and sent him east to clean up the Eklund mess.

It was anxiety.

Sally wet a cloth and placed it over her face. Eleanor's constant pacing was making her feel nauseous, and she needed a clear head to think. Eklund had given her the names of all those to whom he had spoken in the course of his investigations, and she had cross-checked them against the material on his laptop. Had Routh succeeded in securing whatever other material Eklund stored in his home, then Sally might simply have let those other parties be, because with Eklund gone all that remained would be whispers and lunatic theories. But now Routh was dead, murdered – that much Eleanor had made clear – by an unknown assailant close to Eklund's house. The only conclusion to be drawn was that someone dangerous was also interested in Eklund, or possibly Routh himself. Until the facts became known, Sally had to assume that the individual or individuals concerned might continue to follow Eklund's line of inquiry, or delve into Routh's life, either of which eventualities might conceivably lead them to the Brethren.

The solution, it seemed to her, was to remove from the game those among Eklund's contacts who posed the greatest threat, just in case he had sown seeds that might later bear fruit. The books and files that Eklund admitted to keeping in his basement were dangerous, and it would have been better had they been burned to ash, but they were not in themselves enough to warrant a serious investigation. Eklund had a personal stake in his inquiries because of his family history, and no uninvolved parties should have been capable of making the imaginative leaps required to empathize with him, yet Eklund had managed to rally at least two others to his cause. If they died, the likelihood was that the investigation would die with them. Along the way, the Brethren would try to discover who had killed Routh, and make them pay for it. The resulting deaths would also help the Brethern in the long term. They would be the equivalent of money in the bank, and many years might pass before more killing was required. Sally herself could even be dead by then, or elderly enough to relinquish responsibility to the next generation.

With the decision made, Sally removed the cloth from her face.

'Don't be afraid,' she said softly, so that Kirk would not hear. 'I can deal with this.'

Eleanor stopped pacing and turned to face her. Even after so many years of her company, Sally still disliked looking directly into her eyes. They reminded her of what awaited all of them down the line, and so served as an unwelcome memento mori. She tried to focus instead on Eleanor's freckles, fixing her gaze on her nose and cheeks as she shared her plans. Slowly the black glow turned to ivory, and the blue to a pale blush, but that sliver of indigo continued to wind through both, like a worm in the flesh of an apple.

'You're still frightened,' said Sally. 'You have no need to be. We have faced worse in the past.'

You died amid flames and gunfire, she thought. *You know this better than anyone.*

The bathroom window was fogged with condensation. As Sally watched, Eleanor walked to it and reached out a finger.

Sally held her breath. Eleanor rarely interacted with the physical world. But now she was writing on the glass, her finger moving painstakingly to form letters in the moisture, the effort causing black blood to leak from Eleanor's nose and ears, to weep from the corners of her eyes and bubble from between her lips. When she was done she vanished, leaving only the message on the window: nine letters, two words.

HOLLOW MEN

36

Parker's first impression of Mother was that a squat black spider had just scuttled into the room.

The woman before him was shorter than he was, but appeared to be almost twice as wide. Her hair was entirely silver and cut in a bob to which a series of extensions had been added that hung over her back and shoulders like the legs of a dead crustacean. The head beneath was tiny, the skin pale, the eyes heavily kohl-lined to save them from being lost entirely to a combination of the deep hollows in which they sat and the swollen purple bags below. Her mouth was a thin red slash, and her chin was a dowel for the folds of loose flesh that descended in tiers down her neck to be swallowed up by her black gown. Curiously, though, her face was emaciated, as were her arms, which poked like twigs from her sleeves, and her calves, visible below the hem of her dress. Her feet couldn't have been more than a size two or three, and were concealed by black velvet slippers. Only her torso was oversized, its fullness emphasized by the contours of her clothing.

Her son joined her. Just as Philip bore clear traces of his patrimony, so too he was his mother's child: it was apparent in the eyes and chin, and in the unwrinkled skin drawn tight over the bones of her face.

'Mother,' said Philip, 'these are the men I told you about.'

Mother didn't speak, but silently took in Angel and Louis before her bright, clever eyes moved on to Parker and lingered on him for long enough to make him feel uncomfortable, like a fly waiting for the inevitability of the bite. It was an impres-

166

sion heightened by the realization that Mother had begun to move toward him almost without his noticing, her slippered feet making a slight hissing sound as she crossed the rug. He resisted the urge to take a few steps back to compensate. As she drew nearer, he picked up her scent. She smelled exactly like her son. Either they shared the same cologne, or they exuded a common odor through their pores.

Parker, uncertain of what else to do, stretched out a hand in greeting, but Mother's dainty fists remained by her sides. Philip, tagging behind as if bound to her by a length of silk, explained: 'Mother dislikes unnecessary physical contact.'

Parker made a point of not catching the eye of either Angel or Louis, but he heard the latter give a small cough, and Angel appeared to have found something interesting to look at on the ceiling.

Mother spoke for the first time. Her voice had a dry timbre that was not unpleasant.

'Mr. Parker,' she said, 'would you and your friends care to take a seat?'

She gestured at the nest around the table, waited for them to approach, then perched herself on the smaller of the couches. All four men sat, Philip on the same couch as his mother, Angel and Louis on the couch opposite, and Parker in one of the occasional chairs. Philip picked up the teapot, inquired if anyone wanted milk, and – in the English manner – added it to the cups accordingly before pouring the tea. It was all very sociable, Parker considered, if one left aside the fact that sixty percent of the company was present under a degree of duress.

Mother sipped her tea and nibbled on a cookie. Philip didn't eat, and neither did he touch his cup after filling it. Angel took a cookie and managed to consume half of it successfully while leaving the rest in the form of crumbs on the couch, the floor, and his clothing. Mother was more successful in the endeavor, but she'd probably had practice. Nobody spoke.

Finally, Mother finished eating, carefully tapped the cookie residue from her fingers into her saucer, and began.

'What were you doing at Jaycob Eklund's house?'

Parker put down his cup. He didn't know from tea, but whatever had come out of that pot tasted pretty good to him. He might have to ask Mother what it was, assuming they ended the night on good terms, which was far from guaranteed, especially with the bluntness of her opening question.

'First of all,' said Parker, 'you have us at a loss, Ms . . . ?'

If she had a name, then she clearly wasn't in the mood to share it. She looked at Parker with faint surprise, as though he had just suggested something mildly inappropriate.

'This,' said Philip slowly, 'is Mother.'

Parker decided he now knew how Alice felt when she stumbled into the Mad Hatter's tea party.

'I can't call her Mother,' he explained to Philip, in almost the same tone.

'You don't have to call me anything at all,' said the woman herself. 'You just have to answer the question.'

'I'm working on behalf of a client.'

'The name?'

'I'm not in a position to reveal that.'

'And does this client sanction burglary?'

A twist of the mouth; a moue of disapproval.

'You might be surprised at what my client is prepared to tolerate.'

Mother took a sip of tea.

'I once watched a man being skinned alive,' she said, when she was done. 'Very little surprises me.'

If Mother expected anyone in her present company to look shocked, she was destined to be disappointed.

'You appear to lead an interesting life,' said Parker.

He was wondering about the nature of Mother's relationship with Caspar Webb. Obviously the existence of Philip suggested a sexual component at some point, but he got the feeling there was more to it than that. This woman now appeared to be taking care of Webb's affairs, even if her son chose to regard his late father's influence, even existence, as ongoing.

'I spent many happy years with Mr. Webb,' she replied, as though picking up on Parker's thoughts.

'Sitting around the fire,' said Louis, 'skinning folk.'

Mother smiled indulgently at him.

'I know all about you three,' she said. 'You have a lot of blood on your hands.'

She raised her little finger at Louis, singling him out.

'You may be interested to hear,' she continued, 'that this is the first time we've had one of your race in our house.'

'That's certainly progress,' said Louis.

Mother's eyes remained fixed on Louis. Parker began to wonder if, like Philip, the woman ever blinked. As far as he could tell, she had not done so once since joining their company. It might have been genetic.

'Did you ever have any dealings with Mr. Webb?' Mother asked Louis.

'No, Mr. Webb didn't hold with us coloreds, as it seems you know.'

'I don't believe he had ever seen a black man until he came to the United States,' said Mother. 'He was a product of his time and his environment.'

'And what environment would that have been?' asked Parker.

'Mr. Webb was from the Baltic region. He was very private about his origins.'

'Shame?'

'Discretion. He left enemies behind.'

'He left enemies in the ground, if the stories are true.'

'Such tales, if indeed they are true, are all in the past. Mr. Webb is in the next world, and beyond such concerns.'

If even one-tenth of what was whispered about Caspar

169

Webb was accurate, Parker thought, then his precise location in the next world was probably very much a matter of concern for him. Wherever he was, it would certainly be hot.

'He created a considerable operation down here,' said Parker. 'I hope someone is keeping up the family tradition. Pity to see all that hard work go to waste.'

'Actually, we are currently in the process of divesting ourselves of his business interests,' said Mother, and Parker detected a response to this from Philip, a minute change in his posture.

There's disagreement here.

'Really?' It was Louis who spoke. 'And how does Vincent Garronne feel about that?'

Vincent Garronne, from the little that Parker knew of the operation, was Webb's enforcer and the public face of his master's enterprises while Webb was still alive. Garronne was violent when necessary, and both intelligent and ambitious. During the period of Webb's decline, Garronne was believed to be responsible for the day-to-day running of the empire.

But Garronne hadn't been seen in a while.

'Vincent Garronne is dead,' said Mother.

'Ah,' said Louis. 'Was it sudden?'

'It was when he hit the ground,' said Philip.

'He fell from a tall building,' Mother elaborated.

'A man has to be careful on high ledges,' said Louis.

'I don't think being careful would have helped him,' said Mother, thereby putting an end to any further speculation on the nature of Garronne's demise.

Philip offered her more tea. She declined. He didn't bother offering it to anyone else.

'Mr. Webb left a considerable bequest,' said Mother. 'He had certain charities he wished to support, some galleries and museums of which he was fond.'

Mother paused.

'He also had a brother.'

Parker waited. They were coming to it now.

'They were estranged. Mr. Webb's brother did not approve of his lifestyle. He had a wife and son, and believed that if the connection between himself and Mr. Webb were to become known, it might put his family at risk. He changed his name – he then took his wife's name after marriage, placing a further degree of separation between his brother and himself – before breaking off all contact with his sibling and living a blameless life.'

'I notice you're speaking of him in the past tense,' said Parker.

'He vanished almost a year ago. Mr. Webb engaged investigators, and called in favors from law enforcement, but no trace of his brother was ever found.'

'What about his wife?'

'There was no reason to suspect her of any involvement in the disappearance. In fact, it was she who approached Mr. Webb to seek his help in finding her husband.'

'But Mr. Webb checked on her anyway, just to be sure.'

'Of course. He came up with nothing, as he had anticipated.'

'And did he have any more success in establishing the fate of his brother?'

'None, but Mr. Webb was already busy dying by then. Had he been in better health, he might have been able to take a more personal interest in the investigation.'

She examined her nails. They were unvarnished, and cut so short that the tip of the nail bed was visible on each finger.

'I'll ask you again, Mr. Parker: Who are you working for?'

'And I'll remind you that I can't divulge the name.'

Mother's right hand tightened into a claw. Parker knew he was antagonizing her, but this was an exchange of information, and he didn't wish to be short-changed.

'But,' he added, 'I can tell you that I was engaged by

someone who is interested in finding Jaycob Eklund and wishes him no harm.'

'You're certain of that?'

Parker considered Ross: *Not entirely.*

'Yes, I am,' he said. 'I assume you know that Eklund's missing, or else why would you be watching his home?'

'Mr. Webb acquired the alarm company that monitors the house. When the alarm was activated earlier this evening, our people went to check. They found the jammer. Your car was picked up by the cameras trained on the house and street.'

'Cameras.' Parker gave Angel a look. 'Call yourself a professional.'

'Don't blame your friend,' said Mother. 'They're small and well hidden. Once we had the make, model, and license plate number of your vehicle, it wasn't hard to track you down. We made calls, accessed surveillance cameras. By stopping in Massachusetts, you saved us a trip to Maine.'

'Why go to all this trouble for Eklund?'

'Because when he went missing, we anticipated that someone might take an interest in his property.'

They were entering dangerous ground. Parker didn't want to ask her outright if she'd been responsible for Eklund's disappearance. He didn't want to go the way of Vincent Garronne, or the unfortunate who was flayed in Mother's presence.

Mother understood his concerns.

'We didn't do anything to Mr. Eklund,' she said. 'But we are eager that he should be found. His disappearance may be connected to what happened to Mr. Webb's brother and his family.'

'His family?'

'Mr. Webb's sister-in-law and nephew both died in the last twenty-four hours. Their names were May and Alex MacKinnon. They were stabbed to death in their home in Millwood, New Hampshire.'

The mention of the MacKinnon name brought Parker back to the contents of Eklund's basement, and the most recent of the disappearances added to the map on its wall.

'You see,' said Mother, 'shortly before he passed away, Mr. Webb was approached by Jaycob Eklund. Eklund believed they might have certain interests in common, the disappearance of Mr. Webb's brother among them. Mr. Webb, naturally, was wary. Intermediaries were employed, including Philip, and eventually a meeting was arranged between the two men in this very room. I was present for their discussions.'

Philip went to the fire and threw a pair of logs on it. They sibilated as they settled on the embers, like living things consigned to the flames.

'And what did Eklund want to talk with Mr. Webb about?' asked Parker.

'He wanted,' said Mother, 'to speak to him of ghosts.'

37

The Collector was parked a discreet distance away from the offices of Agave Associates. He had intended exploring the house that had attracted the interest of both Parker and the late Donn Routh, but then the alarm went off and continued to sound for some time. The ruckus attracted a private security cruiser, followed not long after by two BMWs, one of them driven by a man who was not unfamiliar to the Collector: Philip, the understandably unclaimed offspring of the late Caspar Webb.

A short discussion took place, followed by a series of phone calls. The security guard remained at the house when the BMWs departed, so the Collector stayed with Philip, a decision that had so far taken him across the Massachusetts border and then back to Providence behind the convoy formed by Parker, Philip, and the others. In the interim, the Collector called his father and asked him to establish the ownership of the Fox Point house. Parker, it appeared, was interested in a private investigator named Jaycob Eklund. Unfortunately for him, so too was Philip; and where Philip went, so went Mother.

The Collector was aware of the failings of the late Caspar Webb, but they were largely without significance for him. Webb was barely a step above a common gangster, even if he cultivated an air of mystery. His sins were a consequence of his greed and fear, because all powerful men are secretly fearful. Webb was unpleasant, but he lacked the streak of depravity that might have drawn the Collector down upon him, and then death had settled the matter.

Mother, meanwhile, had a certain core of iniquity, one worthy of remark yet not of immediate action.

But the son?

Well, he was really very interesting indeed.

38

Kirk was dozing on the floor, stretched out like a dog with his head on a cushion, when Sally eventually emerged from the bathroom with one towel wrapped around her body and another covering her hair. It was probably as well that he was not attentive to the expression on her face, because he would have found no love there: pity, perhaps, and frustration, but not love.

She nudged him with her foot.

'Wake up.'

He stirred and opened his eyes.

'You were in there for a long time.'

'I had a lot to think about. Go downstairs and pour me a glass of wine. I'll be with you in a moment.'

Sally went to her bedroom. She and Kirk kept separate rooms, coming together only when the urge struck one or the other, although the decision was generally Sally's to make. Just as she reached the threshold she let the towel drop, giving her brother a brief sight of her body, but there was nothing flirtatious about it. Kirk wasn't sure if she was even aware of the timing, or the effect.

He glanced into the bathroom as he passed. The air was misty, but he could see that the bottom pane on the window had been imperfectly wiped with a hand, and he thought he could discern parts of letters at the edges. He was still puzzling over this when the skin on his face and hands began to prickle, and the warmth of the bathroom was infected with a damp cold.

Which one of them is it? Eleanor, probably.

176

He didn't retreat, not immediately. Instead he stared into the dissipating steam, as if to say *I have my place, and my purpose. I am not an insignificant figure.* It was a small gesture of defiance.

Something brushed against his lips, like the touch of an insect, and he tasted rot and dead flowers. He gagged and stumbled back, rubbing his sleeve against his mouth in an effort to remove the pollutant. It was no use, though: it was on his tongue and his palate, and he had just enough time to turn and grab a vase – because he wasn't going to try to get to the toilet, not through what was standing in the doorway – before he puked into it.

'You fucking bitch,' he whispered, once he'd finished, ending with a burp that tasted and smelled of marsh gas, but he felt that Eleanor was already gone. The hall was warmer, the bathroom slightly brighter.

He took the vase downstairs with him and washed it in the sink. He poured Sally's wine, before emptying a couple of fingers of Four Roses into a glass and drinking half of it to cleanse his mouth. It was a mean trick, what Eleanor had done, the bite – the kiss – of a low dog. There'd been no call for it. All he'd done was stand his ground.

Suddenly, he found himself weeping. It was, he knew, partly a consequence of contact with Eleanor. It didn't do a person good to spend too much time in the proximity of the dead: Sally would be like an antichrist for the rest of the night, and wake in the morning with a bitch of a headache. But touching them, or being touched, brought on bad blues, like being offered a brief, profound insight into one's own inevitable mortality.

Kirk's moment of despair was not solely Eleanor's fault. He didn't want to end up like them. He didn't want to spend the next life trapped as they were, his fate in the hands of the living just so he could continue to drift through the gaps between worlds, like a rat hiding in the hollow walls of an old house. Nonexistence would be more desirable than that, but nonexistence wasn't an option: it was either damnation or concealment, sequestered with the rest of the departed Brethren who were seeking to escape punishment for the sins of generations. And yet he certainly didn't want to pass eternity, or any portion of it, in the company of Eleanor. Whatever she might have been like in life, death had brought about a serious deterioration in her temperament.

But he couldn't stop the cycle. He was afraid even to think about how it might be done while Sally was around. She had always been able to guess the direction of his thoughts. They showed in his face. He would have made a lousy poker player. Then again, he was lousy at most things.

He heard Sally's footsteps on the stairs and wiped away the tears just before she got to the kitchen. She was wearing her red bathrobe. It looked like silk, but wasn't. They lived a parsimonious existence, because all wealth was shared among the extended family. It was important to their continued security that no one should feel deprived or excluded.

'Are you okay?'

'I drank too fast,' he said. 'Burned my throat.'

She picked up her own glass.

'You should have had wine.'

'I wanted something stronger.'

She nodded and took a long draft from her glass. Instantly, the wine stained her lips and teeth. She was standing so close to him that he could smell it on her breath. She reached up and brushed some of the moisture from his cheek.

'I'm sorry,' she said. 'Eleanor shouldn't have done that.'

He didn't even bother to ask how she knew. *Fucking Eleanor.* He nearly began crying again. This mess, this whole sorry mess . . .

'Sit down,' she said.

He did. She took his left hand in her right and squeezed it reassuringly.

'She's gone,' she said. 'It's just us.'

'She's mean,' said Kirk. He sounded like a five-year-old.

'She's worried. Our Cousin is dead. We may be at risk.'

'So what are we going to do?'

She released his hand and produced a sheet of paper from the pocket of her robe.

'These are the names Eklund has given me so far, the people with whom he spoke,' she said. 'We're going to call a family meeting—'

She took another sip of wine.

'And then we're going to kill some of them.'

39

Mother stared at the painting of Caspar Webb above the fireplace for what felt to Parker like an unconscionably long time. He tried to read the expression on her face, but could only conclude that he didn't detect much love in it. When he turned his attention briefly to Philip, who was following Mother's gaze, he saw no love there at all.

'As you already know,' Mother said, 'Mr. Webb came from a different culture than our own. He was also an intensely religious man, from an orthodox tradition of which I had no real understanding. At the end of his life, he told me that he knew there were those who were convinced he would burn in hell for all he had done, but he believed they were mistaken. For him, heaven and hell were not created realities: he understood that he would look upon God, and perceive his presence as a great fire through which all must pass, the righteous and unrepentant alike. The former would emerge unscathed, but the rest would be consumed. On his deathbed, Mr. Webb repented of his sins. It is in accordance with his final instructions that we are disassembling the structures he created, and putting to good use much of the wealth that has accrued from their operations.'

There it was again: an imperfectly restrained reaction from her son. Any mention of the winding down of Webb's business enterprises was like pricking Philip with a pin.

'I didn't realize that was how salvation worked,' said Parker.

'It is never too late to repent.' Mother's hard eyes dared him to contradict her.

'Unfortunately, barring a message from the next world, you have no way of knowing if Mr. Webb managed to pull off his escape act.'

'Meanwhile,' added Louis, and Parker knew that he too had been registering Philip's responses, 'all those years of effort to carve an empire in the Northeast are being undone in the name of a man who's already burning, one way or another. It's like selling shares when the stock price is still going up.'

'We will not be poor,' said Mother. 'Mr. Webb ensured that we would be well looked after.'

Louis shrugged. 'Not my money.'

He looked away, indicating that, for him, the subject was closed. They'd learned something about Philip, which was enough.

'What does all this have to do with Eklund?' asked Parker.

And Mother explained. Over a period of hours, Eklund had suggested to Webb that a series of unconnected killings and disappearances, spread over more than a century and a half, might be linked to sightings that were both potentially paranormal in nature and strikingly similar in detail. Mr. Webb's brother experienced such sightings in the weeks before he vanished. Apparently, these 'hallucinations' were mentioned in the police report, but only in passing, and as an indication that MacKinnon might have been in a disturbed state of mind before his disappearance. They also found their way into certain newspaper reports, and thence to specialized websites, which was how Eklund picked up on them.

'What did MacKinnon claim to have seen?' Parker asked.

'Variations on three figures: an older, bearded man, flanked by two younger women. MacKinnon was quite specific about their appearance and apparel. He told his wife that he first saw them as he was pulling into the garage, and almost ran into them, they appeared so suddenly. He braked, they lingered for a couple of seconds, and then were gone.'

'And he continued to see them?'

'Yes, according to his wife. She said they were always open with each other about everything. Her husband was not sleeping well. He would wake to noises downstairs, and strange odors, but no one else in the house heard the sounds, or smelled what he smelled. He had made an appointment to see a psychiatrist shortly before he vanished, but was gone before he could attend the first session.'

'And was Webb aware of these incidents?'

'*Mr.* Webb was privy to every step of the investigation into his brother's disappearance. He devoted considerable resources to his own private inquiries, but had no more luck than the police.'

'And then Eklund appeared.'

Parker continued to keep a watchful eye on Philip. He was no longer giving much away, and even appeared bored by the conversation, so it was hard to tell how he felt about all this. Neutral, maybe. At best.

'Mr. Webb was not a skeptic when it came to the paranormal,' said Mother. 'He found Mr. Eklund's theories interesting, to the extent that he was prepared to bankroll him. Mr. Eklund accepted a small amount of financial support, and agreed to inform Mr. Webb if he discovered anything that might shed light on Michael MacKinnon's fate. One of the stipulations in Mr. Webb's will was that Mr. Eklund should continue to be assisted in his work, and monitored. A sum of money was set aside for this purpose.'

'But now Eklund has dropped off the radar.'

'Mr. Eklund traveled frequently in the course of his work. We didn't become concerned about him until very recently. Part of his agreement with us required weekly reports, and Mr. Eklund was very scrupulous about adhering to our terms.'

So Eklund was taking money from Webb, as well as banking the occasional check from Ross. Those were very different masters to be serving. At the very least, Parker concluded, Eklund was being unwise.

'Did you search his house?' he asked.

'We entered it to make sure that no harm had befallen him,' said Mother, 'but nothing appeared to have been touched or removed. You, on the other hand, had no such reservations.'

'You can have it all if you want it,' said Parker.

'What about your client?'

'My client won't be happy, but for him it's an ongoing existential state. It may take him a while to register the incremental increase.'

'And what will he do then, this client?'

'I suspect he'll come after whoever has the material in question. You don't want that.'

'You make him sound like a criminal.'

'He'd be happy in the present company if he was, but he's not. Just the opposite, in fact.'

Parker let the words hang. He'd given Mother as much as he was prepared to, but he wasn't lying. If it came down to it, he was sure Ross would eventually come after what was left of Caspar Webb's operation in order to secure any information that might lead him to Eklund.

Mother nodded in understanding.

'Whatever you may think of us, or of the late Mr. Webb,' she said, 'his concern for his brother was genuine, and was no less for the well-being of his wife and child. I believe that Michael MacKinnon, like his wife and child, is dead. We who remain have an obligation to them. I'm prepared to offer one hundred thousand dollars to you and your friends if you find those responsible for what occurred and bring them to me to face punishment. I have no interest in the workings of the law. I am concerned only with justice.'

Parker saw no reason even to consider the deal.

'That's not going to happen.'

'Is the reward not sufficient?'

'It's not about money.'

'Nor is it about the law, not for you. As I explained earlier, I know something of your past.'

'I already have a client. I don't want another. It would lead to conflicts of interest.'

'One does not have to know about the other.'

'Oh, I suspect my client already knows more about you than you might like.'

'Ah,' said Mother, but nothing more.

Parker stood. Angel and Louis did the same.

'Where are you going?' said Philip. 'Mother didn't give you permission to leave.'

Parker didn't even glance in his direction. 'I think Mother already knows our conversation is at an end.'

'Mr. Parker is right, Philip. Let them go.'

'You trust them?'

'I see no reason not to.'

'But they haven't agreed to help us!'

'They don't have to agree. They're looking for Mr. Eklund anyway. If he is in trouble, and it is linked to what befell the MacKinnons, they will be acting in our interests regardless of any agreement between us. And if Mr. Eklund's fate is unconnected to the MacKinnon family, then it is no concern of ours, beyond ensuring the return of any documentation removed from his home in case it might aid us at a later date. Have I summarized the situation correctly, Mr. Parker?'

'I think you have.'

'Then Philip will see you out. He will also give you a number to call, should you wish to visit with me again.'

'I don't believe that will be necessary,' said Parker.

'Indulge an old woman,' Mother replied. Her hand stroked her cleavage in a grotesque parody of flirtation, but there was neither lust nor joy in her eyes. 'After all, I have few pleasures left to me.'

A log burst in the fire, and the flames cast a shadow on the wall like the legs of a dangling man, the darkness of his form hiding the excoriated ruin.

'I'm sure you'll find something,' he said, and followed Angel and Louis from the room.

40

The Lexus appeared to be as they had left it, but Louis disabled the alarm and checked the trunk. Although to a casual observer it remained untouched, he was in the habit of leaving the faintest strip of clear tape at either side of the trunk's removable base. He could see that both were no longer attached. He didn't bother to lift the base itself. While Philip's men might have succeeded in getting into the car without activating the alarm, the locks on the compartments beneath the lining of the trunk were carefully concealed, and required an electronic code to open. Their contents were safe, although Louis remained annoyed at the trespass.

Parker joined him.

'All okay?'

'As good as.'

Louis took in the four men who were watching them from behind Philip.

'At least you didn't shit in it,' he said.

Nobody responded. Louis didn't care. He just didn't want them to think he hadn't registered the intrusion. He was also pretty certain that they'd fitted a tracker somewhere on the vehicle, because that was what he would have done under similar circumstances. It wouldn't take Angel long to find it. When he'd done so, maybe Louis would have him attach it to a garbage truck or delivery van, let them follow it around in circles for a while.

'You will, of course, inform us if you intend on returning to Providence,' said Philip.

'Your momma's calling you,' replied Louis. 'Better run now, 'fore she decides to give you a whuppin'.'

Somebody in Philip's vicinity snickered, but he didn't look to see who it might have been.

'She's old,' said Philip. 'She told you so herself. Things are going to change around here soon enough.'

'It didn't look like it from where we were sitting,' said Parker. 'You'd be advised to start saving your nickels and dimes for the rainy day that's coming. Whatever your daddy left you, it won't be enough for your tastes.'

This time, Philip didn't even try to hide his reaction. His mouth opened, displaying small, white teeth – a child's dentition – that snapped at the night air. The effect was like watching the deformation of a wax head. And then, in his fury, he spit at the car. Louis took a step forward, and Parker's hand fell on his right arm.

'No,' he said.

Louis took a breath and relaxed.

'I'll remember you did that, boy,' he said.

'Don't you call me "boy", you fucking—'

The word was about to be spoken. Parker could see Philip's tongue pressed against his palate to form the 'n'.

'Go on,' Louis told him. 'Say it.'

But Philip did not. Some vestige of common sense prevailed, for which Parker was grateful. He and Louis were still unarmed. Only Angel, already in the car, had access to a weapon. If guns were produced, it would not end well.

'Get out of my city,' said Philip.

Parker climbed in the front passenger seat, and Louis took the wheel. Neither of them bothered to remind Philip that it wasn't his city – not yet, not ever. The question was: how much damage could Philip do before the reality of his situation was revealed to him?

A lot, Parker thought. *A whole hell of a lot.*

187

41

The Collector watched the Lexus drive away. He wished he had been privy to the final exchange between Mother's son and the three visitors, almost more than the conversation that must have taken place in the rooms above. Words that provoked Philip into a display of unrestrained emotion would be worth hearing, although if anyone were capable of goading someone into revealing himself, it was those three men. Angel and Louis in particular could have catalyzed a coma victim back to consciousness.

He knew where Parker and the others were going: Parker's car remained at the motel, and they still had rooms, even if it was unlikely that they would choose to spend the night in them after what had transpired in Providence. They would by now be aware of Philip's unpredictability – which was a diplomatic way of referring to his obvious madness – and would certainly sleep easier by putting 160 miles between him and them.

The Collector could, of course, have followed them once again to the motel, and spoken to Parker there, but he was still inclined to avoid Angel and Louis whenever possible. Parker, for better or worse, was prepared to engage with the Collector on a mutually beneficial level, even if he struggled at times to hide his distaste for the arrangement, but Angel and Louis would happily have tried to cut the Collector's throat if the opportunity presented itself. He didn't believe they would succeed, but there was no percentage in leaving an opening, and the Collector had no desire to spend time with men so openly hostile to him. He would think about contacting Parker over the next day or two, either by arranging a meeting or simply presenting himself in person at an appropriate moment, yet he had no obligation to do so. Parker believed he had made the Collector his vassal, and this possibility held enough truth to be vexing. The Collector thought that it might be amusing to follow the threads connecting Eklund to Donn Routh, snipping them as he went, leaving Parker to taste failure.

For now, though, he waited in the shadows, and kept his vigil on Agave Associates. Philip bummed a cigarette from one of his lackeys, and smoked it some distance away while they waited for him to calm down. In the third floor above, one of the shutters opened fractionally, and the Collector caught a glimpse of Mother peering into the dark, searching for her son.

You were too indulgent of him, thought the Collector, *and Caspar Webb was not indulgent enough.*

It was a bad combination, and had contributed to the creation of a lusus naturae, a freak. 'Women in their uncleanness will bear monsters' – was that not how Second Esdras put it? The Collector was quite the student of the Apocrypha: after all, it had given him the name by which he sometimes went: Kushiel, the angel of punishment.

Philip was a bad enemy for Parker to have made. He would need to be monitored, and even dealt with, eventually. But to target him would be to draw down the wrath of Mother, and the Collector was not sure that he could yet justify her murder solely because she was unwilling, or unable, to curb her son's excesses.

The Collector turned away. When it was safe to do so he lit his own cigarette, drifting into the night's darkness until only the burning ember was visible.

And then that, too, was swallowed by the night.

42

Parker felt a sense of relief as Providence receded in the rearview mirror. The encounter with Mother and Philip had been like wandering into the wrong carnival sideshow, the kind that left one feeling sick and slightly soiled.

'That,' said Angel from the backseat, 'is not an experience I want to repeat.'

'I liked Philip,' said Louis. 'He had character.'

He raised his right index finger and tapped his ear, then spun the finger in the air in a gesture that encompassed the interior of the vehicle and any listening devices it might now contain.

'Handsome, too,' said Angel.

Parker turned on the radio, and they drove without speaking until they reached the motel. Both of their rooms had been tossed in their absence – Philip, or Mother, must have made some calls – but they didn't think anything was missing. Not that there was much to take: they had traveled light, and everything important was concealed in the compartments of Louis's car. Parker's Mustang had also been unlocked and searched but – again – would have provided slim pickings.

They moved the vehicles to a quiet corner of the motel lot, but one that was lit by an overhead bulb. Angel first searched the Lexus, and then the Mustang. It didn't take him long to find the GPS trackers: both were concealed in the right rear wheel wells.

'Amateurs,' said Angel.

He handed the trackers to Louis, who, in the absence of a

garbage truck or an obliging rodent, stuck one on a U-Haul trailer and the other on a rental with Canadian plates. They would have to wait until they got back to Maine before Angel could sweep for any listening bugs. Analog devices were relatively easy to find using a spectrum analyzer to pinpoint RF signals, and a directional antenna to narrow down the location, but digital bugs were more problematic because they used the same frequencies as cell phones and wi-fi. Angel would need a clear space, unpolluted by other signals, to find out if their vehicles had been compromised in that way. For the present, they'd just have to keep their opinions about Philip and Mother to themselves while driving.

They moved the material they had taken from Eklund's house to the trunk of Parker's car, returned their motel room keys, and headed back to Portland. Parker spent the journey contemplating Webb, Mother, and Philip, and their links to Jaycob Eklund. Another conversation with Ross was already overdue. Parker wondered just how surprised the FBI agent would be by the news that Caspar Webb was casting a posthumous shadow over the case. Ross might already have been aware of Webb's connection to Eklund, but it seemed unlikely. Even Ross wouldn't have allowed Parker to venture into that particular nest of vipers without some warning.

He felt that he was beginning at last to know Eklund better. He now also had two promising avenues of inquiry based on his night's work: the disappearance of Claudia Sansom, and the subsequent discovery of her body; and the lattice of connections that Eklund had made from what he believed to be a series of hauntings, an investigation that had ultimately brought him to Caspar Webb's door. The next day's work would involve finding out what he could about the disappearance of Michael MacKinnon and the killing of his wife and son, but Parker was already troubled by two issues.

While he had yet to establish if Eklund's absence was related to either the Sansom case or his stranger interests, he recog-

191

nized that each might have led someone to seek to put an end to the private investigator's inquiries. But it was also possible that Eklund's obsessions could have brought him to May MacKinnon's door, and Parker didn't yet know enough about Eklund to rule him out as a murderer.

43

Parker stayed behind Louis and Angel for most of the trip back to Maine, turning off only when the Scarborough exit appeared before him. He flashed his lights in farewell, and encountered no other vehicle after leaving Route 1 for the winding road that led to his home. A single lamp burned in the downstairs room he maintained as an office. He kept the lamp lit for Jennifer, his lost daughter, that she might see it from the dark and know he was thinking of her, and use it, if she wished, as a beacon to find her way back to his presence.

He took a moment before he turned into the drive to check the alarm status on his phone. It was one of the modifications to the system added in the aftermath of the attack that had almost killed him. It now recorded any activity on the property larger than the movements of a medium-sized mammal, and cameras fitted to the house immediately responded by making a video record of the intrusion capable of being accessed from his cell phone. On this occasion, the only visit had occurred shortly before noon, when a UPS driver had dropped off a delivery, placing it against the front door instead of in the mailbox by the road. It was a thin envelope, and the sight of it made Parker feel unaccountably uneasy.

He parked, emptied the trunk of the car, and deposited the Eklund material in his office before he opened the envelope. It contained a sheaf of legal documents, informing him that Rachel had begun proceedings to formalize visiting and custody arrangements for Sam. Parker read the papers once, with the realization that Rachel must already have set this process in motion before their most recent meeting. He took a seat by the window of his office and stared out at the moonlight and the marshes. He did not stir, and in time fell asleep with his face to the dark. His rest was unsettled, but he still did not witness Jennifer's approach through the trees, nor did he wake to see her standing before the glass, gazing upon him with eyes that were too old for her face. After a time she sat on the porch, her back to the wall of the house, and there she kept vigil over her father until dawn came.

44

Parker woke stiff and cold in the chair, and feeling worse than if he hadn't slept at all. The clock read 6.00 a.m. He almost considered just heading to bed and pulling the comforter over him behind closed drapes, but he was worried he might never get up again. The papers he had received from Rachel's lawyer were not entirely unexpected, and their arrival left him more sad than angry, but also disappointed at what he perceived as a certain duplicity on Rachel's part.

It should not have come to this, he thought. *But it's my fault that it has.*

He went upstairs, stripped and showered, then dressed himself in fresh clothes and made some coffee and toast. He'd go see Moxie Castin later about the whole business, and find out what he was supposed to do next. Whatever it was, he wanted it to cause as little upset as possible for Sam. He knew Rachel would want the same.

With a piece of toast jammed in his mouth, and a mug of coffee in his right hand, he went back to his office to give Eklund's documents his full attention. Although it was cold out, he opened the window slightly because the room smelled of sleep. The action dislodged something red and black from the frame, which fell to the porch outside. He went to retrieve it. When he returned to his office, he was carrying a chain of winter pods and stems, the kind a child might have assembled in a quiet moment.

The kind that Jennifer had loved to put together, and offer to her mother and father.

Gently, Parker placed the chain around the neck of his lamp to hang beside him as he worked, as the light changed and the shadows altered, and he learned of the Capstead Martyrs and the end they met. But this was the name given to them by others, and not the name by which they called themselves.

To their own, they were the Brethren.

45

Tobey Thayer knew of only one other person familiar with
Jaycob Eklund's investigations, or only one with whom
he could trust his concerns. He was aware, through Eklund,
of Michael MacKinnon's familial connections to the late
Caspar Webb. The name hadn't meant anything to Thayer,
but Eklund had shared enough of Webb's history with him
to make Thayer grateful that they'd never met, and he had
no desire to make the acquaintance of those whom Webb had
left behind, namely the ones known as Mother and Philip.
He couldn't, and wouldn't, turn to them for advice.

But now MacKinnon's wife and child were dead, and
Eklund's whereabouts remained unknown. Thayer could have
gone to the police to share what he knew, but at best he'd
be dismissed as some kind of lunatic, and at worst he might
bring down some suspicion on himself.

So he made the call, and spoke with the woman named
Michelle Souliere. He felt only a little better for the conversation. Souliere wasn't a believer, not like Eklund, and certainly
not like Thayer himself, but she agreed that they should both
be careful. Unlike Thayer, she remained hopeful for Eklund's
safe return.

Thayer hung up the phone feeling that Souliere hadn't
grasped the extent of the threat they were facing. She still
believed that the Brethren, if they existed at all, were purely
mortal in nature. He, by contrast, did not.

He had often argued with Eklund about the Brethren.
Eklund believed they were hopelessly corrupted before they

arrived on these shores, and the New World had simply provided them with richer pickings than the Old. Thayer was not so sure. He wondered if there was something in the soil of the Americas, something elemental that drew creatures like the Brethren and fueled their worst appetites. He envisaged it as a kind of hidden fire, like the coal flames that burned unseen in this very state beneath the town of Centralia, manifesting themselves only in billows of sulfurous gas and fractures in the blacktop while deep down they blazed and blazed.

Thayer sank into his favorite armchair. He could find the dead Brethren again. He knew where they were hiding, and he believed that he also knew why. All he had to do was close his eyes and dream.

But he would not close his eyes.

46

To the north, Parker read on.

The Brethren were scavengers, or began as such: a handful of brutal men and brutalized women who had found the promise of America to be less golden-edged than they had hoped; or maybe they had always anticipated as much and were already preparing to feed upon the weak even as their ships were tossed on seas so dark they differed from night only in the half-glimpsed fissures of the foam.

Eklund had done what he could to trace their origins, but they came from different countries, and changed their names almost as soon as they reached dry land, for many were fleeing retribution for crimes committed in Europe, and feared that their pursuers might have a reach that spanned continents. Call it fate, or bad luck, but slowly these disparate individuals came together under the aegis of a single man. Call it something more, if you were Jaycob Eklund and those who shared his fascination.

Call it the work of older gods.

Call it the intent of angels.

The leader of the Brethren was named Peter Magus, a name Parker recalled from some of the notes on the wall of Eklund's basement. According to the information assembled by Eklund, he almost certainly came from somewhere in the area along the English-Welsh border known as the Welsh Marches. He possessed a certain level of skill in metalwork, suggesting that he might have been apprenticed, or even worked, as a blacksmith. A process of elimination had narrowed down his true identity to one of three men, of whom Rhydderch ap Rhys seemed the most likely candidate. Rhydderch meant 'reddish brown' in Welsh, and early contemporary accounts of the Magus referred to this as the color of his hair. Meanwhile, ap Rhys meant 'son of Rhys,' and the only son of a blacksmith named Rhys ap Madoc had disappeared from the local parish records of the town of Monmouth five years before the appearance of Peter Magus in the United States in the first half of the nineteenth century. What Rhydderch might have done in the intervening period was unclear. The only hint came from a survivor of his clan, a woman named Nessa Perry, who was probably one of the Magus's lovers, and was subsequently hanged for her crimes. Perry claimed that the Magus told her he had spent many years 'studying the runes' and 'reading gallants' – a reference, according to Eklund, to occult volumes. The Magus appeared to have no religious affiliations, or none that any established church would have recognized. He spoke of the lore of angels, was well versed in the apocryphal scriptures, and claimed to consort with spirits in the night.

'I do not pray,' he once told Nessa Perry. 'I speak with the angel as an equal.'

Exclusive relationships between his followers were discouraged. Men and women changed partners as a matter of routine, although some relationships lasted longer than others. Jealousy was not permitted. If it raised its head then, like that of the serpent, it was cut off.

None of this particularly concerned those who were drawn to him, as few regarded a stable domestic life as a priority. What mattered was that the Magus – through his charisma and hospitality, and the adroit use of women and, later, children to create the illusion of a God-fearing family man, a leader of an extended clan seeking only a new home in a strange land – was able to gull travelers into lowering their guard, at which point they became easy prey: solitary horsemen, stagecoaches, even, toward the end, entire wagon trains, fell to the Brethren. That they escaped notice for so long was due, it seemed, to planning and brutality. No one was spared, and no one escaped. Bodies were buried, wagons cleansed of distinguishing marks, horses subtly rebranded. Wealth was carefully sequestered away, with riders dispatched far from the scene of their crimes to sell on any items of value that might otherwise have been easily identified.

What separated the Brethren from other brigands, their inhumanity apart, was a willingness to wipe out entire lines. Those traveling alone did not die before revealing details of families and homesteads left behind, to which, in time, the Brethren came. A house without an adult male made for easy pickings, and the more isolated the better. In those cases, the favored mode of operation was simply to strip the abode and make the entire family disappear. Ideally, the desired impression would be that the settlers had just given up and moved on, but the Brethren were also content simply to leave their disappearance a mystery. Infants were often kept alive, and passed on to those of the Brethren's women who were barren or had lost children of their own, or merely to add further credence to their pretense of normality. As the Brethren grew, they separated into smaller groupings so as not to attract attention, with some becoming settlers themselves, attaching themselves to communities, watching all who came and went, and feeding them, when appropriate, to those who remained nomads.

It could not last, of course. Despite all their efforts, the Brethren began leaving traces of their passing. They grew careless. Witnesses survived. The net began to close on them. By then, the Magus had established his own settlement at Capstead, near the confluence of the Mississippi and Missouri rivers. There he had dug himself in, his followers living in homes more akin to redoubts, with slit windows and earthen floors dug below ground level. In early 1860, amid snow and ice, they fought off the first of two incursions by posses, one

201

of which was supported by a contingent of soldiers, but it was clear that the end was approaching. A gunboat, the *Pioneer*, was sent upriver, and shelled Capstead to provide cover for a final assault, but before the settlement could be breached, smoke began to rise, then flames. It remained unclear whether the bombardment or those inside had started the fire, but the result was immolation for all but a handful of the Brethren. Most of the survivors, apart from the very youngest, were shot or hanged, many without even a cursory nod at a trial, since the soldiers were either unwilling or unable to protect them from the vengeance of civilians.

But the actions of the military, combined with the failure to provide a fair trial for the Brethren, however guilty or innocent they might have been, caused discontent. Suspicion of a crime was not reason enough for women and children to be burned alive, and there were those who wondered, quite rightly, if what had been visited on the Brethren might not someday be visited on themselves, should they fail to bend the knee to the government. Thus it was that the name 'Capstead Martyrs' came into being. Capstead, it seemed, was the Waco of its day.

Parker rose and stretched. There was more material about the period in Eklund's files, but he didn't need to look at it now. What interested him was the conclusion reached by Eklund and the various amateur historians with whom he had consulted, or whom he had read: Capstead might have marked the end of the Brethren's predations, but it had not wiped them out. The rest, the ones who had blended into civilized society, remained. The question was: what became of them?

This was the point at which Eklund's theories spun off into a whole new realm of oddness. Parker had transferred to his computer the photos taken of the wall in Eklund's basement, and assembled them into a coherent representation of the map. By flicking through the notes, and cross-referencing, it became clear that Eklund believed the alleged paranormal occurrences around each murder and disappearance were echoes of the original Brethren, including Peter Magus. How Eklund had decided this was not entirely clear, and appeared to be based largely on anecdotal evidence: mostly testimony provided by surviving friends and relatives who were willing to speak of the apparently impossible, if only because of what had befallen their loved ones. Eklund recorded their experiences with a degree of objectivity, although not skepticism, but even Parker had to admit that the similarities in the accounts were striking. It was possible, though, that Eklund had manipulated the data, or was recording a form of shared hysteria, with various interested parties exchanging information that in turn contaminated their own recollections, either deliberately or unwittingly, and facilitated by the Internet.

Parker also noticed absences in the files. Some entries and references were incomplete. It meant that Eklund kept more material and updates elsewhere, probably on his laptop. Neither did anything Parker had read so far reveal a reason why more recent killings and disappearances should be linked to a group that had, for the most part, been wiped out in the nineteenth century.

Unless, of course, some vestige of the Brethren continued to engage in criminal behavior, old habits dying hard, but these were not the same crimes. The historical Brethren were thieves: vicious ones, but thieves nonetheless, with murder as a by-product. Leaving aside unexplained disappearances of persons, the crimes recorded by Eklund appeared to involve murder as an end in itself.

Parker felt, not for the first time, as though he had wandered into a ghost story. But even if this were true, it was a tale for which real people had suffered and died.

47

Angel and Louis arrived shortly before noon, the former carrying his toolbox.

'There was a bug in the Lexus,' he confirmed, 'although I bet Philip is sorry he had it installed.'

'Why would that be?' Parker asked.

'Because Charley Pride here played his shitkicker music all the way to our parking garage. I put up with it just because I figured that listening to it would be worse for Philip than for me. I'm almost numb to it by now.'

'What was the range of the bug?'

Parker asked because, depending on the limit, it might have required Philip to send someone to tail them. If that was the case, that person might still be nearby, and Parker didn't like the idea of anyone involved with Philip and Mother being closer to Portland than Providence.

'Pretty much limitless,' said Angel. 'It was hooked up to the electrical system, so there was no need for them to worry about batteries, and it would send out an alert when the car was started. The signal is transmitted over a 3G network. Philip could pick it up from the comfort of his mother's bed.'

That wasn't an image Parker particularly wanted to entertain, so he did his best to erase it from his memory. Meanwhile, Angel went to work on the Mustang. Since he now knew what he was looking for, it didn't take him long to find the second transmitter. It was a small black box with a gray microphone wire.

'What do you want me to do with it?' Angel asked, once they'd stepped away from the car.

'What did you do with yours?'

'Left it where it was until we'd spoken to you. It's not like we discuss anything important when we're on the road. You never know who might be listening.'

Parker realized it wouldn't take Philip long to figure out they'd found, and disposed of, the GPS trackers, but Philip might assume that they'd been content to get rid of those and hadn't considered the possibility of listening devices. If they removed these as well, then Philip might simply try again, and Parker didn't want to spend every morning sweeping his car for bugs. But having a direct channel for the transmission of information – or, more probably misinformation – to Philip might be useful.

'Let's keep them in place for now,' said Parker. 'Come into the house. We need to talk.'

Parker made a fresh pot of coffee, and found Fig Newtons that hadn't expired too long before. Louis, who had a nose for such matters, took one look at them and passed, although Angel was untroubled. He reached for the box, but Parker whipped it away before he could lay a hand to it.

'Did you make that medical appointment yet?' Parker asked him.

Angel's shoulders sagged.

'Yeah, I made the appointment.'

'For when?'

'Next week. Is that okay, *Mom*?'

'Good. Now you can have a Fig Newton.'

'Jesus,' muttered Angel. He proceeded to eat and sulk simultaneously, while Parker told them of what he had managed to glean from Eklund's files so far.

'It's not much,' said Louis.

'Eklund found a pattern of a kind. He just couldn't figure out a reason for it all, or if he did it's on his laptop. What he did seem certain of was that everything somehow connected back to the Brethren.'

Louis looked skeptical. 'So he showed pictures of folk from the nineteenth century to people who'd claimed to have seen ghosts, and they said, "Yeah, that's them." I don't think that qualifies as scrupulous research.'

'That's not exactly how he worked,' said Parker. 'Anyone who claimed to have experienced a sighting was already dead. He was relying on whatever their friends and relatives could remember of what they'd claimed to have seen.'

'Hey, that's worse.'

'Maybe all these folk were in touch with one another,' suggested Angel, 'or exchanging notes on the Internet.'

'I considered that, but Eklund didn't think so. Some of the people he spoke with were so old they might have considered computers sorcery.'

'So,' Angel continued, 'random individuals, all of whom later died violently, or just went missing, claimed to have seen similar ghosts, identified by Eklund as members of an extended family killed during a siege in the nineteenth century. Have I got that straight?'

'As straight as I do.'

'Well then, the solution is to track down the descendants of the Brethren and ask them just what the hell they think might be going on.'

'Eklund was ahead of you. He just couldn't find them. If they're still around, they've hidden themselves well. And it's not exactly the kind of family history about which one likes to boast.'

'But otherwise there's nothing to connect the victims?' asked Louis.

'Not until we get to Caspar Webb's brother, and the wife and child.'

'Could be coincidence.'

'True, but it's the first point of contact I can find between cases, and it resonates with something I found in Eklund's notes:

when they could, the Brethren would go looking for the family of an earlier victim, figuring they'd be vulnerable.'

'Smart,' said Louis. 'Not classy, but smart.'

'So it seems like the best place to begin. Eklund spoke with a man named Tobey Thayer when he first began looking into MacKinnon's disappearance. He runs a discount furniture business. He's also, according to Eklund's notes, a psychic.'

Angel paused in the consumption of a second cookie.

'A furniture salesman?' he said. 'You've got to be fucking kidding. Aren't psychics supposed to be, like, little old ladies?'

'Might be onto a good thing,' said Louis. 'He could rent out his own tables for séances.'

'Funny,' said Parker. 'Maybe you can suggest that to him when you meet him.'

'I don't want to meet him.'

'You want me to do this alone?'

'Hey, you're the one who decided to take Ross's nickel.'

'You think the deal with Ross doesn't buy you two some breathing space as well? Anyway, there's Philip and Mother to consider. Mother in particular strikes me as a goal-oriented person.'

'And Philip?'

'I suspect his goals are self-oriented, and he may also have father issues.'

'From what I know of Webb,' said Louis, 'he never owned up to any kids.'

'If Philip was your child, would you?'

'Possibly not. Then again, I'm not sure I'd have got close enough to old Mother to do the deed.'

'She might have been prettier when she was younger.'

'Maybe. Still don't mean she was pretty.'

Parker had been considering the problem of Philip.

'Here's my take on it. Webb has a relationship with Mother, which becomes sexual at some point, although for how long is anyone's guess. Long enough to produce Philip, in any case. But Webb doesn't acknowledge the boy, although he provides for Mother and for him. Mother, meanwhile, develops into something more than a lover to Webb, or ceases to be a lover entirely and morphs into a part of the operation. Eventually, she manages to make herself indispensable, and it's to her that he entrusts the disposal of his operation after his death. She's probably happy to do it because she doesn't want to be Ma Barker. She's put a little aside for her old age, and Webb has left her more in his will, so she can look after herself and her son.

'Except Philip doesn't want to see his father's business liquidated. He'd like to take on the running of it, if only to piss on his old man's grave. He suggests as much to Mother, but she isn't biting, either because she's smart or afraid, and one goes with the other, because she'd be smart to be afraid. A lot of people out there, some only as far away as Boston, would regard her as an easy target. The sooner she divests herself of all Webb's interests, and the income flow begins naturally to redirect itself into other pockets, the more likely it is that she'll survive long enough to buy a condo in Miami or Tucson, and not end up dumped in Narragansett Bay as bait for crabs.'

'But her son isn't as clever as she is,' said Angel.

'I think we've established that her son is crazy, and crazy cancels out clever every time.'

'You figure Mother knows?'

'That he's ambitious? Oh yeah. That he's crazy? That's a whole other conversation. She might suspect it, but I haven't met a mother yet who'd admit her child was out where the buses don't run, not without a fight.'

'But Mother must have signed off on Vincent Garronne taking an unscheduled flight off the top of a building,' said Louis.

'Probably because Garronne wanted the same thing her son does, except Garronne was too obvious about it.'

'And Mother was watching her back.'

'And her son's.'

'But now she's exchanged one problem for another,' Louis noted, 'because while Garronne is no longer around, her son is, and Garronne's absence could be viewed by Philip as a power vacuum. If he steps up, Mother might be reluctant to have him thrown from a great height.'

'But would he be as reluctant when it came to Mother?' asked Parker.

'I think Philip could spend an afternoon throwing puppies from the top of the Empire State and only stop when his arm got tired.'

'It's not the same as killing your mother. You need cold blood to do that.'

'I wouldn't like to commit until we have Philip's DNA examined by a herpetologist.'

'But if Philip hates his father, and might not be averse to killing his mother, why did he go to the trouble of bugging our cars?' asked Angel.

'Because Mother told him to?' Parker suggested.

'Possibly, but that doesn't mean he had to do it.'

'Let's assume the listening devices and GPS trackers were his idea,' said Parker, because the possibility was interesting. 'Why would he be anxious to find out who might have killed his aunt and cousin, or caused his uncle to disappear?'

'Because if it's something personal to do with Webb,' Louis offered, 'then Philip could be next.'

'But the possibility that Philip is Webb's son isn't common knowledge, because Webb kept himself so far in the background that only a handful of people knew for sure what he looked like. I mean, the first we heard of it was when we met Philip, saw his old man's picture, and joined the dots. So, if it is personal, he's not the next one in the sights. Mother is.'

'Then,' said Louis, 'Philip, like a good son, wants to make sure nothing happens to his mommy.'

'Or that something does.'

'Families,' said Angel, with some feeling. 'Can't live with them, can't have them killed without complications.'

'So we avoid Philip, keep Mother at a safe distance, and then go see Thayer, the furniture-dealing psychic?' Louis asked.

'The discount furniture-dealing psychic,' Angel corrected. 'He's low rent.'

'That's the plan,' said Parker, 'in the absence of anything better.'

'And what about Ross?' Angel reminded him. 'What are you going to tell him?'

'Everything. He's paying the bill.'

'Even about Mother and Philip?'

'Especially about Mother and Philip.'

'Gonna bring trouble down on their heads,' said Louis.

'You feel like that's a shame?'

'Only because I won't get to watch.'

'Maybe he'll send pictures.'

'We can only hope.'

48

Not only did Kirk and Sally Buckner discourage their fellow parishioners from entering their home, they rarely entertained at all. Their nearest neighbors, the Ferriers, could count on the fingers of one hand the number of times they had seen strangers come to the Buckners' door and actually be admitted for any length of time.

The Ferriers were not particularly religious, beyond making an effort at Christmas because they both liked carols and enjoyed the decorations in St. Joseph's Catholic Church. Their two kids were raising families of their own, and were no more observant in their faith than their parents. If the Ferriers – parents and children – believed in anything, it was that people should try not to be assholes most of the time. End of lesson.

But even bearing that principle in mind, David Ferrier found it hard to warm to the Buckners. Oh, they were friendly enough, and didn't do anything that could give cause for complaint. They weren't holding wild parties, and kept their home and yard well looked after. Kirk designed and maintained websites, and Sally made fancy cakes and pastries that she sold to some of the stores, cafés, and restaurants in town, as well as taking special orders for birthdays and other celebrations. Ferrier had learned to identify her creations by sight, just so he wouldn't accidentally ingest them.

Etta, Ferrier's wife, thought he was nuts. She figured he had too much time on his hands, and should never have retired as early as he did. She also believed that he was too reclusive, and if he took the time to socialize a bit more, and involve himself in the institutions of the community, then he might not find cause to judge others so easily. It was true that Ferrier liked his own company, admittedly a little too much, but there was a lot to be said for a man's capacity to be comfortable while alone, and Ferrier was never bored or lonely. There were books to read, movies to watch, poetry – okay, bad poetry – to write, and walks to take with his dog. As things stood, he barely had enough hours in the day to fit in all this important stuff without getting distracted by damned meetings and committees. He had enough friends for his needs – four, two of them close – and wasn't about to start auditioning more at this stage in his life. He actively disliked very few people, and most of those were lawyers, politicians, golfers, and preachers.

So locally it was really only the Buckners who set his teeth on edge, and if a gun had been put to his head, and the hammer cocked, he still wouldn't have been able to explain why. His wife might have thought him an old curmudgeon, and in that she wouldn't have wanted for company, but David Ferrier was an observant man, and something of a student of humanity, even if only from a distance. He'd been a good accountant, and a stickler for detail. You could tell a lot about people from how they managed their money, and Ferrier had spent more than forty years examining the financial minutiae of the lives of others.

He'd like to have seen the Buckners' accounts because he was certain they'd be clean and neat, without a single detail amiss to bring the IRS to their door. This would be in character for them, because that was what Ferrier was convinced the Buckners were: characters, façades. They were playing roles. Their smiles never lit up their eyes, and they were always watchful. He also caught a dissonance in their interactions with each other, a kind of emotional and physical distance that made him wonder about the nature of their relationship and the state of their marriage. He didn't doubt that they were clever. The town was small enough for Ferrier to have learned how they'd managed to secure themselves a position of authority and influence within their own church without appearing to have tried too hard to do so, and that was no easy trick to pull off.

But clever wasn't the same as honest.

Ferrier had tried researching the Buckners on the Internet, but hadn't come up with very much: some links to Kirk's website, and the same for Sally's. He couldn't discover where or when they'd tied the knot, or even where they'd come from before settling in Turning Leaf. He'd tried raising it once with Kirk, just in passing, shortly after the Buckners first moved into the neighborhood. They'd both found themselves working in their yards on the same warm day, and Ferrier decided to offer Kirk a cold soda as an opening gambit. The conversation didn't last long – just enough time for Kirk to down his soda and exchange some observations on the weather – and all Ferrier could get out of him on the subject was that Kirk and his wife had moved around a lot.

'You know,' said Kirk, all smiles and dead eyes, 'like free spirits.'

'Hippies,' Ferrier offered.

'Nah, not for us. Don't like pot, and never could listen to the Grateful Dead for long.'

Kirk scrunched up his empty soda can and tossed it over by his front door to pick up later.

'Thanks for that,' he said. 'Got to be getting back to work. This lawn won't mow itself.'

He flipped the switch on his mower and it growled to life. Ferrier continued sipping his soda, but didn't move.

'My wife would like to have you and Sally over for dinner some evening,' he said, over the sound of the machine.

'Yeah?'

'You've been here awhile, and we haven't really gotten to know one another.'

'Oh, we're pretty quiet. Not much interesting about us.'

He was guiding the mower away from Ferrier, who gently kept pace with him, even though it meant intruding not only on Kirk's personal space but also his private property.

'All the interesting people say that,' Ferrier told him.

'Except that in our case it's true.'

'We don't even know how long you two have been married.'

'No?'

'Well, you never said.'

Kirk tried to make a joke of it, but it didn't take.

'Too long,' he said, but he seemed to be struggling with his smile more than usual.

'I hear that,' said Ferrier. 'Etta and I got married at St. Joseph's, right here in town. We could have got married in the city, but we already had our eye on a house so we decided that we should exchange our vows in the same place we were going to live. Like putting down a marker. What about you two?'

'City clerk's office. Nothing fancy.'

'But you two are Baptists, right? I thought you'd be pretty strict about these things.'

'We had a church ceremony later.'

'Really? Huh. Where was that?'

Kirk killed the mower. The air smelled of freshly cut grass, underpinned by gasoline. It was one of those heavy days when even birds appeared reluctant to fly, but Kirk didn't seem to be sweating much.

He looked at Ferrier. He wasn't smiling any longer.

'We're really very private people, Mr. Ferrier,' he said. 'I don't mean to be rude, but we just want to keep to ourselves. We don't socialize much beyond church. We like our own company just fine.'

'Yeah,' said Ferrier, very slowly, as though Kirk Buckner had just flashed a gun at him. 'Well, I'll be getting off your lawn, then.'

'Thanks again for the soda.'

'Anytime.'

Ferrier crossed the road and returned to his house. He wasn't feeling angry or offended in any way. He was actually kind of pleased with himself. He believed he had confirmation of a suspicion, and that was enough.

The Buckners were hiding something.

Later that same evening, when his wife returned from a lecture on integration at the local community center, he told her about how he'd gone over to speak with Kirk Buckner.

'I invited him to dinner,' said Ferrier.

If his wife didn't quite keel over with shock, she still paused in the act of adding hot water to a herbal tea bag, just in case she burned herself, and considered her husband with surprise.

'You did *what*?'

'I asked him and his wife to dinner.'

'Did aliens come and abduct my husband while I was away?' asked Etta. She raised a fist and shook it at the ceiling. 'Damn you, space monsters, bring him back!'

'Very funny.'

'What did he say?'

'He avoided the invitation.'

'Were you rude about it?'

'How can I be rude about an invitation to dinner?'

'I don't know, but if anyone could, it's you.'

'I wasn't rude. He told me they were private people who wanted to keep to themselves. He didn't run me off his property, but he came close.'

'And why would you have asked them to dinner? I can't even get you to take *me* to dinner.'

'Just curious, I guess.'

'Oh, David!'

'What?'

'You wanted to pry into their affairs. What else did you ask him – his shoe size, how often he goes to the bathroom? You really are something, you know that?'

'I only wanted to know where he got married. And, uh, when.'

'Jesus. I'll have to apologize to them both next time I see them.'

'For what?'

'For being married to you!'

She took her mug of tea and stormed out.

'I only asked them to dinner,' said Ferrier, but there was no one to hear him except Slipper, their basset hound.

Slipper looked at Ferrier. Ferrier looked at Slipper.

'I was trying to be polite,' said Ferrier.

Slipper closed her eyes.

Across the street, Kirk had stood by Sally's bed and told her about his conversation with Ferrier.

'It's natural that he'd be curious,' she said. 'We're his neighbors.'

'I don't like him.'

'You don't have to like him. You only have to tolerate him.'

'I think he's been trying to find out about us.'

'Let him.'

'There may be gaps, details we'll have to lie about.'

'Then we will.'

'You don't understand. It's harder now because of the Internet.'

'Don't speak to me like I'm an idiot.'

She turned her attention from him and back to the book she was reading. It was one of those Oprah novels, the kind he always avoided.

'I'm sorry,' he said. 'I didn't mean to suggest anything of the kind. But Ferrier *was* prying.'

'I'll speak to his wife. She seems okay.'

'Right.'

He lingered at the door.

'Do you want me to stay?' he asked.

She didn't even glance up.

'I think I'll just read for a while longer before I go to sleep. I have a big order to prepare in the morning.'

Kirk turned away, closed the door behind him, and returned to his room.

We don't exist, he thought. *There is no Kirk and Sally Buckner.*

We are already ghosts.

49

The Collector did not head north to Maine and Parker, but south, back to his refuge in Delaware. It was compromised, this final lair, this sanctuary. Parker had tracked him down to it, but he was alone in doing so, and showed no inclination to share his knowledge of the Collector's whereabouts with others. This, at least, was good. The Collector had no desire to sell the house and try to move on again, not yet.

His father, the lawyer Eldritch, was growing frailer. He had appeared to rally for a time after the injuries he sustained during an attack on his old offices back in Massachusetts, but that upturn had been followed by a gentle decline. He now slept for most of the day, and often struggled to recall names and details from old cases. Consequently, his efforts to reassemble his destroyed records from memory had ground to a halt. Without his vocation to spur him on, Eldritch seemed to have given up. His eyes, once clear and bright, were now yellowed and rheumy. He no longer shaved every morning, and had dispensed with the neckties that had previously finished off the careful assemblage of his wardrobe. Even were he considering moving locations, the Collector would have been reluctant to do so for fear of the effect such an upheaval might have on his father.

But in Eldritch's moments of lucidity, his former powers were revealed, even if his flawed file on Routh had given only a hint of the dead man's singularity. The more his father uncovered about Routh, the more ultimately unknowable the man appeared to be. There was his elusiveness, his impenetra-

218

bility. He had not been as easy to read as so many others that the Collector had punished. Perhaps the fault did not lie with Eldritch. Perhaps there was no fault at all. Routh was simply unusual, and if the Collector required further proof of this then it lay in the reaction of the Hollow Men. They had not wanted to touch this one. They had no desire to welcome him into their number. Routh bore some deeper, odder taint that now made his past worthy of further investigation.

In the quiet of his study, his father dozing in a chair in the next room, the TV silently broadcasting inanities, the Collector went back over the Routh material, detail by detail, but by the end of the process he had merely confirmed what he already suspected: Donn Routh had, for decades, managed to hide an innate strangeness from view, and in death had left no clues, or none that the Collector could follow.

The afternoon light was fading, and darkness was rousing from its slumber. He heard a sound from behind. Eldritch laid a hand on his son's shoulder, like a bird alighting.

'What are you doing?' Eldritch asked.

'Thinking about this man.' The Collector gestured at the file, and his father stooped to view the picture attached to it, because he was not wearing his spectacles.

'Routh.'

'Yes.'

'Where is he now?'

'Dead.'

'You did it?'

'Yes.'

'Then why should his file be on your desk, and his fate on your mind? He is gone, done with.'

'He was different.'

'How? Don't tell me you're feeling regret at his passing.'

'Only that I did not interrogate him before he died, except I don't believe he would have told me anything, even under the knife. He was hiding a secret. He'd been hiding it for most of his life, I think.'

'And what was this secret?'

'I haven't discovered it yet. Possibly the fact that he was worse than we imagined.'

Eldritch's grip tightened on his shoulder, the talons of the bird tensing in preparation for flight.

'Then to hell with him.'

Each stared at the other's reflection in the window. Snow lay heavy on the lawn, the bare branches of bushes poking through in places like the browned fingers of buried men.

'I'm dying,' said Eldritch.

'I know.'

His tone betrayed no feeling.

'You've never told me.'

'Told you what?'

'About what lies beyond. About what awaits me.'

'You're in no danger. You'll sleep, and when you wake you will be transformed.'

'Will I remember?'

'Only if you want to.'

'I don't think that I do, or not this.' And the Collector knew he meant all that they had done, and the taking of lives in which Eldritch had conspired. 'I don't want to forget your mother, though. I don't want to forget everything.'

'And me?'

The silence that followed was broken only by the rattle and wheeze of his father's breathing.

'I treated you like my son.'

'Am I not your son?'

'My son died. You took his place. You wore his skin, spoke in his voice, looked at me with his eyes, but you were never my boy. You were a changeling.'

'You raised me. I called you "father". If I was not the son you might have had, then I was, at least, a son.'

'I suppose that's true. Whatever the facts of it, there's no point in arguing about them now. I'm hungry. There are cold cuts in the fridge. I'm going to make a sandwich. You want one?'

He did not, but heard himself say that he did. He knew that Eldritch would do no more than peck at the bread, leaving most of it for the trash. He was eating so that his son would eat, and his son was eating so that the father would eat. If it was madness, it was of a gentle character.

'Then I'll take care of it,' his father said. He moved away, his reflection fading, but he stopped before it vanished entirely.

'You were a good son,' he said. 'I could not have asked for better.'

The Collector did not answer. He stared beyond himself, into the gathering shadows, and thought that grief, for so long alien to him, might soon be a stranger no longer.

50

Moxie Castin operated out of a compact suite of offices on Portland's Marginal Way. He had been married and divorced three times, and continued, by some miracle, to be on good terms with all his ex-wives, even if he displayed no inclination to make it fourth time lucky. He never wanted for female company, despite his unprepossessing exterior. He was overweight – or undersized: as he liked to tell Parker, 'My weight is fine, it's just my height that's the problem.' He wore expensive suits that never fit properly, and paired them with either black or brown brogues, regardless of whether or not the color of the shoes matched the outfit. He smoked enough cigarettes to merit a Christmas card each year from Philip Morris, and took his nickname from the carbonated beverage he consumed in similar quantities to oxygen. Although born Oleg, no one in Portland ever called him by that name. Even the newspapers had dispensed with putting his nickname in quotation marks. He was Moxie Castin, and that was the name they would carve on his gravestone.

Parker had called ahead to make sure Moxie was around, and found him running the numbers with his secretary on a personal injury case in which a man had lost his right arm in an industrial accident. From what Parker could tell, as Moxie waved him into his office, the insurance company was playing hardball because the man was reported to be left-handed, and consequently it had made an offer that was about thirty percent lower than Moxie's own estimate.

'Vampires,' said Moxie, with some feeling. 'Leeches. Snakes in the grass.'

Moxie's secretary nodded Parker a greeting. She wasn't the talkative kind; that, or she'd simply given up long ago on trying to get a word in when Moxie was around, and this silence had infected all of her dealings with the world.

'What will you do?' Parker asked.

'I'll say he was ambidextrous. Good luck to them proving he wasn't.'

He finished scribbling some notes, handed them to his secretary, and asked her to type them up. Moxie ran a bijou, personal business. He had a couple of people he could draft in if needed, but he prided himself on the fact that anyone who availed themselves of his services got looked after by him. Parker did some work for Moxie on occasion, mainly process serving and pretrial investigations. Moxie paid well, and on time. When he died, the people of Maine would have to club together to erect a statue in his honor, if only to remind themselves, and the majority of his profession, that you didn't have to be a jerk to be a lawyer. Then again, Parker supposed it all depended on whose side Moxie happened to be. Somewhere, an insurance lawyer would soon be cursing Moxie's name and wondering just how one could prove conclusively that a one-armed man had not, until recently, been ambidextrous.

Moxie told Parker to take a seat, opened a can of soda, and asked what he could do for him. In return, Parker handed over the documents from Rachel's attorney. Moxie read through them, slowly. Parker didn't disturb him. When he was done, Moxie placed the paperwork on his desk and scowled.

'It's pretty standard stuff at this stage. How are you and Rachel getting along?'

'Could be better. I wouldn't be here otherwise.'

'Yeah, kind of goes without saying. What I mean is, you're not throwing stuff at each other, or exchanging gunfire?'

'No.'

'Is she doing this as a last resort?'

'I guess so.'

'Did you feel it coming?'

'Kind of. After what happened with Sam, it was always going to be bad.'

'Yeah. Still, at least it sounds like she's playing fair. If you're getting fucked, then you're getting fucked. But if you're getting fucked by someone who's smiling, then you're *really* getting fucked.'

'Words to live by.'

'I like to think so. I'll make the call and get the ball rolling with her attorney. I don't know her, but if she's in Vermont she probably wears beads and has someone to cleanse her aura. Best thing to do in these cases is find out what the other party wants, and what she'll settle for, and then you tell me what you want, and what you'll settle for, and when everyone's equally unhappy, we have an agreement that we can present to a judge.'

'I just want what's best for Sam.'

'Sure, but you don't need to get hosed. You may think Rachel won't hose you, but if it comes down to it, she will. You were never married, you live in different states, and people seem to shoot at one of the parties, namely you, on a regular basis. At the risk of casting a pall over proceedings before we begin, you're not starting from a position of strength. I take it you contributed to the child's support?'

'Yes.'

'Was it a formal agreement?'

'No. Rachel and I decided it between ourselves.'

'You keep records?'

'No.'

'Damn.'

'She won't lie about it.'

'You sure?'

'Yes.'

'You got stubs, copies of cashier's checks, anything?'

'I told you: Rachel won't lie.'

'I hear you, but just find what you can and pass it along to me, okay?'

'Okay.'

'In the meantime, take a few days. Think about what you really want out of this, your daughter's happiness aside.'

Parker opened his mouth to speak, but Moxie held up his hands to quiet him.

'I know, I know: you want what's best for her, but if you aim to crucify yourself, find another lawyer to hammer in the nails. I'm not in the business of facilitating the creation of martyrs. That's why I'm telling you to let this sit for a while and figure out what you can live with. For now, try not to shoot anyone, and if anyone looks like he's going to shoot at you, ask him not to until we've been before a judge. You staying around town?'

'I may have to leave for a couple of days.'

Parker told him about his meeting with Ross, and the investigation into Jaycob Eklund's disappearance. Moxie, thanks to his work on the contractor agreement, was one of the few people who knew of Parker's arrangement with Ross, and he didn't like it.

'Have I told you I don't like it?' he said.

'About a million times.'

'Then I'm telling you again. This won't end well. You think you're using Ross, and Ross thinks he's using you. That requires a delicate equilibrium for both parties to remain satisfied, and that equilibrium is never going to be sustainable for long. It's like a marriage.'

'I can see now why you're thrice divorced.'

'"Thrice"? Jesus, who are you: William Shakespeare?

Whichever attorney let you sign that contract should be ashamed of himself.'

'I'm not sure he has that capacity.'

'Really? I like him more already.'

Parker stood to leave. They shook hands.

'We'll get this thing with Sam worked out,' said Moxie. 'I promise.'

'I trust you.'

'And I know that it sucks. No one ever wants to end up in court arguing over a child. If we can find a way to avoid that, we'll both have done a good day's work.'

'See you around, Moxie.'

Parker left and closed the office door behind him. He was almost at the lobby when Moxie's door opened again.

'Hey, did I ever tell you that you shouldn't have made that deal with Ross?'

Parker drove up to Middle Street and found a spot near Bull Moose. The store had expanded, and now seemed to have more space for DVDs and Blu-rays than before, although the CD racks had stayed pretty much the same, and there was more vinyl. Whatever the balance, Parker was just glad to see a business that was still thumbing its nose at the death of the record store, and appeared to be doing okay out of it. He even liked the smell of the place, a funk of paper and plastic. He dropped enough money to feel that he was helping the cause, then headed over to Arabica, bought a coffee, and took a seat in the raised area at the back of the café. He was alone.

He watched the cars go by on Spring Street. He thought about Sam. He remembered the night Rachel told him she was pregnant, how he had held her until she slept, almost overwhelmed by feelings of gratitude and fear. He had lost one daughter, and had never imagined being the father to another. Now his life, in ways that he could not entirely explain to another, revolved around Sam.

He was glad to be leaving town. It would distract him from his personal problems. He still wasn't angry. That, at least, gave him some satisfaction. Getting angry wouldn't help.

He finished his coffee and got up to leave. The floor felt thin and hollow beneath his feet, as though it must surely disintegrate if more weight were placed on it. Below it – below everything – was only darkness.

Darkness, and the creatures that moved through the honeycomb world.

51

Philip watched Mother pour herself another cup of tea. When she eventually died, and the flesh rotted away, he believed that her revealed bones would be stained brown.

He loved his mother.

He hated his mother.

Although not as much as he hated his father.

'I have a job for you,' said Mother.

Philip did not bristle, even though she spoke to him as if to a messenger boy. He had worked hard to develop an exterior that would not show emotion. Whenever it failed him, as it had when Parker mocked him about his parentage, he felt an intense disappointment with himself. He had not slept well the night before, his mind tormenting him with alternative permutations of his confrontation with the detective and his friends, each ending with them on, or in, the ground. Every display of weakness made it harder for him. If he wanted to be a leader, he would have to learn to behave like one.

'Of course, Mother,' he said. 'What do you want me to do?'

'I want you to go away.'

She was working her way through a sheaf of documents: annotating some, adding colored adhesive notes to others, and laying aside a handful to be shredded. He fought the urge to wrench the papers from her hands. This was his future being divided up and disposed of before his eyes, and she did not have the decency to consult him about it. She even appeared to take a certain pleasure in making it clear that she was excluding him from these decisions by working while speaking with him, when she could just as easily have taken care of business matters in the privacy of her own small office.

But now Philip was confused.

'What do you mean by "go away?"'

'I'm concerned that the final disposition of—' The pause was barely perceptible, but Philip had spent too long in his mother's company not to notice.

Go on, he thought, *say it, even if only once: my father.*

But Mother, as always, refused to acknowledge her son's male progenitor. It was a strange game they played. Ever since he was a boy, he had suspected that Caspar Webb was his father, even though the man showed him no particular affection and displayed little interest in his activities, present or future. For much of his life, he and Mother occupied a wing of the house on Block Island, but it was only in his midteens that Philip came to understand that Caspar Webb, the man for whom Mother acted as secretary, was something more than a wealthy recluse.

Philip suspected that his conception had been the result of a brief liaison, a moment of weakness and lust on the part of Mother and Webb. He did not believe he was the product of rape, because his mother's devotion to Webb made no sense in that context, but he could not recall witnessing a single moment of intimacy between them.

As he mused, Philip found himself cradling his malformed fingers as though to conceal them. They were, for him, an outward manifestation of his blighted pedigree, a physical symbol of his failure. He would sometimes catch Webb glancing at them with disgust, or perhaps this was just a trick of Philip's mind, a justification for the actions that followed.

Webb had remained a distant, aloof figure in Philip's life until right at the end, when his illness restricted his movements and he chose to relocate from Block Island to these

229

apartments in the Jewelry District, where he soon became bedridden, and numbed by medication. Although a roster of nurses maintained a near-constant vigil, and doctors visited, most of his care devolved to Philip's mother, and, on occasion, to Philip himself, who would take his turn at the old man's bedside. By the end, Webb was being fed oxygen through a mask, and was conscious for only a few minutes each day. Death would be a final small step, a simple transition from being to nothingness.

So Philip helped him on his way. A simple pinch of the oxygen line. A gasp. A spasm.

Gone.

The alarm sounded, but by then Philip was already calling for help. The nurse, who had been taking a break in the next room, tried to revive Webb, but his heart had given out at last. It was not unexpected, and Philip thought the nurse's efforts at resuscitation were little more than perfunctory. Mother was not present. She was resting in their smaller accommodations in the building next door. When she appeared, she held the dead man's hand. She did not weep. Neither, though, did she look at or speak to her son.

In the months since, she had given no indication that she suspected Philip of any involvement in Webb's death. And why should she? Webb was sick and old. Even the doctors admitted they were surprised he had lasted so long.

But Philip thought that Mother knew.

Because Mother knew everything.

All this in a single pause.

'—Mr. Webb's assets and business interests may be causing you undue distress,' she finished.

'I've told you how I feel about it,' said Philip, 'but I've resigned myself to the inevitable.'

'Have you, though?'

Those sloe eyes regarded him neutrally. Mother was good at that. She was capable of turning her emotions on and off in an instant, even with her son. It permitted her to examine any problem with equanimity.

'Yes, Mother. Really, there's no need to send me away.'

'When this is done, you'll be comfortable for the rest of your life.'

'Comfortable': what a mealy-mouthed word. Comfort was for the old, the dying.

'I know. We've had this conversation before.'

'We keep having it because I don't think you really listen.'

'It's hard for me. It's hard not to be trusted.'

'With these matters?'

'With anything. Even my share of the bequest is tied up with conditions and allowances. It will be drip-fed to me, and I'll have to beg for more.'

'It's still a great deal of money.'

'It's not just about the money.'

'I understand.'

'If you understood, you'd change things.'

'My hands are tied. How many times do I have to say it? There are legal stipulations. Mr. Webb's will was very clear on his final wishes.'

'That's not entirely true, Mother, and you know it. Many of the business interests under discussion are not legal at all.'

And there it was, over and over. An empire was being cast to the wind, and with it Philip's dreams of becoming an emperor.

'Philip, I love you, but you are not Caspar Webb.'

'I have his blood.'

Mother winced.

'What you have,' she said, 'is ambition.'

'You've seen what I can do.'

She had. She could still remember the summons to the warehouse, and Philip standing before the dangling figure of Terry Nakem, Vincent Garronne's wingman. Mother had ordered Garronne's death, because Garronne was plotting against her. Nakem should have fled when Garronne died. Mother would not have pursued him. Instead Nakem stayed around, which suggested he might be of a mind to cause trouble. Mother had instructed Philip simply to find Nakem, not to excoriate him. The vision of her son, stripped to the waist and mired in gore, a filleting knife in his right hand while what was left of Nakem pulsed redly behind him, had come close to threatening her own sanity.

But it was the look on Philip's face that remained with her, and returned in the depths of night. It was the expression of a child expecting to be praised for an act of destruction.

Look, Mother. See what I have made.

And yet she had stayed to watch him finish his work.

'Yes,' she said, 'I have witnessed what you're capable of.'

'I'm harder than you think. I can be ruthless.'

'Ruthlessness and savagery are not the same thing.'

'I can learn. I—'

'Philip, enough. It is decided. You have a choice: stay and be silent, or leave until all this is done. You can go anywhere in the world. You'll travel well – I'll make sure of it. Take Erik with you.'

Of the men who remained, Erik Lastrade was the most loyal to Philip. They were of similar age and temperament. In Philip's disturbed mind, clogged with imperial visions, Erik was Hephaestion to his Alexander.

'I would be happier to remain, Mother, if it's all the same to you.'

'It's not, but have it your way, and let this be the last of it.'

She returned to her papers. Philip allowed some minutes to go by, if only to ensure that he had his emotions under control. His eyes were warm, and he knew his voice would crack if he spoke too soon. Only Mother could do this to him, reduce him to the level of a child. Eventually, when he felt certain of his self-possession, he said, 'What about Parker?'

'What about him? I made him an offer, and he turned it down. He will do what he has to do. If it serves our ends, so much the better.'

'I don't like him. Or his friends.'

Mother did not look up as she replied, but Philip did not need to see her face. The mockery in her tone told him all he needed to know.

'I would keep that opinion to myself, if I were you,' she said. 'The tolerance of such men for those who cross them is even lower than mine. Now please, leave me to my work.'

Philip stood, walked to the desk, and kissed Mother on the crown of the head.

With her free hand, she reached out and stroked his cheek.

'It really is for the best,' she said.

'I told you, Mother. I'm resigned to the inevitable.'

'Good.'

And he was: Mother would have to go.

52

Parker had been putting off calling Ross, mostly because he was still trying to assimilate what he had learned about Eklund and his crusade, although if anyone might be willing to listen to a tale of ghosts while keeping his skepticism in check, it was probably the FBI man. Parker called him on the number he'd been given, but it went straight to voice mail after two rings. He didn't bother leaving a message. He figured Ross was only using this number for one purpose. Two minutes later, his call was returned.

'Sorry, I was in a conference.'

Parker heard traffic and shouting in the background – nothing alarming, just the sounds of a city.

'I figured you might like a progress report,' he said.

'I would, but not over the phone. I'm in Boston. Can we meet?'

Parker didn't ask why Ross was once again north of his New York stomping ground. Whatever the reason, it meant bad news for someone. Still, Parker wasn't about to haul himself down to Boston just for the pleasure of Ross's company. If he wanted to spend time having people swear at him and sound their horns, he'd just stop dead in the middle of Congress Street during what passed for Portland's rush hour. At least then folks would have a reason to be annoyed with him. He didn't need to go to Boston and have them feel that way for no reason at all.

'Boston's kind of, well, Bostonian at this time of year,' said Parker.

'It's Bostonian at every time of year,' replied Ross, not unreasonably.

'Yeah, that's its problem.'

'Would you like to suggest a compromise?'

'How about Portsmouth?'

'Don't you have something against the citizens of New Hampshire as well?'

'Not like Massachusetts. They're unstable in New Hampshire, crazy but they're not angry with it.'

'Such subtle distinctions. I'm taking the last shuttle back to New York tonight. I can be in Portsmouth in, uh, two hours. Where should we meet?'

'They have a bookstore that sells booze.'

'They would. What's it called?'

'Portsmouth Book and Bar.'

'Fine, I'll find it.'

He hung up.

Yeah, and you drive safely too.

Ross, Parker felt, should probably retire to Massachusetts.

As things turned out, Ross was about an hour late, which gave Parker plenty of time to browse, drink a late afternoon coffee, and think about Sam and Rachel. When he got tired of beating himself up, he bought a pristine copy of *Man on the Run*, a biography of Paul McCartney that began not with the Beatles, but with what McCartney did after they broke up. Parker had always preferred McCartney's work to John Lennon's, whatever effect it might have had on his standing with the cool kids. Lennon could only ever really write about himself, and Parker felt that he lacked empathy. McCartney, by contrast, was capable of thinking, or feeling, himself into the lives of others. It was the difference between 'Strawberry Fields Forever' and 'Penny Lane': although Parker loved both songs, 'Penny Lane' was filled with characters, while 'Strawberry Fields Forever' really had only one, and his name was John

Lennon. Parker might even have taken the view that Lennon needed to get out of his apartment more, but when he did, an idiot shot him. He'd probably been right to spend the best part of a decade locked inside.

Ross appeared just as McCartney was growing his beard long and getting it together in the country. The FBI agent didn't look happy, although with Ross it was always hard to tell. He also wasn't alone. Parker spotted his shadow, a young woman wearing a jacket that was too warm for indoors, but which she didn't remove. She took a chair facing the door as Ross went to the counter and ordered two coffees, one of which was to be sent to her table, before joining Parker.

'Sorry I'm late,' he said. 'I'd have been on time if we'd met in Boston.'

Parker closed his book. Ross pointed a finger at it.

'I always liked John Lennon more.'

'It figures,' said Parker.

Ross didn't bother asking why, which Parker put down to his innate solipsism.

'What's with the escort?' he asked.

'An indulgence to put others at ease. There's another waiting in the car.'

'You're moving up in the world – that, or you've been kicking beehives again.'

Ross's coffee arrived, but he waved it away.

'On second thought,' he said, 'just bring me a glass of wine. Red. Strong. You want one?'

'Sure,' said Parker. 'The same.'

The decision to order wine seemed to relax Ross a little. He removed his jacket and reclined in his chair. There were fine lines at the corners of his eyes. Parker hadn't noticed them before. Parker thought they might be new: stress, and on a government salary too.

'We've been speaking with someone you know,' said Ross. 'Garrison Pryor.'

Garrison Pryor was the head of Pryor Investments, which was under investigation by the FBI's Financial Crimes Section, the branch specializing in securities and commodities fraud. More interestingly, Ross and Parker both believed Pryor was the bagman and intermediary for a group of individuals known as the Backers, men and women who were directing the hunt for the Buried God. Of course, Parker guessed Ross had neglected to share the more esoteric and arcane of his suspicions with the FCS, and had instead found sufficient justification elsewhere for them to take an interest in Pryor.

The actions of the FCS had begun as an attempt, at Ross's instigation, to increase the pressure on Pryor in the hope of forcing him to turn informant. That was as much as Parker knew, but he was aware that Ross was deliberately piquing his interest, because Ross never revealed anything without a purpose.

'And how did that go?'

'As of this afternoon, he's under indictment.'

'On what grounds?'

'Certain of his company's transactions did not stand up to the scrutiny of the Financial Crimes Section.'

This didn't surprise Parker. His own late grandfather had been the most honest man he'd ever known, an individual of utter moral probity, but the FCS would still have found a way to make him look like a crook.

'How did he react?'

'His lawyers begged to differ with our assessment. They're stonewalling.'

'Then it looks like you're in this for the long haul.'

'Our investigations are ongoing.'

'I'm sure they are.'

'This began as a fishing expedition, and one not entirely unconnected to you, but it seems that the hook has snagged on something.'

Ross had used the gun attack that left Parker fighting for

his life to increase the pressure on those with reason to want him dead. Parker might have been more touched had it been an act of genuine concern instead of an excuse to flex some federal muscle.

'Snagged on what, exactly?'

'That remains to be conclusively established. Let's just say it caught on Pryor, and he's starting to squirm. He's vulnerable, whatever his lawyers may say.'

The wine arrived – a good Cab Sauv. Ross didn't bother with a toast, or even a raising of his glass, but just dived in. Parker thought he caught Ross's minder gazing a little enviously at him over her cappuccino.

'Is Pryor on your list?' Ross asked, once he'd surfaced again.

'No,' said Parker, 'Pryor isn't on the list.'

'You really should consider handing it over to me.'

'I have considered. I decided against it.'

'You still believe you'll find something we can't?'

'Maybe I just like frustrating you.'

'That possibility grows more likely with each passing day. If you do find the name you're looking for, be sure to scribble it on a note and paste it to the back of your refrigerator so we can discover it when you're dead.'

'I'll do that. Is the Pryor business why you're traveling with armed company?'

'As I told you, it was at the insistence of others.'

'You really think the Backers might come after you over Pryor? It would be a big step, killing a federal agent.'

'The people we're looking for are not typical.'

'So I'm taking my life in my hands just by being in your company?'

'Now you know how the rest of humanity feels around you.'

'Funny. While I'd hate to write off killing you as a solution to anything, it would be easier for them just to get rid of Pryor.'

'That possibility had crossed my mind.'

'Pryor's too, I'll bet.'

'We did raise it during our discussions with him. His shit-eating grin barely faltered.'

'He does have a shit-eating grin, now that you mention it. Do you think he knows something you don't?'

'A great deal, I imagine, but he's prepared to try and wait us out. A case like this could take years to go to trial. Who knows what might change during that time?'

'I take it you have some ideas.'

Ross drank more of his wine. Music played softly in the background. Through the window, Parker watched the breeze carry snow from the roofs of buildings and deposit it on the unwary passing below.

'If Pryor doesn't break,' said Ross, 'then perhaps I'll threaten to cut him loose. All charges will be dropped.'

'And?'

'And I'll let it be known, through unofficial channels, that he has been cooperative, and is planning to be more cooperative still. I may prevail upon you to share with us some more names, ideally those with a connection, however peripheral, to Pryor's line of work. We'll begin squeezing them.'

'Which, in turn, will squeeze Pryor.'

'Exactly.'

'It may also get him killed.'

'That's a risk that he – and we – will have to take.'

'I think you just like tethering goats.'

'Well, be sure to tell me when your rope begins to chafe.'

'My lawyer thinks I should never have made that agreement with you.'

'Mr. Castin? I spoke to some of our legal people who were forced to deal with him. They're hoping to recover from the experience sometime soon.'

'He'll be pleased to hear it.'

'I presume he has also warned you of the ultimate consequences of not surrendering the list,' said Ross. 'The Backers, and those in league with them, will eventually realize you're in possession of it. The ones you've picked off will form a pattern, and it will be noticed. They're not stupid. When that happens, they'll come for you. If you're lucky, they'll just kill you.'

'I remember. Note. Back of refrigerator.'

Parker tried his own wine. It was good, but he didn't plan on finishing it. Just a taste was enough. He wanted to keep a clear head.

'You're still not getting the list,' he said.

'I will, eventually. Over your dead body, but I will get it.'

Parker raised his glass.

'To a long life, then,' he toasted, but Ross conspicuously failed to respond in kind. Instead, he said: 'Tell me about Eklund.'

Parker gave Ross what he knew. First, Eklund's obsession with a series of alleged manifestations of figures that might or might not be linked to the group known as the Brethren, and Eklund's belief that these sightings were in turn connected to murders dating back to the nineteenth century; and second, the discovery of Claudia Sansom's body three years after her disappearance, and three years older than when she'd vanished, with the concomitant mystery of where she had been during the intervening period.

'The rest of Eklund's caseload is pretty much what you'd expect,' said Parker, 'which doesn't mean there might not be aspects of it capable of causing resentment. He took on divorce work, fraud investigations, embezzlement, skip tracing. It all looks mundane, but any part of it could be the potential source of a grudge. There are no small cases, not for the people involved in them. But Eklund was fixated on the Brethren, and the Sansom woman's file was on his desk when we searched his house, so he'd obviously returned to that recently.'

Ross didn't take any notes. He didn't need to. In Parker's experience, Ross had a good memory for bad news.

'Could the two cases be related?'

'There's nothing to suggest Eklund thought so, and he was meticulous in his research.'

'So how do you propose to proceed?' he asked.

'I'd like to talk to Oscar Sansom, if only because he's just a few hours' ride from here. It makes no sense to start chasing old ghosts farther afield before trying to establish if the clue to Eklund's disappearance lies with the Sansoms.'

'Agreed,' said Ross. 'Anything else?'

'There is one other detail, relating to the Brethren,' said Parker. 'Hardly worth mentioning, really.'

'Why do I feel you've been saving the best until last? Go on.'

'Guess whose brother turned up in one of Eklund's case files?'

'You have me on tenterhooks.'

'Caspar Webb's.'

Ross's eyes widened minutely in a manner that Parker could only think of as satisfying.

'Maybe you need to order another glass of wine,' said Parker, 'while I tell you about Mother . . .'

53

Sam was searching for a stapler. She was putting the finishing touches to a school project on mountains, which involved collecting photos and maps, and adding drawings of her own alongside whatever facts and figures she and her grandfather assembled from books and the Internet. Her grandfather had enjoyed the project more than Sam, who thought it was kind of dumb. She was supposed to be working on it with Stacie Mayer, but they fell out over who got to write about Mount Everest. Their teacher, Ms. Howard, decided – with Solomonic wisdom, or that was how Sam's grandfather described it, once the nature of the rift became clear – that the two girls might be better off working alone, and both could include Everest in their projects. Sam believed that Stacie Mayer should have been prevented from any involvement with Mount Everest due to her being a dork, and had set out to provide the final word on the mountain. The result was that her project now consisted of ten pages on Everest and a couple of paragraphs on various peaks of lesser interest.

She wasn't allowed in her mom's office without permission, but her mom was out with Sam's grandmother, her grandfather was taking a nap, and Sam really, really wanted to get the stupid project finished so she could play games on her iPad. She knew where her mom kept the stapler anyway, so it wasn't a big deal.

With her project under one arm, she opened the correct drawer, found the stapler, and was about to get to work when her eye was caught by her name on a letter poking from a file on her mom's desk. She put the stapler down and checked instinctively behind her to make sure that her mom or anyone else had not mysteriously manifested in the room without her noticing before pulling out the paper.

The letter came from a law firm. Sam didn't understand a lot of the words, but she didn't have to. She knew what *custody* meant, and she kind of knew what *restrict* and *access* meant, too. She looked at the letter for a while longer before returning it to the file. Then quietly, calmly, she stapled her project, put the stapler away, and left the office, closing the door behind her.

Back in her room, she sat on the edge of her bed, her chin on her hands, her face turned to the smaller of the two windows. Her grandparents had ordered it made especially for her. It was clear in the center, but the edges were stained-glass squares of various colors, and as the sun moved through the day, it cast beads of variegated light along the walls of her room.

Sam stared hard at the window, and one by one the panes of glass began to crack.

54

The first of the vehicles started arriving at the Buckner house shortly after four p.m. It was a freezing day, and few people were outside. Had a photograph captured the sky and the houses below, it would have been impossible to tell if one were looking at a picture of summer or winter without recourse to a glimpse of bushes and trees, because a flawless expanse of blue stretched across the horizon. But step outside and the answer would immediately have presented itself: the air was painfully cold, the chill rendered more agonizing still by a wind that appeared to direct itself with particular ferocity at the nose, the ears, and the fingertips, and caused eyes to water in a simulacrum of grief.

David Ferrier, being a sensible man, was not outside. He was sitting at his desk, trying to remember which sonnet rhyming scheme was Petrarchan and which was Shakespearean. He could just have looked it up on the Internet, but that would have been an admission of failure. Also, like many who considered themselves cerebral individuals, he lived in fear of losing his memory, although his physician had advised him not to be overly concerned about forgetting facts and names, and he should begin to worry only if he stopped noticing that he couldn't remember them – if, in essence, he forgot that he was forgetting. Ferrier didn't bother to point out the logical flaw in this particular piece of advice, since he was sure that Dr. Cyr had spotted it long before now, and if he hadn't, then he had no business advising anyone on anything.

Ferrier rummaged in the attic of recollection for a line of Shakespearean poetry, and dredged up something about chimney sweepers and dust, and 'dust' rhyming with 'must', which meant that a Shakespearean sonnet went AB-AB-CD-CD-EF-EF-GG. He tapped his pen triumphantly against his notebook and was about to start work on another poem that no one else would ever read when he saw the van pull into the Buckners' drive. It wasn't an RV, but a commercial vehicle that had been adapted to provide accommodation in back, with drapes on the windows. The paintwork was green, but obviously a spray job, and an amateur one at that, rendered even less appealing by the spots of rust and Bondo. It didn't look like anything in which Ferrier would have wanted to spend a night, but then he was unique among his peers in never having taken his family camping, on the grounds that he wouldn't force his wife and children to do something he wouldn't have wanted to do himself. And even when his kids had commenced asking him to consider a camping vacation, or even just a weekend away under canvas, he decided that they had been spending too long in the hot sun, and ignored them until, after some years, their urge to punish him in this way passed.

A pair of fiftysomethings stepped from the van. They looked to Ferrier like they ate bad food to match their bad taste in clothes and wheels. The woman's hair was dyed an unnatural shade of red, while the man could have dyed his in every color of the rainbow and it still wouldn't have cost him more than a few bucks for all that he had left on his head. Both wore loose blue jeans, matching fleeces, and white sneakers.

Rubes, thought Ferrier.

Sally Buckner came out to greet them, her husband appearing at the door seconds later. Sally hugged the woman, then the man, but there was something almost consoling about the way they embraced, like mourners at a funeral. Sally led them inside, one arm around the woman's waist, or as much of it as she could encompass, which Ferrier reckoned was about fifty percent, give or take. Kirk shook hands with the man, kissed the woman on the cheek, and the door closed behind them, although not before Ferrier caught Kirk glancing over in his direction, even though the net drapes helped conceal anyone inside the Ferrier home from view.

All thoughts of poetry were now set aside, not only because this was one of the rare times Ferrier could recall seeing anyone enter the Buckners' home apart from the couple themselves, but also because he'd always taken Sally for a cold fish. He found it hard to imagine her letting Kirk anywhere near her body, even fully clothed, never mind anyone else, yet here she was hugging and touching someone, and – hell – acting almost like a regular human being.

Over the next hour, three more vehicles arrived at the Buckners'. Two of them disgorged couples, both in their midforties. From the last emerged three younger people – two girls and a guy – who might have been siblings. More hugs, more handshakes: it was a regular outpouring of emotion.

Just as the kids were about to head inside with Kirk and Sally, Ferrier's wife turned onto the street in her Subaru. She stopped and rolled down her window, and she and Sally spoke for what might have been a minute before Etta moved on and parked in the drive.

Her husband was waiting for her when she entered the house.

'What's all that about?' he asked.

'All what?'

'The thing with the Buckners. Are they having some kind of party over there?'

She bristled. There was no other word: it was an honest-to-God bristle. If she'd been an animal, her hairs would have been standing on end.

'No, they are not,' she said. 'Their great-aunt died, the last of that generation of the family. Sally says it's like a little bit of their history just faded away. She lived alone, and there's a whole mess of stuff that needs to be sorted out. She's called her kin, or the ones who live near enough to make the trip, to mourn the old lady together, and figure out how to get started on what needs to be done. A party! God, I hope you're even just a little bit ashamed of yourself.'

Ferrier wasn't, but he composed his features into a semblance of contrition, if only for a quiet life, and said that he was sorry. His wife's response was 'Huh,' which spoke volumes. She went off to gather together a selection of cookies, wine, candy, and whatever else she could lay her hands on to give to the Buckners. Ferrier watched her bustling around.

'Why are you giving them cookies? The woman's a damn baker.'

'Oh, keep quiet.'

'And they're Baptists. Do Baptists even drink wine? I'm pretty sure they don't.'

'I'm warning you.'

Ferrier returned to his desk and looked out at the assembled vehicles. He wasn't an unreasonable man, or an entirely insensitive one, but he still couldn't bring himself to feel anything for the Buckners or their rube relatives in their time of loss.

He was still standing by the window when his wife appeared and placed a basket of provisions right on top of his poetry notebook.

'Hey!' he said. 'Watch what you're doing.'

'No, you watch. I'm sick of this. The Buckners have done nothing to offend you but mind their own business. You're a nosy, uncharitable man, but I'm going to give you this chance to redeem yourself in my eyes, and prove to the Buckners that you're not a complete jackass. You bring this basket over to them, and offer your sympathies like a decent human being.'

Ferrier knew better than to argue with his wife when she was in this kind of mood. Slipper appeared at the door and began barking. The dog was overdue a walk anyway. Ferrier could use her as an excuse, so he wouldn't be forced to show up at the Buckners' door with a basket of cookies like some weird, gender-conflicted Girl Scout.

'Fine,' he said. 'I'll go.'

His wife turned on her heel and left him to it.

Kirk Buckner looked surprised to find Ferrier on his doorstep, and Ferrier could hardly blame him. Since the whole soda/lawn incident years earlier, they'd managed to be civil to each other, but not much more than that. Now Ferrier awkwardly extended the basket to Kirk while trying not to yank Slipper up by the neck in the process. Ferrier could see Sally standing in the kitchen doorway ahead of him, a bowl of chips in her hand, and through the living room door to the left he glimpsed one half of the rube couple with what looked like a beer. Maybe the Buckners weren't such strict Baptists after all, or their relatives didn't much care one way or the other.

'Etta told me about your loss,' said Ferrier. 'I'm very sorry. We thought these might come in useful – you know, for your guests.'

Kirk hesitated for a moment before taking the basket.

'That's real nice of you both,' he said. 'We appreciate it.'

Sally advanced, and Kirk moved aside to make room for her. Once again, Ferrier was struck by who wore the trousers in the relationship, and it wasn't Kirk.

'Please thank Etta for us,' she said, and something in her tone, and the way she put the emphasis on his wife's name, was like a poke in the eye to Ferrier, as though Sally knew that this whole damned basket had been none of his doing.

'I'll do that,' he said.

Fuck you and your shit-heel kin.

Ferrier turned so quickly that Slipper didn't have enough time to adjust and gave a small yelp as she was forced to deal with the sudden maneuver. The door closed behind him, but Ferrier didn't look back. He walked Slipper as far as the golf course, upon which dogs were forbidden to tread, and out of spite let her slip through a gap in the fence and take a crap near the eighteenth hole. By now it was completely dark, so Ferrier turned for home, stopping in front of the Buckners' along the way. The drapes on the living room window were not quite fully closed, and a sliver of light showed through the gap.

Ferrier had a pen in his jacket pocket. He always kept a pen and paper with him in case he was struck by an idea or, more usually, to remind himself to complete whatever errands his wife had assigned him. Hidden by the dark, and largely shielded by the bulk of the van, he quickly scribbled down the make and license plate number of each of the vehicles in or near the Buckners' drive. One of them, a beige Chevy Blazer, had a sticker on the trunk that read SUPPORT YOUR LOCAL EDUCATOR, which struck Ferrier as an invitation for some disaffected student to key it or douse it with corrosive.

'Come on, Slipper,' he said, when he was done. 'Time to go home.'

He crossed the street, whistling to himself.

And from her bedroom window, Sally Buckner watched him go.

55

Ross knew of Caspar Webb only by reputation, but his understanding, shared by the bureau, was that Webb's operations were being wound down, and the resulting fragmentation of his criminal endeavors was probably good news overall. He made some calls from the relative privacy of the bookstore's performing arts section to confirm a couple of details, then returned to the table.

The feds, it emerged, had regarded Philip as simply another cog in Webb's machinery, and Mother as a glorified secretary. Her given name was Lydia Orzel, although Ross's people weren't certain that this was genuine, Lydia Orzel seemingly having popped into existence a few decades earlier, fully formed and without a past.

'So much for the FBI's insights into the criminal underworld,' said Parker. 'You guys have really gone downhill since Hoover died.'

'We had no proof that Webb was a criminal at all, only suspicions and guesses. He emerged from the shadows with a degree of wealth, and managed his activities on a cell basis – there were men and women working for him who had no idea he was their ultimate employer – so an infiltration was out of the question for us. He probably had three or four people he kept close, and we can only guess at the degree of trust he placed in any of them.'

'Mother excepted.'

'If she's to be believed.'

'I didn't see anyone else stepping up to the plate, and Vincent Garronne is dead.'

'That we knew, and his lieutenant, Terry Nakem, has vanished from sight.'

'Mother mentioned that she'd watched a man being skinned alive, but she didn't say who it was, or when.'

'Whether Nakem went into the ground skinless or not, that's almost certainly where he is. Both men had eyes on Webb's throne. With them out of the way, "Mother" has a clear run to act as she deems fit.'

'You're forgetting Philip.'

'You're sure he's Webb's son?'

'He has his father's distinctive good looks, like a badly made crash test dummy. He also smells like a funeral parlor, but that may be incidental.'

'He's Mother's problem, not ours. Are they expecting you to report back on the matter of Webb's brother and his family?'

'My sense was that adhering to Webb's final wishes, including the matter of his brother, was of importance to Mother, but less so to Philip.'

Ross finished the last of his wine. Parker still had most of his glass left. He felt pleased with his self-discipline.

'If I were to express a preference, it would be that a channel of communication remain open,' said Ross. 'We like predictability. With Webb in place, and the Italians corralled in Boston, the Northeast was mostly in balance. The dissolution of Webb's interests would mean a redistribution, but along existing lines. It would also offer an opportunity for state and federal authorities to find an entry point and start a process of disruption. Mother's interest in your investigation could prove useful to this process.'

'Do I get a Junior G-Man badge too?'

'No, just my undying gratitude, and the continued payment of your retainer.'

There are moments to play a card. This was one, and Parker had been waiting for it.

'I'm not going to try to get information out of Mother just so you can pad out your end-of-term report. You haven't met her, or her son. Their company isn't the kind I'd choose to keep. And unless I'm missing something, you're using agency funds to investigate a disappearance that you don't want your friends in Federal Plaza to know about. I'm also aware that you're probably keeping pertinent information about Eklund from me, for reasons I don't even pretend to understand.'

Ross's aspect, already less than warm, grew noticeably colder.

'So what do you want?'

Parker reached into his satchel and removed a sheaf of papers. They represented Aimee Price's last professional involvement in his affairs.

'You're not just using me,' he said. 'You're also using my friends.'

'And?'

'A token of your gratitude wouldn't go amiss.'

'More money? I don't think that's going to happen.'

'They don't need money, but you can offer some practical assistance that might help your cause. Louis doesn't have a record. Angel does.'

'Which, let me remind you, has required me to clean up more than one mess, and calm any number of representatives of local and state law enforcement. As for Louis, just because he has never been convicted of a crime doesn't mean he's not on the radar.'

'Louis isn't the issue. Angel is. My price for going after Eklund just went up. This is it.'

He handed the papers to Ross, who glanced through them.

'Proceedings to seal his criminal record in the state of New York,' he said, when he was done. 'You and Ms. Price have been busy.'

'Angel's record complicates certain areas of his life, including possession of a firearm. We'd have gone for expungement, but that isn't an option in New York. A lot of favors have been called in to fast-track this. As you'll see, there's also a degree of confusion about Angel's age at the time of the commission of the offense that got him put in Rikers – and for burglary, a nonviolent felony.'

'All very affecting, but I don't see how this involves me.'

'I'd like you to support the application.'

'Officially or unofficially?'

'We'll settle for the latter, as long as we get the right result. We're also aware that Angel's details are in the FBI database, and the FBI, as a federal agency, is not bound to follow any order issued by a state court. We'd need to know that the state decision would be implemented by all appropriate institutions.'

'Just so another of your friends can continue shooting at people with impunity?'

'No,' said Parker, 'so he can shoot at the *right* people with impunity.'

One thing that could be said for SAC Edgar Ross: he didn't go in for a whole lot of hemming and hawing.

'I'll have to talk with my superiors. I'll see what I can do. You can throw in some pages of that list of yours. It may help to sweeten the deal.'

'I'm sure I can find two.'

'I'm sure you can find five.'

'Three it is.'

It was a good deal. Parker had been prepared to offer Ross much more than that.

Ross put on his jacket, and they shook hands.

'The Webb business is interesting,' Ross reminded Parker, 'but Eklund remains the focus.'

'On that,' said Parker, as Ross was about to turn away.

'Yes?'

'You told me that my investigation into Eklund had to be kept off the FBI's books, yet you show up here with two federal agents in tow. It doesn't make sense.'

Ross frowned.

'Who said they were federal agents?'

Parker drove back to Portland. He got delayed near the Kennebunk Service Plaza, where a tractor-trailer had skidded on the road ahead and ended up on its side. He used the opportunity to pull in and pick up a coffee, more for something to do while the accident was cleared than anything else. When he returned to his car, he turned on the interior light and located the bug. He'd play Mother's game, but not Philip's.

'Screw you, Philip.'

He pulled the bug and ground it into fragments beneath his heel.

56

Sam was quiet at dinner that evening. Rachel didn't notice; she was tied up with preparations for a meeting the next day that would determine the funding of her biobehavioral research, and wasn't even looking at her food as she ate, so concerned was she with the screen before her.

They were in the kitchen of the converted stables that served as their home. They usually dined with Sam's grandparents only every second or third night, and on weekends. Despite their proximity, they didn't want to be living in one another's pockets.

Sam pushed some vegetables around on her plate. She'd eaten most of her chicken, and some of the rice, but she wasn't very hungry.

'Can I leave the table, please?' she asked.

Rachel looked up.

'You haven't finished your food.'

'I don't want any more.'

'Are you feeling sick?'

'No, I just don't want to eat anything else.'

'Well, if you're sure. What are you going to do now?'

'Go to my room.'

'Are you sure you're okay?'

'Yes.'

'Then come over here and give me a hug.'

Sam did, but she kept her eyes open, and didn't hold on to her mother for long. She went to her room and looked at the cracked panes of glass. She'd pulled the drapes after the glass had cracked, but the damage would be discovered the next day, when her mom or grandmother came in to clean the room or put away fresh clothes. Even if she left the drapes closed, they'd just be opened again.

She undressed and went to bed. When her mother arrived to check on her, she pretended to be asleep, and stirred a little for show when she felt the kiss on her cheek. She was still angry, and still sad, but after a time she slept for real, and dreamed of fire.

57

Madlyn was the last to arrive at the Buckner house, when it was already after seven p.m. Her son, Steven Lee, drove her, but David Ferrier wasn't around to witness their welcome. By then his wife had announced that she'd had enough of his ways for the evening – and every evening for the foreseeable future – and forced him to join her in the kitchen, where they were playing a series of bad-tempered games of gin rummy, made only slightly more tolerable by two glasses of actual gin. With the door closed, and the window facing out on his backyard, Ferrier was cut off from all activity at the Buckner house.

Madlyn was the de facto matriarch of the Brethren. There were members of the family older than she, but they weren't capable of doing much more than eating, sleeping, and mostly getting to the bathroom on time. Madlyn was seventy-nine, but looked a decade younger. She was tall and thin, and favored an obscure French perfume that reminded Kirk of dead chanteuses.

Madlyn still saw the ghosts, but not as often since Sally had come to the fore. Steven Lee, her only child, fat and shiny like a statue of the Buddha, had never married, and was devoted to his mother. When Madlyn died, it was widely believed her son would have to be buried alongside her, living or dead.

Kirk was in the basement when they turned up. He'd been showing off his plastering to Sumner, who worked in construction. Sumner thought it a miracle that Kirk and Sally's whole house hadn't started to crumble around their ears if this was the quality of Kirk's efforts throughout, but he did his best to keep this opinion to himself. He thought he might say something about it to Sally before he left, if only to suggest that it would be a good idea if every tool Kirk owned were suddenly mysteriously lost, never to be found again.

Sumner was drinking a beer, while Kirk stuck to soda. Some of that Baptist shit seemed to be sticking to Kirk, in Sumner's view. They all had their ways of blending into communities – volunteer work, neighborhood watch, Rotary Club, whatever – but Kirk and Sally had favored churches right from the start. It was one thing using them for cover, but another entirely to start taking anything they said seriously. It wouldn't make any difference. There would be no salvation for any of them.

The two men went upstairs to greet Madlyn and Steven Lee, and the entire group squeezed into the Buckners' living room, some of them forced to sit on the floor, or perch on the armrests of sofas and chairs. It was a long time since so many had gathered for an occasion that wasn't a funeral or a wedding, and the latter tended to be only superficially happy affairs, especially if someone from outside were being drawn into the family. That was why the Brethren generally married distant cousins, with no secrets to be kept. When they did marry outside their own – and it was good for the bloodlines, at least – they tried to keep the truth from their spouses. Untold generations of those who married into the Brethren had spent their entire lives ignorant of what would befall them at the moment of death, unaware that they had cursed themselves from the moment of consummation, just as their children were cursed, and their children's children.

Those gathered in the Buckners' home were all related by blood, although Kirk and Sally were the only siblings in a relationship. Such unions were not unknown among the Brethren, and it was generally felt to be for the best in this case. It meant that Sally didn't have to bear the burden alone.

They all knew why they were present. Donn Routh was dead, his body still missing. The women had experienced the moment of his passing, even – in the cases of Sally and Madlyn – sharing some of the pain of it. Now they had come together to discover how it might have happened, and what steps should be taken in the aftermath.

Sally had not told anyone but Madlyn about the private investigator, Eklund. Obviously Kirk knew, because he'd been present when Eklund arrived at their door, but it wasn't as if Sally needed to consult the others before acting. She understood immediately the threat Eklund posed, and the only piece of good fortune about the whole affair was the fact that fucking David Ferrier and his bitch wife had been away for the weekend when Eklund showed up, and so nobody had seen him enter the house, just as nobody had witnessed Kirk later driving away in Eklund's car, which he'd taken by back roads to the wrecking yard owned by Steven Lee, where it was reduced to scrap before the sun was given time to set on it.

Now, as the Brethren listened, Sally explained all that had happened, up to the point where she dispatched Routh to purge Eklund's home of any incriminating evidence. She omitted the words Eleanor had written on the bathroom window. She didn't know what they might mean, only that Eleanor had communicated anger and fear as she wrote them. Until she could find out more, she thought it better not to cause alarm. They had enough to be concerned about as it was. The exception was Madlyn: Sally would quietly share everything with her later.

'So what should we do?' asked Jeanette. She had arrived with her younger sister, Briony, and their older brother Art. Their parents had died in a car accident while Jeanette and Briony were still in their midteens and Art was barely twenty-one. The boy had looked after his sisters with the help of the rest of the Brethren, but Jeanette was the one who had always demonstrated the greatest maturity. Sally thought that she and Art might soon begin sleeping together, if they had not done so already. It was in the way they looked at each other, and in how Art's hand rested on his sister's thigh. Sally would question the girl about it before she left. It might be that the next leader was emerging at last, and in time Sally would be able to hand the reins to Jeanette, aided by her brother. The arrangement had a pleasing symmetry to it.

'Eklund spoke to many people over the course of his investigations,' Sally replied, not quite answering the question. She had to move cautiously on this. They needed to be led to a point from which there could be no turning back. 'He spent years looking for us, even if he didn't determine until recently that we, the living, were the real object of his pursuit.'

'If he was so intent on finding us,' said Sumner, 'how come we weren't aware of him until he showed up on your doorstep?'

Sally detected an accusatory tone, which she didn't like. Murmurs of agreement accompanied the question from the two older couples in the room – Esther and Allan, who had been the first to arrive, and Sophia and Richard. Richard and Allan were brothers, and had married sisters from an ailing branch of the family in Iowa. Sometimes, the Brethren's marital arrangements made even Sally's head swim. Esther and Allan were followers, not leaders. Whatever the majority decided this evening, they would fall in behind. If, by some small chance, they showed any signs of individual thinking, Sally knew she could steer them back in the right direction. Richard and Sophia were brighter, but still easy to manipulate. Sumner, by contrast, was a smart-ass, although his wife, Jesse, was okay.

'I don't have an answer to that,' Sally replied. 'I think he was just lucky, but we have always hidden our tracks well.'

'What changed?'

'He received an influx of funds, which enabled him to

concentrate solely on his obsession, and he started speaking to some of the right people. Which brings us to the reason why you're all here. We're still under threat, and we must respond. We have to deal with those who helped lead Eklund to us.'

This news wasn't met with universal approval. With one exception, the Brethren gathered around her weren't killers, although they had killing in their genes. They were ordinary folk, with ordinary jobs and ordinary lives. Esther had early-onset arthritis. Allan had beaten stomach cancer, and would be three years clear come April. Richard and Sophia were both teachers, and their two kids had brains to burn. Richard had cheated on Sophia a year or two back, and she'd found out about it, but they'd come through it and were working at getting along better. What united them was a bargain that had been struck in their name more than 150 years earlier, and all because the Magus was afraid of the justice he and his brood might face in the next world. His descendants had been paying the price for that bargain ever since.

Donn Routh had done all their dirty work for them in the past, but he was dead. Steven Lee had his uses, but he was reactive, not proactive, and didn't like to leave his mother. He also preferred killing women, which concerned Sally.

'Do you have names?' asked Allan.

'Yes.'

'How do you know that Eklund wasn't lying to you, or keeping something back?' asked Sumner.

Fucking Sumner.

'That,' said Sally, 'I can prove to you.'

The room lay off the basement. Sumner reckoned it was no more than ten feet by twelve, but of sufficient build quality to suggest that Kirk hadn't been involved in the construction. Sally said that the previous owners had tiled it and installed plumbing for a shower and toilet, but then sold up before the work could be completed. The floor was unfinished concrete, and the wall tiles were cream. Both were heavily stained with blood.

They couldn't all see the man who lay chained to a pipe in the corner, so the ones at the front had to make way for those at the back after they'd finished gawping. The room wasn't too cold because the boiler stood on the other side of the wall, but the man was still shivering. He was naked apart from a pair of stained boxers, and the tips of his remaining fingers and toes were blue. The stumps of the rest had been crudely cauterized. Cotton gauze covered his eyes, held in place by bandages, and his mouth was taped shut. He turned to face the new arrivals, and tried to say something, but the tape muffled his words.

'God, the smell,' said Esther.

Even Sumner, who was familiar with sewer pipes, had to admit it was pretty bad.

'We've been hosing him down once a day,' Kirk explained. 'It helps some.'

'Who cut off some of his fingers and toes?' Sophia asked.

'I did,' said Sally.

'Was it hard?'

'Only the thumbs.'

She turned to Sumner.

'Now do you see why I believed him?'

'I surely do,' Sumner replied. A man would give up a lot of information to avoid further amputations.

'He had a laptop in his car. He gave us the password. I used it to double-check everything he said.'

'Why did you keep him alive?' It was Allan. 'Why didn't you, you know . . . ?'

'Kill him?' said Sally.

Allan nodded. He looked appalled at what he was seeing. He'd be no use to them for what was to come, not that Sally had expected anything better from him.

'I wanted to wait until Donn finished his work, just in case we had any more questions for him.'

'And now?'

'It might be best to get rid of him, but I'm not doing it.'

'Why can't Kirk take care of it?' Esther asked.

'Kirk's no killer. Anyway, don't you think we've done more than our share already? It's time for others to do theirs.'

Sumner was the first to understand.

'So this is some kind of test?'

'If you want to put it that way.'

Eklund was moaning and shaking his head. He might not have been able to see or speak, but he could certainly hear.

They regarded him in silence. Then Richard spoke.

'Okay, I'll do it,' he said. 'I have a gun in the car.'

'You own a gun?' Sumner was shocked. He'd always taken Richard for one of those tree-hugging liberals. Hell, he'd wept with joy when Obama was first elected, then wept even harder the second time.

'Yes,' said Richard, '*and* I know how to use it.'

'He's a really good shot,' said Sophia. 'I keep telling him he should enter competitions.'

Sally was surprised. After all these years, Richard was showing some spunk.

'You can't use a gun,' said Sally. 'Someone might hear, even down here.'

'What, then?'

Sally was wearing a long sweater over her jeans. She raised the sweater, reached into one of the pockets, and pulled out a knife. Richard took it and flipped the blade. It wasn't long – only four inches – but it was sharp.

He licked his lips, and blinked hard behind his black-framed spectacles.

'I might need someone to hold him,' he said.

'I'll help you,' said Sumner.

Esther announced that she didn't want to watch. Richard

said that was fine, because he didn't want an audience. Kirk shooed everyone upstairs, with the exception of Sally and Madlyn, who declined to leave.

Eklund was crying – a high keening sound, like a woman in pain. He heard the two men approaching and tried to kick out at them with his ruined feet, but they were too quick for him. Sumner sat on Eklund's legs, but Richard wanted him facedown: 'I don't care to get blood on me.'

Sumner managed to get Eklund turned, and Richard caught hold of him by the hair, pulling his head back to expose his neck. Richard gritted his teeth and placed the blade to the left of Eklund's lower jaw.

'Hold him still, dammit.'

'Just get it finished.'

For a moment, Sumner thought Richard was going to chicken out. His hand was shaking, and his face was all scrunched up. Then he took a deep breath, dug the blade in, and slashed once, quick but deep.

Sumner had never seen so much blood. He looked away, but stayed where he was until Eklund stopped flopping around and grew still.

Richard rose and pushed up his spectacles. He had some blood on his hand, and the movement spread it to his nose and left cheek. He stared down at Eklund's body before dropping the knife, covering his mouth, and stumbling up the stairs to the guest bathroom. Seconds later, they heard him puke.

Sumner felt himself start to sway. The smell of blood was heavy and intense. Hands gripped him, and Sally helped him up.

'Well,' said Sumner, when he had recovered himself, 'I guess Richard passed.'

58

The Brethren began to disperse. There were babysitters to be paid, and chores to be done in the morning, the mundane coexisting with the extraordinary, although sometimes days, or even weeks, could go by without most of them giving even a passing thought to the strangeness of their lives. It was different for those like Sally and Madlyn, the ones who were haunted, but if any of the others began to waver, or needed a reminder of what it meant to be born or wed into this family, then the two women would always be happy to give them a sense of those who had gone before. All it took was a brief summoning, a touch, and once experienced, no one was ever in a hurry to ask for a repeat performance.

Richard and Sophia remained at the Buckners', along with Sumner and his wife, Jesse, and Madlyn and Steven Lee. Richard had recovered from his initial reaction to the killing of Eklund, and now appeared energized by it. Sally guessed that he'd enjoyed what he'd done, or was juiced by the fact that he'd managed to do it at all, which might be useful for what was to come, even if it did raise serious questions about Richard's psychological makeup. She hadn't particularly enjoyed hurting Eklund, and she'd stopped once he told her what she wanted to know. She'd have been forced to kill him herself, if nobody else was willing – that, or convince Steven Lee to do it for her, which would depend on his mood – but she was glad Richard had taken care of it instead.

They drank coffee and herbal tea while Sally produced a list of three names: the furniture salesman, Tobey Thayer;

Lydia Orzel, known as 'Mother', who was bankrolling Eklund's investigation through the bequest of a man named Caspar Webb; and an academic and historian named Michelle Souliere, who lived in Waterbury, Connecticut, and was a visiting lecturer at NYU and Bowdoin College in Maine. Souliere's background lay in psychology, particularly the history of extra-religious beliefs in the United States. She specialized in debunking psychics and other hucksters, and had published a number of books, including a well-regarded feminist history of witchcraft. She was single, and Eklund's notes indicated that she owned a cat. Sumner took this as evidence that she was a lesbian, since it would serve to confirm everything he had ever suspected about feminists. He was nothing if not unreconstructed in his opinions.

Thayer, the first individual on the list, had a wife and children, and appeared in his own TV commercials and newspaper adverts. Sally found a couple of the commercials on the Internet, and showed them to the others.

'He looks like a clown,' said Sophia.

It was a fair assessment. Thayer favored check suits and loud ties, and ended every pitch with an invitation to 'Come talk to Tobey!' He had a comb-over, which he made no effort to disguise, and the production values on his commercials were so poor that they could only have been a deliberate decision. Richard suggested he wouldn't accept the time of day from a man like Thayer without double-checking it with someone else first, and Sophia agreed. Richard grinned at her, seemingly in surprise, and Sophia gave him a more tentative smile in return. The wounds left by Richard's affair were still raw with Sophia, and Sally supposed that Richard was grateful for any scraps of apparent forgiveness Sophia might throw in his direction.

'And Eklund claimed this man was a psychic?' said Jesse.

'It's in Eklund's notes,' said Sally, 'but there isn't a single reference in the media to anything of that nature in connection with him.'

'Could Eklund have been lying?' asked Sumner.

'Not unless he falsified all the notes on his laptop, and why would he do that? No, I think Thayer may really have some kind of gift. Eleanor thinks so too. The Brethren have felt him looking for them.'

'On our side?' asked Madlyn.

'No, on theirs.'

This was unusual, and troubling. Even Madlyn was unable to walk the paths of the dead.

'It seems that he'd been making inquiries of his own before Eklund got in touch with him,' Sally continued. 'They were coming at the same problem – us – from different directions. It was probably inevitable that they'd meet up at some point.'

'And the academic?'

'According to Eklund's records, she may be working on a paper, or even the chapter of a book, about the Capstead Martyrs. She didn't accept everything Eklund told her, but she was open to considering his central thesis.'

'Which is?'

'That setting aside any suggestion of paranormal phenomena, it was possible that at least some of the killings referenced by Eklund might have been carried out by descendants of the original Brethren, or individuals influenced by a cult of Peter Magus.'

'Fuck,' said Madlyn.

Kirk winced. She might have looked like some East Coast Brahmin, but Madlyn had a whore's mouth.

'Which leaves Lydia Orzel,' said Sally. 'According to Eklund, this man Caspar Webb was a criminal, and a wealthy one. Caspar Webb wasn't even his real name, although Eklund didn't know what it might be, except that he was probably Eastern European by birth. He was estranged from his younger brother, who went by the name of Michael MacKinnon.'

'Fuck it twice,' said Madlyn, recognizing the name.

'Come on, Madlyn,' Kirk pleaded. 'Do you have to?'

Madlyn regarded him with something like pity.

'You have a body in your basement, we're conspiring to murder three more people, and you're complaining about my language? You're a milksop, Kirk. Unless you have something sensible to offer, just keep your fucking mouth shut.'

Kirk noticed that Sally didn't leap in to defend his honor. He couldn't blame her, not where Madlyn was concerned, but it still hurt.

'The cousin's murder of MacKinnon was an error in judgment,' said Sally. This was understating the case. MacKinnon, while on a business trip, had crossed Routh's path, and a simple argument over a parking space had erupted into a full-on shouting match. Sometimes that was all it took with Routh. He'd simmered for a few weeks, his growing rage drawing the worst of the Brethren to him like vultures to meat, then, with them whispering in his ear, he'd gone looking for the object of his ire.

'Had he known who MacKinnon was, he'd have stayed away, but unfortunately nobody outside MacKinnon's immediate family knew he was related to Webb. When he disappeared, and the police failed to find any trace of him, his wife eventually turned to her brother-in-law, who was already dying. But instead of Webb's death putting an end to any interest in MacKinnon's fate, responsibility devolved to this Lydia Orzel, who continued to fund Eklund, encouraged by MacKinnon's widow. And so Donn killed MacKinnon's wife and child, just as he would eventually have taken care of Orzel, Thayer, and Souliere for us, if required.'

'Maybe he shouldn't have killed the MacKinnons,' said Jesse. 'Wasn't that just likely to attract more attention?'

Sally glanced at Madlyn, who gave the tiniest of nods. Sally felt a strange sense of relief. Until now, only she and Madlyn had known what they were about to share with the rest.

'If not them, then it would have been someone else,' said

Sally. 'Silencing the MacKinnon woman offered a temporary solution to not one, but two problems.'

'What was the other?' asked Sophia.

It was Madlyn who replied – Madlyn, who monitored the debt owed by the living and the dead, the price of the deal struck by Peter Magus as the flames rose at Capstead. It was a bargain made with an entity that called itself an angel, a curse on every generation of the Brethen to come. They would be spared punishment for their sins. The angel would hide them and their descendants from divine justice. All it asked in return was blood. Refuge in the next world would be bought by the killing of innocents in this one. The Brethren would spread suffering, and thus avoid suffering in turn.

'It's getting harder to do what we have to, to feed the flames. Technology, cameras, DNA – they all mean that killing is much riskier than it was in the past. Every death buys us time, but as our family has grown, and new generations are born into it, our efforts have not commensurately increased in turn. Donn acted on our behalf, and Steven Lee helped out where he could, but it wasn't enough. If we were dealing with a bank, we'd almost be out of credit. The ones who have gone before us are uneasy. If we don't hold up our side of the bargain, well, I don't need to tell you what the consequences will be – for all of us.'

'So if we kill these three, on top of Eklund and the MacKinnons, we can stave off trouble,' said Sally.

'For how long?' Sumner asked.

'A decade. More.' She didn't know for sure, but that felt about right. By then, Jeanette would be old enough to include in these discussions, and mature enough to act. Sally and Madlyn had spoken to her before she left, and she confirmed that she and her brother had 'grown closer', as she put it. Jeanette also told them she'd had sightings of a girl. The girl was still keeping her distance, but was slowly drawing nearer.

It was good news, because it confirmed everything Sally had hoped about Jeanette.

The various couples exchanged looks with their respective partners, and with one another. Sumner shrugged.

'Then it looks like it's decided,' he said.

'Who do we begin with?' asked Richard.

'The academic, Souliere, ought to be the easiest,' said Sally. 'But I feel that we should deal with Thayer at the same time. Eklund believed in him, and the fact that we can find no reference to his abilities means that he's been careful to keep them hidden. Only frauds boast.'

'What about Orzel?'

'She'll be the most difficult to kill. She told Eklund that she hardly ever leaves her building, not since Webb's death.'

'Do you think she's afraid?' asked Richard.

'No, I think she's in mourning.'

'Does she live alone?'

'She has some of Webb's people around her.'

'A criminal's associates? They'll be armed.'

'Most likely. But she also has a son.' Sally smiled. 'And according to Eklund, he may have *very* mixed feelings about his mother.'

So it was agreed: Sally – aided, as best he could, by Kirk – would deal with Souliere, on the grounds that a woman might find it easier than a man to gain her trust, while Richard, assisted by Sumner, would kill Thayer. Sumner worked for himself, while Richard's exclusive school had just commenced a short break. Sally and Kirk were flexible, as long as Sally made arrangements to have her baking orders filled by someone else. A woman named Patti Best helped her with bigger batches, and covered for her when she took vacations. Patti would be glad of the extra money.

Thanks to Eklund, they had addresses for the three targets. It would take some coordination on all their parts, but it wouldn't be too difficult to get rid of Souliere and Thayer within a day of each other. After that, they could turn their attentions to Lydia Orzel.

The final farewells were made. Sally looked across at the Ferrier house, but it was after midnight, and all the rooms were dark. Steven Lee backed his car up to the Buckners' garage door so that Kirk and Richard could bring up Eklund's body, concealed by black garbage bags, and dump it in the trunk. Eklund's remains would go the way of his car, compacted to shit and lost amid the rest of the junk in Steven Lee's yard in West Abbot, about thirty miles from Turning Leaf.

Sumner and Jesse departed, followed by Richard and Sophia. Madlyn stayed back to speak with Sally, Steven Lee sitting behind the wheel of the car, as silent and implacable as ever. Sally suspected he might be the craziest of them all.

'Eleanor wrote something on my bathroom wall,' said Sally.

Madlyn's pinched features, the skin stretched drum-tight over the bones, somehow managed to register surprise.

'Eleanor *wrote*?'

'Two words: Hollow Men. What are they?'

'I have no idea.'

'I think she's frightened of them, whatever they are.'

'It could be linked to the bargain. Perhaps it will fade after the killings.'

'Perhaps.'

Madlyn laid a hand on Sally's arm.

'You've done so well,' she said. 'I'm very proud of you.'

'Thank you.'

They hugged, and Madlyn climbed into the car beside her son, Kirk holding the door and helping her in. He and Sally waved goodbye, and waited until they were out of sight before heading back inside, donning gloves, and scrubbing the final traces of Jaycob Eklund from their walls and floor.

271

59

Louis woke to find the other side of the bed empty. The clock on the nightstand showed 3:30 a.m. He waited, but heard no sounds from elsewhere in the apartment. He rose, put on his robe, and walked down the hall to the living room. One end was effectively a glass wall that looked out over Casco Bay, and because of the orientation of the apartment the adjoining properties were not visible from the window. As their block was the last building on the outcrop of land, and they owned the penthouse, standing at the window during the day was like standing on the prow of a great ship. At night, it was like floating among stars.

Angel was sitting in an armchair, facing into the darkness. It took Louis a few seconds to spot him, curled up as he was with a blanket around his shoulders.

'Are you okay?'

'I couldn't sleep.'

'Pain?'

'I wouldn't call it pain. Discomfort, maybe.'

'Is it getting worse?'

'Nah. Usually I just toss and turn for a while, then go back to sleep. Can't figure out why it didn't work this time.'

'Because it *is* getting worse.'

'Everyone's a doctor now.'

Louis joined him at the window, but did not sit. He discerned the beacons of a tanker moored out to sea, waiting for dawn to break before being guided in. Farther out, the streetlights on the nearest islands glowed like fireflies. He reached down and slipped a hand beneath the blanket so that it rested against the bare skin of Angel's shoulder. It felt hot to the touch, like an infected wound.

These were not gentle men. Each had suffered, and made others suffer in turn. Because of this, their devotion to each other was unconditional, and untroubled by concealment or illusion. It was a hard love, but love nonetheless.

'I'm scared,' said Angel.

'I know.'

'I can't even say of what. Everything. Of knowing, and not knowing; of what's to come. Not the pain so much – I can deal with pain – but being sick. I don't want to be one of those people, the gray kind, all worn down by poisons.'

'Don't get carried away. It could be a hernia.'

'It's not a fucking hernia.'

'Oh, so now you're at death's door? Couple of nights ago, sitting in the bar, you were trying to convince us it was nothing.'

'It's different in the dark.'

'Yes, I guess it is.'

Angel shifted position, and Louis saw him wince.

'You want me to stay here with you?' he asked.

'You got anything better to do?'

'Just sleep.'

'That would be a no, then.'

'Probably.'

Louis moved a second armchair so they were sitting side by side, like a pair of old farts waiting for daybreak, except they were not old, and if this was mortality, then it should not be taking such a form. They had faced down guns. They had been cut, and shot. The end, when it came, was always destined to be a violent one, not some creeping pollution of the body.

Louis was not a religious man. He named no gods. But because of Parker, he was conscious that what lay beyond

273

this life was not a void, although it was possible that a void might be less troubling. Now he communed in silence with whatever waited, and made his obeisance to it.

Let it be nothing, he asked. *Let this not be the end.*

When he was done, he spoke aloud.

'If you die,' he told Angel, 'I'll kill you a second time myself.'

But Angel, no longer alone, had fallen asleep.

To the south, a similar vigil was being kept. The Collector sat by his father's bedside while the old man, lost in a delirium, recited a list of names, only some of which were familiar to his son: clients, friends, relatives, a litany of those who had crossed his path. Among them were some he had fed to his son's justice. It was as well, the Collector thought, that his father was here and not in some old age home. Who knew who might have been listening to his ramblings otherwise?

The nurse had been summoned, and would arrive the next morning to take up permanent residence. His father had objected, but the Collector was no longer able to care for him unaided, and there was work to be done. He had decided that he would not entrust to Charlie Parker the identity of the man he had killed in Providence. Call it what you would: a small act of rebellion, a hunter's pride, or a refusal to feed any longer on scraps from Parker's table.

He dearly wanted to view whatever had been removed from Eklund's home. It was possible that not everything of interest had been taken from the house in Fox Point, so searching it thoroughly was one option. No alarm went off while Parker and Angel were in the house, which meant they had disabled it upon entering. Yet in the aftermath, Philip had quickly managed to track them down to their hotel, which indicated some form of surveillance: cameras, perhaps. The Collector could deal with most security systems, but he was wary of alerting Philip or Mother to his presence. He would deal with them if he had to, but only once this more pressing matter was settled.

The other course of action was to enter Parker's house and see what he could scavenge, but he quickly dismissed this as foolhardy in the extreme. After the attack that had almost taken his life, Parker's home would now be protected in every imaginable way. The Collector doubted he could even set foot on the property without activating some form of alarm, which would draw Parker, the police, or – worst of all – Angel and Louis. No, he would try Eklund's home, and see what might be revealed there.

His father stopped speaking. His eyes were fixed on his son.

'I heard voices,' said Eldritch.

'You imagined them. There is no one here but us.'

Eldritch looked around the room, seeking the speakers in the shadows, as though doubting the truth of his son's statement.

'Don't leave,' he said.

'I won't. I'll stay with you until you sleep.'

'I meant don't go. Let the mystery of this man Routh remain unsolved. Allow whatever he was hiding to remain concealed.'

The Collector brushed a stray hair from his father's forehead.

'You don't have to be concerned. The nurse will take care of everything, and there is a physician on call in Rehoboth. He's being paid well. If he's needed, he can be here in minutes. You'll be well looked after in my absence.'

Eldritch pushed his son's hand away in irritation, and the spark ignited something of his old fire. The Collector could see it in his eyes.

'I'm not worried about myself. It's you I fear for.'

'Me?' The Collector almost laughed. He was the one to be feared.

And just as soon as it caught, the flame went out again.

Eldritch frowned, and put the fingers of his left hand to his dry lips, like one experiencing a moment of doubt.

'Don't you hear them?' he said. 'They're whispering.'

'Who? Who is whispering?'

'The Hollow Men,' Eldritch replied.

The Collector leaned forward. Eldritch knew of them – his son had told him – but he had never seen them, and never would. Even had the old man committed the worst of sins, the Collector would never have delivered him to these scavengers. And they were silent: death had taken their tongues. The Collector was sure of it.

Wasn't he?

'What do they say?' he asked.

'They're speaking your name. And that sound . . .'

'What is it? Tell me!'

'I think – I think it's laughter.'

60

Parker woke shortly after seven thirty a.m. His bag was packed, and the drive to Natick would take only a couple of hours. He had called ahead to inform Oscar Sansom that he was coming. Sansom sounded weary, but agreed to meet Parker at his home. His tiredness wasn't surprising. Parker knew that he would have been juggling police, the media, and lawyers ever since the discovery of his wife's body. Although Sansom now at least knew for certain that she was dead, which would bring some small, conditional peace, the mystery of her missing years, the trauma of the retrieval of the remains, and the lingering grief of mourning would prove a drain on the energies of the strongest of men.

Parker made a small pot of coffee, put some bread in the toaster, and walked down to retrieve the newspapers from the box by the road. He read them at the kitchen table, then checked his e-mail, and wrote some checks to mail along the way. Finally he made a call to the Natick PD, identified himself, and was put through to a detective named Dawna Hall, who had been involved in the Sansom case since the beginning. He told Hall that he was looking into the possible disappearance of Jaycob Eklund, and would be speaking with Oscar Sansom later that day. The call was as much a search for information as an act of professional courtesy on his part: he wanted to find out what he could about the progress of the investigation. Hall told him that she'd call him back, so Parker waited at the table while the detective did a background check on him, and was speaking with her again within a half hour. There wasn't much she could give him, except to confirm that wherever Claudia Sansom had been for those three years, she wasn't living rough. The autopsy could find no evidence of malnutrition, or not the kind of mistreatment and suffering that came from a life on the streets. Only her teeth were in poor condition.

'Her teeth?'

'Untreated cavities, and evidence of an abscess. She must have been in a good deal of pain toward the end of her life.'

'So either she couldn't afford to see a dentist, or—'

'Yeah. Or.'

Neither of them needed to say anything more about it. A woman being held against her will couldn't be permitted to see a doctor or dentist.

'Anything else?' Parker asked.

'Her body was stripped and cleaned before it was put in the ground, and by "cleaned" I mean soaked in bleach. Officially, we're following a number of lines of inquiry. Unofficially, we're banging our heads against a wall. We're going to be reduced to monitoring the funeral service, just in case someone can't resist being a spectator at the end.'

'And Oscar Sansom?'

'Opinions differed at the start – I never made him for it, others did – but those missing years mean that even the diehards have pretty much admitted he couldn't have had anything to do with what happened to his wife.'

Parker thanked her for her time, and promised to inform her if he found out anything useful in the course of the Eklund investigation.

His inquiries into the more recent killings of May MacKinnon and her son had to be more discreet, but he was helped by Ross, who provided him with all relevant material courtesy of the taxpayer. If the Sansom investigation was floundering, the MacKinnon one was dead in the water. The only DNA discovered in the bedroom came from

May and Alex MacKinnon. Footprints were found outside the house, but they revealed no make of shoe, or even an imprint that could be checked later. A small fragment of blue plastic was found caught on a stone, suggesting that the killer might have been wearing boot coverings or overalls, and marks on one of the locks indicating entry through the back door, but that was the sum total of the evidence for now.

With that, Parker was ready to leave for Natick. Angel and Louis would make straight for Greensburg that afternoon, where Parker would eventually rendezvous with them prior to approaching Tobey Thayer. He could simply have called Thayer on the phone, but whenever possible Parker liked to conduct interviews in person. Eklund had thought highly of Thayer, according to his notes, and they had been in regular contact. Of all those referenced in Eklund's records, Thayer was the most interesting.

But Parker was also curious about the Waterbury-based academic, Michelle Souliere. The previous evening, he'd spoken about her with Ian Williamson, who taught at Bowdoin and knew Souliere from her work there. Williamson liked her, he said, but they had a fundamental difference of approach.

'I believe in lots of things,' Williamson had told Parker over the phone, 'and want to give credence to even more. But Michelle, she doesn't believe in very much at all, feminism apart. To paraphrase Einstein, even if she saw a ghost, she still wouldn't believe it.'

'I'll tell her you said hello.'

'Perhaps even give her a playful pinch on the cheek from me.'

'Really?'

'Absolutely. At least you'll have a good story to tell about how you lost a hand.'

Parker was putting his bag in the trunk of his car when

his cell phone rang. The caller ID showed Moxie Castin's name.

'I spoke with Rachel Wolfe's lawyer,' he said.

'And?'

'She doesn't do yoga, and I doubt she wears beads. Look, I hate to be the bearer of bad news, but they're going to seek an injunction to prevent you from seeing Sam until a judge rules on visiting arrangements. After that, they'll be pressing for supervised visits with a third party present at all times. If they have their way, you won't be able to spend time alone with your daughter.'

Parker slumped against his car. He couldn't find any words. The temperature seemed to drop, the cold entering his bones.

'I'll get in touch with Rachel,' he said finally. 'I'll try to find out what's going on.'

'No, don't do that. Her lawyer and I are still talking. I'm hopeful we can stave off the injunction, and reach a compromise on visitation prior to a hearing. But if you call Rachel now, it could complicate the situation. I'm going to take a ride to Burlington this week, and try to sit down with the lawyer over a drink. Maybe I can find out where this is coming from.'

'It's not Rachel,' said Parker. 'She wouldn't do this.'

But even as he said the words, he recalled her rage in the aftermath of Sam's abduction. When he arrived at the hospital in New Hampshire where Sam was undergoing checks by a pediatrician, Rachel had hit him, slapping his face twice until he gripped her wrists. She'd been too angry and scared and relieved even to cry. She just stared at him as he held her, then turned away when she was released. She apologized later, and he told her that he understood, and didn't blame her, but nothing between them had been the same since.

'Leave it to me,' said Moxie. 'It seems like the end of the world now, but it isn't. I guarantee it. Go do whatever it is you have to do, but remember what I said: don't shoot, and don't get shot. I got this.'

They said goodbye. Parker put his phone away.

He wanted to throw up.

V

A man is a very small thing, and the night is very large and full of wonders.

Lord Dunsany

61

Sam lay in her bed, the blanket pulled up to her chin. She'd told her mother that she wasn't feeling good, and Rachel had been in too much of a rush to get to her budget meeting to investigate further. Sam's grandparents assured Rachel they'd keep an eye on her, but Sam declined their invitation to come to the main house and curl up on the couch, so her grandfather was sitting in the living area of the stable building, reading his newspaper and listening to the radio.

Sam wasn't lying when she said she felt sick. Her tummy had been sore since she discovered the letter from the lawyer. She'd had the sense that something was up with her mother, even before she found the letter, but she put it down to work, and her mom's worry and anger at what had happened to Sam at the end of the previous year. Ever since the bad man had taken Sam from near their home, her mother had been reluctant to let her out of her sight. Sam wasn't even allowed to play outside unless she stayed close to the house, where one of the three adults could keep an eye on her. Nothing Sam said led to a relaxation of the restrictions. After all, it wasn't like she was going to be taken again . . .

None of them could understand why Sam wasn't more troubled by the abduction. She didn't have night terrors. She wasn't clinging to her mother or grandparents, or refusing to go out alone, or acting up in school. She seemed almost totally unaffected by what she had endured.

Sam could have told them why. She'd known the man was coming. She'd waited for him – him, and the thing he was carrying inside – and prepared. She'd been a little bit scared when he put her in the trunk of the car, and later when he carried her into the motel room, because he didn't appear to be growing weaker, but when the blood started flowing from him she knew she'd be safe. She did have some bad dreams in the days and weeks after, dreams in which he'd stayed strong and started to hurt her, but they went away after a while.

The other reason she was sick to her stomach was because of the broken window. She shouldn't have allowed herself to get annoyed. It was important that she kept her temper – and her secrets. The window would be hard to explain. She could tell everyone that she'd broken it with a toy, or the corner of a big book, but then she'd have to offer a reason why. Whatever she came up with, she was certain of two things: first, she'd be in trouble, and second, she'd quickly be back in Ms. Ferguson's office, sitting in a big chair and being asked about her feelings.

She didn't want to do what she was about to, but she couldn't think of another way out. She pushed back the sheets, walked to the window, and opened the drapes. Birds were flying among the trees at the edge of the back garden. Her grandmother kept them supplied with seeds and nuts in feeders that hung from the bare branches. Sam waited. Eventually, a pigeon came to eat. It was big and plump, and didn't look like it was starving. It used its claws to cling to the larger of the two feeders while it pecked at peanuts.

Sam focused on the pigeon, its feathers and its warmth. The bird stopped eating. It flapped its wings and rose into the air, circling for a moment, increasing its velocity.

'I'm sorry,' said Sam.

And the pigeon flew straight into the window.

Her grandfather stood beside Sam, staring at the damage. The bird hadn't shattered any of the individual glass panes, but each was cracked all the way across, and a smear of blood marked the point of impact. The pigeon lay dead on the ground below, its neck broken. Sam could see it through the fractures in the glass, although her grandfather told her to stay back in case she accidentally leaned on the window and cut herself. At least it hadn't suffered. She'd made sure of that.

'It happens,' said her grandfather. 'They get disoriented, or mistake their reflections for another bird.'

'Can we bury it?' she asked. It was the least they could do. She didn't want it to be thrown in the garbage.

'Sure we can, if it'll make you feel less sad.'

He examined the stained glass, but didn't touch it. Sam held her breath.

'That's damn strange,' he said. 'Every one of those squares has its own crack. Must be to do with how they're held in place.'

He took Sam by the hand.

'We're going to go over to the main house, and I'll call a glazer. It'll have to be all plain glass for now, until we can arrange to have another special one made.'

'You don't have to,' said Sam.

She felt guilty. She hadn't thought about the cost of replacing the whole window.

'Of course we do. It's Sam's Window.'

Together they headed to the main house. Sam hadn't eaten breakfast, and her grandparents were now even more worried about her than before. She didn't want them calling a doctor, so she ate most of a soft-boiled egg and some toast. While she was finishing the last of the toast, she began to cry. She didn't mean to, and tried to hide it, but the tears came too fast, like a flood rising and swallowing her up.

Her grandmother rushed over from the sink, and gathered Sam up in her arms.

'What's wrong, honey? What is it?'

Her grandfather appeared at the kitchen door.

'It's the dead bird,' he said soothingly, 'and she's under the weather anyway.'

'No,' said Sam. 'No, no.'

'Hush . . .'

'I want my dad,' said Sam. She sobbed the words out, tripping over them as the breath caught in her throat. 'I want my dad and you can't keep me from seeing him.'

'Nobody—'

'I want my dad,' she repeated – louder, no longer stumbling. 'I want my dad, I want my dad, I want my dad, I want my dad . . .'

Now Sam was screaming, and all the pain that she had convinced herself she didn't feel, all the fear, all the loss, found a voice at last. She was many things, this child, and would be many more, but most of all she was a little girl whose mother wanted to keep her from her father.

And that couldn't happen. She would not allow it.

'*I want my dad!*'

62

Jennifer, the dead daughter, sat on a rock, staring but not seeing as the departed flowed past, an endless river of souls flowing into the waiting sea.

A little boy was approaching. He was about five years old, and looked scared. The youngest were always the most fearful; still children in spirit and mind, not yet transformed. They grew confused, and tried searching for their parents, and in doing so some of them went astray. The unlucky ones, the saddest of them, ended up caught between worlds, little bubbles of rage and fear moving through rooms now rendered unfamiliar by the passing of years, too desperate to let go.

The boy opened his mouth to speak, to ask the way, but Jennifer's attention was elsewhere. She was listening to her half sister scream.

And then she was gone.

The boy remained standing at the foot of the rock, his feet almost touching the water. He regarded the dead, searching the faces for one that might be familiar, but found none. A woman reached out a hand to him, sensing his turmoil, but she was swept away before he could react.

The boy left the shore and walked into the foothills. For a time he remained visible, a small white presence against the darkness, until the shadows absorbed him and he was lost.

Sam lay on her side beneath the comforter on her grandmother's bed. The drapes were drawn, and an untouched glass of warm milk stood on the nightstand. Her mother was on her way home. She'd picked up the message about Sam as soon as she came out of her meeting.

Sam's grandmother peered into the room, but neither entered nor spoke. She could see Sam's lips moving, forming words but not speaking them aloud. Sam would not let anyone come near her, not since they had put her to bed. If they tried, she screamed. All they could do was watch their granddaughter stare into space, speaking to an unseen presence.

Her grandmother went away.

Jennifer was sitting against the bedroom wall, talking with her half sister.

you have to be careful

'I know. I'm sorry.'

you mustn't break things and you mustn't hurt things

'I was angry. She wants to take me away from him.'

she's frightened because of what happened

because of the Dead King

'I'm safe. I was always safe.'

no you weren't

'It doesn't matter. It's done now.'

she loves you

they both do

she just wants you to be safe

'I'm safer with him, and he's safer with me.'

she doesn't know that

'I could make her do what I want.'

Jennifer didn't reply to this immediately. Sometimes it was easy to forget just how dangerous Sam could be.

you mustn't

'Why?'

because it would be bad and you mustn't be bad

Sam did not reply, but closed her eyes and hid her face from view.

63

Parker was still no calmer by the time he reached Natick. He'd simmered all the way down I-95, and it took every ounce of self-restraint not to dismiss Moxie Castin's advice against contacting Rachel. He felt powerless, the fate of his relationship with his daughter now lying in the hands of others. Worse, he was truly furious with Rachel for the first time that he could remember, but he was also angry with himself. Rage, grief, loss: these were the emotions he had permitted to govern his existence for so long. They had been the dominant forces in his life ever since his father's death, and when Susan and Jennifer were taken from him, he had given them free rein. Now he believed he had them under some form of control, but still they called to him, and he fed them in his way.

Meeting Rachel, and the birth of Sam, represented a divergent path, the opportunity for a second chance. He could have chosen another way of living. He might have continued to work as an investigator, but in areas that would not have put his family or himself in harm's way. Had he done so, he might still have been with Rachel. They might have had another child together. He saw grandchildren. He saw himself growing old in peace, with a woman who loved him. He saw—

A fantasy. He let it slip away. He was not that man, and some of those choices had been made for him. And Sam? He could have pretended to believe that she was just a regular child – precocious, perhaps, but no more than that – but he knew better, just as he knew that he was not mad, and the

291

occurrences he had witnessed over the years, and of which he had been a part, were not the conjurings of a disturbed mind.

But this price, the loss of Sam – it was too much to ask, too high to pay.

Yet what could he do to change it now?

Nothing, was the answer. He could do nothing.

Oscar Sansom was a Realtor. He lived in Natick in a house that was almost as big as Parker's own, which meant that it was too sizable for one man. He opened his front door as the investigator walked up the path, and Parker wondered how long Sansom had been waiting for him to appear. All thoughts of Sam and Rachel were set aside. His anger could be directed. He would use it to power his search for Eklund, and hope that by doing so he could expend the worst of it.

Sansom was a small man, which made his home appear larger still. Even the doorway dwarfed him. He was slightly stooped, but in the manner of one who is too tired, and longs to sleep. Parker had seen men and women physically diminished in this way before, weighed down by suffering. Grief has its own gravity.

They shook hands, and Sansom led Parker to the kitchen. The doors they passed at either side of the hallway were closed so Parker couldn't see inside the rooms, but he didn't have to. He knew what he would find: variations on a theme of absence. This was a house bought with the intention of filling it with children. It was built for a family, and Sansom had remained within its walls in the hope that some version of this life might still be possible. To sell it would have been to admit that all hope was gone, and his wife was not coming back. So he held on to it, gliding through its empty spaces, using only a handful of rooms, keeping the others closed up but clean, just in case she returned; a small man, shrinking with the years, as the space around him increased. All this

Parker saw in a matter of moments, loss attuned to loss.

The kitchen was open plan, with a table and chairs at one end, the stove and cabinets at the other, and a nest formed of a couch and big armchairs down a small flight of steps in between, looking over a garden sheltered from view by hedges and evergreen oaks. A flat-screen TV hung on one wall, with books, newspapers, and magazines on a table before it, along with an empty coffee cup. One end of the table was covered with documents, and a pair of bedroom slippers sat beside a dining chair with worn cushions tied to the seat and back for added comfort. The space was untidy but homey, and Parker guessed this was where Sansom spent most of his time.

A few prints brightened up the walls, mostly reproduction posters from the sixties and seventies featuring Hendrix, Neil Young, and the Rolling Stones. The exception was a large black-and-white photograph, professionally mounted and framed, featuring people walking through a park in late fall, judging by the leaves on the ground. Women, children, a couple of dogs running around, but no men. It was a perfectly ordinary scene, if expertly captured, apart from one detail: all the faces were blurred, so that it was impossible to identify any individual features. Every person caught by the lens was reduced to the status of a ghost.

Sansom, who was making coffee with some fancy Italian machine, caught Parker looking at the photograph, but said nothing.

'Who took this?' Parker asked.

Sansom didn't answer immediately, just continued fussing with cups and beans.

'I did,' he said at last.

'It's very good.'

Eerie, Parker thought, but quite beautiful. The more he looked at it the more he was drawn into it, as though he might move among these frozen figures, staring into their blurred faces, until—

Well, until he became one of them himself.

'I thought I needed a hobby,' said Sansom. 'I took some classes, bought a lot of photography books. I don't use a digital camera. I'm happier working with film. I have a dark-room in my basement.'

'This isn't a digital image?'

Parker was surprised, given the degree of manipulation of the faces.

'No, that was all done the old-fashioned way. I just had to make sure the faces got less light than the rest of the image. It wasn't so hard, but it took a lot of attempts. Trial and error. I thought it might seem conceited to have it framed and put on the wall, but it's not like a whole lot of people get to see it. I don't get many visitors.'

Parker didn't have to ask why Sansom had chosen this image to display, aesthetic judgments apart. It said everything anyone needed to know about the man and his pain.

They sat at the kitchen table, and Parker asked Sansom about Eklund.

'When did you first consult him?'

'I didn't,' said Sansom. 'The initial approach came from him, after Claudia had been missing for maybe two years, but no money ever changed hands. He just offered to help where and when he could. I was suspicious at first, of course. I'd been bitten badly before, especially after Claudia first disappeared and the police started to think that maybe I'd done something to her. People, some of whom I'd considered friends, sold stories to the newspapers, and then there were all kinds of others who claimed to know something about what happened, or wanted money in return for information. I'd get letters, e-mails, calls to my office, some of them just so abusive. People can be pretty fucking shitty, you know.'

'But Eklund wasn't.'

'No, he was the real deal. When he had a little spare time he'd nose around, or get in touch with his police sources.

Mostly I think he was just nudging them, making sure they didn't let the case grow any colder than it already had. There was nothing Eklund could do about that, but if he heard anything, or I did, we'd meet or talk over the phone. I finally convinced him to let me pay his expenses, but it was really only a few bucks here and there.

'When they found Claudia, he was one of the first to come to my door. He helped me deal with what came after. He knew his way around the police, the media. He stayed in the background, but he always gave me the right advice. He told me it was good for the investigation that Claudia's body had been recovered. It would add a new impetus. It's hard to investigate a crime without a body. Except—'

'Except,' said Parker, 'now you have a body, but nobody's sure of the crime.'

Sansom nodded.

'Claudia's remains showed signs of neglect, but she died of natural causes: septicemia, from an injury to her leg. A deep cut, down to the bone. The autopsy indicated that proper medical treatment might have saved her, but obviously she didn't get it. The police have all kinds of theories. It was suggested that she could have had some kind of breakdown and fallen off the radar. It happens more often than you might think. Those folk living rough, sleeping under bridges, they're not all forgotten. There are people looking for them – friends, families – but some are just too far gone to realize it. When they die, their bodies lie around until someone finds them, or they get buried by the people they knew, or whoever was with them at the end.

'But that wasn't Claudia. She was the most balanced person I ever knew. She wasn't dull or boring – or not to me she wasn't. If she'd sensed something was wrong with her, physically or psychologically, she'd have mentioned it, or sought help. I know these things can happen without warning, and maybe I was fooling myself by trying to pretend it might have been different for Claudia because, well, she was mine, but the breakdown hypothesis never sat right with me.'

Parker recalled what Mother had told him of Mike MacKinnon's character, and his disappearance. His personality sounded remarkably similar to that of Claudia Sansom.

'And Eklund – what did he think?'

'He didn't believe it either.'

'Did he have his own theory?'

'Yes. He was always straight with me. He thought she might have been abducted. Some of the detectives agreed with him. Now it looks like they were right, because of how she was found.'

He spoke with no emotion in his voice. It was probably the only way he could talk about it. Parker didn't tell him that he had been in touch with Dawna Hall about the progress of the investigation. He wanted to hear Sansom's take on events.

'Claudia was wrapped in plastic, but otherwise she was buried naked,' said Sansom. 'They found no DNA apart from her own, nothing at all. If she'd been put in the ground by homeless people, they wouldn't have been so careful. They'd have left clues. That's what Eklund told me.'

'Did he offer to continue looking into the case?'

'He promised to keep an eye on it, but now that the police had a body to work with, he said they were best equipped to investigate.'

'Have they indicated when Claudia's remains will be returned to you?'

Sansom looked away.

'In a day or two. I'm going to have her cremated. It'll be easier to keep private.'

He turned back to Parker. His eyes were soft.

'You know, some people still think I did it, that somehow I made my own wife vanish, then magicked her up again years later. It's why I work for myself. No Realtor would employ me. I don't even sell many properties in the state. Mostly I act as an agent for wealthy buyers seeking second homes in Europe. They don't know who I am, or don't care as long as they get the property they want at the right price. Even some of my neighbors made it clear to me that they'd have preferred if I sold up and left the city, but I wouldn't go. It would have been like an admission of guilt, and I knew I hadn't done anything wrong. And if I abandoned this house, how would Claudia have found me if she came looking?'

He glanced at his watch.

'I'm sorry, but I have an appointment with a client in Boston in about an hour, and you never know how bad the damned traffic is going to be. You said on the phone that Mr. Eklund hadn't been seen in a while.'

'That's right. I was wondering when last you heard from him.'

'About two weeks ago, I think. I met him for a drink at the Fairmont.'

'May I ask what you talked about?'

'The same as always. Claudia, mostly. In a way, it was kind of a farewell drink.'

'Why do you say that?'

'With Claudia found, it was as though our connection was coming to an end. Like I told you, the investigation was back with the police, and Mr. Eklund didn't feel that he'd be able to contribute much from this point on, although he told me to call if there was ever any way he could help.'

'Did he mention any other cases he was working on?'

'No, he rarely spoke about things like that, maybe for reasons of confidentiality, just like I trusted him not to share anything private I might have told him about Claudia and me.'

'What about matters of personal interest to Eklund?'

There was only the slightest of pauses, a shifting of position by Sansom, but it was enough.

'That depends on what you mean.'

Sansom wasn't putting up a wall, exactly, but it was clear that he wasn't going to betray a confidence either. He waited for Parker to go on.

'What I mean is, did he ever talk about ghosts?'

Sansom stayed very still.

'Yes.'

'And the Capstead Martyrs, and linked deaths?'

'Yes.'

'And how did you react?'

'I thought he was joking at first. But I came to realize that he wasn't, so I started to think that maybe he was crazy. But he wasn't crazy either.'

'Did you believe him?'

Sansom shrugged.

'How should I put it? I believed that he believed, but it wasn't like he was spouting all kinds of other wild theories, or carrying one of those Ouija boards under his arm. He talked about it in a completely matter-of-fact way. It was a puzzle, and he was trying to solve it: why did a series of killings and disappearances share sightings?'

'Did you get the sense he was coming close to an answer?'

'Possibly. I think it was part of the reason why he was happy to let the police deal with my case, and limit any further involvement he might have with it. But that's all I can tell you. He didn't share much with me; it was just that there was a sense of, oh, excitement about him when we met at the Fairmont. Anticipation.'

'Did he ever suggest that Claudia's disappearance might be connected to his own inquiries into the Capstead Martyrs?'

'No.'

'And he didn't tell you of travel plans, or mention the names of anyone he might have intended to meet?'

'Not directly.'

'I don't understand.'

'He asked me if I knew of any Realtors in West Virginia. I inquired if he was planning on selling his home in Providence and moving on, because brokers in Massachusetts have complete reciprocity with West Virginia, and I'd have been glad to take care of buying or selling any property for him. I'd have looked after him, too, especially after all he'd done for me. But he said that he just wanted to find someone who might have local knowledge of transactions in the Turning Leaf area. I made some calls and gave him a couple of names.'

Turning Leaf, West Virginia: Parker tried to recall any mention of it in Eklund's notes, but was pretty sure there was none. It was something, at least. He made a note of the names of the Realtors to whom Sansom had referred Eklund.

Sansom stood, indicating that it was time to leave. Parker gave Sansom his card and asked him to call if he thought of anything else. He wondered how many times in his life he'd said that to people – a lot – and how often they actually got back to him with something useful: a lot less. Sansom grabbed a coat and a briefcase and walked him to the door. Parker waited while he locked up, then watched as Sansom hit the button to open the garage. A new red Kia Forte stood waiting, and beside it, leaning against the wall, was a batch of FOR SALE signs.

'One of those is going to be out here pretty soon,' said Sansom.

'You're selling?'

'This house is too big for me. It always was, but I couldn't put it on the market, not until I was sure Claudia wasn't coming back.'

'Where will you go?'

'Europe, I think – France, or Italy. I've spent years buying and selling nice properties over there for other people. It's time I considered finding one for myself. I want to go where nobody knows me. I'll have Claudia's ashes interred somewhere nearby once I've settled on a place to live.'

'What about the investigation?'

'What about it? It'll go on without me. There's nothing more I can do or say that will help. But deep down, I don't believe they'll ever find out what really happened to my wife. If uncovering her body couldn't provide them with clues, then what will? And it won't bring her back. I hope that whoever took her from me dies kicking and screaming, and burns in the next world, but I won't let it destroy me. All I have left of Claudia is what I can remember of my life with her, and every day it seems like I forget a little bit more of it. So I'll go somewhere new, and I won't work so hard, and I'll wait for the time when I can be with her again.'

They shook hands once more.

'I hope you find Mr. Eklund safe and sound,' said Sansom. 'He was a good man.'

'Yes,' said Parker, 'it sounds like he was.'

64

If it is true that nature abhors a vacuum, then criminality regards it as a business opportunity. The death of Caspar Webb had left a void that, in another time, might have been ruthlessly exploited by both his rivals and elements within his own network.

But Webb was no ordinary criminal. His connections to illegal activity were complex and nebulous, which was why he had never even been formally interviewed by any law enforcement agency, let alone charged with any crime. Only a handful of those closest to him were even aware of the machinery behind his operation, and most of those, with the exception of Mother and Philip, were now dead. The secretive nature of Webb's business arrangements was the first obstacle presented to those from outside who might have wished to fight over his spoils.

The second obstacle was the absence in the region of anything resembling the organized crime families of old, of traditional structures capable of absorbing or dividing most of Webb's business without undue bloodshed. The death in 2015 of Frank Angiulo, the accountant for the Mafia crew led by his brother Jerry, had provoked in the Northeast waves of nostalgia more usually associated with the death of a beloved entertainer. Frank was the last of the Angiulo brothers, who had ruled Boston from an office in the North End for more than two decades until the actions of Whitey Bulger and a cabal of rogue FBI agents succeeded in royally screwing the pooch for venerable criminal conspiracies in New England.

The Angiulos were the mobsters of legend, who greeted each other with kisses and savored espressos in the cafés of Hanover Street, who left bodies on sidewalks and in the trunks of cars out by Logan Airport, but were scrupulous about not killing women, civilians, or cops. They kept the North End free of crime – apart from their own criminality, obviously – just as fear of Whitey Bulger ensured that the streets of South Boston, and later the rest of the city, remained safe for anyone who didn't cross him. But now all those old certainties were gone: Frank Angiulo had joined his brothers in the ground, and Whitey Bulger's reign was over. Organized crime had been replaced by disorganized crime conducted in a Babel of languages, and the remnants of the old order could aspire only to survive in reduced circumstances, and reminisce about better times.

It was Erik Lastrade who made the initial approach, confirming to Philip that a channel of communication was open. The two men headed up to Boston in a car rented in the name of one of Erik's girlfriends, but had to drive around for a while before they found a parking spot off Commonwealth Avenue. Philip didn't want to leave the vehicle in a parking garage. Even the best of them were dark, and if everything went south he didn't want to end up anywhere they could be hemmed in. Lastrade tried to reassure him that he had nothing to worry about, that this was just a chance to talk, but like all duplicitous, unreliable men, Philip saw his own moral imperfections reflected in every face he met.

The meeting was to take place in a tony bar and restaurant on Newbury Street, far from the North End or any of the usual haunts of the men they were meeting, who existed in a state of barely restrained paranoia about the surveillance capabilities of law enforcement. Lately, according to Lastrade, they had become obsessed with drones, to the extent of shooting one down with a pistol somewhere near Revere

Beach, necessitating the payment of compensation to its owner once they'd confirmed his address and warned him against reporting the incident to anyone in uniform.

Three of them, all men, were seated at a table in back when Philip and Lastrade arrived. Two were in their early thirties and dressed in shirts and sweaters. *No guinea chic for these guys*, Philip thought. The third was in his late sixties and looked less comfortable than the others in these surroundings. He wore a wool jacket over a cardigan, and a red tie so wrinkled that it was beyond help from any iron. His head was mostly bald and blotched with psoriasis. An old cap lay on the chair beside him. Philip guessed he might have been happier keeping it on, but didn't want to look like a – well, like what he was, which was the right guy in the wrong place.

Lastrade knew one of the younger men, Stefano – or Stevie. It was through him that the meeting had been arranged. Stefano made the introductions to Anthony, the second member of the youth wing, and Bernardo, the older man. He didn't need to bother with any family names. The quintet made some polite small talk about the weather while half glancing at menus. The restaurant was new, with a vaguely Mediterranean edge to its food, so they ordered plates of appetizers to share, and Bernardo asked for a bowl of soup as well, because he was feeling the cold. Nobody wanted to drink wine, so they stuck to water and soda.

They didn't begin speaking in earnest until the food came. Stevie did most of the talking, Anthony nodding along with him. Bernardo seemed more interested in slurping his soup, and barely looked up from it as the conversation went on around him. Philip wasn't fooled, but he still wished that the old man would just dispense with the theatrics, or at least eat his fucking soup quietly.

'Our understanding,' said Stevie, 'is that Caspar Webb's operations are being wound down. In light of this, we've made alternative arrangements, although as a gesture of goodwill – a thank-you for our business and cooperation over the years – introductions to useful contacts were provided by Mr. Webb's representatives.'

Philip hadn't been aware of this, but didn't react beyond a closing of his right fist under the table in a spasm of frustration. Mother must have authorized it. Jesus, she was handing over contacts worth a fortune to these people as a *thank-you*?

'Crumbs from the table,' said Philip.

'Very good crumbs,' said Stevie. 'Potentially very lucrative.'

'What I'm offering is more valuable.'

'You say.'

Philip gave him the pitch. He could offer women from Eastern Europe and Africa to put out as whores, and access to desperate refugees from enough countries to fill half an atlas, because as far as Philip could tell, everyone everywhere wanted to be someplace else and was prepared to pay well for the trip. He threw in counterfeit clothing, perfume, liquor, and whatever else he could think of to pique the interest of these men.

'All that we got,' said Stevie.

'I'm offering more, and better, at a cheaper price.'

Stevie looked skeptical. It was clear he wasn't interested, or not enough.

'You called it,' he said. 'These are crumbs, and we're already full up on them.'

'What about drugs? You full up on them, too?'

That caught their attention, and now that he had it, he wanted to keep it.

'Here's how I see it,' said Philip. 'You got cocaine, and you got marijuana, both through Sinaloa, but it all got fucked up with that fruit thing.'

The Mexicans had taken over operations in the Northeast from the Dominicans, who had long controlled the market.

The 'fruit thing' referred to an elaborate FBI sting in 2012, in which feds posing as Italian gangsters offered to set up fake fruit distribution companies, ostensibly to ship Sinaloa cocaine from the Northeast to Spain in return for a twenty percent cut of the product. The sting led to arrests in Spain and Massachusetts, and the seizure of 760 pounds of cocaine. Sinaloa had been badly burned in the process, and relations with the Italians had suffered, all because of a bunch of feds wearing cheap leather jackets.

Meanwhile, the 'Ndrangheta in Calabria had overtaken the other criminal organizations, including Cosa Nostra, to become the dominant force in cocaine trafficking, extending its reach to Australia and the United States. Its *locali* in these countries answered to similar *locali* back home, creating a global cooperative network. The rumor was the 'Ndrangheta now had more money than it knew what to do with. These men sitting with Philip and Lastrade were not Calabrian. That was one of their biggest problems.

'What are you offering instead?' asked Stevie.

'Heroin.'

Bernardo continued supping his soup, but his eyes flicked to Stevie. The nod, when it came, was barely perceptible.

'Caspar Webb didn't deal in heroin,' said Stevie.

'Because the network wasn't in place when he started out, and he was too sick to take advantage of it by the time it was. But we have the means of transport, and the suppliers.'

'When you say "we", who do you mean?' asked Anthony, giving up on nodding along. 'Vincent Garronne is dead, and no one has seen Terry Nakem in months. Nobody expects to see him again, neither.' He waited, realized that nobody was going to bite, then went on. 'With them gone, and Webb dead, that just leaves a couple of lawyers, an old lady in Providence signing checks, and you two. No offense, but last time I looked, you were just spear carriers.'

Philip waited a beat or two.

'I'm Caspar Webb's son.'

Stevie laughed.

'The fuck you are. He didn't have no sons.'

'None that he acknowledged.'

'And we're supposed to take your word for this?'

'There are people in Europe with blood ties to Caspar Webb, and they won't deal with anyone from outside his circle, because that's how they work. The truth of what I've told you will lie in my ability to supply you with product.'

Bernardo put down his spoon and wiped his mouth with a napkin.

'And where will this heroin be coming from?' he asked. His voice was a mixture of Boston and the old country, and he slurred a little, like he'd had some kind of stroke.

'Afghanistan,' said Philip. Where else did he think opium came from – Philly? The route was clear: Badakhshan-Doshi-Bamiyan-Herat, then through Iran and into Turkey.

'And refined in Turkish labs?'

Philip nodded.

'If it's coming from Turkey, then it's those ISIS mother-fuckers who are supplying it.'

'Is that a problem?'

'It will be when they fly a plane into a building over here, or go shooting up an office or a school.'

'They're not over here,' said Philip. 'They're over there.'

Bernardo looked at him closely.

'If you're Caspar Webb's son,' he said, 'how come you're so fucking stupid?'

'Hey, hey!' said Lastrade. 'Come on.'

Bernardo raised a finger, Stevie shook his head at Lastrade in warning, and the table went silent.

'I only agreed to speak with you because my nephew vouched for your friend here, and your friend vouched for you, but we're done now,' said Bernardo. 'I don't know what you're trying to pull here, but you should listen to me, because this is free advice. I don't care whose son you are, but you try bringing in heroin from Turkey and you'll end up dead or in a federal jumpsuit. They won't just try you on trafficking charges, but for aiding terrorists. You got some short memory if you don't remember what happened here in 2013. In case you forgot, the Boston Marathon got blown up by Islamists. Now you want us to put our money into their pockets, just so you can live out some fucking fantasy about being a big-time drug dealer? Get the fuck out of here. Go back to Providence, and maybe I'll forget I ever saw your face.'

Bernardo stood, grabbed his cap, jammed it on his scarred head, and started for the door. Anthony joined him, leaving Stevie to stare at Lastrade in disappointment.

'Jesus, Erik,' he said.

'Hey,' said Philip. 'Don't look at him, look at me.'

'I don't—'

Philip didn't let him continue.

'We'll be talking again, whatever the old man thinks. I'm not going away.'

'You ought to pay attention when people offer you advice,' said Stevie. 'Especially when it comes from someone like my uncle.'

He followed the others from the restaurant. Philip waited until they were gone, then tossed some bills on the table. His face burned with humiliation, but he hadn't lied to Stevie. He wasn't about to go away, and he wouldn't forget what had just happened, or what had been said.

'What now?' said Lastrade.

Philip patted Lastrade on the back, to show that he wasn't mad at him.

'We make some calls.'

65

Rachel sat on the edge of the bed. All she could see of her daughter was the back of her head. Sam's face was buried in the pillow, the way it would be when she pretended to be upset as part of a game, or wanted to hide her laughter, but neither was the case now.

Rachel felt worn out. She had been tired ever since Sam was abducted, and each day the exhaustion dug deeper and deeper, like a dampness seeping into her bones. She'd spoken about it with her therapist, and he'd suggested a course of medication, which she rejected. She was already experiencing life at one remove, distanced from her parents, her daughter, even her old self. A course of antidepressants wasn't going to bring her any closer to them, and it wouldn't solve the underlying problem, which was her rage at the damage that had been done to her world by the events of the previous year. Jesus, her daughter had almost died. The man who took her was maybe only minutes away from killing her when he—

When he what, exactly? That was the question. Technically, he'd suffered a series of massive hemorrhages, simultaneously yet independently occurring, as though unseen devices had exploded inside him, bursting blood vessels in his arms, legs, chest, face, and ultimately his brain. A full explanation was still not forthcoming; the best anyone could come up with was some form of systemic collapse, but Rachel understood enough about medspeak to know that this was the equivalent of a mass shrugging of shoulders, another great don't-know added to the pyre.

Not that Rachel cared much either way. Her only regret was that the man who had abducted Sam didn't appear to be in any pain, and was likely to remain in a persistent vegetative state until he finally died. What mattered was that her ex-lover, Charlie Parker, had brought this horror down on them all by participating in what amounted to a paramilitary assault on the abductor's community, even if that community deserved everything that had befallen it, and certainly much worse. Parker had also done so mere months after their daughter watched a policewoman being shot and seriously injured, and the individual responsible die moments before he could turn the same weapon on her father. Twice his actions had put their daughter at risk. There wasn't going to be a third time.

But how to explain the legal implications to the child before her, and how had she found out about them anyway, if that was what the current hysteria was about? Rachel didn't think Sam had overheard any phone calls, but she couldn't be sure. The child was beyond smart for her years, with a stillness and quietude to her, when she chose. She was the only kid Rachel knew who could vanish in a small room, yet she was still just a little girl, and she couldn't protect herself. No matter how hard it might be, she'd have to be made to understand that her mother was only trying to do what was best for her. If anything happened to Sam, Rachel didn't think she could go on living.

'Are you going to talk to me?' Rachel asked, but received no reply. 'If you won't talk to me, how I am supposed to know what's wrong?' She almost said 'what I've done wrong', but caught herself just in time. She wasn't about to give that hostage to fortune.

The voice, when it came, was muffled by the pillow.

'Why are you stopping me from seeing Dad?'

So that was it. Jesus.

'Why do you say that?'

'Because it's true.'

'No, it isn't.'

'I saw the letter, in your office.'

Again, Rachel stopped herself from asking what Sam thought she was doing going through her mother's private papers. They could come back to it later. Also Sam, for all her quirks, was very conscious of boundaries, both her own and those of others. If she'd come across the letter, then it was certainly because she'd been looking for something else, something perfectly innocent. But how much of the lawyer's letter could she have comprehended? Enough, apparently.

'Did you understand everything the letter said?'

'No. I understood a lot, though, and I looked some of the other words up online.'

Despite the awfulness of the situation, Rachel had to stop herself from laughing. God, this child! She reached out to stroke Sam's head, and an odd detail muscled its way to the forefront of memory.

The bird.

When the police had arrived at the motel room, they found the man who'd abducted Sam lying on the bathroom floor. Someone had burned the remains of a bird in the sink. Sam said the man had done it, and the detectives ascribed some ritualistic element to the action, especially given what they'd learned about his community. But later, when Rachel brought Sam home from the hospital, she found a book of matches in the pocket of her daughter's jacket, along with a couple of small brown feathers.

It's not important, Rachel told herself. *It doesn't matter.*

But another voice that sounded almost like her own said, *Oh, but it does.*

'I want you to be able to see your father,' said Rachel, 'but we have to take precautions. There are people who would like to hurt him, and if they can, they'll try to do it through you. That's what the man who took you wanted. You'll still be able to spend time with your dad. He can come here and see you at the house, just like he used to, and we can go visit him in Portland. It's just that the two of you can't hang out together in the same way you once did. It's not possible, not after what almost happened. You know this, Sam. Your father does, too.'

'You mean that Dad says it's okay?'

Sam couldn't help herself. She looked up. Her eyes were red from crying, and her face was desolate.

Rachel could have lied and said that, yes, her father agreed, but she had vowed never to lie to her daughter.

'I haven't spoken to him about it, but he'll agree. He'll do whatever is necessary to keep you safe from harm.'

'Then why do you need a lawyer?'

It was like being in a boxing match. You never knew where the next jab was going to come from.

'Because it has to be formal. It's how these things work.'

'Dad won't let this happen.'

'Sam—'

'He won't! I don't want to live with you anymore. I hate you. I want to live with him. I want to be with my daddy!'

And with those words, the dam that Rachel had placed around all her sadness and anguish in order to keep functioning was breached. The sound she heard herself make was like the yelp of a wounded animal, its paw pierced by a spike or broken in a trap. She tried to stand, but her legs wouldn't move. Her stomach heaved, and she tasted stale coffee. She wanted to scream, but her throat seized up. An aspect small and fragile broke deep inside her, and she knew that it could never be repaired.

Sam saw her mother go pale, then sway as though she were about to faint. Tears began to fall from her eyes, but her face remained absolutely still, her lips parted in a little oval of shock. It was like watching a doll cry, and Sam knew that she had done this, all with a few words that were out of her mouth before she even knew what she was saying. She wanted to take them back, to swallow them down like bad medicine, rewinding time. She'd set out to wound her mother, and now that she'd succeeded she wanted nothing more than to unwound and unspeak.

'I'm sorry, Mommy,' she said. 'I didn't mean it. Don't cry. Please, don't cry.'

She scrambled across the bed and wrapped her arms around her mother, whispering her name, saying 'Sorry' over and over, but Rachel's arms remained by her side, and whatever her eyes were fixed upon was not in the room with them. Sam heard the bedroom door open, and her grandmother entered just as her mother began to pull away from her. Sam tried to hold on, but Rachel was too heavy. She fell from her daughter's arms and dropped to the floor.

66

Parker hadn't learned much from his conversation with Oscar Sansom, although he was reasonably content to dismiss, for now, a connection between Eklund's interest in the mystery of Claudia Sansom's disappearance and the private investigator's own vanishing act. From what Sansom had told him, it sounded as though Eklund was in the process of disengaging from any real involvement in the case by the time he went missing, and his previous efforts appeared to have been tangential in the first place, as well as largely ineffective.

In the meantime, he wished Oscar Sansom well. Sansom exhibited a peculiar combination of resignation and optimism: resignation to the likelihood that the years-long path his wife had taken from disappearance to death might never be revealed to him, and optimism that it might be possible to start again, or at least live out the rest of his days in the knowledge that his wife was no longer lost in this world.

It was time, therefore, to forget Sansom, and move on to Michelle Souliere and Tobey Thayer, but even as he left Natick, Parker couldn't shake a sense of disquiet. *Why Claudia Sansom?* he thought. *Why should this case, of all others, have attracted Eklund's interest?*

He thought that he might come back to the Sansom business, given time.

Most of what Parker knew about Waterbury, Connecticut, could be summed up in two words: brass and watches. Brass manufacturing was the foundation of the city's wealth in the nineteenth and twentieth centuries, but that came to an end in the 1960s when Chase Brass moved its operations to Ohio. The watch industry grew alongside the brass, Waterbury being responsible for the manufacture of Robert Ingersoll's one-dollar *Yankee* pocket watch in the late 1800s, and later the Mickey Mouse watch, too. An Asian company now owned the Ingersoll brand, which was, to a certain kind of person, an example of modern America's problems in a nutshell.

As with Sansom, Parker had called Michelle Souliere ahead of time to make sure she was willing to meet with him, using Ian Williamson as a reference if required. Souliere sounded interested, but asked him to give her a call when he was an hour out of town. She told him she had a busy schedule over the coming days and didn't want to leave him waiting for too long, or be forced to wait on him in turn. Parker made the call when he reckoned he was about fifty minutes from Waterbury, but Souliere's cell phone went straight to voice mail. He left a message, and tried again as he was entering Waterbury, with the same result.

It was growing dark, and not only because the afternoon light was fading: gray clouds were moving in from the west, and more snow was forecast. It wouldn't be heavy, but it would make driving a bitch for a while. Even if he managed to make contact with Souliere in the next hour, Parker didn't think there would be much point in later inching his way through bad weather just to have to spend the night in some roadside motel. He decided he would find somewhere in Waterbury to spend the night and wait out the latest storm.

Souliere lived in South End, a large neighborhood originally settled by French-Canadian immigrants, but their descendants now shared the area with a big Latin-American community, judging by the signs and storefronts Parker glimpsed as he drove through. He also saw a lot of empty factories and deserted lots, a reminder of how far Waterbury had fallen from its glory days.

Souliere lived not far from St. Anne's Church, in a two-story wood house that was neither the best nor the worst kept on the street. The paintwork was fresh enough not to be a blight, but not so new as to attract the attention of anyone looking for signs of obvious prosperity as a prelude to a burglary. The front porch was empty of junk, and a white fence surrounded the garden. Parker could see no lights burning inside, and there was no car in the drive. He parked outside and called Souliere's cell phone a third time, but ended the connection as soon as he heard her voicemail message begin again. He drove downtown and took a room at the Marriott. He checked in with Angel and Louis, who were already most of the way to Greensburg, PA, home of Tobey Thayer. Like Parker, they'd decided that it was smarter to wait out the weather, and make better time in the morning. They were staying somewhere called the Prescott Inn on the New York-Pennsylvania border, in the Emily Dickinson Suite – or, as Angel put it, the 'Depressed Poets Wing.'

'We got a lot of chintz,' he said. 'Expensive chintz, but still chintz.'

'How expensive?'

'Four hundred bucks a night expensive, although we did also go for the champagne upgrade.'

'Of course you would.'

'Is that sarcasm?'

'It might be.'

'We figured Ross would want us to be comfortable. Where are you?'

'Waterbury. In a Courtyard by Marriott.'

'Ask for an upgrade.'

'It's a Marriott. They already gave me free water.'

'Well, then you got no cause to complain.'

Parker conceded that he had a point.

'How are you feeling?' he asked Angel.

'I'm worried about the direction our country is taking, and

I hope rehab works for Sabathia or the Yankees will be another twenty-five million in the hole.'

'Very funny. Your health, idiot.'

'I'm okay. A little sore.'

'Maybe you should have stayed in Maine.'

'And done what, waited for summer? I need distraction. You hear any more about the Sam thing?'

Parker told him the latest. Angel sympathized.

'Moxie's right,' he said. 'You have to keep your distance, and let him play your hand for you.'

'I think I need distraction, too,' said Parker. 'It's a mess.'

'Look at it this way: if you require bodyguards every time you meet Sam, we can do it. Tell your lawyer to keep that card up his sleeve. It could be what wins the game.'

Parker tried to imagine Rachel's face if that was the best suggestion he could offer. It took some of the edge off his anger, and dulled the sadness.

'I should be with you by tomorrow evening,' he said. 'When you get to Greensburg, see if you can shadow Thayer.'

'Are you worried for him?'

Parker had his cell phone on speaker. He glanced at the screen, but there was no sign of a response from Souliere.

'Not yet,' he replied, 'but consider it a fluid situation.'

67

The Collector stood in the basement of Jaycob Eklund's home, staring at the map and notes on the wall.

He had gained entry by the simplest of expedients: repeatedly activating the alarm. The first time he did so, by shaking a window at the back of the house, it took just ten minutes for someone to arrive to investigate: a man in a gray BMW, whom the Collector recalled as being among those who had escorted Parker and his friends to their meeting with Mother. He checked the exterior of the house before entering and resetting the alarm. The Collector waited until he left, counted to twenty, then activated the alarm from the same window. The same man returned, made another circuit of the property, went into the house a second time, and returned to his car. He did not drive away immediately, but first made a call.

When the Collector shook the window again, the alarm did not go off.

Now, in the basement, he wondered what additional material Parker might have discovered and removed from there. He found it only slightly curious that Philip and Mother had not reclaimed what was taken. Presumably they had reached some accommodation with Parker, recognizing that his aims might equally serve their own, while remaining cautious enough to ensure that Eklund's property continued to be secured. The Collector examined each location on the map, and read the details variously handwritten and typed beside them. From what he could gather, they represented a summary of information contained elsewhere, probably in the files acquired by Parker. Still, there was enough in the names and dates on the wall to enable the Collector to build a picture of Eklund's thoughts, and suggest answers to some troubling questions, principal among them being why Donn Routh was so careful to conceal himself, and why his death had sent a ripple through the hollow brood that followed the Collector.

The Collector was unfamiliar with the Brethren, and the name Peter Magus meant nothing to him. Before the night was out, he intended to fill both gaps in his knowledge. He made a cursory search of Eklund's home before leaving, but found nothing else to interest him, and didn't even bother to hide the evidence of his trespass. He dumped the contents of drawers on bedroom floors, and scattered paperwork across desks and chairs. It didn't matter: Eklund would never be returning to this house, because Eklund was almost certainly dead.

Parker ate at Diorio's, an Italian restaurant on Bank that had been around, in one form or another, for almost a century. He tried Michelle Souliere twice more, but had no more luck than before. He didn't know the woman, so he had no reason to sound the alarm just yet. There were all kinds of reasons why she might have her cell phone powered down, and their agreement to meet was relatively informal. He was still working on the McCartney biography he'd picked up in Portsmouth. McCartney was in a Japanese prison, and deeply regretting his attempt to bring a half-pound of marijuana into the country. Apart from being kind of dumb when it came to weed and Japan, Parker decided that the book hadn't altered his opinion about McCartney much at all. He still liked him a lot.

He walked back to his hotel after the meal, thinking that he wouldn't sleep, but he was out as soon as his head hit the pillow. It wasn't physical tiredness so much as emotional exhaustion, and he didn't dream.

Rachel Wolfe lay in a hospital bed at the University of Vermont Medical Center, feeling like an idiot. She'd tried to tell her parents, and later the emergency room doctor, that she had just fainted, and needed to rest, but the hospital insisted on keeping her under observation for at least one night. Sam's hysterics made the whole incident more traumatic, and she had only become marginally calmer once it became clear her mom wasn't about to die. Rachel tried to convince Sam that it wasn't her fault, but she didn't think the message was getting through. Reluctantly, Rachel agreed to let a pediatrician give Sam something to help her sleep. She hated the idea of medicating her child, but she was genuinely concerned about Sam. Sam wouldn't, or couldn't, stop crying.

The TV in the room was dark. Rachel didn't feel like watching anything. She had a book and some magazines by her bedside, but the thought of even looking at print made her dizzy. The attending physician had asked her if she was under any particular stress at the moment, and she couldn't help but laugh. She warned her parents not to say anything to Parker about her collapse if he called, although she doubted he would. They were also under orders to keep Sam away from phones, just in case she took it upon herself to inform her father of this new development. Again, Rachel doubted that Sam would try to call Parker. She was ashamed of what had been said, and she wouldn't want to share that shame with him.

God, Rachel thought, *every child is probably duty-bound to say I hate you to her parents at some point. I just thought we might get as far as adolescence before Sam did it.*

She had the strangest urge to discuss Sam with Parker. It was the kind of incident she would have shared with him had they been on better terms. But now the man with whom she instinctively wanted to speak about the child they had created together – the man with whom she had always spoken about such matters, even after they'd separated – was the last to whom she could turn.

She wasn't going to cry again. She'd cried enough for one day.

She was about to settle down to sleep when she heard footsteps from the hallway outside her room. They were light, and fast. She glanced up and saw a child pass by, a girl with blond hair. She couldn't have been more than five or six, and was barefoot. It was late. If she was a patient, what was she doing out of bed?

'Hey,' Rachel called. 'Are you all right?'

The footsteps stopped, but the girl did not reappear. Carefully, Rachel got out of bed and walked to the door.

'Honey, I was—'

The hallway was empty except for a nurse standing at the station, reading a file. She looked up when she saw Rachel.

'Ms. Wolfe, can I help you with something?'

'I saw a little girl pass by my door. I think she might be a patient.'

The nurse shook her head.

'You must have been dreaming. There are no children in this wing.'

The nurse came to her and gently led her back to her bed.

'I'm certain I saw a girl,' said Rachel.

'I was there,' said the nurse, 'and I didn't see anyone but you.'

Nevertheless, at Rachel's insistence she agreed to check the adjoining rooms.

'I told you,' she said upon her return. 'No children. Now try to sleep.'

And after a time, Rachel did.

Philip was drinking alone in a bar on Washington Street, in the part of Providence known as Downcity. The bar was old school; the music wasn't loud and the TV above in the corner was on mute. Philip scratched at the crook of his left arm, where Lastrade had removed the blood to be couriered to New York, the final step in authenticating his claim to be Caspar Webb's son. Lastrade professed to know what he was doing, but the needle hurt like fuck going in, and the skin around the hole was bruised and tender.

A couple of students were sitting in a booth, drinking some overpriced foreign beer with a name Philip couldn't even pronounce. His phone had rung three times since he started drinking, and he'd ignored it each time. He didn't want to talk to Mother.

He'd been bullshitting Lastrade when he said he was going to make some calls after the meeting with the Italians. He didn't have anyone he could call. Bernardo and his people, for all the diminution of their power and position, were still men of influence: no other parties could offer the kind of score he needed to prove himself. Philip had been at the periphery of other deals over the years, and knew the names of half a dozen individuals who'd dealt with Webb, but they were all bit players, little fish. Only Mother had access to the names that mattered, and she wasn't about to share those with her son. Without Lastrade's connections, Philip wouldn't even have been able to get to Bernardo and his people, and look how well that turned out.

When he was halfway through his third drink, he began thinking about taking Mother up on her offer. He could go away for a while, live it up. When he returned, he'd be able to enjoy a life of comfort. He wouldn't have to work, not if he didn't want to. He could go to college, study something. He was able to draw. His art teacher in high school had been convinced of his potential. He could apply to Rhode Island School of Design. If they turned him down, he might convince Mother to make a donation, see if that might change their mind.

'Fuck it,' he said aloud, and one of the students turned and stared at him.

'What are you looking at, bitch?'

She turned away. He'd killed their conversation, though, that was for sure. Within a couple of minutes, they were gone.

No, he wasn't going to take Mother's dime. If he did, he might as well just cut his own balls off and throw them in the river. The world would look at him like he was just a momma's boy, and he was more, much more. Terry Nakem had learned that, right at the end; Vincent Garronne, too. They'd died within days of each other, both by his hand. He'd shown Mother what he could do, and it was more than just putting old men out of their misery. But did it make any difference to her?

No, so whatever followed would be on her head.

His phone started vibrating again. This time it wasn't Mother calling, but Lastrade. He decided to pick up. Erik might want to join him. They could find a club, talk to some girls – proper local girls, not those stuck-up student whores. Philip didn't have much interest in women, but he knew it would piss off Mother if he brought a girl back to their apartment.

'Yeah,' he said.

'Where are you?'

Philip named the bar.

'I'm coming to get you,' said Lastrade.

'Why?'

'Stevie got in touch with me. It's on. You hear me? It's *on*.'

68

Michelle Souliere was an unlikely debunker of psychics, ghost hunters, and apocalyptic conspiracy theorists. She loved fantasy and horror literature, and was an associate member of the Horror Writers Association and the H. P. Lovecraft Historical Society. That she was also a member of the American Humanist Association and the Skeptics Society caused her no difficulty whatsoever, as she was quite capable of distinguishing between fantasy and reality. Just because something entertained her didn't mean she had to believe in it. Actually, it was all the more entertaining if she didn't.

She was a dark, pretty woman, and despite Sumner's suspicions to the contrary, contentedly heterosexual. She enjoyed an interestingly eccentric relationship with a games designer who couldn't quite believe his luck in landing someone like her, but who wasn't so smitten that he threatened her privacy or independence. She was proud that her home was furnished only with gently used items, which included much of her extensive collection of books. For regular companionship, she had a cat named Creswell.

Her cell phone sat on the table before her. A series of meetings, both personal and professional, had run late that day, with the last not concluding until after nine p.m. As soon as she turned her cell phone back on, she was greeted by messages from the private detective named Charlie Parker. She decided to wait until she got home, or even the next morning, before returning his calls, mainly to ensure that she wouldn't have to meet him that night. She was tired, and had survived the day on bottled water, bad coffee, and worse pastries. She wanted a bath, a glass of wine, and a hot meal. Parker could wait.

Oddly, her first meeting with Jaycob Eklund had been similarly delayed, although on that occasion it was he, not she, who was responsible. Still, they'd been destined to meet – not in a romantic sense, or even on any significant level of friendship, as they'd never grown close, but because, like him, she had for a number of years been quietly and discreetly collating information on the Capstead Martyrs and their leader, the one who called himself Peter Magus.

The reason for her caution was initially different from Eklund's. He had convinced himself that some vestige of the Capstead Martyrs – or the Brethren, as he generally termed them – still existed, both physically present in the form of descendants and as something more ethereal. Consequently, he was wary of drawing attention to his inquiries.

She, by contrast, saw in the story of the Martyrs the potential for bringing together any number of subjects with which she was fascinated, among them nineteenth-century American frontier history, murder, false preachers, and esoteric belief systems – in the case of the Martyrs, a potent compound of alchemy, eschatology, the apocryphal scriptures, angel lore, and demonology that, as far as she could tell, was entirely the creation of Peter Magus himself.

What Eklund's theories added to this already heady brew was more bloodshed, and Souliere was savvy enough to realize that blood sold books. She made it clear to him that she still wasn't fully prepared to accept his view that all of the disappearances and killings pinpointed by him were linked to the Capstead Martyrs, but at least a few were interesting in that regard. As for the sightings, she'd encountered enough instances of collusion, hysteria, and miscommunication to be able to dismiss that part of Eklund's tale virtually without a second thought, although the consistency of the witness statements was a factor worth addressing in her book, perhaps in a chapter relating to the contaminant potential of mythologies.

But the figure of the Magus fascinated her. He would have been worthy of examination if only as an example of the transformative power of the immigrant dream, and the possibilities for reinvention offered by the United States in pioneer times.

Few images of the Magus existed. Given his activities, and those of his followers, he was reluctant to permit himself to be photographed, even allowing for his distinctive appearance. But perhaps in a moment of vanity, and spurred by a recognition that his pursuers were closing in for the kill, he consented to having a daguerreotype made of himself shortly before the retreat to Capstead. Souliere possessed a copy of it, as did Eklund. It depicted a tall, thin man dressed in the black suit of a preacher, his hands hanging loosely by his sides. His hair was long and red, and his skull was misshapen and pitted, a consequence of the violent existence that he led. In the photograph, the Magus was facing the camera, his distinctive beard disguising the weakness of his chin, and the angle of the lens hiding the flattened profile of which contemporary records spoke.

The Magus's left eye bulged, which Souliere believed might have been a symptom of Graves' disease, or even a form of cancer: the Magus was said to have suffered diarrhea and fevers in the final months of his life, which, like the bulging of the left eye, were symptoms of neuroblastoma. DNA analysis of the Magus's remains might have provided a definitive answer had his body not been badly burned during the Capstead siege, and the corpse thrown in the Mississippi, denying him a proper burial as further punishment for his sins. Meanwhile, the right side of the Magus's face was almost entirely covered by scar tissue, a souvenir of the Brethren's attack on the Kjellson homestead near Marietta, Ohio. The patriarch of the family, Bjorn Kjellson, turned out not to be quite as dead as was thought, and managed to get off a shotgun blast that left the Magus near blind in one eye. Kjellson's sister, who lived in Chillicothe, was named Agata, and she married a man named Christer Eklund, who was Jaycob Eklund's great-great-great-grandfather. For Jaycob, therefore, the Capstead Martyrs were a matter of personal interest, with a specific connection to his family's past.

Souliere blinked, and a single droplet of blood exploded on the kitchen table. She coughed, and the droplet was lost in a greater spray of red, but she barely noticed. She had already forgotten about the two people behind her, even though one of them – the woman – had stuck a knife in her. Souliere had put up a good fight before the end, though, and managed to land one particularly sharp blow to the bitch's cheek. Souliere might have taken her, too, if the bastard with her hadn't rabbit-punched her on the back of the head, leaving Souliere momentarily stunned and open to the blade.

None of that was of consequence now. She was dying, and her attention was fixed on the man standing before her. The Magus didn't look quite as he did in the daguerreotype. That version of himself was wounded and tired, corrupted by years of predation and rapine. This one glowed. The scarring to his face was gone, and his head was perfectly smooth. Only his eyes were cloudy, with a milky-gray cast to them like water mixed with bleach. She saw other figures moving behind him, mostly women. Given time, she might have been able to put names to them.

The knife had felt very cold when it entered her, which surprised her. Even as the coldness spread through her system, her body remained warm. She didn't know how that could be. The Magus might have been able to tell her, but she didn't want to ask him. She didn't like having him in her kitchen. His presence made her feel dirty.

She heard a mewing sound from the back door: Creswell returning from his evening wanderings. The cat flap was broken, and she'd been forced to seal it up temporarily to keep out the cold until she could get around to replacing it. She willed the cat to go away. She didn't want them to kill Creswell.

The Magus was watching her. He was very still. She thought she could detect some residue of dark pupils in the pale fathoms of his eyes. They reminded her of frogspawn.

She coughed again. It hurt, but not as much as before. She wished that she'd replied to the detective's messages. He might have been able to save her from this.

The cat stopped mewing.

The Magus and his people vanished.

The cold went away.

It was done.

69

Parker woke shortly before eight a.m. It didn't take long for his concerns about the situation with Sam to gather like clouds on the horizon, but he did his best to set them aside. He had work to do, and his personal problems wouldn't help him to do it any better.

He reached for his phone. He always left it on because, like any parent, he lived in fear of being out of contact in the event of a problem with his child. There was still no sign of contact from Michelle Souliere. He called her number again – he knew it by heart now, even with a redial button – and was surprised to hear it ring. He waited, but nobody picked up, and eventually the familiar voice message sounded in his ear once more.

He grabbed a coffee in the lobby of the hotel, checked out, and drove over to South End. A car now stood in Souliere's drive: a lovely old blue VW Beetle that, judging by its condition, was clearly its owner's pride and joy. Parker pulled up to the curb, opened the front gate, and walked up to the house. He rang the doorbell and waited, but nobody answered. He tried again, this time holding down the bell for long enough to be considered rude if Souliere did respond, but there was still no response from inside.

Parker called Souliere's number and heard it ring twice: once in his ear, and the second time from somewhere in the house. The ringing in the house ceased, and he heard Souliere's by now familiar voice speaking from his phone: 'Hi, this is Michelle. I'm sorry I can't pick up right now, but . . .'

He silenced her. He peered in the window at the front of the house and saw a small room furnished with a pair of armchairs, a lot of bookshelves, and not much else. Connecting doors led into the next room, but they were closed. He followed the left side of the house to a small yard, and heard a mewing from beside the kitchen door. A white cat was sitting by a closed flap. While Parker watched, the cat scratched at the plastic. Parker drew closer, but the cat didn't appear frightened. It just mewed again, and looked up at him expectantly as he reached the door. He knocked hard and called Souliere's name. The drapes were closed on the only window, so he couldn't see inside.

'Can I help you with something?'

A man had emerged from the neighboring house. He was big and broad, with a sallow complexion and a long mustache that made him look like a Mexican revolutionary. Two small children peered from the kitchen behind him.

'I was looking for Michelle Souliere.'

'Well, that's where Ms. Souliere lives, but most people, they wait to go in by the front door.'

The word *honest* remained unspoken before 'people', but Parker heard it anyway. He identified himself as a private investigator, and Souliere's neighbor introduced himself as César Valenzuela.

'I was due to meet with Ms. Souliere yesterday,' said Parker, 'but I never heard from her. I assume that's her car in the drive.'

'Yes, that's hers.'

'Did you hear her come home last night?'

'No, I work late. I think it was there when I got back, but I couldn't say for sure.'

'What time would that have been?'

'After eleven.'

Valenzuela shifted nervously from foot to foot, and looked over Parker's shoulder at Souliere's home.

'You think she's all right in there?' he asked.

'I hope so, but I don't want to call the cops only to find that she's been in the bathroom, or took a sleeping pill and zonked out.'

The children were still watching through the open kitchen door. Valenzuela told them, in English, to go inside, then added '*Hace frío.*'

Parker waited.

'I got a key,' said Valenzuela. 'She's asked for it maybe twice in five years, when she locked herself out.'

'Get it, please, and I'll stand with you while you open the door,' said Parker. 'We'll call her name, and if we get a reply, then fine. If we don't – well, let's just hope that she replies.'

Valenzuela went into his house to find the key. While he was gone, Parker paced the yard and called Ross. The FBI man answered on the second ring.

'We may have a problem,' said Parker, and explained about Souliere's failure to make their meeting, or return his calls. 'I'm outside her house now. Her cell phone rings inside, but nobody answers. Her neighbor's gone to find the spare key, but if she's run into some trouble, then the police are going to become involved.'

The silence over the phone was not an easy one, and went on a little too long for Parker's liking.

'If I have to call the police, they'll ask me what business I had with Souliere,' Parker prompted. 'That means telling them about Eklund, which will raise the question of who hired me to look for him.'

'I'd prefer, and you might also find it beneficial, if Eklund's disappearance was not mentioned,' said Ross. 'The same goes for my involvement.'

'With respect, your preferences could land me in a jail cell.'

Through the kitchen window, Parker could see Valenzuela waving a key fob at him, and indicating that he would come around from the front of the house, as a fence separated the properties. He frowned at the sight of Parker talking on the phone. Time was running out.

'Give them Eklund, but only if you have no other choice,' said Ross.

'And when they ask who hired me? In case you needed reminding, I don't have any kind of protection here.'

Communications between private investigators and their clients were not privileged. If something had happened to Souliere, and the police asked Parker about his efforts to contact her, he would have no option but to provide answers.

'Refer any questions that you don't want to answer to Moxie Castin,' said Ross.

'I'm not employed by Moxie on this.'

'I'll rectify that situation.'

That didn't make Parker much happier. Even in the case of an investigator working for an attorney, privilege only applied to communications relating to advice or strategy on a court case, and there were no legal proceedings involving Eklund for Moxie to fall back on. But Parker understood what Ross was doing: delay, delay, delay.

'Moxie's not going to like it,' he said.

'Then he should never have started working with you,' said Ross. 'From experience, I can attest that there's not a great deal about it to like.'

'The feeling's mutual.'

'I thought it might be,' said Ross, then added: 'Understand something: when I said I would prefer if Eklund's current nebulous status was kept out of this, I should clarify that, in my world, the word *prefer* is generally construed as an instruction.'

Ross hung up without another word, and Valenzuela appeared. The key fob in his hand was shaped like a white cat, a plastic miniature of the one that continued to cry at Souliere's back door. It was clear that Valenzuela was curious about whom Parker might have been speaking with, but didn't want to ask. Discreetly, Parker deleted Ross's number, flicked to his contacts list, and called Moxie Castin. He let the number ring twice before ending the call and slipping the phone into his pocket. If the police had to be summoned, and Valenzuela subsequently mentioned witnessing Parker having a telephone conversation, the list of recently called numbers would show only Souliere's and Castin's. If the police decided to investigate further, they'd need a court order. It was another imperfect solution, but then it was an increasingly imperfect world.

Parker and Valenzuela went to the back door together. Parker picked up the cat and held it in his arms while he knocked hard a couple of times and called Souliere's name, to no result. He was wearing a sweater under his jacket, so he pulled the sleeve down until it covered his hand and tried the door. It was locked.

'Put the key in,' he told Valenzuela, 'but don't touch anything else, okay?'

Valenzuela nodded. He inserted the key and twisted. The lock clicked, and Parker opened the door.

Michele Souliere was sitting in a chair, her head on the kitchen table, her hands hanging almost to the floor. Parker recognized her from photographs on the Internet. Her face was turned to the door, and her eyes were closed. The surface of the table and the floor around her chair were sticky with blood.

'*Híjole,*' whispered Valenzuela. He covered his mouth with his hand and backed away. From somewhere in the distance, Parker heard the sound of approaching sirens and realized that Valenzuela had probably called the police while he was searching for Souliere's spare key.

The cat was wriggling in Parker's arms, and its cries blended with the noise of the sirens.

It's just hungry, Parker thought, as he stared down at Souliere's body. *It can't know.*

Then the little cat grew still, and wailed and wailed.

70

Parker didn't have much time. He handed the cat to Valenzuela, who was leaning against the fence taking deep breaths, and stepped away to make another call. He remained in Valenzuela's sight, mostly so there would be no issue with the police when they arrived. He didn't want there to be any question about his possible intrusion on a crime scene.

He called Angel.

'Where are you?'

'About half an hour out of Greensburg.'

A Waterbury PD patrol car pulled up outside Souliere's home. He only had seconds left.

'Michelle Souliere's dead. Get to Thayer, and keep him safe. I'm going to be tied up with the police for a while. Let Moxie Castin know when you have Thayer.'

He hung up, deleted the number, and put his phone away. The approaching officer had his right hand on his weapon, so Parker made sure to keep his own hands clearly in sight. He was about to tell Valenzuela to do the same, but Valenzuela was already ahead of him.

For the second time that morning, Parker identified himself as a private investigator, then indicated the open back door.

'You've got a body,' he said. 'Her name is Michelle Souliere.'

He corrected himself. Everything about her would be in the past now.

'*Was* Michelle Souliere.'

*   *   *

The Buckners had checked into a chain motel a couple of miles off the highway. They had discussed heading straight back to Turning Leaf, but neither of them had ever killed before, and Sally was surprised by how exhausted she felt. Thanks to TV and the Internet, they were reasonably familiar with forensics and DNA. They'd scrubbed Souliere's hands thoroughly after she died, and checked the floor for any stray hairs that might have fallen from Sally's head during the fight. They found a couple, helped by the fact that Sally's hair was so red, and now were certain they'd left few, if any, traces of their presence at Michelle Souliere's house – with the obvious exception of a dead body, as Kirk noted while they worked on the clothing they'd worn at the scene. They soaked everything in water mixed with Clorox in the motel tub, and sealed the items in separate bags. When that was done, Kirk showered then drove around for a time placing the bags in trash cans and Dumpsters. He returned, and they slept for a few hours.

Sally was impressed with Kirk. She'd always considered him to be kind of a pussy, although he made up for it with his computer smarts, but he'd shown some spirit when Souliere fought back. Still, the bitch had hit Sally hard, and she was now sporting a hell of a bruise, which she'd have to hide with makeup.

They had Souliere's laptop, and a box file of her material on the Martyrs. Kirk went out and bought coffee with sausage and egg sandwiches for breakfast, and together they set to work on Souliere's laptop and documents. Sally was shocked at just how much Souliere had discovered about the Martyrs' past, including aspects of their history of which even she was unaware. More worryingly, Souliere had made some progress on tracing family lines among the Brethren, undaunted by changes of name, and aided by gossip and hearsay. It was clear that her information, combined with Eklund's, had brought the investigator to their door, although Eklund realized too late just how close to the Brethren he actually was.

Kirk copied anything that might be useful from the computer before removing the hard drive and piercing it repeatedly with a screwdriver. He would toss it in the furnace when they got home, along with Souliere's papers. The laptop itself he'd take to Steven Lee's junkyard.

Eklund's laptop, on the other hand, he had retained, although not by choice. The investigator had collated so much data that Sally was still working her way through it, but to safeguard the material, Eklund, who was smarter than he appeared, had employed someone to build him an OS and install it in a Frankenstein machine made from the salvaged parts of others. The system was incompatible with any driver that Kirk could find, and even with the authentication codes tortured from Eklund, any attempt to copy the files risked a fatal crash. Kirk was afraid that if he screwed around too much with the laptop, they might lose everything on it. Finally, to ensure that the hard drive couldn't be removed, Eklund had stripped the screw heads holding the case together. It was a perfect storm of protection, and so Kirk was stuck with dragging the bitch device around with him, in case either Souliere or Thayer gave up information that needed to be cross-checked.

During their time with Souliere, Sally had taken the opportunity to go through the contents of the woman's iPhone. They didn't bother taking it with them – they knew how easily it could be traced, which was why they were carrying only primitive burner phones themselves; they didn't want to risk even removing the iPhone from the house and dumping it somewhere along the way – but she deleted all the messages after listening to them, just as a precaution. Kirk tried telling her how easily they could be retrieved, but she told him to shut the fuck up. Most of the messages related to college business, and one to Souliere's proposed book on the Capstead Martyrs.

A book! A fucking book!

But a couple of the messages, along with a bunch of missed calls, came from a man named Charlie Parker, who'd been due to meet with Souliere on the evening she died. Sally was concerned he might try to come by Souliere's house, which was why she'd gone to work with the knife so quickly, once Souliere had given up her laptop password and cell phone passcode.

The Parker name was familiar to Sally from somewhere, but she couldn't recall how, not at first. She had to wait until they were in the motel, and Kirk had finished copying the material from Souliere's computer, before she could access the Internet. Now she googled Parker, and the cell phone number he had left with his message. She did so almost absentmindedly. She was thinking about taking Kirk to bed before they left. It would be a reward for both of them.

A page of results came up. As soon as she began scrolling through them, all thoughts of sex with Kirk left her, and she recalled where she had first come across Parker's name.

It was on Jaycob Eklund's laptop.

'Shit,' she said. 'Shit, shit, shit.'

71

Richard collected Sumner shortly after five a.m. Initially there had been some discussion about using a vehicle other than Richard's, perhaps a salvage from Steven Lee's yard, but Steven Lee didn't have anything reliable on hand, and the last thing anyone wanted was a breakdown either heading to or, worse, leaving Thayer's place, so Richard's Chevy Blazer it was.

Richard had picked up two coffees at a Dunkin' Donuts before he arrived, along with some crullers, and that kept them going for a couple of hours. Richard told Sumner that he usually listened to political discussion programs while he was driving, but Sumner didn't have time for that talk radio shit, liberal or conservative. If he wanted to hear folk agreeing with their own opinions for hours on end, he could just stay at home and listen to his wife. They settled on Deep Tracks for the first part of the drive, stopped for a late breakfast at an IHOP off the highway, then switched to Classic Rewind for something a little more modern. They agreed that pretty much all music made after 1983 sucked, even if it meant they were becoming a pair of stubborn nostalgists.

Richard had always taken Sumner for a loudmouth. Richard concealed a secret terror of those who could build and fix things, as they made him feel less masculine by comparison. But Sumner turned out to be quite the thinker, and if he was loud then it was because his was a big, generous personality. Richard discovered that Sumner was planning to head over to South Africa at the end of the fall to build houses for some

337

charity. Jesse would be going with him, although Sumner said she was kind of nervous about it, which he understood. Richard wasn't sure just what Jesse would be doing when she was over there, since she was even less adept with a hammer and nails than he was. Sumner confessed he wasn't sure either, but she didn't want to stay home alone.

Sumner, in turn, had never spent a lot of time in Richard's company, but gradually found that what he had mistaken for standoffishness, or even superiority, was actually a kind of shyness. Richard didn't strike Sumner as the kind of guy who'd cheat on his wife, but if there was an adulterous type, then greater minds than Sumner's had failed to pinpoint it. It was Richard who raised the subject of his affair, as they were nearing the Ohio-Pennsylvania line. They were passing one of those wedding venues, the sort Sumner always associated with Irish marriages: lots of guests, bad food, and buyer's remorse once the hangovers wore off. The sight of it seemed to spark a series of associations in Richard.

'It's been a shitty year or so,' he said. 'Real shitty.'

'Yeah?' said Sumner, because what else could one say to that? 'Work, or . . .'

He let it hang.

'The "or" part,' Richard confirmed.

The affair was common knowledge among the Brethren. The closeness of their relationships meant they could have few secrets. Affairs were regarded as unwise, and were tacitly discouraged. Any unhappiness had to be tackled – they couldn't risk the urge to confess that might come with analysis, or conversations with pastors or priests – but flaws in marriages carried very particular risks: no extramarital affair could survive without some degree of pillow talk, and who knew what confidences might be exchanged at such moments?

When Sophia found out about her husband's dalliance, it was to Sally she turned, and pressure was immediately placed on Richard to put an end to the relationship. The girl was young, too. She wasn't one of Richard's students, but she'd graduated a few years earlier from the high school at which he taught. They'd hooked up after some Lions Club event for underprivileged kids, which the girl was attending with her younger sister. Their home life was a mess, and Sumner could only assume that Richard had taken pity on her, and then one thing led to another, as one thing often did.

'Jesse said she thought you and Sophia were getting on better now.'

'Yeah, we're okay,' but the way he spoke the word *okay* spoke only of sadness and regret. 'But we don't . . . you know. We have separate rooms.'

'I'm sorry to hear that. She'll come around. She's just angry and hurt.'

'It's been six months since we last slept together.'

'How long have you been married?'

'Fifteen years come April.'

'Then six months isn't so long.'

'No, I suppose it isn't.'

Richard continued to stare out the window, watching fields and trees and life pass him by.

'I miss her.'

'Sophia?'

'No, Lucie. The girl. I miss her.'

Sumner resisted the urge to smack Richard across the back of the head. For a teacher, he wasn't very bright.

'I wanted to contact her again,' said Richard. 'Dumb, I know. I just needed to tell her I was sorry for how it ended, and find out how she was.'

And fuck her one last time for the road, Sumner wanted to add, but didn't. Instead he said, 'And did you?'

'This between us?'

Sumner nodded, and he meant it, for now. They were on their way to kill someone, and a degree of trust was imperative in such situations.

'I tried,' said Richard, 'but she'd moved somewhere else. Her father was an asshole, and her stepmom wasn't much better, so she'd always talked about getting away from them. I feel sorry for Vicki, her sister, but I think she'll be all right. She's stronger than Lucie was.'

'Do you have any idea where she went?'

'I spoke to Vicki, but she didn't know. Lucie just told her to finish high school. Once Lucie was settled, and had a place to live, then Vicki could come join her. Vicki said she'd like that.'

I bet she wouldn't, thought Sumner, *not unless she wants to be crushed and buried somewhere in Steven Lee's wrecking yard. You killed her, Richard. Donn Routh might have been the one who strangled her, tracking her down to some shithole apartment in Jersey, but she died because you couldn't keep your pecker in your pants. Whatever you did or didn't say to her wasn't the issue: she was your weakness, and an end had to be put to her.*

'Did her sister know about the two of you?' Sumner asked.

'No.'

'You're sure?'

'I made it clear to Lucie that no one could know. I told her that when we first started seeing each other. I said I might be able to take care of her and her sister, but I wouldn't be able to do it if anyone found out. I needed time to make a plan and move some money around.'

'You mean you told her you'd leave Sophia for her?'

'Yes.'

'Did you mean it?'

Richard's voice cracked.

'Yes.'

What an idiot.

'Christ, Richard, if her sister even suspected there was something between the two of you, it could cause problems.'

'You mean if the police came looking for Lucie?'

Sumner turned to stare at him. Their eyes met, and in that instant Sumner understood that Richard knew the truth about what had befallen his lover, or suspected it. Maybe Sophia had thrown it at him in the course of an argument, or he was just smart enough to realize that a girl who loved her sister, and wanted to protect her, wouldn't just head into the sunset, breaking off all contact.

'Why would they do that?' he asked, but it wasn't a question to which either of them expected an answer, and they didn't speak again until they neared Greensburg.

72

Philip and Lastrade met Stevie in Newburyport. It meant a drive of almost two hours from Providence, but they didn't care, and it was smarter not to meet in Boston. Newburyport in February was quiet, and the chances of being seen by anyone known to the parties involved were next to none.

Stevie was waiting for them at Angie's on Pleasant, which was all black-and-white tiles and clean Formica, and reminded Philip of vaguely recollected diners from his youth, when he still regarded Mother with adoring eyes. He'd avoided her that morning, just in case she started asking him about his plans for the day.

Philip thought Stevie looked more like an Italian lizard than last time: leather jacket, jeans that hung too low on his ass, a big patterned sweater to ward off the cold. He was also a lot less relaxed, which, oddly, made Philip trust him more. Over coffee and eggs, Stevie explained how he respected his uncle Bernardo, but that sometimes he was too cautious, and it was time for new thinking if all that was to be left of a great criminal heritage was more than a couple of bakeries in the North End.

Frankly, Philip could have given two fucks for Stevie's talk of Italian heritage and tradition, because what it came down to was goombahs fighting for territory with spics and Africans and Russians and anyone else with a dog in the fight. What mattered to him was that Stevie's pitch wasn't a million miles away from his own, and a man's greed could always be relied on. But it was clear that old Uncle Bernardo, the patronizing, soup-slurping fuck, tended to frown on people going behind his back and cutting deals after he'd laid down the law. This had to be kept between the three of them. Also, Stevie didn't have the same financial resources as his uncle, so he'd be coming in at a lower level, but Philip was farsighted enough to recognize that profits from the first deal would be plowed into the next. He was in this for the long haul, and it sounded like Stevie was, too. And, like Mother, Uncle Bernardo couldn't live forever.

As a sign of his bona fides, Stevie paid the bill and walked them to his car, a Dodge Challenger in black and red that couldn't have done more to invite unwanted attention from the law if it spewed crack smoke in place of exhaust fumes. But Philip decided to be forgiving of this particular quirk when Stevie produced a block of bills encased in plastic wrap: $100,000, including a contribution from Anthony, who also saw no reason to pass up a good thing because their uncle couldn't tell one Muslim (the good kind that sold drugs) from another (the bad kind that flew planes into buildings). Philip, who took an interest in affairs beyond the borders of New England, didn't bother to explain to Stevie that those Muslims were pretty much one and the same, because it wouldn't have made the Italian any happier, and would probably just have confused him.

'How long?' asked Stevie, once they'd stowed the cash away in Lastrade's latest rental.

'The stuff comes in by ship,' said Philip. 'Three weeks. Could be a little more, could be a little less.'

'Three weeks is good,' said Stevie.

They shook hands. The deal was on. Philip didn't bother to tell Stevie that the three-week estimate was probably bullshit. He was sure that the heroin was already in the country, which meant that Stevie could be supplied within days, not weeks. Philip would keep him waiting for a week at least, though. Stevie would still be happy when the heroin reached him sooner than anticipated, but Philip didn't want Stevie to start thinking the whole business was too easy for his partners. He wasn't concerned about Stevie trying to discover the identity of Philip's supplier in the hope of cutting a better deal behind his back. The men involved didn't break bread with Italians, or Hispanics, or anyone else. They dealt only with their own, and Philip was one of them. He'd proved it with blood. That was how they worked, these people.

No, not these people.

His people.

73

Sumner and Richard had performed a considerable amount of due diligence on Tobey Thayer. They knew he kept his office at the main store and warehouse on Greensburg's west side, so they parked in a lot across the street and made the call from there. When a woman answered, Sumner asked to speak with Mr. Thayer and was told he wasn't available. Sumner gave her some bullshit about wanting to make a bulk purchase from the damaged stock in Thayer's warehouse to replace a quantity of his own that had been lost in a fire. He was informed that Thayer might be in later, but it would probably be tomorrow.

After he laid on the charm, she revealed that Thayer was working from home that day, although she couldn't give out either Thayer's residential or cell phone number. If Sumner left his own number, she assured him, she'd be sure to pass it on. Sumner, seeing no harm in supplying the burner number, gave it to her. He figured that if Thayer did call him back, they'd be able to glean a little more information from him, and confirm that he was actually home like the woman claimed. Then again, why would she have lied about something like that? So there it was: Sumner and Richard now knew where Thayer could be found, and they had his home address, thanks to the late Jaycob Eklund.

'What do you think?' Sumner asked Richard.

Richard, who had read enough about Tobey Thayer's business and personal life to ghost his memoirs, was watching a girl walk by, her hair tied up in a loose bun, a pair of big headphones acting as makeshift ear muffs. She wore a white padded jacket that came down only to mid-thigh, just above the hem of her navy skirt. Her legs were clad in white tights, her feet hidden by impractical ankle boots. Nice-looking kid. Nineteen, maybe twenty.

She must, thought Sumner, *be fucking freezing.*

The expression on Richard's face as he followed the girl's progress was equal parts regret and lust. Richard, Sumner decided, had severe problems. He'd have to talk with Jesse about him when all this was over, and maybe even Sally and Madlyn, too. His opinion of Richard might have softened, but he still didn't care enough about him to miss him if he disappeared. Right now, he wasn't sure if Sophia did either. If Richard were to fuck up again . . .

Then what? Routh was dead. It didn't matter that his body hadn't shown up yet. Sally said he was gone. Eleanor had told her so, and you could take that to the bank right there. It was because of the Cousin's demise that he and Richard were about to kill Tobey Thayer, but Sumner didn't plan on making a habit of doing the Brethren's dirty work. There was always Steven Lee, but he wasn't much of a planner. Richard, meanwhile, had done an efficient job of dispatching Eklund, but Eklund was under restraint when the blade was taken to him, and already on nodding terms with death as things stood, thanks to Sally. Nevertheless, how things went with Thayer would go some way toward determining if Richard could be relied on in the future – assuming he could keep his dick in his pants for five minutes – although Sally had promised that this spate of killings, even if born out of necessity, could buy them years of peace.

The girl turned a corner and was lost from sight, breaking the spell.

'Huh?' said Richard.

'I said, "What do you think?"'

'I think we should do it,' said Richard. 'That's why we're here, right?'

'Okay, then,' said Sumner. 'The sooner it's done, the sooner we're home.'

With luck, he and Richard would be back by nightfall.

74

Michelle Souliere's property was alive with police. A curious crowd had gathered on the sidewalk, and various neighbors were leaning on gates and watching the comings and goings.

It didn't take the Waterbury PD's Criminal Investigation Bureau long to finish nibbling at Valenzuela and move on to the entrée represented by Parker. After speaking initially with the first responding officer, he'd been placed under the care of the second uniform that arrived, before being passed on to CID. Following a brief conversation with a detective named Alicia Kohner and her partner, Emile Rolde, he wasn't entirely surprised to find himself in the back of an unmarked car being taken to the Waterbury PD on East Main, where he was placed in a room with a table, a couple of chairs, and a cup of lukewarm coffee. He wasn't cuffed, and it was made clear that he wasn't under arrest, but he was still sitting in a room behind a locked door, waiting to provide what were likely to be unsatisfactory answers to some very direct questions. He'd spent a lot of time in rooms like this, on both sides of the table. He enjoyed being the questioner more than the questioned, but it wasn't really much of a contest.

His phone had been taken from him, which made him glad that he'd deleted Angel's number from the call list. Parker wondered if Angel and Louis had managed to get to Tobey Thayer and apprise him of the trouble he might be in. He'd find out when he next got the chance to call Moxie Castin.

The subject of Moxie brought him back to Ross, and his continued reluctance to involve the police in the search for Jaycob Eklund. Parker knew that Ross was protecting his own back, but despite their earlier conversation, the Eklund situation had changed with the discovery of Michelle Souliere's body. It was entirely possible that Eklund might have killed Souliere. Even if he hadn't, he would become a suspect the moment Parker mentioned his name to the police.

Yet Ross had also suggested that it might be better for Parker if the police didn't take an interest in Eklund's whereabouts. But Parker had never met Eklund. Their only point of connection was through Ross. He could only conclude that he was possibly being royally screwed over by Ross, a man who might now constitute a rogue element within the FBI. Parker wondered what the penalty was for aiding and abetting the undermining of a federal institution: probably something really bad, and without a view.

The door to the interrogation room – *hey, call it what it is* – opened, and Kohner and Rolde entered. Both carried pens and writing pads, but the room was certainly wired for recording anyway, so any notes were simply for their own information, or for show. He hadn't been Mirandized, since he wasn't under arrest, but he still needed to talk to Moxie Castin, if only to confirm that he was free to stretch the principle of privilege to breaking point.

Kohner was pretty in a blond way, and Rolde was handsome in a dark way. Both were of a similar age, and at least a decade younger than Parker. If they ever decided to hook up, they could make beautiful children together.

The dance began. Rolde asked Parker to explain again what he had been doing at Michelle Souliere's house. Parker asked to speak with Moxie Castin. Kohner spoke up to remind him that he wasn't under arrest, and had no need of a lawyer. Parker in turn pointed out – as he'd explained before they put him in a car and drove him over here – that he had been engaged in a professional capacity through a lawyer, and was obliged to clarify with Mr. Castin what he was permitted to say about the client. A brief debate on the nature of privilege followed, but Parker held firm. Eventually he was led to a phone and allowed to call Moxie. He was put through as soon as he identified himself to Moxie's secretary, which he took as either a very good or a very bad sign.

'You,' said Moxie, without preamble, 'are a troublesome and troubling man, and your work brings you into contact with individuals of dubious principles and low character. And I think you know who I'm talking about.'

'Did you receive some paperwork?'

'I received a lot of paperwork, and I'm still not entirely sure what it all means. What I do know is that none of it will protect either of us in a court of law, but it contains enough flimflam and doublespeak to tie experts in jurisprudence up in knots for weeks, maybe months. For what it's worth, until someone starts pulling at threads, you are employed on a third-party basis by this firm to pursue inquiries relating to the disappearance of one Claudia Sansom and the subsequent discovery of her remains in a shallow grave. This firm has, in turn, been subcontracted by the Federal Bureau of Investigation to follow up – quote "at your discretion", unquote – all relevant leads and contacts relating to the Sansom case.'

'Does it explain how Sansom falls under the jurisdiction of the FBI?'

'She disappeared in Massachusetts, and was found in New Hampshire. Geography is our friend.'

Parker had to concede that it was clever of Ross. It would allow him, if necessary, to explain how he had ended up at Souliere's door, and to mention Eklund without admitting that Eklund himself might be under investigation. Eklund had provided professional assistance to Oscar Sansom. He had also spoken with Souliere. Parker had simply been trying to establish if Souliere knew anything about the Sansom case. He was doing what any good investigator, police or private, would do: chase down every lead, reinterview every witness, if only to rule out their testimony as irrelevant.

'What about Angel and Louis?' he asked. 'Have they been in touch?'

'Your lunatic friends? No. Should they have been?'

Kohner appeared in the hallway and tapped her watch. Time was up.

'I think we need to ensure the safety of a man named Tobey Thayer. I asked them to take care of it.'

'You could pass on this information to the police.'

'I might be mistaken.'

'Nevertheless.'

'It's complicated.'

'You mean FBI complicated?'

'Exactly.'

'I'll call Angel and Louis. When I know something more, I'll get back to you. I take it the Waterbury PD has your phone?'

Parker gave him the names of the two detectives, so Moxie would know whom to contact.

'Call me,' said Parker.

'I will,' said Moxie. 'And don't end up in jail down there. I charge mileage.'

The coffee was replenished. Parker put the issue of Angel, Louis, and Tobey Thayer to the side, and concentrated on the questions being put to him. Kohner did most of the talking, Rolde interjecting when required. They might have looked neat and clean, but they were bright too. Parker could tell they smelled something off in his story about Eklund, but they couldn't figure out what it was. It helped that Parker didn't have to lie, except by omission. When he found himself on treacherous ground – for example, Rolde homing in on why he would have come all the way to Connecticut to interview a woman who appeared to have no direct connection to the case in hand when a simple phone call might have served just as well – he referred the detectives to Moxie Castin.

'So in all this, you were just doing what Mr. Castin asked?' Kohner offered.

'That's correct.'

'Following orders,' said Rolde.

'But not in a Nazi way.'

'Does that count as one of your principles?'

'If it does, it's not much of a boast.'

'Mr. Parker, we know exactly who you are, and what you do. We're also aware that no law enforcement agency has ever received a straight answer to a question directed at you. You appear to be allergic to transparency.'

'Maybe I'm turning over a new leaf with you,' said Parker. 'You have to believe in a man's capacity for change and personal development.'

Kohner snorted. It was kind of cute, in a gross way.

'Tell us about Jaycob Eklund,' said Rolde.

Back to Eklund. Rolde, in Parker's opinion, had moved from 'smart' to 'really too smart for his own good.' The only consolation was that the system would eventually knock it out of him.

'I don't know a great deal about Eklund, apart from what I've discovered from walking in his footsteps.'

'Were you aware that he's believed to be missing?'

'I've never spoken with him.'

'That's not answering the question.'

'I only know that he hasn't been around in a while.'

'He hasn't been seen at his home or office in over a week. He doesn't answer calls. His mailbox hasn't been emptied.

Curiously, though, the receptionist at his serviced office building remembered receiving a call from him during that time, asking two men to be permitted entry as soon as they arrived. What's odd about it is that Eklund doesn't actually appear to have been in the building when the call was made. What do you think about that, Mr. Parker?'

'I think you've been hard at work while I was sitting here all alone.'

'As has already been suggested, I don't believe you're being entirely forthcoming with us. Are you looking for Jaycob Eklund, Mr. Parker?'

'I'm looking into the disappearance and death of Claudia Sansom. Eklund was close to her husband. As part of my investigation, I'd be interested in speaking with him. So far, I haven't had a whole lot of luck.'

'Were you recently at Eklund's office building?'

'I made inquiries about him, just as you did.'

'Did you gain entry to his office under false pretenses?'

'No,' Parker lied. Good luck to them with tracing the call that supposedly came from Eklund, and he hadn't broken any laws by entering the building, or not in any way that could be proved. It was only when he got to Eklund's office door that the trouble started.

'You're sure about that?'

'Yes.'

Eklund's office building was run as a cheap operation, with minimal security camera coverage, and he would bet good money that the young receptionist wouldn't be able to conclusively identify him if the police decided to show her a photograph. He wasn't happy about lying to the detectives, but it was the first real lie he'd been forced to tell, and a calculated gamble. If he admitted wrongdoing, he could potentially find himself having another awkward conversation in another euphemistically titled 'interview room', this time with the Providence PD.

'Could Eklund have killed Michelle Souliere?' Kohner asked.

'I don't know any reason why he would,' said Parker, which was true, but still didn't mean that Eklund wasn't a suspect.

He could see that Kohner and Rolde were growing frustrated. At least they could say he hadn't confounded their expectations.

'I know it doesn't seem like it,' he said, 'but we're on the same side here. I'm not sheltering Eklund. I don't know where he is. If I find him, I'll inform Mr. Castin, and he will, in turn, pass those details on to law enforcement. Neither of us has any interest in obstructing the course of justice.'

Kohner snorted again. It wasn't quite as cute the second time around. She looked at her partner. He shrugged. Parker had committed no crime in the city of Waterbury or the state of Connecticut, as long as one glossed over the matter of any small lies told to the police, and as many more sins of omission. They couldn't hold him, and they knew it, but that didn't mean they had to look happy about it.

'Then I guess you're free to go,' said Kohner.

She led him to the door and opened it for him. Rolde stayed where he was while Kohner escorted Parker from the building. Along the way, she said softly, 'Seriously, and between us, what the fuck are you doing here?'

Parker didn't break stride, but he decided that it was worth leaving some bridges unburned in Waterbury.

'Looking for Eklund.'

'Is he suspected of a crime?'

'He wasn't until I saw Michelle Souliere's body.'

'Will Castin be straight with us?'

'He's a lawyer: he couldn't be straight if you tied him to a rack. But he's one of the good ones. He'll tell you what he can.'

'And you? Will you be straight?'

Parker paused. They were at the final door before the main lobby.

'I don't want to see what happened to Michelle Souliere go unpunished.'

'Then I guess that'll have to do, won't it?' said Kohner.

'I guess it will.'

75

P arker's phone and gun were returned to him. Connecticut did not have a reciprocity agreement recognizing pistol permits from Maine, but Parker had nonresident permits for most states. His weapon was not an issue, but Kohner had advised him that they'd checked his status, just to be sure. The news didn't make him feel any more loved in Waterbury.

No one had offered to give him a ride back to his car, which remained parked near Michelle Souliere's house. It wasn't too much of a schlep: the Waterbury PD building was on East Main, and from where he stood he could almost see the spire of St. Anne's Church on South Main, just across the Yankee Expressway. He could get back to Souliere's house on foot, but it wouldn't have killed Kohner or her partner to save him the walk.

He still had his cell phone in his hand, ready to call Angel and Louis, when he saw the car. It was a black 1966 Chrysler Imperial, in perfect condition. For a moment, Parker was worried that he might just have experienced a blow to the head, and would soon find himself with a hallucinatory version of the Green Hornet standing before him. Then the tinted window on the passenger side rolled down, and he realized, if he hadn't already, that this was to be one of those days in which he was destined never to catch a decent break.

Mother was sitting in the back of the car.

Parker stared at his phone. He really, really wanted to talk with Angel and Louis, but it seemed inadvisable to keep Mother waiting, although she hadn't as yet glanced in his direction, and if the cold breeze blowing through the open window was bothering her, she didn't show it. Still, the implication was clear: his company was required. At least, he figured, he now had his ride.

The driver got out as Parker approached. Parker didn't recognize him, as he hadn't been part of Philip's coterie back in Providence. He was in his fifties and broadly built. He appeared old-school hard, the kind of guy who had delivered so many threats and beatings in his life that he could no longer even take communion without looking intimidating. He put out a hand like a shovel and waited. Slowly, Parker removed his gun, ejected the clip and the round in the chamber, put the ammunition in his jacket pocket, and restored the gun to its holster.

'That's as good as you get,' he said. *And more than I wanted to give*, he might have added.

The driver looked to Mother for confirmation that this was acceptable and received it in the form of the barest of nods. He opened the door for Parker, and closed it again behind him before returning to his seat. The window rolled up, and the car pulled away from the curb. The interior smelled faintly of old leather and Mother's scent.

'I thought you might like us to take you back to your vehicle,' said Mother.

'As long as the two hundred and thirty mile round trip isn't too far out of your way.'

In the rearview mirror, the eyes of the driver shifted to Parker, as though to warn him against inappropriate displays of humor in Mother's company.

'I heard about the Souliere woman,' said Mother. 'Did you have the opportunity to speak with her before she died?'

'No.'

'It doesn't matter. I'm not sure that you'd have learned much more from her than Eklund already had.'

Which confirmed to Parker that Mother, or someone close

to her, must have gone through the material in Eklund's home before, or shortly after, Parker commenced his own search of the property with Angel; before, most probably, as Mother didn't strike him as the kind of person who liked playing catch-up. He doubted that it was Philip who had been entrusted with the task. Philip would have left a mess.

Parker watched Waterbury go by. He felt as though he needed a shower. Being stuck in an interrogation room, in any role, always left him feeling unclean. Perhaps it was something that emanated from one's pores under stress, or maybe it was just three people in close proximity in a room where too many others had sweated before them.

'Just in passing, I'm still not sure what I should call you,' he said.

'Excuse me?'

'As I said before, I can't really address you as "Mother".'

He knew her name, thanks to Ross, but he didn't want to confirm to her that he'd made inquiries about her, even if she must have realized that he would.

'It's not an issue,' she replied. 'We're never going to be close.'

Parker tried not to look hurt. It was easier than he'd anticipated, and he'd anticipated that it would be very easy.

'So how far have you progressed in your inquiries?' Mother asked.

'They're ongoing.'

'Don't be facetious, Mr. Parker. I don't have the patience for it.'

'The last time I looked, I wasn't employed by you.'

'When last we met, you declined my offer of employment, and I advised you that I'd continue to take an interest in your activities. My obligations to Mr. Webb remain in place, and therefore they also affect you.'

Parker gave up.

'I believe that somewhere out there are individuals connected to the Capstead Martyrs, or the Brethren, or whatever you or anyone else might choose to call them,' he said. 'For some reason, they don't want people delving into their history, and that's why Souliere was killed. If Eklund is dead, then he died for the same reason. If he's not dead, then it's possible he may have killed Souliere. While he's missing, he'll remain a suspect, for the police if not for me.'

'You don't think he could have murdered her?'

'It seems unlikely.'

'And what about Mr. Webb's brother and his family? How do they connect to these Brethren?'

'If we accept that Michael MacKinnon is dead, then possibly just bad luck in his case, and punishment in the case of his wife and son. She kept looking for her husband, and they wanted to stop her. But I still don't understand why they'd target someone who wasn't a threat to them. If they killed MacKinnon, then his death caused more trouble than it was worth.

'And there are a lot of missing people: MacKinnon, Eklund, even Claudia Sansom, at least until her remains showed up. In addition, Eklund had marked any number of other disappearances as being of interest. If even a quarter of them involve the Brethren, then that's a significant figure, and it suggests deliberation. It's hard to make a case without a body, although they've left some of those in their wake as well.'

He had purposely included Claudia Sansom, just to hear what Mother might say.

'You believe there's a link between Claudia Sansom and the others?'

So Mother knew about Sansom, which confirmed that she'd gone through Eklund's records.

'Eklund is the connection.'

'But Eklund didn't uncover any sightings in her case. There are no ghosts where Claudia Sansom is concerned.'

Parker was tempted to correct her. In his experience, there

were ghosts where everyone was concerned, if rarely of the uncanny kind. Instead he contented himself with saying, 'She was important to Eklund, and whatever was important to Eklund is important to me.'

They were already long past Souliere's house, with the driver heading south along the Naugatuck River. Parker hoped that he intended to turn north again before they left the state, or else the walk back to his car would put the trot from the Waterbury PD building into grim perspective. Although it was bleak outside, Parker tried unsuccessfully to roll down his window. In the contained environment of the car, Mother's scent was moving from cloying to nauseating. But even as the smell grew stronger, so too did the stink of what it was designed to hide. Mother reeked of sweat, sickness, and disease, but whether it issued from her or her clothing wasn't clear. Parker had a terrible suspicion that, for the most part, it might be the latter. Up close, he could see stains on her dress: food, what might have been oil or grease, and other fluids that weren't immediately identifiable without the aid of a laboratory, but were almost certainly bodily in origin. If they weren't her own, then they came from Caspar Webb. How long had she been wearing that dress: since his death? Perhaps she just kept it for special occasions. Parker had to fight the urge to move farther away from her, or break the glass. He opted for breathing through his mouth, and tried not to focus on the particulate nature of odors.

'You still haven't told me who hired you to look for Eklund,' said Mother, 'although I have my suspicions.'

'I'm not going to confirm them.'

'Julian could make you.'

She gestured at the driver, who again glowered at Parker from the rearview mirror.

'Julian?' said Parker. 'For real? No wonder he looks so unhappy.'

Julian smiled. It wasn't a nice smile. If Mother let him off his leash, he was likely to do some damage, but Mother didn't pursue the matter, leaving Julian – or Julie, as Parker now thought of him, albeit silently – to simmer away.

'I do have one question to which I need an honest answer,' she said.

'I'll do my best.'

'How much did you tell the Waterbury PD about Mr. Webb, or about me and my son?'

'Nothing. You didn't come up. Unless, of course, you had Michelle Souliere killed, in which case you probably should have.'

'I'm pleased to hear you kept us out of your conversation.'

Parker didn't bother to tell her that he'd discussed everything about her circumstances with Ross, since that wasn't the question he'd been asked. He also noticed that she hadn't responded to the second part of his answer.

'And Michelle Souliere?' he prompted.

'I think you know I wasn't involved.'

'What about your son?'

It was like watching an iceberg shudder from some unseen collision in the ocean depths.

'My son doesn't care enough about any of this to become involved.'

'What does he care about?'

'His reputation.'

Mother kept her face turned away as she spoke, although Parker could see it reflected in the window. It bore an expression he'd seen before: love poisoned by disappointment.

'I wasn't aware that he had a reputation.'

'That would be part of the problem.'

'And does he care about you?'

'He loves me.'

'Which would be another part of the problem.'

'Love covers a multitude of sins.'

Julian turned into a lot overlooking the river and brought

the car to a halt. Parker didn't like this one bit. All it would take was for Julian to turn around with a gun in his hand, and all his worries would come to an end. The body of the Chrysler would muffle most of the sound, suppressed or otherwise. With low velocity ammunition or hollow points, his death wouldn't even leave a stain on the upholstery. But Julian kept his hands on the wheel, and his eyes on the river.

'I'm concerned about Philip,' said Mother.

'Please don't take this the wrong way,' Parker replied, 'by which I mean don't think that I'm not serious, but if he was my son, I'd be concerned too.'

'We have issues to resolve. It's important that we be given the time and space to do so.'

'Without the police asking awkward questions, you mean.'

'Without anyone asking awkward questions.'

'Caspar Webb was a criminal, and you're engaged in the disposal of a criminal empire. Nothing you do will be unobserved. A lot of people are curious to see what happens next.'

'Including your employer?'

She turned to face him, and he looked her in the eye as he answered. He'd had enough of Mother's company. He shifted position. If Julian made a move he didn't like, he'd be able to land a blow to his temple that would stun him for long enough to ensure he could be hurt more seriously in the aftermath.

'My employer cares only about Jaycob Eklund,' said Parker. 'You could say he sees the bigger picture, and Eklund is part of that. You and your son are not. Neither was Caspar Webb. Like him, you'll die, and your son will die, and you'll all be forgotten. Your pond is going dry, but your son isn't smart enough to spot it. He'll only realize it when he's gasping in the mud, but I won't be there to see it. If you're lucky, neither will you. But it won't matter in the end, not any of it.'

He stopped talking, but remained wary of Julian, even though the driver's hands had still not moved from the wheel.

When it came, Mother's reply was not what he had anticipated.

'Good,' she said.

She patted the back of the driver's seat. Julian turned the Chrysler around, and they headed back to South End, stopping at the end of Souliere's street. Parker's car remained just beyond the police cordon, surrounded by TV trucks and gawkers. He was fairly certain that no one in the local media would have any idea who he was, but he intended to keep his head down, just in case.

Julian got out and opened Parker's door.

'When you discover what happened to Mr. Webb's brother-in-law and his family,' said Mother, 'I'd appreciate it if you'd call and let me know.'

'*If* I find out.'

'I have faith in you, Mr. Parker,' she said. 'You aspire to completeness.'

The door closed. Julian bestowed one last scowl for bad luck, then returned to his seat and drove away. Parker restored the ammunition to his gun, and the gun to its holster, before at last calling Angel and Louis.

It was Angel who picked up.

'It's me,' said Parker. 'What's the situation?'

In the background he could hear sirens, and a woman screaming.

'Well,' said Angel, 'I have good news and bad news . . .'

76

Sumner had always thought of himself as a rational, organized man; it was hard to remain successful in the construction business and be any other way. On the other hand, he occasionally found it hard to balance the physical world of wood and cement, of feet, inches, and angles, with a state of existence that encompassed the existence of ghosts. He'd never killed anyone, but he was complicit by blood in more deaths than he cared to consider, and was about to become intimately involved in at least one more. It was strange, he thought, what the human mind could inure itself to, if required.

Sumner was now behind the wheel of the Blazer. Beside him, Richard was humming to himself, and bouncing with excitement in his seat. Richard, Sumner felt, had a lot of rage in him. While it was nice that he'd discovered an outlet for it, his obvious enthusiasm for making Tobey Thayer his second victim suggested that he had simply exchanged an old set of problems for a whole new set.

Thayer lived far outside town, in a big, isolated house set back from the road and surrounded by trees and bushes for added privacy. The ornate wrought iron double gates stood open as they passed, and they could see a short driveway leading to the house itself. Sumner, whose own home was just the right size for the needs of his four-member family, looked at Thayer's and decided that it was exactly the kind of house in which he would have expected to find someone who made tacky adverts for discount furniture: six bedrooms at least, he reckoned, and enough bathrooms for a man to be able to take a dump once a day for a week and never use the same one twice. Two cars were parked in front, and to the right was a separate two-car garage with the doors closed.

They knew from a newspaper profile that Thayer and his wife now lived alone. Thayer had spoken about how his kids had left home, and maybe it was time to consider downsizing. There were mentions of vague aspirations to visit Europe, or even Asia, which would never come to pass, not if Richard and Sumner had anything to do with it. At no time, though, did Thayer refer to the abilities that had brought death to his door. He was, to all appearances, just another successful businessman with a wife who had been forced to make the aging woman's choice between her face and her body, and had, judging by the photographs accompanying the article, opted for the body. She was okay from the lower neck down – a bit scrawny for Sumner's liking, and with the kind of raised veins on her arms that would have given him the shivers to touch – but her features had the drawn, rapacious look of someone who spent too much time wishing she could eat more.

Thayer had returned Sumner's call just fifteen minutes earlier. He sounded like he was nursing a head cold, although he described it as flu, which Sumner, who was no doctor, could have told him it wasn't. Sumner had been laid low with the real thing a couple of years back, and it took him a week to work up the strength to get out of bed, never mind call a stranger to shift a couple of sticks of chipped furniture. At least it had confirmed for them that Thayer was at home. In an ideal world, his wife would have been elsewhere when they came for him, but from the cars in the drive – a Lexus and a chick-car BMW Z4 Roadster – it looked like she was in the house with her husband.

Richard was untroubled by the wife's presence. He had no problem killing both of them, he assured Sumner, which didn't make Sumner feel any easier about the workings of Richard's mind. Sumner suggested waiting until nightfall before going in, but Richard pointed out that the couple was in the house now, and the trees and bushes provided plenty of cover from the road. He also noted that the longer they stayed in the area, the more likely it was that someone might notice and – later – remember them, which struck Sumner as sensible, and suggested that Richard might not be completely nuts after all.

So it was decided: they'd kill the Thayers early, and have done with it.

Tobey Thayer hung up the phone after commiserating with the man on the other end about his recent losses to fire, and reassuring him that he would be fighting fit in a day or two and was committed to fulfilling all his discount furniture needs. He was dressed and sitting in his den, where he was half watching a movie while adding to the pile of mucus-sodden tissues in the wastebasket by his feet.

He felt a headache coming on, and not just from his clogged sinuses. His fingers and toes were prickling, and he tasted metal in his mouth. The room was swimming around him, and the phone rang again, except this time it wasn't the familiar electronic beeping but an older sound he remembered from his childhood: the double bell of his parents' old black rotary dial model.

He picked up the handset. He heard waves crashing and – distantly – a woman singing a song. Instantly he was transported back to a bedroom in Philadelphia's Fishtown, where his father's family had lived for generations, the earliest of his ancestors being among the German-Americans who bought up the fishing rights on the Delaware River at the end of the eighteenth century. His mother, though, came from English stock, a heritage that set her apart in what was a predominantly Irish Catholic neighborhood. It was she who used to sing to him long after he should have been too old for lullabies, and it was she who sang to him now, across time and space and death:

> *Do not fear the sound of a breeze*
> *Brushing leaves against the door.*
> *Do not dread the murmuring seas,*
> *Lonely waves washing the shore.*

God, he knew that air: 'Sleep My Baby', it was called. His mother used to lull him with it as a child, and he was overcome with the most desolate sense of loss and longing. He found himself calling his mother's name, but in return received only the sound of the sea, and the voice fading, growing indistinct, and he could not tell if he was still hearing the words or just filling in the gaps from memory:

> *Sleep child mine, there's nothing here,*
> *While in slumber at my breast,*
> *Angels smiling, have no fear,*
> *Holy angels guard your rest.*

She faded away, and was gone. The crashing of the waves became an electronic rasp in his ear. The loneliness was replaced by terror, because the meaning behind the song lay not in its words of consolation, but in the emphasis the voice had placed on 'fear' and 'dread'.

Something was coming, but there would be no angels to guard his rest.

And then the doorbell rang.

77

Sumner and Richard found a side road by Thayer's property. In the distance was another house on what looked like farmland, although Sumner saw no sign of livestock. Maybe they were all indoors because of the weather, although what Sumner knew about farming could be written on the palm of his hand. But even from a distance, the house and outbuildings looked run-down. That suited him just fine.

Once he and Richard were content that they had not attracted even cursory attention, they turned back on the empty road, hung a right, and drove up Thayer's drive. Richard already had the gun in his hand: a Glock 19 with some fancy attachments which Sumner, who knew even less about guns than he did about farming, thought looked like overkill, and certainly would have made it hard to carry in anything other than the little case Richard had brought with him. The gun, Richard explained to Sumner, was fitted with a Unity Tactical ATOM slide, a Trijicon RMR red dot sight, and a SureFire X300 Ultra WeaponLight, the latter of which Sumner, with tongue only partly in cheek, convinced him probably wouldn't be required since he'd be shooting in daylight. The gun was loaded with polymer-copper projectiles that would, according to Richard, 'tear apart soft tissue but won't overpenetrate.'

Jesus.

'Well, put it away until we get inside the house,' Sumner told Richard. Anyone glimpsing that thing in Richard's hand would barricade the doors and call the cops, or possibly just preemptively open fire.

Richard had put on a coat, and somehow managed to slip most of the gun into one of the side pockets. He turned to Sumner and smiled.

'I brought this one for you,' he said.

He rummaged in another pocket of the coat and withdrew a small hammerless revolver. Sumner thought it looked like a lady's gun, especially when compared to Richard's.

'I don't want it,' said Sumner.

'You can't go in with your hands hanging by your sides.'

'I don't know how to shoot.'

'This one, you just point and fire.'

'You don't understand: I don't *want* to know how to shoot.'

'Look,' said Richard, 'it's just for show. If both of us are armed, Thayer and his wife are more likely to sit tight and do as they're told.'

Reluctantly, Sumner took the gun. It was shiny and didn't weigh much at all.

'What is it?' he asked.

'A Smith & Wesson Model 642. Five rounds.'

'What about a safety catch?'

'It doesn't have one.'

'Isn't that kind of dangerous?'

'You want to have that discussion now?'

Sumner decided that he didn't.

'Should I keep my finger on the trigger?'

'I wouldn't. Keep it outside the trigger guard. Remember: it's just for show. I'll take care of everything.' Richard grinned at him. 'It's all going to be fine.'

Sumner's heart was racing. He was scared, but had to admit that he was thrilled as well.

They pulled up outside the house, and Sumner turned the car so that it was facing toward the gate. Whatever happened next, they'd be leaving fast, and he didn't want to panic and risk a collision with the house or one of the Thayers' cars. At best, it would leave evidence, and at worst it might result in the kind of damage that would disable the vehicle. They'd debated whether or not Sumner should just stay in the driver's seat while Richard took care of the Thayers, but reached the conclusion that it would be better if both of them entered the house, as two men would be more intimidating than one. It was decided to keep the motor running, though, just in case.

They got out of the car.

They walked to the front door.

They rang the bell.

78

Thayer heard his wife coming down the stairs in response to the doorbell. He only owned one gun, a Taurus Public Defender revolver that had been recommended to him by his brother-in-law, a retired local judge. He'd never fired it outside a range, and stopped carrying it years earlier after he hired a security company to take care of cash runs. It mostly sat in a safe at the bottom of his bedroom closet because his wife hated the sight of it.

Thayer tried calling to Laurie, but his damn throat was clogged up with phlegm, and all that emerged was a kind of croak. He wasn't sure what he would have said to her anyway, other than to advise her not to answer the door. She knew of his gift. She didn't like to talk about it any more than she liked to think of that gun in his closet, but she understood that his abilities were real. If he warned her about something, she'd pay heed to him.

He stumbled to the door of his den, barking his shin painfully against the corner of a table along the way, and got to the hall just as his wife reached the front door. They had a camera system, but it didn't record. It was supposed to, but it had gone on the fritz a couple of weeks earlier after they changed ISPs, and Thayer hadn't got around to calling the guy who'd installed it in order to get it fixed. There was a screen in the kitchen, and another upstairs, but he wasn't near either of them. He could only assume that his wife had checked and decided it was okay to answer the door.

Except it wasn't. He could feel it.

371

The door was solid wood, with thin panes of glass at either side. He could see no one.

He tried to speak again.

His wife reached for the door.

And Tobey Thayer's world went black as he fell to the floor.

79

Sumner and Richard rang the bell a second time and waited. When no one answered after thirty seconds, Sumner began to feel uneasy. Thayer was in there – he had to be. Maybe he and his wife were out in the yard and hadn't heard the bell. If so, he didn't know what they might be doing. They could hardly be gardening.

He turned to Richard.

'I guess we go round back.'

80

Thayer opened his eyes. He was sitting against the wall, his feet outstretched. His wife was kneeling beside him, wiping his face with a damp cloth. Laurie he recognized, but the two men standing behind her he did not. One was tall, black, and dressed in the kind of suit and jacket combination that rarely graced the floor of Thayer's Discount Furniture Sales, or of a discount anything. The other, smaller and of uncertain racial heritage, was the kind of guy Thayer would have dispatched a security guard to keep an eye on if he ever set foot in his store. He looked like someone who could steal out with a sofa under his shirt while your back was turned.

'Who are you?' asked Thayer.

'My name is Angel,' said the smaller man.

Thayer blinked.

'I think,' he told his wife, 'I may have hit my head.'

Richard and Sumner were in the Thayers' garden. The whole first floor at the back of the house was a combination kitchen and dining room, with a glassed-in area furnished with chairs and couches that extended out into the yard. Most of it was lawn, with a surrounding line of mature trees that provided shelter from the wind.

Sumner was nervous now. They had given the Thayers no cause for alarm, or not before they'd started prying around the back of their property, so he could see no reason they might have retreated into the depths of their house and refused to answer the door. If their suspicions had been raised, then the police were almost certainly on their way, and he and Richard would be better off putting as much distance as possible between Greensburg, Pennsylvania and themselves. But why should the Thayers have been concerned by the appearance of a car in their driveway? If they were that paranoid, the gate wouldn't have been wide open to begin with.

Maybe the Thayers weren't home after all, and owned more than two cars between them. If that was the case, he and Richard could find a way to hide their own vehicle and wait for them to come back. This might be their only chance to deal with Thayer. Sally had texted a seemingly innocuous message to let them know that Michelle Souliere was dead, and if Thayer wasn't already aware of her murder, then he soon would be, and might make a connection between her killing and the possibility of some harm befalling him. No, Thayer needed to be dealt with as quickly as possible. Sumner certainly didn't want to have to face Sally and tell her that they'd failed, not after she and Kirk had managed to kill Souliere.

Richard glimpsed movement in the house: a man moving from the stairs to a room on the left, from which he did not emerge again.

'There's someone inside,' he whispered.

Sumner's bowels contracted. He needed a restroom like he'd never needed one before. Now he understood why burglars sometimes took a dump on the floor of people's homes. They weren't simply being assholes, although some of them undoubtedly were; the call of nature was just too much for them.

Richard gestured at the glass door, and Sumner tried the handle. The door opened under the pressure of his gloved hand. He stepped aside, allowing Richard to enter first. Richard held the gun in a two-handed grip. To Sumner, he looked like he knew what he was doing, which was good, because Sumner wasn't capable of killing another human being. He wasn't like Richard. The Smith & Wesson was starting to feel heavy in his hand. Sumner wanted to be rid of it.

In a brief, final flash of sanity, it struck Sumner that he should never have agreed to this.

Richard was halfway across the kitchen floor.

Sumner, already doomed, followed him.

VI

It is terrifying to see, but it is the movement of shadows, only of shadows. Curses and ghosts, the evil spirits that have cast entire cities into sleep.

Maxim Gorky, 'On a Visit to the Kingdom of Shadows' (1896)

81

Angel explained to Tobey Thayer why they had come. Thayer had never met Michelle Souliere, but he had spoken with her over the phone, and thought that he might have enjoyed spending time with her face-to-face, if only to tell her just how wrong she was about the pathways between this world and the next. It would never happen now.

He and his wife were sitting in the den with Angel and Louis. Laurie had made coffee. To a casual observer, the situation might have appeared almost normal.

'I see things,' said Thayer. 'I guess that's the best way to put it, although it doesn't really cover it. I get flashes, images. Sometimes I perceive colors, or hear sounds, and I have to extract meaning from them.'

'You ever get lottery numbers?' asked Angel.

'No.'

'Sucks.'

'Yeah. I did predict the score of the 1993 Super Bowl, though. Dallas against Buffalo, 52–17.'

'I'm not psychic and I could have predicted that,' Angel pointed out.

'I guess,' said Thayer. 'Pity I don't gamble.'

'How long have you known about the Brethren?' asked Louis.

'I feel like I've always known about them. I saw them in dreams when I was younger, but it wasn't until much later that I started to recognize a pattern. I'd glimpse them reflected in glass, or in water. Maybe I'd be writing something on a piece of paper at work, and then look down to find I'd drawn a face, or a house. I started keeping a record of dates and times, and gradually I was able to connect some of my sight-ings – or "attacks", as my wife calls them – with incidents. It's not easy, though. It never was. There are about forty murders every day in this country. It would be hard to experi-ence a sighting and *not* find that it coincided with a killing somewhere. And then, if you start factoring in disappearances, it becomes impossible. It's nothing I could go to the police with, and this gift that I have, it's not something I speak about with others. If I could find a way to rid myself of it, I would. It only brings pain.'

'And then Eklund found you,' said Angel.

'Actually, I found him. I read something he posted on a message board about a year ago, and I got in touch. I was cautious at first, and so was he. Makes it sound like a date, doesn't it?'

Louis raised an eyebrow.

'Except,' Thayer added hurriedly, just in case anyone got the wrong idea, 'it wasn't. Between us, we began making progress. We established what were almost solid correspond-ences, and I—'

He paused, and it was clear to Angel and Louis from the look he cast at his wife that this was not something he had previously shared with her.

'Go on,' said Louis.

Thayer gulped some coffee.

'I'd always tried to smother what I could do, or ignore it. It used to be that, when I had an attack, I'd just lie down for a while, or distract myself with the TV until it passed. It's like a muscle, you know? If you start using it, you develop it, and it gets stronger. I didn't want it to get stronger.

'But Eklund, he convinced me to open myself to it. He wanted me to go deeper, to find clues about the people who were doing these things. So that's what I did.'

'Oh, no,' said his wife.

Thayer ignored her. He was unburdening himself of this, perhaps for the first time. He was no longer looking at any of them. Whatever he saw was both deep inside and far away.

'I began searching for them,' he said. 'I'd wait until Laurie had gone out, and I'd sit in here where it was dark and quiet, and I'd close my eyes and try to relax. It was like willing myself to dream. And sometimes, if I did it right, I'd find myself walking down twilight streets, moving through a shadow city. I had to be careful, though, because once I opened myself they began calling to me, all the voices. There are so many of them, and you don't want them to get into your head, because they'll drive you mad. You have to keep moving, and not acknowledge them, but it's hard because they're in so much pain. Most of them are just lost, but some . . .'

He was trembling. His wife reached out, placed her hands over his, and calmed him.

'Some of them are hiding. That's what the Brethren are doing: they're hiding.'

'From what?' asked Angel.

'From judgment.'

Louis knew that they should already have been moving the Thayers away from their home. They were at risk here, and would be safer in a motel. But he also understood that what he was hearing was important. Parker would want to be told of it, and if they interrupted Thayer now it was possible he might clam up and never speak of it again, or not so openly.

'It makes you sick, being in that place,' said Thayer. 'It's not for the living. It's not even for the dead. It's a kind of limbo, a crawl space between worlds. It's full of cracks and crevasses and dark, dark corners, all places to conceal and be concealed. That's where the Brethren have sequestered themselves. They've made a lair there, far from the ones who've just gone astray. It's a fortress, and it's theirs. They only emerge if they have to, when there's killing to be done in their name, and that's when I catch flashes of them on this side. But they had no idea I could see them, not at first. They're almost blind in our world, but not in theirs. That was the mistake I made. I shouldn't have gone looking for them. Eklund was wrong to ask.

'Because they sensed my coming, and now they know.'

It was like walking through a city made of smoke: that was how Thayer described the place in which the Brethren were hidden. There were houses, and streets, and buildings, but they resembled projections on mist. They shimmered, and their lines and dimensions were not fixed. The sky was red, and the distant hills were little more than patches of darkness against the firmament. He recognized some of the architecture, especially on the skyline, which combined elements of any number of great American cities, and he understood instinctively that this landscape had been created from the combined memories of all those who moved through it. That was why the great skyscrapers were less detailed than the small houses: the latter were important and intimate, while the former were simply backdrops to daily life.

The city was filled with wraiths, figures as indistinct as the environment through which they moved. Some wandered aimlessly, calling out the names of loved ones, while others sat in the windows and doorways of the homes they had conjured up from what could be recalled of their old lives, staring emptily at eternity. But the children were the worst: Thayer could feel their distress, and could not help but respond to it. When he did, they turned to him, reaching out, and as they touched him he experienced a leaching of his own life force, and was acutely aware that it would be possible to die in this place. The furniture salesman seated in a chair in his den would be found lifeless, and his death blamed on a heart attack, or a stroke, but the truth of it would lie elsewhere, and no one would ever know. He had to disentangle himself from the small hands, and force his other self, the one in the chair, to wake. He did so suddenly, like a man shocked into consciousness by a dousing with cold water. Only a minute or two had gone by, but it took hours for his fear to ebb.

That was the first time.

'And you went back?' said Angel.

'Eklund told me we had to learn more. He was right, I guess, but he didn't know what it was like for me over there, or didn't want to know. All he cared about was tracking the Brethren. He talked me into it, over the phone. But, you know, I was also curious. It wasn't just Eklund. It was my fault as well.

'The second time I explored farther, and drew closer to where I sensed they were, but when I tried to return I couldn't. I'd gone too deep, or spent too long on the other side. Either way, I couldn't seem to wake. That was when the children came back, and this time there were others with them – adults, but they wanted the same thing as the kids. I think I was like a beacon, and they believed if they followed me they might find a way out. And even if I couldn't help them escape, I represented light and heat. I was *life*.

'I began to panic, and that saved me. When I came to in my chair, I thought I was having a seizure. My chest hurt, and I swear that my face had gone purple. Eventually, I found the strength to crawl up to my bed. When Laurie came home, I told her I was feeling unwell. You remember, honey? That was back in December.'

'I remember,' she replied. She looked like she wanted to slap her husband across the back of the head for this foolishness, and only the presence of the two visitors prevented her from doing so.

'I'm sorry for it,' said Thayer.

'So you should be,' she replied, but Angel noticed that she did not take away her hands, and retained her grip on her husband. She might have thought him a fool, but he was her fool.

'And you told Eklund about this?' said Angel.

'I did. We came to an agreement: I would only go searching for the Brethren if he was with me, and we'd set a limit on the time I'd spend over there. He came here shortly after New Year's, when Laurie was away visiting our daughter in Boston, and we gave it a trial run. I sat in this very chair, Eklund beside me, and I traveled over. Eklund said he could tell when I was gone because my eyes opened, which he said was the damnedest thing – to be stared at by someone who wasn't seeing you. He counted to ten, then brought me back.'

'How?'

'It was just like waking a sleeper. He shook me hard, I closed my eyes, and when I opened them again I was back here. I felt like Dorothy in *The Wizard of Oz*, but without the ruby slippers.

'So with Eklund to help, it seemed safer than before. I wouldn't have only myself to rely on. There'd be someone else looking out for me. We agreed on twenty minutes, which was twice as long as I'd ever spent there before, but I knew where I had to go. I'd developed a sense of the place, and recalled the route that would get to where they were.'

'And you trusted Eklund?'

'I had no reason to doubt him, and he didn't let me down. He kept his word.'

Louis and Angel noticed that Thayer had started shaking again. It was just the faintest of tremors in the hands, arms, and jaw, like a man in the early stages of Parkinson's, but it was enough to cause his wife to raise a hand to his face in an effort to calm him. Thayer's eyes grew large, and a great desolation filled them, as though he had been forced to gaze into a pit filled with the remains of innocents.

'What happened wasn't Eklund's fault,' he said. 'He couldn't have known. Neither of us could.'

'Known what?' whispered Angel.

'How bad they are.'

Which was when the doorbell had rung for the second time that afternoon.

82

Sumner stopped breathing as soon as the man appeared, and it took him a few seconds to start again once the figure had vanished into the room off the hall. When he released his breath, it emerged in a rush that sounded like a wave breaking on rocks, and caused Richard to cast a warning glance in his direction. Sumner raised a hand in apology, but this was all wrong. The doorbell worked. They'd heard it ring twice inside the house, yet no one had responded.

But someone should have.

They ought to leave.

Now.

But Richard was moving again.

Into the kitchen.

Past the table.

Past the door.

Into the hall.

From behind the drapes in a second-floor bedroom, Thayer and Louis had watched the two men leave the front door and move to the rear of the house. Farther back, Angel was trying to keep Thayer's wife from panicking. Thayer could clearly see the guns in the hands of the men outside, but decided not to mention this to Laurie, just as he didn't see fit to tell her that a renewed bitch of a headache had just come upon him with the force of a brick falling on his head. She was already pissed at him for opening his gun safe and removing the

Taurus, especially when she smelled the oil on it and knew that he'd been keeping it clean, just in case.

'You recognize them?' asked Louis.

'No,' said Thayer, 'but they're Brethren. Trust me on it.'

Louis saw no reason not to. It was possible they were the same ones responsible for killing Michelle Souliere. If so, they were engaged in a serious clean-up operation. He cursed himself for not removing Thayer and his wife from their home earlier. He had allowed Thayer's wife to call the police, but only reluctantly. Police meant questions, and Louis didn't like answering questions, especially not the kind asked by law enforcement. He had already instructed Angel to hand over his weapon: the New York hearing wasn't for another week, and Louis didn't want to complicate matters with another gun. He, by contrast, had never been convicted of a crime, despite having committed enough of them to land him in prison for ten lifetimes. The weapon in his hand was registered, and all his paperwork was in order. However, that didn't make the prospect of police attention any more inviting.

'Don't take this the wrong way,' Thayer said, 'but which side of the law are you on?'

'That depends, but mostly the other side.'

'I thought as much, when you asked your friend there for his gun.'

'Don't worry about it,' said Louis. 'This is what we do.'

'Not in my home it isn't.'

'I don't think those men are going to give us a whole lot of choice.'

'You're wrong. I can choose. You stay here with my wife. You keep her safe for me.'

'Mr. Thayer—'

'Sir, this really isn't open for discussion.'

Louis looked at the gun in Thayer's right hand. The earlier shaking had ceased entirely.

'We'll compromise,' said Louis. 'I'll back you up, but you call it.'

Thayer acquiesced, but Louis knew this could end only one of two ways: with the men outside captured, or dead. His priority was to ensure that Thayer came through it all unscathed.

Because Parker would want to speak with him.

'Hey,' said Sumner.

'What?'

'I think that guy we saw was black.'

Richard paused. He hadn't managed to get a good look at the man who had passed through the hall, only registering his presence at the last moment. Richard spotted that he was tall, but so was Thayer.

'You certain?'

Now Sumner started to doubt himself.

'Not certain, but—'

A woman's voice shouted to them from somewhere above their heads.

'You need to get out of here now,' it said. 'We've called the police.'

'Shit,' said Sumner, but the warning only served to spur Richard into action. If the police were coming, then it was all the more reason to deal with the Thayers. Alive, the Thayers would be able to identify him and Richard, and give details of their vehicle, assuming they hadn't done so already.

Richard was halfway down the hall when a male voice said 'Fuck this.' Sumner heard a shot, and Richard stumbled against the wall to his left. Sumner's ears were still ringing as he watched Richard raise his weapon and fire, and suddenly the house was filled with a barrage of noise – gunfire, shattering glass – that only ended when a shard of Richard's skull detached itself from the whole and landed close to the kitchen trash can.

By then, Sumner was running.

*   *   *

Louis stared across the hall at Thayer, who was standing in the doorway of the dining room with the smoking Taurus in his hand. The plan, for what it was worth, and mainly at Laurie Thayer's insistence, had been to see if the intruders could first be warned off. If not, Louis had given them just enough sight of himself to draw them toward the den, which would put them under his gun, and Thayer's. Instead, Thayer decided to take matters into his own hands, with the result that one of the men now lay dead in the hall while the other was getting away.

'Stay there!' Louis ordered, although Thayer showed no signs of moving. He seemed mesmerized by the corpse, his face ashen, and Louis was certain that Thayer would soon end up back on his ass. He called to Angel to come down, and headed to the front door in order to intercept the fleeing man, but it had been double-locked with the deadbolt in place, and it took Louis precious seconds to get it open. He emerged just as the Blazer was accelerating down the drive, but he didn't fire. Already he could hear the sound of approaching sirens. He went back to the hall where, as predicted, Thayer was sitting on the floor again, with Angel beside him. To avoid any awkwardness, Louis placed their weapons in the hidden compartment of the Lexus. The sirens were louder now. The police would be here in moments. He returned to the house just in time to hear Angel's cell phone ring, and Laurie Thayer start to scream.

83

Parker got most of the story from Angel, but the tale was abruptly cut short when it became clear that Thayer hadn't just slumped to the floor from shock, and was suffering what might well be a heart attack. Parker had just enough time to advise Angel that, in case of any awkward police questions, they were working on behalf of Moxie Castin, and all inquiries should be directed to him, before the call ended. Thankfully, neither Angel nor Louis appeared to have broken any laws that day – what was seldom was wonderful – and so Parker didn't anticipate too many difficulties. With luck, he thought, the police would apprehend the second gunman, which might enable everyone to find out just what was going on.

Angel hung up and immediately dialed 911 to inform the authorities that an ambulance would be required in addition to the imminent police presence, and that the car in which the two attackers had arrived was now back on the road, minus fifty percent of its original occupants. Laurie Thayer had stopped screaming at the sight of the corpse bleeding all over her carpet, or at her semiconscious husband – Angel wasn't sure which of the two stimuli had set her off – and was concentrating on keeping Thayer comfortable. Through the open front door, Angel could see the first of the police cars pulling into the drive.

He looked around him. The floor was a mess of broken glass, shards of china, pieces of plaster, and wood splinters.

The wall above his head was pockmarked with bullet holes, and a dead man lay in a spreading stain of red.

'You see?' he said to Louis. 'This is why we can't have nice things.'

Sumner, through good luck alone, initially managed to head in the opposite direction from the approaching police vehicles. He fought his instinct to put his foot to the floor and get away as fast as possible, just in case, by some small miracle, the police didn't yet have the make and license plate number of the Blazer. For now, it was all he could do to hold himself together: it was as though he could still hear the echo of the gunshots, and see the wound that had appeared in Richard's back as the first of the bullets exited. He wondered what he was going to tell Sophia. Richard said she'd been on Valium since the affair. Sumner hoped she still had some left.

He forced himself to take deep breaths, and considered his situation. He was driving Richard's Blazer, but he was hopeful that no one at the Thayer house had managed to get a good look at him, so there was nothing beyond the vehicle itself to connect him to what had just gone down. The risk of discovery, therefore, was greater behind the wheel than it was on foot. If he could just get close enough to the next town, he could ditch the vehicle, walk in on foot, and maybe catch a bus or a cab somewhere else. That still left the problem of DNA and fingerprints inside and outside the Blazer. He could wipe it down, although it might be better to burn it, but then the sight of rising smoke would inevitably—

The road ahead inclined gently. Two police cars now appeared at its apex. Sumner couldn't continue in that direction, and he couldn't go back the way he'd come. To his left was thick woodland, but he saw a service road ahead about halfway between him and the approaching cops. He accelerated, turned sharply, and drove as far as he could along the winding dirt track until he came to a chain barrier. He stopped the Blazer, got out, and started running. He heard sirens, and an amplified voice ordered him to stop. Sumner paid it no heed. He was thinking about his wife and kids. He wanted to go home. He hadn't hurt anyone, and Richard was dead. Couldn't they just call it quits and let him go?

He glimpsed movement in the trees to his right: a man in uniform. He risked a glance behind and saw more police approaching on foot. He had a stitch in his side. He was out of condition. He wasn't going to make it to the next town. The way he was feeling, he wasn't going to make it to the next tree. Fuck it. Maybe he could find a way to blame it all on Richard, invent some tale of an imaginary grudge against Thayer over a shitty couch or a crummy dining room set, claim that he didn't know what was happening until Richard produced a gun. He couldn't keep on running. He'd collapse.

Sumner stopped. The blood was pounding in his ears. The police were shouting at him again, but he barely heard what they were saying. It was over. He was done. He started to raise his hands only to realize he was still holding the gun that Richard had given him. He'd been holding it ever since he left the house: holding it while driving, holding it while opening the car door, holding it while running.

Now he would hold it while dying.

A fusillade of shots rang out, but Sumner heard only the first.

84

David Ferrier returned from walking his dog and noticed that the Buckners still hadn't come back from whatever trip they were taking. It was unusual for them to be away overnight. Hell, if they didn't get back soon they might miss Sunday services, and their whole damn church would fall apart without them. Or worse – at least for the Buckners – maybe it wouldn't, and then their true position in the universal hierarchy would be revealed to them. Ferrier realized that his distrust of the Buckners had become an obsession: if they ever pulled up sticks and left, he'd be lost. He'd have nobody to dislike within an easy walk of his home.

He hung up his coat, put away the dog's leash, and decided to grab a beer and watch some TV. His wife, who didn't approve of drinking before sundown, wouldn't be home until after six, and therefore would never know, although Ferrier thought that he might hide the empty bottle under some other containers in the recycling bin, just in case she was counting, because she didn't really care much for him drinking, period, on account of some foolish notions she'd picked up from his physician. Then again, if she was counting, she'd certainly notice that the six-pack of Leinie's in the refrigerator was lighter by one bottle, so it would all be for naught.

Once he'd been through the various permutations, all joy was sapped from the idea of a beer anyway, so he settled for a soda. He spent the better part of an hour channel surfing, so it was a while before he stumbled on the story about the attack on the home of Tobey Thayer, the furniture king. The coverage flicked to woodland, and a beige Chevy Blazer parked with the driver's door standing open. A cloth hid the license plate, but the decal on the trunk was clearly visible.

Support Your Local Educator.

'Holy shit,' said Ferrier.

Parker was almost at the Pennsylvania border when Moxie Castin called him.

'Well, your boys aren't behind bars, although it was all I could do to stem the tide of police curiosity about them,' he said. 'Tobey Thayer had a heart attack, and is under observation. Before he lost consciousness, he and his wife corroborated Angel and Louis's version of events, and Thayer confirmed he killed one of the men who entered his home. Apparently the cops have a name, but they're not releasing it. You want to know what it is?'

'I thought you said they were keeping it to themselves.'

'They are, but that didn't stop Angel from taking a look in the dead guy's wallet before the cops got to him. Richard Franklin. I have an address for him in Lima, Ohio, but by now his home probably has more police in its vicinity than the White House.'

'What about the other guy?'

'That one I had to call in a favor to get. His name was Sumner Chase. He ran a construction company out of Findlay. In case you're wondering, Lima and Findlay are about thirty-five miles from each other. Neither of these guys had so much as a parking violation between them before they came gunning for Thayer, assuming that's what they set out to do. But here's the thing: from what I hear, the cops believe they came to Greensburg from the west, not the Northeast. They were picked up on some tollbooth cameras. Whoever killed Michelle Souliere, it wasn't these two, not unless they took the scenic route.'

'Anything else I should be told?'

'Just that Ross wants to know if you and your – and I'm quoting here, "goons" – actually understand the meaning of the word *discreet*?'

'Yeah? When you speak to him again, ask him if he understands the concept of honesty. Whatever is bothering him about Eklund, he's not sharing it with me.'

'Well, I'm sure you'll be hearing from him in good time, and he's not going to like the size of my bill when he gets it.'

'Add on an extra zero,' said Parker. 'Tell him I said it was okay.'

'You think?'

'Sure. It's the federal government: they won't even notice. And they're your tax dollars anyway. Consider it a rebate.'

'I'll think about it. In the meantime, I'm still working on that other matter.'

Parker had temporarily forgotten about Rachel and Sam. The realization came with a stab of guilt.

'I appreciate it.'

'And finally, I just need to make sure you're still clear on the importance of not shooting—'

Parker hung up.

85

Kirk and Sally Buckner were a few miles out of Turning Leaf, and Sally was getting antsy. She wanted to know that Richard and Sumner had done what they were supposed to, but she didn't want to risk calling them. The agreement was that either Sumner or Richard would text 'OK' when the job was done, and then they could all dispose of their phones, but so far Sally had heard nothing.

Kirk was dozing in the passenger seat, which made her want to grab a handful of his hair and smash his face against the window because he had no business sleeping, not with all that was going on. Ahead of her, a highway patrol car had stopped some guy in a truck, and Sally glanced anxiously in the rearview mirror before changing lanes.

Eleanor stared back at her from the backseat. The dead girl's lips were moving rapidly, but Sally couldn't read what they might be saying. Then Eleanor began shaking her head in warning, her mouth still forming soundless words, and Sally took the next exit and pulled into a gas station with a Starbucks next door, which caused Kirk to wake up.

'We out of gas already?' he said.

Sally turned to him. 'Eleanor's in the car. She's frightened. Get on the computer. Check the news feeds. Find out what's happening.'

Kirk didn't argue, although he couldn't stop himself from looking back. He could feel Eleanor's presence as a coldness at the top of his spine. It brought back the memory of her taste.

He fucking hated Eleanor.

Kirk used the wi-fi at Starbucks to get on the Internet, googled Thayer's name, and quickly scanned the results before displaying them for Sally. She read them without comment. Now she knew what Eleanor was trying to tell her.

'We have to run,' she said.

'How do you know? Maybe we should wait and—'

Sally slapped him hard across the face.

'Don't you dare argue with me, you fucking useless piece of shit. Richard and Sumner are dead, and the police may already be on their way here, otherwise Eleanor wouldn't have come to warn us. Do you understand?'

It took Kirk a moment to answer.

'Yes,' he said. He wouldn't look at her. He was rubbing his cheek with his left hand, but his right was balled into a fist. Sally thought he was close to striking back. When his eyes flicked to her, she knew it. Maybe he still had some spirit left in him after all. Good: he'd need it.

'I'm sorry I hit you,' she said, although she wasn't. The words were just required to mollify him.

He didn't reply, just said 'Most of what we need is in the house.'

'We can't go back there. Somehow, we've been tied into what's happening.'

They were always prepared to move at short notice, even after all these years. It was why the house was rented, and they owed nothing on their car, although if Sally were right then they wouldn't be able to hold on to it.

'Then we'll have to risk going to Donn's.'

In the event of a disaster, Kirk had anticipated having at least some time to gather what they needed. But just in case, he had left some essentials at Routh's place, hidden in an airtight bag in his basement: cash, drivers' licenses, and birth certificates in new names – Jesus, those had cost him a lot of money and effort – spare phones, and a couple of changes of clothing. There was also a wig for Sally; she kept her hair short, maybe for just that reason, although he had never asked. He could cut his hair and shave off his beard. It wouldn't take long. They'd have to separate, of course – the police would be expecting them to travel together – but they had clean e-mail addresses with which to stay in contact, and the burner phones at Routh's home had never been activated.

On the other hand, no one had ventured into Routh's house since he'd made his final trip to Providence. Sumner had made a couple of passes and detected no signs of intrusion or surveillance, but it was possible that whoever was responsible for Routh's death might now be watching the property. It was a risk they'd have to take. They could also leave their car in his barn, and exchange it for the battered Camry that was the latest in a string of vehicles Routh always kept for discreet use. It would get them wherever they needed to go before they were required to split up. They could argue about who got to keep the Camry once it was safely in their possession.

But Kirk still didn't want to believe Sally was right, and that their home was no longer safe for them. He'd grown accustomed to it, and had started to enjoy being part of the community. For Sally, it was all a pretense: she was good at dissembling. She didn't have any affection for the church folk, or even the people who supported her business by buying her pastries. He wouldn't have put it past her to piss in the cake batter, just to spite them.

But Kirk wasn't like his sister – and was this really so surprising, given that he wasn't the one who saw Eleanor and the others on a regular basis? For that much, at least, he was grateful. It enabled him to maintain a certain objectivity, and permitted him to retain a little of his sanity. In his private moments, especially when Sally was being particularly hostile toward him, Kirk often entertained fantasies of cutting himself off from his kin and leaving them to their bargain. He knew that he could easily manage to hide himself; he was the creator of identities, the provider of false names and histories. In recent years, he had even gone so far as to lay the groundwork for a new, unconnected life, although he was careful to work on it only when Sally was occupied by Brethren business, because when Sally was distracted it meant Eleanor and her kind were distracted too. That was the problem with being haunted: you could never be certain that an unseen presence wasn't looking over your shoulder, and Kirk didn't like to think about what would happen if his subterfuge was discovered. Sally, he believed, would have him killed. In the absence of Routh, she might even choose to take care of him herself; that, or hand him over to the placid, permanently grinning figure of Steven Lee, who would crush him inside a cube of metal as a favor to the family.

So Kirk had opened a couple of new bank accounts, one of them in his own name and one in the name of Edward Dempsey, his chosen alias. He now had eight thousand in the first account and almost twenty thousand in the second, thanks to the doctoring of invoices, and taking on jobs for cash, including a couple that were highly illegal but distinctly lucrative. He kept telling himself it was just in case everything went south for both of them, in which case he'd share the proceeds with Sally, because he didn't have any intention of leaving her, not really. But if that were truly the case, he'd have told her about the money, and Edward Dempsey. Instead he remained quiet, and waited.

He knew that he would never have another chance like this one: enforced separation from Sally, with the necessity of remaining apart for a considerable period of time. It would enable him to go deep, and when he surfaced again it would be somewhere far from here, with a new name and a new background. He didn't think the Brethren would find him, either. From what Sally had shared with him over the years, he knew that their link was always with only a handful of family members. Sally wouldn't have been able to hide from them, but he probably could.

And what of the next world? It existed – Kirk had no doubts about that – but wherever the Brethren roamed wasn't somewhere he wanted to be, in the life to come or any other. He had long wondered if the need to curb dissent among the Brethren was linked only to fears of discovery, and might not also conceal a greater repugnance for repentance.

And who could say with certainty that they were all damned to the same fate, that the pact could not be broken? Kirk was now infected by the Baptist faith that he and Sally had initially embraced only as a front, to the extent of reading much of the work of Albert Mohler, the president of the Southern Baptist Theological Seminary. Mohler, like other evangelicals, believed in the reality of the devil and demons. For him, evil was not an abstraction. He had given a talk on exorcism and exorcists at the Southern Baptist Convention in 2010, which Kirk was privileged to attend. 'The powers that the forces of darkness most fear,' Mohler informed his audience, 'are the name of Jesus, the authority of the Bible, and the power of his Gospel.' If Kirk could get to Mohler or someone like him, and convince him of the truth of what he had to tell . . .

He realized that Sally was speaking to him, and forced himself to pay attention.

'I said, "Do you know where he keeps his guns?"'

Kirk nodded.

'There's a safe under the floor of the barn,' he replied.

'Keys?'

'It's a combination lock.'

'I don't suppose you remember the combination?'

'Actually, I do.'

Recalling numbers and passwords was one of Kirk's talents. It came with his job, not that Sally had any fucking appreciation of it.

He looked out the car window. It was cold and hazy beyond. Wherever he ended up after this, it would be warm. He'd had enough of harsh winters.

'How do you suppose they found us?' he asked. He had a vision of police cars surrounding their home, of detectives going through their possessions. Once they began examining the details of the latest of their invented lives, the loose threads would become apparent.

'I've been thinking about that,' said Sally. 'I bet it was that nose-poking son of a bitch Ferrier, always hanging around, asking questions. I promise you, once this has all died down, we're going to come back and deal with him.'

Kirk glanced at Sally, but she was staring straight ahead, working at the inside of her cheek with her teeth, the way she always did when she was agitated. He knew how to conceal and reinvent himself, but she didn't. Without him to help her, she'd be found. Would she keep quiet when she was? Possibly. Then again, if he ran away and cut off all contact with her, she'd have no reason to be loyal to him. She could just blame everything on him: Souliere, Eklund, all of it.

He returned to looking at the landscape. He hadn't liked hitting Souliere when she went for Sally, but it wasn't as difficult as he might have anticipated. Had he been forced, he could probably have hit her some more. It was all a matter of getting one's blood up. He touched his cheek where Sally had struck him. It still smarted. He'd have a mark there.

And outside, the cold ground waited.

86

The lawyer Eldritch was in the ebb tide of his days. Even if he hadn't felt the failing of his body and mind, he would have known by the manner of the nurse who was caring for him. She hid it well, but Eldritch had spent decades descrying truth in the faces of others, and none could conceal it from him for long.

Yet as he prepared to leave this life, his concerns were not for himself but for his son, whoever or whatever he might be. Everything to do with this man Routh and the Brethren disturbed Eldritch. He had listened intently as his son described the contents of Eklund's basement, and used this information as a springboard for his own researches. It was a slow, difficult business: his eyesight was now so poor that he had to magnify individual words on the laptop screen in order to read them, and could only concentrate for short periods on what he read, or was told, before he was forced to rest. Even then, most of what he had accumulated amounted to rumor and conjecture, but from it he had established this much: somehow, Peter Magus had struck a deal with an entity powerful enough, or so the Magus believed, to hide him and his descendants from divine justice.

What little was known of the Brethren came from those who survived the Capstead siege and the extrajudicial killings that followed it. All were young women and children, and their testimonies were not entirely reliable, but those statements formed part of the historical record, and were held in the archives of the University of Missouri. The records had been digitized, but not shared, yet Eldritch accessed them all in a matter of minutes.

According to the witness testimonies, Peter Magus claimed to be in contact with an elemental force, an angel. Eldritch had no time for the foolishness and sentimentality about angel lore that had birthed a lucrative industry involving imagery that owed more to fairy tales and the Pre-Raphaelites than the Bible. It was an angel that slaughtered the firstborn of Egypt, an angel that was sent to punish Israel for David's numbering of the people, and an angel – specifically an 'evil spirit', to distinguish it from a demon – that God sent against Saul for looting the Amalekites, while a single angel was credited with destroying 185,000 in the camp of the Assyrians. Eldritch had always been particularly fascinated by the various translations of Psalm 78:49: 'He unleashed against them His hot anger, His wrath, indignation, and hostility – a band of destroying angels.' But in the King James Bible, the angels were described as 'evil.' He had spoken with the Collector about this, but had never received a satisfactory answer, just as only rarely did his son allude to his own true nature.

'What if I were an angel?' he had once asked Eldritch.

'Is that what you are?'

'In truth, I can no longer tell. Perhaps I am only what others wish me to be.'

It took a long time for Eldritch to discover what this might mean, and the revelation came from a most unexpected source: the rabbi named Epstein, who visited Eldritch while he was recovering from his injuries, before his son spirited the old lawyer away to safety. In the course of a conversation that seemed to last only minutes but in fact went on for almost two hours, Eldritch forgot his pain amid talk of the Buried God, of the angelic Watchers who sinned against the Divine by taking wives on Earth, and of the blurring of the distinctions between angelic and demonic during the period of the Second Temple, when divine messengers became tempters, tormentors, and punishers. It was Epstein who tried to explain something to Eldritch of the Kabbalah's teachings on angels, of how they were not physical beings but more akin to emotional states controlled and personified by the Divine, so that those visited by them saw, in effect, what they wished, or were meant, to see. Thus similar entities might provide visions of comfort, of revelation, and of punishment, or so Eldritch understood it, although he had to admit that he was under the influence of painkillers and sedatives at the time, and could not have sworn to his ability to recall every detail.

But this he knew: the ones who had rebelled, the fallen angels, were beyond the purview of the Divine . . .

Beside him, the nurse read on. Her name was Berenice. The Collector had assured him of her discretion, and Eldritch had no reason to doubt his son's judgment so he had entrusted to her the task of recapitulating the trove of new information. She was tall and dark, and although her individual features were without flaw, they had somehow combined to form an unattractive whole, as though she had been created from the scavenged pieces of others.

Eldritch felt himself drifting off, and tried to remain conscious. Soon, he knew, he would drift for the final time.

The nurse was reciting from a batch of documents e-mailed to him from the Boone County Historical Society. Why had he sought them? He could not recall. Something to do with one of the men involved in the final confrontation with Peter Magus, was that it? Yes, he believed so. A transcript kept by his family, a record of the dying whispers of one of the Brethren.

His eyes closed. A woman stretched out a hand to him from the dark, but he could not see her face. She spoke, but he could not understand what she said. If he took her hand, he would die. This alone he knew. She would draw him into the void, and his life would end.

The nurse paused to yawn. Eldritch heard her, but did not

open his eyes. Her recitation resumed with descriptions of bodies, and the smell of burning wood and flesh, and a young girl who had not even reached her teens lying scorched in the ruins, babbling amidst her final agonies. A word brought him back with such force that he grabbed the nurse's wrist, causing her to start violently.

'What was that?' he asked.

'What do you mean?'

'The name spoken by the girl. Read it again.'

She put a finger to the screen and pinpointed the reference.

'Belial,' she said.

Belial.

'Find my son,' said Eldritch.

87

Jennifer, the dead daughter, stood beneath a rocky promontory, the shape of her concealed by its shadow, with only the glimmer of her eyes to give her presence away.

Below her lay the city. She had known about it for a long time, ever since she decided to follow a man and woman who had separated themselves from the great wave of the dead to vanish instead into the hills. Jennifer did not know what could have caused them to turn aside from the deep ocean that awaited them. Perhaps they were afraid of what might lie beyond it, intimating a subsummation into the whole that would result in a loss of self and, consequently, of each other. Whatever the reason, they found their way to the city, there to hide from the was and the yet-to-be. Jennifer wondered if they now regretted their decision. The city, shimmering darkly on the boundary between the real and the imagined, was a landscape of hurt, formed from the memories both of those who had wandered and gone irrevocably astray, and of those who had chosen to conceal themselves from the consciousness that lay beyond the sea.

So much pain. So much badness.

As she watched, a figure appeared at the southern boundary of the city, where the walls melted away to be replaced by scorched, barren earth, with a series of emplacements at its heart like a primitive fortress. The man's pate was bald, but even from this distance she could see the frill of long red hair beneath it, and the curtain of beard that ran from ear to ear. Although she should not have been visible to him, still she felt his gaze upon her. He knew she was out there. He wanted her to come down.

And then he would take her.

More figures emerged to join the first, the Magus, so that in time a great crowd of the Brethren, generation upon generation, was watching her, all unmoving.

Come. Come to us.

But she remained where she was, waiting for another force to move against them.

88

Kirk was driving. Sally was in the backseat. Beside her, to her left, sat Eleanor. Sally's left hand was outstretched. Invisible to Kirk, Eleanor's right hand lay upon it.

Eleanor didn't speak. She was mute; death had silenced her. But she could convey emotions, and pick up on Sally's own thoughts and feelings. Now Sally showed her the photographs of Parker from Eklund's laptop, and felt Eleanor give a kind of shiver in response, flashing warning colors of red and purple. Sally didn't know much about Parker beyond what she had discovered from the Internet and Eklund's computer, but she recognized that to draw his attention was not dissimilar to having an unerring bullet fired in one's direction, a projectile that would maintain its trajectory and velocity without diminution until it found its target. Sally tried to make Eleanor understand this, but the signals Eleanor was giving out were confusing, and Sally couldn't be sure that she was reacting solely to Parker, or if some other factor was influencing her. Sally could only be certain that Eleanor was afraid.

An image flashed in Sally's mind, and Eleanor's grip on her hand tightened.

The shape of a man, then emptiness.

I don't understand.

It came again: man and emptiness, two separate projections that then coalesced into a single image. Now Sally understood. Not empty, but hollow.

Hollow Man.

The image multiplied, one becoming many.

Hollow Men. Who are they?

Another image, this time of fire and destruction, and Sally felt Eleanor's skin burn as the final moments of the Capstead community were re-created for her. Then the flames were sucked into a point of infinite density, and darkness prevailed.

The end. But of what?

Eleanor's mouth moved, struggling to form the words. It took two tries, but Sally finally understood.

Of us all.

89

Philip had made the arrangements. Now he and Lastrade were just waiting for the handover. In addition to the $100,000 from Stevie, they had another $35,000 they'd pooled from their own resources. Philip was optimistic they could triple or quadruple their investment, depending on how much they stepped on the heroin before they sold it. They'd also agreed an agent's cut of $10,000 with Stevie, which meant they would ultimately emerge with anywhere from $120,000 to $150,000 apiece. All being well, they would reinvest most of that in another batch of heroin, and maybe a little coke if they could negotiate a good price from the right suppliers.

But they'd been forced to make a long journey to get to the point of purchase. Philip's contact had insisted on meeting at Willets Point in Queens, popularly known as the Iron Triangle, which meant an eight-hour round trip for a destination that looked like Philip's idea of hell: a landscape of rusting vehicles waiting to be cannibalized by the auto shops that lined its mostly unpaved streets, a stinking vista broken only by the occasional waste-processing plant. Redevelopment of the area was imminent, but Philip still thought it might have been better just to nuke the Triangle and walk away. As daylight began to fade, they waited, as instructed, by a disused lot in the shade of the Whitestone Expressway. They'd already been ordered to move position three times by two different callers, first over to Railroad Avenue and then up to Overlook Park. At Overlook Park they were told to change vehicles, and ditched Philip's BMW in favor of a piece of shit Sebring, once Philip had found a 24-hour-garage in which to leave his car. Neither of the callers had sounded like Slaven, the main contact. An hour had gone by since the last communication. Philip twice tried calling the number he'd been given, but it went straight to voice mail.

No, make that three times.

'Well?' asked Lastrade from the backseat.

'Nothing. They're not answering.'

'Jesus. We ought to go.'

'And do what?'

'I don't know, but we can't stay here much longer.'

The money was in a pair of sports bags by Lastrade's feet. He couldn't get comfortable, no matter how he tried to position his legs, but he thought that it might have been nerves as much as anything else.

Philip wasn't nervous, just irritated. He wanted the heroin. He also wanted to conclude the deal to have Mother killed. He knew he wouldn't be able to do it himself. He loved her too much for that. He'd made it clear to Slaven that a job might need to be done, although he hadn't named names – not that he felt it was necessary to do so, since he'd dropped enough hints to make the object of his animus fairly clear. He also had a good idea of the going rate. Ten grand would cover it. He could probably get it done for less – even for free, if he waited long enough and gave Slaven and his people enough business – but it would be difficult for him to establish himself while Mother was still alive. She'd find out. She had her ways. It would be better if she were no longer around.

'I need to take a leak,' he said. He also wanted to stretch his legs, and give himself time to think away from Lastrade. He got out of the car and walked to the corner of the lot, which was surrounded by a wall with a spiked fence running along the top. Near the corner was the recessed entrance to a garage, accessed via a pair of locked steel doors. It gave him a little privacy, so he unzipped himself there, pissed, and

411

lit a cigarette. He tried Slaven again. This time the phone was answered on the second ring, and Philip recognized Slaven's voice.

'Where are you?' Philip asked.

'Right behind you,' said the voice in his ear, just after the same voice spoke to him from behind.

Philip turned to see Slaven holding a phone in one hand, and a gun in the other. With him was a second man, also armed, with a face like an assemblage of blades. Philip heard the Sebring start up at the same time as the garage doors were opened.

'Inside,' said Slaven.

The Sebring appeared behind them, but Lastrade was no longer alone in it. There was a stranger at the wheel, and another in the backseat holding a gun. Lastrade looked frightened as the car drove into the garage.

'What is this?' asked Philip.

'That,' said Slaven, 'is what we are about to find out.'

90

The call came as Parker reached the outskirts of Greensburg. He recognized the number. Few others knew it.

'Hello?' he said.

The voice of the lawyer Eldritch came over the Bluetooth connection. His breathing was labored.

'Mr. Parker, I want you to listen to me. In Kentucky is the home of a man named Donn Routh . . .'

VII

To the house wherein the dwellers are bereft of light,
Where dust is their fare and clay their food,
Where they see no light, residing in darkness,
Where they are clothed like birds, with wings for garments,
And where over door and bolt is spread dust.

'Ištar's Descent to the Underworld,'
trans. E. A. Speiser,
Ancient Near Eastern Texts (1950)

91

The Collector moved through Donn Routh's near-empty house, with its spoiled food in the kitchen, its unused rooms, its life half-lived. It smelled bad, and only the continuing cold spell prevented it from smelling much worse. It was not just the pot of old stew on the stove, or the vegetables that had begun to soften to mush. Routh's home stank of neglect and foul habits. It reeked of moral decay.

The Collector wondered if Routh had killed the Chinese girl here. He thought so, but he did not believe Routh had killed many other women in the same way. He had sensed an emptiness to Routh, a joylessness. He might have murdered the girl simply to see what it felt like to take her life, and the Collector could almost pick up the lingering aftertaste of his disappointment, even after all this time. The music collection was interesting, though. It suggested some form of aesthetic sensibility, and a desire, if not an actual ability, to take pleasure in the sublime.

His phone vibrated in his pocket, but he ignored it. Somewhere in this house there had to be a clue to the identities of the surviving Brethren. He needed to concentrate.

The Collector first went through all the vinyl records, emptying them from their sleeves and tossing them to the floor, barely noticing if they broke or not. They had clearly been precious to Routh, and therefore it was possible he might have hidden other items of value among them. In the end, all the Collector found for his troubles were some letters to Routh from a dealer in rare vinyl, stored away in a copy of

Verdi's *Requiem* featuring the Philharmonia Orchestra conducted by Carlo Maria Giulini, with the voices of Christa Ludwig, Nicolai Gedda, and Elisabeth Schwarzkopf. The Collector was about to discard this record, too, when some instinct caused him instead to set it aside intact. His father always claimed that Schwarzkopf was the greatest interpreter of lieder he had ever heard, although he admitted to being troubled by what appeared to be her enthusiastic membership of the Nazi Party. The Collector thought that this particular example of her work might bring Eldritch some pleasure.

He continued his search of the house, moving from room to room, finding little of interest, until finally all that was left was the basement. He stood at the top of the steps, looking down. An earlier brief glance had revealed boxes and assorted junk. Now he had little choice but to tackle it. First, though, he wanted a drink of water. His mouth felt dry and dusty.

He stepped into the kitchen. A woman was standing before him, a man hovering at her right shoulder. The woman held a kitchen knife in her hand. The Collector raised his left hand and opened his mouth to speak, even as he tensed his right wrist to release the blade concealed along his forearm. The woman advanced a step, and the Collector felt a sharp pain in his chest that, like a flame igniting and feeding on oxygen, grew in intensity until it was all that he knew. He dropped his left hand to the handle of the knife, even as the blade on his wrist snicked from its scabbard and landed uselessly on the floor. The kitchen door stood open, and beyond it he could see the last of the day's sunlight fading into evening. He began walking, and the woman and man stepped out of his way. The blade in his chest cut at his insides with each step he took, but he did not stop. He wanted to die in the light. He made it to the door just as his legs gave out, then dropped to his knees as the sun grew dark and the world bled red around him. Shadows converged. He tried to keep them at bay, but he no longer had the strength. The shadows took on a terrible solidity as he moved from his world into theirs, and he found himself surrounded by the Hollow Men.

The falcons have no love for the hunter, he thought. *He is simply a provider.*

They fell upon him, and he was devoured.

92

Sally and Kirk looked down at the body before them. The stranger lay on his side, his eyes barely open in death, his lips forming an oval of shock. He was still holding the handle of the knife, as though it were he, and not Sally, who had delivered the fatal blow. As they stared at him, marks began to appear on the exposed skin of his face and hands: puncture wounds, as of the insertion of needles.

Or sharp teeth.

A kind of gray mist seemed to swirl around the dead man, and in it Sally thought she could discern faces materializing and vanishing.

None of this was visible to Kirk. All he saw was a dead man who appeared to be conspiring in his own rapid decay, his face mottling where he lay. He didn't look like a cop. That was all Kirk knew for sure, which was good.

'What's happening to his skin?' Kirk asked, but Sally barely heard him. Eleanor had appeared. She was standing by the old barn, and shaking so violently that she was little more than a blur. She radiated fear, and Sally felt it break upon her in turn.

And then Eleanor vanished from view.

'We have to get away from here,' said Sally. 'Like, right now.'

For once, it was Kirk who was the calm one. He retrieved the cash and documents from the basement, gathered some food for the road, and took the keys to the Camry from a hook in the hall. By the time he was done, Sally was over at the barn, keeping as much distance as she could between herself and the man she had killed. Kirk joined her, and removed a board from the barn floor, revealing Routh's gun safe. He unlocked it, and took out a pair of pistols and some ammunition before replacing the board. Finally, he opened wide the barn doors, drove the Camry out, and parked their Focus in its place. He had to help Sally into the passenger seat, all thoughts of abandoning her forgotten for now. She was retreating into herself, and he struggled to get any sense out of her.

'Eleanor's gone,' she said. She started to cry. 'She's gone, and she won't be coming back.'

Good, Kirk wanted to say, but he kept this opinion to himself.

'Where should we go?' he asked.

'It doesn't matter,' said Sally. 'It's all coming to an end.'

'It matters to me.'

He wasn't about to give up. They had money and new identities. They just needed some time, and a place to hide. A hotel was out of the question while they were together, and they couldn't turn to any of the family because they were all in danger now.

He was halfway to the highway when he figured it out.

He turned the car at the first opportunity, and headed northeast.

Many hours later, Parker pulled up behind the home of Donn Routh, and the beams of his headlights caught the body on the ground. Parker stepped from the car, a flashlight in one hand, his gun in the other, and took a moment to stand over the remains. He then checked the house, established that it was unoccupied, and returned to the body.

It seemed impossible that the Collector should be dead, and Parker was surprised at the sadness he felt. In death, the ogre was diminished, but also humanized. Whatever he was, or whatever he might have believed himself to be, he had died alone and in pain.

Across the yard, the double doors to a barn stood fractionally ajar. Parker slowly advanced on it, and used the door on the right to shield himself as he made the gap wider. He identified himself as an armed investigator, but received no reply. He risked a glance, and saw a red Ford Focus parked inside. He stayed low and touched a hand to the hood. It was warm, but he sensed the emptiness of the barn. He found the registration in the glove compartment of the car, identifying it as the property of one Kirk Buckner, with an address in Turning Leaf, West Virginia.

He called the police, and waited for them by the body of the Collector.

93

In the house by the sea, the lawyer Eldritch woke from a dream of tides. The nurse sat in a chair beside the bed, flicking through a magazine. Eldritch stretched out a hand and touched her leg. She looked up. The old man's eyes stared clearly and brightly at her, and when he spoke, it was without a tremor.

'My son is gone,' he said.

94

Philip knelt on the filthy garage floor. His hands were secured behind his back with plastic ties, and the left side of his face was covered with Lastrade's blood and brain matter. Like Philip, Lastrade's hands had been bound, but he'd barely lived long enough to resent the cinch.

Philip had closed his eyes and waited for the shot that would end his own life, but it did not come. That was hours earlier. No one had spoken to him since then, and a cotton sack had been placed over his head. The warehouse was freezing. Philip couldn't stop shaking. His knees hurt, and his back ached, but he was alive.

There was hope.

Philip drifted. He thought of Mother. When he fell asleep and started to topple, he received a blow to the head for his trouble, and was returned to an upright position. It was torture.

But there was hope.

Footsteps approached, and the bag was removed from his head. The light was dim in the garage, and it did not take his eyes long to adjust. Lastrade still lay on the floor beside him, facing the ceiling with a hole where his nose used to be.

But now Slaven was standing over Philip, the two bags of money at his feet. Slaven reached into one, withdrew a wad of bills, and held it up like a dead fish. He even sniffed at the paper, his nose wrinkling in distaste, before removing a Zippo from his pocket, igniting it, and holding the flame to the corner of the bills. He waited for them to start burning, watching Philip throughout.

'Hey,' said Philip softly. 'Hey.'

The bills caught, a faint blue tinge to the flame.

'Worthless,' said Slaven. 'Fake. Just like you.'

'I didn't know,' said Philip.

More footsteps, this time from behind: the *tap-tap* of heels. He smelled her before he saw her. He knew her scent, had known it all his life. He tried to look over his shoulder, but a gun touched his cheek, forcing him to continue staring straight ahead.

'Mother,' he said, when at last she appeared before him. 'Please tell him. Tell him that I didn't know. Honest, I didn't.'

Mother looked down at her child, and Philip started to weep.

'I don't understand,' he said.

'They set you up,' she said, speaking softly as one would to a little boy who does not understand why the bigger boys were being mean to him. 'They fed you to the authorities so that you would lead them to Slaven and his people, and then Slaven would lead them to the drugs, and the drugs would lead them to the terrorists, or so they believed. You've caused everyone a great deal of trouble.'

'I was going to make us all rich,' said Philip.

'"Us"?' said Mother.

He heard it in her tone. She knew what he had planned to do. Slaven had told her. That was low, spilling another man's secrets to Mother.

Philip stopped crying, the tears instantly cut off as though a faucet had been turned.

'Why couldn't you just have trusted me?'

'Because I knew it would have ended like this: in guns, and blood, and dying.'

She reached for him, and used her thumb to blot the last of his tears, smearing some blood with them, even as the first of her own tears began to fall.

'I won't do it again,' said Philip.

'I know.'

She drew his head to her, and held him to her womb.

'I just want to go home,' said Philip.

'No,' said Mother. 'You can't do that. I can't keep you with me anymore. You must go away for a long time. Arrangements have been made.'

She stroked his hair, and kissed the top of his head. She recalled the scent of him as an infant, the feel of his hair against her skin, the sound of his breathing as he slept. She was too soft. All women were when it came to their sons.

She released her hold on him and stepped back.

'Goodbye, Philip,' she said.

'Mother—'

She turned and walked away. She had taken only three steps when the shot rang out. She did not look back. She did not want them to see her face. It was a mother's frailty.

Had she been stronger, she'd have killed him herself.

95

With the assistance of David Ferrier, the police now possessed a list of the owners of the vehicles present at the house of Kirk and Sally Buckner for the family conclave, and a series of arrests commenced.

The widows of Richard Franklin and Sumner Chase were held in separate interview rooms, advised by a pair of lawyers who instructed them to stay silent for the present, although Sophia and Jesse didn't need to be told that. They understood their best hope was to keep quiet, and beyond confirming that a gathering had taken place at the Buckner residence in Turning Leaf, and professing ignorance of what might have brought their respective husbands to the home of Tobey Thayer, they were prepared to admit nothing at all.

Also in custody were Art, Jeanette, and Briony Montague, all of whom were doing passable impressions of innocence. Their stories were similar to those of Sophia Franklin and Jesse Chase: they had all been brought together by bereavement, the passing of a distant relative. They even had a name to give: Elyse Barlow, who had died recently in upstate New York surrounded by semi-feral cats, and whose body continued to lie unclaimed in a mortuary.

Madyln and Sally had warned them that a day like this might come, and they were well prepared. The attempted murder of Tobey Thayer was problematic for Sophia and Jesse, but there was nothing to link the others to it. Therefore it might have been possible – barely, but sometimes barely is enough – for some, or all, of those being questioned to distance themselves from the accumulating mess of bodies had it not been for Steven Lee.

Steven Lee had been laid up with a peptic ulcer. The ulcer wasn't responding to medication, not helped by his ongoing intake of caffeine, alcohol, and tobacco, and he was now resigned to surgery. But due to his indisposition, somewhere on his lot the remains of Jaycob Eklund lay rotting in the trunk of a 1982 Oldsmobile Firenza, generally regarded as being among the worst cars manufactured in the 1980s, and not likely to be improved by the addition of a corpse. Elsewhere, packed into various cubes of twisted metal stacked by the eastern boundary, were the bones of some of the unfortunates who had passed through Steven Lee's hands in recent times, including Richard Franklin's late, lamented squeeze, Lucie Mossman. Steven Lee should probably have found a means to get rid of them, but in a curious way he liked having them around. They constituted both a memorial wall and a trophy cabinet.

As soon as he saw the cops arrive, Steven Lee panicked and tried to run.

With a peptic ulcer.

When he collapsed, he started shooting. Only one person died in the ensuing exchange of fire, and that person was Steven Lee, his body jammed between two cars. One was a Kia Concord.

The other was a 1982 Oldsmobile Firenza.

More police. More calls to Moxie Castin and to SAC Ross in New York. Parker was questioned about how he came to be at the farmhouse of one Donn Routh. He told the police about the call from Eldritch, which was when he realized that nobody had informed the old man of his son's passing. He tried to do it himself, when he was given a minute, but the phone just rang out.

But perhaps, he thought, *Eldritch already knows.*

Parker didn't hide anything from the police, because he had very little *to* hide. It was an unusual position in which to find himself. He had grown used to avoidance, half-truths, and outright lies. He found the opportunity for relative honesty slightly unsettling.

Sleet fell, slowly turning to snow. The Collector's body remained on the ground, covered by a sheet, and at last it was decided that the time had come to take it away. Parker watched the removal, and eventually the police conceded that he could go too, yet he lingered. He felt a sense of failure. He was surrounded by pieces of a puzzle, but could not make them fit into a coherent whole. Eklund was still missing. Michelle Souliere was dead. Tobey Thayer, at least, was alive. And the Buckners, hosts of a gathering that had, according to the police, resulted in at least four deaths so far – five if Souliere's murder could be linked to them – had dropped off the map.

All investigations have their own momentum. Some are driven by the investigators while others drag the investigators along behind, their impetus a product of factors beyond the influence of those seeking answers. For Parker, this was just such an inquiry: he felt himself always to be a step behind, and had been so from the very start, ever since Ross had chosen to withhold whatever might be the true reason for his interest in Jaycob Eklund.

Parker stood amid the falling snow, the flakes descending like fragments of paper, the detritus of a greater record to which he would now never be privy, tumbling and accumulating to further conceal the missing and the dead, the victims of a belief that somewhere in the past a bargain had been struck to stave off damnation.

Belial: according to Eldritch, this was the name of the entity with which Peter Magus had claimed to commune. Belial, the fairest of all who fell from heaven, fairer even than Lucifer himself; Belial the angel of hostility, the demon of lies. Peter Magus promised his followers that he had made a compact with a spirit, and as a consequence they would not be punished in the next life for their sins. All that was required in return was sacrifice. They would buy the safety of generations with the lives of others. But the deal was struck with a being that thrived on deception, and so was based on deceit. Whether the creature Belial existed or not was inconsequential. What mattered was that Peter Magus managed to convince his acolytes of its objective reality, and their descendants had been killing to protect themselves and their forebears ever since.

Men and women moved through Donn Routh's home, seeking out the secrets of his life. Parker caught the shapes of them, like ghosts against the drapes. He left them to their work, and headed north.

Two sheriff's deputies stood close to Steven Lee's body as it was taken away. His mother had been removed from the little house that she and her son shared. She spoke only one word as she was placed in the car, her son's body visible to her at the far end of the lot.

'Murderers.'

Snow was settling on the deputies. If they remained where they were for much longer, someone would have to mark them with an orange pole so they could be found in the drifts.

'That car stinks,' said one.

'It's a Firenza,' said the other. 'My sister used to have one. Piece of shit.'

'No, it *stinks*.'

They drew closer to it. The interior of the windowless car was empty, the trunk locked. The older of the two men found the release mechanism and popped the trunk.

Instantly, Jaycob Eklund ceased to be missing.

96

The pace of the arrests increased. Esther and Allan Sherwood were detained while making for the Canadian border in their van, their destination clear from the Canadian dollars and travel guides to Quebec found in their possession. Within hours, all those who had been present at the meeting in the Buckner house, with the exception of the hosts themselves, were being interrogated, along with their children, their children's friends, and anyone with whom they happened to be even on nodding terms.

The answers given by the Buckners' immediate kin were similar enough to cause the detectives involved to suspect, not unreasonably, that the various parties had colluded in the creation of a cover story. Even Steven Lee's mother professed to being unaware of how Jaycob Eklund's body had come to occupy the trunk of a car in the family scrapyard, and was therefore unable to clarify the extent of her son's involvement in the private investigator's death, and whether the appearance of a corpse on their business premises might represent an aberration or a more regular occurrence.

But the balance was shifting against the Brethren, in this world and another. Peter Magus had made a blood covenant, but it required successive generations of his family to service the debt. Now four of them – Donn Routh, Richard, Sumner, and Steven Lee – were dead, and it was not yet clear how many of those who remained might find themselves behind bars.

Weakness. Vulnerability.
The predators were circling.

Tobey Thayer woke in his hospital bed. He felt a tingling in
his fingers and toes. He put it down to his current circumstances until a girl's voice, one he did not recognize,
whispered

come see

He closed his eyes again and joined her.

Thayer was back in the city of shadows, but it was different.
The streets were empty, although he sensed movement behind
closed doors and shuttered windows, and a kind of
watchfulness.

Before him lay the fortress of the Brethren. It stood in
isolation, with scorched earth before and scrubland behind.
Figures surrounded it, mostly men with gray skin wrinkled
like rotten fruit, some women scattered among their number,
although gender had long ceased to have meaning for any
of them. They stood unmoving, watching the fortress,
waiting.

Thayer shivered. It was cold here. When he breathed out,
his breath was like smoke from a hidden fire.

A girl appeared beside him. She looked like a child and
spoke with the voice of a child, but her eyes were ancient.
She took his hand. Her touch was warm. He stopped
shivering.

'Who are they?' he asked.

hollow men

'Why are they here?'

the one they hated is dead

A Hollow Man looked back, as though alerted to their
presence by her words, and the empty pits of his eyes were
like holes gouged in old mud.

but without him they're lost

'So they want to join these others?'
no
they want to punish them
And with that, the Hollow Men descended upon the fortress.

97

Kirk and Sally made it to Jaycob Eklund's cabin while it was still dark, and Kirk broke a pane of glass on the back door so they could gain access. They had learned about the existence of the cabin from Eklund, while he was being encouraged to describe the purpose of each of the keys on his key chain so that Donn Routh would have no trouble entering his home. The interior was simply furnished, with a small kitchen adjoining a living area, a bedroom and bathroom beyond, and an insulated extension to the rear made of brick clad with wood. The extension housed a single room with a toilet in one corner, a showerhead to the side, and a drain in the floor. Otherwise, it was entirely empty, and smelled of bleach. It reminded Kirk of a prison cell.

Although neither he nor Sally was hungry, they realized the importance of keeping their strength up, so Kirk made franks and beans from their own supplies and contents of Eklund's kitchen closets. The cabin didn't have a TV or an Internet connection, so the Buckners weren't yet aware that Eklund's body had been found in Steven Lee's yard, but Kirk knew that they wouldn't be able to remain in these woods for long. They'd sleep, stock up on necessities, and do their best to alter their appearance before continuing on their way.

Kirk risked lighting a fire. It was dark, and the cabin stood at the end of a trail, well hidden from the surrounding properties, which were few. Kirk held Sally, and wondered how he could ever have conceived of abandoning her. She lay against his chest, trembling like a bird. She had barely spoken to him since they arrived, but her lips had never stopped moving. Had he not known better, he might have thought she was praying.

Kirk was exhausted. He just wanted to sleep, even if it was only for a couple of hours. He closed his eyes as desire became reality.

Fire was blooming in the heart of the fortress. Thayer watched the Brethren try to flee the conflagration, but none escaped the Hollow Men. The girl never let go of Thayer's hand throughout, but gazed with equanimity on all that was transpiring.

Thayer heard a sound from the black skies, as of the beating of great wings. He looked up and saw nothing, yet he knew that a presence was circling high above. Dark smoke rose in a funnel from the stockade as the Brethren were transformed, and a hole began to open in the clouds to accept them, its periphery ringed with red.

The beating grew louder. Voices screamed, the clouds split, and Thayer glimpsed for an instant a massive form, a being terrible in its flawless beauty and implacable in its animosity. Its wings were those of a great predatory bird, its hands and feet curved like talons, its face rapacious with lust, its androgyny hinting at appetites that could never be satisfied. It shone with a brightness that served almost to disguise the depravity of its features, the outward manifestation of its profound corruption. If this was the creature with which Peter Magus had made his bargain, then Peter Magus was a fool.

And still the flames grew, and still they fed upon the Brethren.

Kirk woke to darkness. The fire in the hearth was reduced to glowing embers, and all the warmth had gone from the room. Sally was no longer beside him. He called her name, but even as he did so he saw her standing by the kitchen doorway. She was staring fixedly at a point in the center of the room, and he knew that whatever she was seeing was not of this world. Sally's face was a rictus of horror, and she was shaking her head, her mouth forming the word *no* over and over, moving from silence, to a whisper, and finally to a scream.

'Eleanor – No!'

Sally was watching Eleanor burn. Fragments of skin flaked from Eleanor's face and ascended, blackening as they went. Eleanor's lips were stretched wide, exposing yellowed teeth, and her eyes were squeezed shut with the agony of her disintegration. Sally extended her hands, and as she did so two forms appeared at either side of Eleanor, their skin gray and wrinkled. One of them grasped her hair, yanking her head back, while the other reached deep into her mouth. It stared at Sally across the gap between worlds, and she heard it speak her name as a promise just before it wrenched Eleanor's tongue from her mouth.

The fortress had crumbled. The screaming had ceased.

Peter Magus stood alone in the ruins, surrounded by the Hollow Men. Above them all circled the angel, so huge that it could only be glimpsed in parts as it moved across the gap in the clouds. As Thayer watched, Peter Magus lifted his arms to the sky and cried out the name of the entity that had betrayed him at the last, even as the Hollow Men tore at him and his spirit began to burn.

Thayer looked away. He tried to let go of the girl's hand, but she would not release him.

'I want to go back now,' he told her.

you can't

'Why?'

you know why

And he did. He had known it ever since he'd been brought to this place by the girl, but had not wanted to admit it.

'I never got to say goodbye to my wife, to my children.'

i am sorry

And she was.

walk with me

i will take you to the sea

98

Dawn came. Kirk woke to a buzzing sound. He thought it might have been a snowmobile, but he could see no sign of it from the windows. The fire was low, but still gave off some heat. Sally must have replenished it while he slept. They'd have to let it die. They couldn't risk someone spotting the smoke.

Sally was sitting in a corner of Eklund's living room, her chin resting on her knees, gazing silently at the light around the drapes slowly growing brighter. Kirk tried to talk with her, but couldn't get a response, and eventually grew tired of the effort. He searched in Eklund's freezer and extracted a loaf of bread with the consistency of a brick, and a pack of bacon. He used the microwave to defrost both, and set about preparing breakfast. He made a pot of coffee while he worked, and listened to the radio. He thought he might go out later and find somewhere he could access the Internet. It was important to establish just how bad their circumstances were.

Music played. A bird passed overhead, large or low enough for Kirk to discern the beating of its wings. He didn't know much about nature, but they were out in the sticks and there had to be some big birds of prey in the woods. Maybe he'd see an eagle. He'd never caught sight of one in the wild, only in zoos.

He wondered what would happen if Sally didn't come out of her daze. He couldn't haul her around like a zombie. If they were to survive this, they both needed to be alert. Maybe it was the taste of the coffee, and the smell of frying bacon, but he was starting to believe that escape might be possible. Eleanor was gone, and probably the others too; that much, at least, he'd managed to get out of Sally. Perhaps it was all over at last, and whatever had taken Eleanor and the rest would be satisfied with their immolation. The old Brethren might be finished, but he and Sally were still here. They were alive. They could start again.

The bacon was about ready, and two slices of the defrosted bread had just popped up from the toaster. He freshened his coffee, filled a mug for Sally, and divided the food between two plates. He'd force her to eat, if he had to. He'd feed her like a child, or a baby bird.

He stepped into the living room. Sally's blanket lay discarded on the floor nearby, but she was nowhere to be seen. He checked the bathroom, and the weird little extension at the back of the house, but both were empty. He went to the front door of the cabin and tried to open it. A weight pulled against him. He yanked harder, and this time the door moved slightly, just enough for him to see what was on the other side.

Sally was kneeling on the ground. She had taken off her blouse, tying one end around her neck and the other to the ornamental metal loop at the center of the door before using her own weight to tighten the noose. Her face was a reddish-purple, and her tongue hung from her mouth. Her skin was still warm to the touch.

Kirk started to untie the knot around the door handle in the hope that he might yet revive her, then paused. If he managed to bring Sally back to consciousness, he would not be able to take her to a hospital. If he left her and called for an ambulance along the way, it might not take the police long to identify her and come after him.

Kirk stood over his sister. He braced himself with one foot against the inside of the door, placed his hands on her shoulders, and pushed down. He thought he heard her make a

439

sound, but he could have been mistaken. Even if she had, Kirk convinced himself that it was probably not a sign of life, only the last of the air leaving her body.

He returned to the kitchen, found a knife, and used it to cut the noose. He dragged Sally into the living room and laid her on the floor. As an afterthought, he placed the blanket over her, covering her face. When that was done, he went back to the kitchen for the last time. He ate some of the bacon and toast, and put what was left in Saran Wrap for later. He dug up a Thermos from Eklund's kitchen closet and filled it with coffee. Finally, he scavenged whatever else might be of use – some books, a Swiss Army knife, a couple of sweaters and shirts, a coat, a pair of jeans that were just slightly too long – and added them to a big tote bag. He placed the bag beside the door and looked back at Sally's body. There was no point in wasting the time it would take to bury her. He'd cleaned up as he best he could, but if the police came to the house they would know from the fire and the stove that someone had been there. His wife's corpse wouldn't make much difference either way.

'Goodbye, Sally,' he said.

He opened the door and found himself staring down the barrel of a gun.

99

It had been a hunch on Parker's part, but a reasonable one based on the discovery of Eklund's body at the wrecking yard, and his own knowledge of the existence of Eklund's cabin. He'd made the call to Art Currier, who had in turn got in touch with Eklund's nearest neighbor. A quick look at the property had confirmed the presence of a car, but Art had taken the trouble to head over himself while Parker was still on the road, just to be sure.

Kirk Buckner didn't try to fight or run – not that there would have been any point, not with Angel and Louis holding guns on him as well. He lay on the ground, just as he was ordered, and allowed Parker to remove the pistol from the pocket of his jacket. It still had the safety on.

'Where's your wife?' Parker asked him.

'Inside. She's dead. And she wasn't my wife. She was my sister.'

Parker didn't even bother exploring the subject further. This wasn't the time.

Angel risked a glance into the house, Louis at the other side of the door. 'We have a body on the floor. It's got a blanket over its upper half.'

Parker secured Buckner's hands with plastic ties from his car while Angel approached the body, Louis covering him. Angel yanked the blanket away, revealing Sally Buckner's swollen face. He checked for a pulse, although he could see that she was dead.

'She's gone,' he told Parker.

'She hanged herself,' said Buckner. 'From the door handle.'
He stared up at Parker.
'I didn't kill her,' he added. 'Not even a little.'

They held off on calling the police. They didn't have much
choice as there was no cell phone signal, so one of them
would have to head back to the main road to make the call,
or prevail upon Eklund's neighbor for the use of his phone.

Parker took the opportunity to search the cabin, but there
wasn't much to look at: just the living room, the kitchen, the
bathroom, and the main bedroom. The bedroom and bathroom, like the rest of the house, showed signs only of male
occupation, but the books on the shelves of the living room,
and the DVDs alongside them, were an odd mix of male and
female tastes, more appropriate to a space shared by a couple.

At the rear of the cottage was a small extension. The single
window was high and narrow, and couldn't be opened.
Ventilation came from a grill in one corner, although the room
was also wired for electricity. The door was made of oak,
with metal panels on either side. It had a single big keyhole,
with another grill at face level, but Parker saw holes in the
metal and in the wood of the frame, as though a bolt had
been removed at some point. Parker checked the lock. It was
scuffed on the outside, but not the inside. He smelled the
lingering odor of bleach, and got down on his knees to examine
the concrete floor. It didn't take him long to pick out the
marks left by a metal bed frame, and what might have been
a table and chair. He'd seen rooms like this before, most
recently in a place called the Cut. This wasn't somewhere to
stay willingly, but somewhere to be held.

He returned to the kitchen and looked at the photographs
pinned to the corkboard on the wall. One of them was a
replica of the photograph on Eklund's office desk: the investigator smiling beside his ex-wife. He had not picked up on
the resemblance before now. It wasn't obvious, not at first. If

it hadn't been for the room at the back of the cottage, he might never have made the connection.

Claudia Sansom looked not unlike a younger version of Eklund's ex-wife.

Parker thought of Eklund's befriending of Oscar Sansom, his offers of help, his desire to stay in touch with the progress of the case. He recalled the details of Claudia Sansom's discovery, the signs of possible neglect, and the mystery of how a woman could vanish for years and then be laid to rest in a shallow grave.

Eklund.

He heard Louis call his name, but could not bring himself to move. He continued to stare at the picture of Eklund's wife, and wondered how one could even begin to distinguish love from hate in such circumstances.

Louis appeared in the kitchen doorway. He was holding an ancient laptop in his hand.

'Man in there looked *real* unhappy when I found it . . .'

100

Parker sat at Eklund's kitchen table, the laptop in front of him. Even without Kirk Buckner to tell him the password, he might have guessed it: Milena, the name of Eklund's ex-wife. The home screen appeared. It contained about twenty files, but only one of them had Parker's name on it.

He opened the file. It contained photographs. Some were of him, but most were of his daughter, and none was more than two months old.

Ten minutes later, Parker returned to the living room. Kirk Buckner was seated against a wall, in almost exactly the same position that his late wife had occupied overnight. He seemed to want to look anywhere except at her body.

'This was Jaycob Eklund's,' said Parker.

'I don't know who you're talking about.'

'I'm not a cop. Nothing you say here is admissible in court. For now, this is between us. I'll try again: Jaycob Eklund. They found his body in a wrecking yard owned by one of your relatives.'

'It's nothing to do with me.'

'Did you kill him?'

Kirk held Parker's gaze.

'No.'

And Parker believed him.

'If the police find this laptop, all your denials will come to nothing. It ties you to Jaycob Eklund.'

Buckner appeared puzzled. He opened his mouth to say

something before closing it again with whatever it was that he was about to say remaining unspoken. Kirk Buckner might have been a lot of things, but dumb wasn't one of them. He was in enough trouble as it was. Possession of the laptop would only add to his problems.

'You know,' he said, 'I don't recall any laptop at all.'

Parker stood and left the house. When he returned, he was no longer carrying the laptop, and the police were on their way.

101

The room in which Mother and Parker had first met was now almost entirely devoid of furnishings, just like the rest of the house. Only Mother remained. She did not interrupt Parker as he told her what he knew, or as much as he wanted her to know. She understood that he was keeping some details from her. She would have expected nothing less. If there was some deeper truth to all that had occurred, she was not sure that even he fully grasped it. Yet she was impressed that he had returned to pay her the courtesy of an explanation, however partial and unsatisfactory it might be.

'A ghost story,' she said, when he had concluded.

'Perhaps.'

'And do you believe in ghosts, Mr. Parker?'

'Only my own. But what I believe isn't important. The Brethren believed, and all the harm that followed came from their belief.'

Mother nodded.

'Then we're done. I'd like to make some contribution toward your efforts.'

'I don't want your money.'

'Because you think it's dirty?'

'Because I know it is.'

'You have some very old-fashioned ideas, Mr. Parker.'

'I like to think so.'

He moved to leave, and she spoke.

'You haven't asked about my son.'

Parker looked down at her. His face was studiedly neutral.

'I hear he went away,' he said.

'It was for the best.'

'I'm sure you must miss him greatly.'

'Yes,' said Mother, 'I really do.'

That evening, in the bar of the Langham Hotel in Boston, SAC Edgar Ross of the Federal Bureau of Investigation also used the term 'ghost story', but seemed less inclined to be dismissive of it than Mother had been. Nevertheless, it was the other tale that interested him more: the tale of Jaycob Eklund.

'You think he abducted Claudia Sansom and held her for years in a room at his cabin?' he said.

'I don't know if she was there for all that time,' Parker replied. 'He might have moved her around, but I think she ended her days in that cell.'

'You've no proof.'

'I'm sure that if someone searched Eklund's cottage and its surroundings long and hard enough, proof could be found.'

'Are you suggesting that's what should be done?'

'No.'

'Why?'

'Eklund is dead. Oscar Sansom is leaving for Europe, and the truth won't bring his wife back. Milena Budny, Eklund's ex-wife, has a new husband and three stepchildren. The truth won't make their lives any easier, and might even destroy them.'

Ross sipped his drink.

'And,' Parker added, 'if an investigation occurs, it could expose Eklund's involvement with you, and you don't want that.'

'No,' said Ross.

'Did you know?' asked Parker. 'About Eklund, and what he might have done to Claudia Sansom?'

'No.'

'Did you suspect?'

'No.'

'Then what was Eklund doing for you that was so delicate you needed me to find him?'

'I don't think that's any of your business,' said Ross.

'I guess I'm just curious.'

'Don't be. It's not always healthy, not even in your line of work.'

Ross called for the check.

'About your friend, Angel,' he said. 'Unsurprisingly, my superiors are uncomfortable with the idea of making a formal representation on his behalf, but we won't raise any objection to the sealing of his records. We have made that clear, unofficially, to the relevant parties in the state of New York, and to the judge assigned to the hearing. I doubt that any problems will arise.'

'Thank you.'

'Don't thank me. It would have been better for both Angel and Louis if they had never come to my attention, but they, like me, will have to live with the consequences. I've also arranged for a bonus to be paid to you via Mr. Castin. You may be glad of it. I hear that you also have a court hearing coming up, something involving your daughter?'

Parker didn't reply. If Ross felt awkward about raising the subject, he showed no sign. The check came. Once again, Ross paid in cash.

'There's still no sign of Eklund's laptop,' he said, as he rose and took his coat from the chair beside him. 'Kirk Buckner claims to have no knowledge of it.'

'Is the laptop important?'

Ross shrugged.

'It might be. I'd be suitably grateful if it was found.'

'I'll bear that in mind.'

Ross regarded Parker for a moment.

'Do that.'

Parker and Ross walked together to the door. They did not shake hands as they said farewell. A car was waiting for Ross. He opened the door himself, and the car pulled away. Parker watched it go. When it was out of sight, Angel and Louis materialized, as though they had formed themselves from shadows and night.

'Well?' asked Angel.

'I think he hired Eklund to spy on my daughter.'

'Then why send you to retrieve the laptop?'

'Because I'm good at what I do. If I found it and handed it over without accessing its contents, then no harm would have been done. If I didn't find it at all, the result would have been the same.'

'And if you did find it, and you decided to look at the contents?'

'Then Ross would have sent a message to me.'

'Which is?'

'That he knows, or suspects, something about Sam.'

'Sometime,' said Angel, 'we all need to have a long talk about that little girl . . .'

102

Rachel was sitting at her office desk, the latest communication from her lawyer before her, when Sam appeared by her side. Her daughter had been especially solicitous toward her since she'd returned home from the hospital. What happened to her mother appeared to have affected Sam deeply.

Rachel was tired. She had not slept well the night before. She'd been dreaming.

Dreaming of Charlie Parker's first daughter.

In her dream, Rachel was standing by the shore of a great lake. On a rock sat Jennifer Parker, dropping stones into the water. A cairn of rocks and pebbles stood next to her, but no matter how many of them she consigned to the depths, the pile never grew smaller.

Rachel looked out over the lake. No wind blew, yet the surface rippled and swelled, as though disturbed from above or below, and she heard a susurration, as of the whispering of many voices.

Jennifer handed her a stone. It had a white line running through it.

here

take it

Rachel accepted the stone.

'Should I throw it?'

keep it

as a memento

And then Rachel woke up.

She touched her fingers to the letter from the Family

Division of the Vermont judiciary informing her of the court date for the custody hearing. She did not try to hide it from her daughter.

'I'm going to ask that the hearing be postponed,' said Rachel. 'You know what that means?'

'Yes,' said Sam. 'Is that why Grandpa is mad today?'

'Possibly.'

'For how long?'

'We'll see.'

Sam hugged her mother.

'I'm sorry,' said Sam, 'for the things I said.'

'I know.'

Rachel kissed her daughter, and held her face against her cheek.

'Sam?'

'Yes?'

'Who do you talk to, when you're alone in your room?'

Rachel counted the silence. One, two, three—

'No one.'

'It's just that I've heard you sometimes, in passing. Do you have, you know, a friend?'

'Like an imaginary friend?'

Sam sounded relieved.

'Yes, like an imaginary friend.'

But Rachel put particular emphasis on the second word.

'Maybe.'

'Is it another little girl?'

The silence again.

'Maybe.'

'Is she—'

But Sam pulled away before she could finish, and began dancing in circles.

'I have lots of imaginary friends,' she said, and Rachel could not tell if her cheerfulness was real or forced. 'I have a pony, and a unicorn, and a rabbit, and a fairy.'

'Sam—'

The dancing ceased. The smile vanished.

'Mommy.' Sam took her mother's hand. 'I'm *not* a little girl.'

And then she was gone.

Rachel added the letter to a folder marked 'Legal'. She opened her desk drawer and slipped the folder inside before locking it, pausing for only a moment to look again at the stone with its single white striation, the stone she had discovered in her closed hand when she woke that morning.

103

Angel buttoned his shirt and put on his sweater. He slipped into his sneakers and tied the laces. He walked through the waiting room and down the corridor. He stepped into the winter sunlight and closed his eyes against the glare.

Everybody dies, he told himself. Everybody.

But not I.

Not today.

Acknowledgments

This odd book – if mine are not all odd books – is as much a product of a lifetime of reading ghost stories as it is any specific research, but two books of recent vintage proved particularly useful: *Ghosts: A Natural History* by Roger Clarke (Penguin, 2013) and *Paranormality: Why We See What Isn't There* by Professor Richard Wiseman (Macmillan, 2011). I'm also grateful to Brian Showers of the Swan River Press, who knows more about ghost stories than is quite possibly healthy, and whose enthusiasm for Irish writers of supernatural fiction provided me with some of the quotations used in the novel. Seth Kavanagh, meanwhile, answered my idiot tech questions without even once losing his temper.

My thanks, as always, to Emily Bestler, my editor at Atria/Emily Bestler Books, and all at Atria and Simon & Schuster, including Judith Curr, Lara Jones, and David Brown; to Sue Fletcher, my editor at Hodder & Stoughton, and Kerry Hood, Swati Gamble, Carolyn Mays, Lucy Hale, Alasdair Oliver, Breda Purdue, Jim Binchy, Ruth Shern and everyone at Hodder and Hachette Ireland; and to those editors and publishers who have released my work in translation over the years, thus bringing it to a new readership and permitting me to see a little more of the world along the way. I continue to be fortunate in having Darley Anderson as my agent, and his staff as my supporters, even if I do occasionally forget to sign all the paperwork. Thanks, too, to Steve Fisher at APA; Ellen Clair Lamb for keeping me on the straight and narrow; and Madeira James at xuni.com for enabling me to pretend that I understand the Internet; and

Michelle Souliere of Portland, Maine's wonderful Green Hand Bookshop for allowing me to use her name. My love to Jennie, Cameron – to whom I owe particular gratitude for one of the incidents in this book – and Alistair.

In the best books, the ending often comes as a shock.
Not just because of that one last twist in the tale,
but because you have been so absorbed in their world,
that coming back to the harsh light of reality is a jolt.

If that describes you now, then perhaps you should track down
some new leads, and find new suspense in other worlds.

Join us at www.hodder.co.uk, or follow us on
Twitter @hodderbooks, and you can tap in to a
community of fellow thrill-seekers.

Whether you want to find out more about this book,
or a particular author, watch trailers and interviews, have
the chance to win early limited editions, or simply browse
our expert readers' selection of the very best books,
we think you'll find what you're looking for.

And if you don't, that's the place to tell us what's missing.

We love what we do, and we'd love you to be part of it.

www.hodder.co.uk

@hodderbooks

HodderBooks

HodderBooks